THE SMALL TOWN

Y0-BDB-466

Step onto Main Street of any small town in America and you feel as though you've come home. Here, neighbor knows neighbor, the shops and businesses are familiar, and people take care of their own. It's an idyllic existence, surrounded by those who share our values.

But don't let the slower pace of life fool you! There's always something happening in these small towns and watch out for the surprises around almost every corner. Whether it's the stranger in town, a secret coming to light or discovering love in unexpected places, there is never a dull moment.

So step onto the front porch, sit down and savor this special 2-in-1 collection of classic romance stories that bring you into the heart of America and remind you of what we love about small towns!

If you enjoy these two stories, be sure to look for more romances set in small towns from Harlequin American Romance.

TANYA MICHAELS

Tanya Michaels is a *New York Times* bestselling and award-winning author of over thirty romances, a five-time RITA® Award nominee and the mom of two highly imaginative kids. Sadly, Tanya's hobbies of reading, oil painting and cooking keep her much too busy to iron clothes. She and her husband are living out their slightly wrinkled happily-ever-after in Atlanta, but you can always find Tanya on Twitter, where she chats with followers about books, family and TV shows ranging from *Dr. Who* to *Project Runway*. Also, visit Tanya online at www.tanyamichaels.net.

Look for more books from Tanya Michaels in Harlequin American Romance—the ultimate destination for romance the all-American way! There are four new Harlequin American Romance titles available every month. Check one out today!

New York Times Bestselling Author

Tanya Michaels

and

USA TODAY Bestselling Author

Marie Ferrarella

TROUBLE IN TENNESSEE

AND

MONTANA SHERIFF

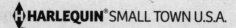

⊕HARLEQUIN®SMALL TOWN U.S.A.

Recycling programs
for this product may
not exist in your area.

ISBN-13: 978-0-373-60671-9

Trouble in Tennessee and Montana Sheriff

Copyright © 2014 by Harlequin Books S.A.

The publisher acknowledges the copyright holder
of the individual works as follows:

Trouble in Tennessee
Copyright © 2007 by Tanya Michna

Montana Sheriff
Copyright © 2011 by Marie Rydzynski-Ferrarella

This edition published by arrangement with Harlequin Books S.A.

For questions and comments about the quality of this book,
please contact us at CustomerService@Harlequin.com.

® and TM are trademarks of the publisher. Trademarks indicated with ® are registered in the United States Patent and Trademark Office, the Canadian Intellectual Property Office and in other countries.

Printed in U.S.A.

CONTENTS

TROUBLE IN TENNESSEE
Tanya Michaels

For Jen, with five years' worth of gratitude. Thank you for everything you've taught me, for laughing at my jokes, for helping me find the right home for this story and for your uncanny ability to always pick the perfect restaurant.

Chapter One

"Please?" The word was simple and dignified. As if it hadn't been preceded by twenty minutes of cajoling.

Even though they were on the phone, Treble James could picture the earnest expression in her half sister's big blue eyes. "Charity, you know I'll make time to visit after the baby is born, but—"

"How would I know that? You've been back home to Joyous all of, let me think, *once* in the past decade."

Maybe that was because Joyous, Tennessee, had never quite lived up to its name for Treble. *Stifling, Tennessee.* That *would have been appropriate.*

"I was there for your wedding," Treble pointed out, keeping a wary eye on the digital clock atop her bedroom nightstand. "You don't think I'd make the trip for you again?"

"Then make it now," her sister begged. It was unlike Charity to request favors, particularly those that inconvenienced other people. "I'm scared. The books say placenta previa isn't all that uncommon, and my OB says mine isn't a severe case and that panicking is no good for me or the baby…but I'm a first-time mommy. Having my big sister here would make me feel better. Besides, being on bed rest is driving me nuts! Come tell me dirty jokes or something, keep me from killing my poor husband."

Charity doing harm to *any* living creature was laughable, but to Bill Sumner? They'd been smitten with each other since high school, as evidenced by their marrying shortly after Charity's graduation. It blew Treble's mind that her sister, at twenty-two, was expecting a child and had already been married four years. She hadn't even been old enough to drink champagne at her own wedding! Treble had taken it upon herself to imbibe enough for both of them.

It had been the best way to cope with being in Joyous two weeks after a bad breakup with the boyfriend who was supposed to have been her date. Twenty-nine-year-old Treble's relationship record—in contrast to Bill and Charity's seven years together—was about six months.

"Charity, I don't want to cut you off, but I need to leave for work, so—"

"You know what being pregnant makes you think about? Motherhood. I'm about to have my own little girl, and I wish Mom… Even though you've never been pregnant, you're my closest female relative. It would mean the world to me if you were here right now. *Mom* would have wanted that, her two girls together."

Treble did a double take, actually staring at the receiver. "I thought you were the good sister. Since when do you use emotional blackmail?"

"Is it working?"

Yes. "I really do have to leave for the station." Charity's soft-spoken barb had found its mark, though. Despite Treble's cynical shell, she retained weak spots for her late mother and younger sister.

"All right." Charity sighed. "I'm sorry to dump this on you. I know you have a career, a life in Georgia beyond all of us, but I miss you, Treb. And I love you."

"Love you, too, brat." The epithet had become a term of endearment over the years, but this evening it seemed particularly applicable. Didn't her sister *know* what she was asking? To go to Tennessee early and just wait around for Charity's due date in July...

Few citizens of Joyous would welcome Treble with open arms. *More like the sign of the cross.* She'd been a somewhat, ah, spirited youth, and folks in small towns had long memories.

Treble hung up, catching sight of herself in the oval mirror on the wall. "Don't give me that look," she chastised her reflection. "You don't want to go back any more than I do."

Talking to herself? Never a good sign. But Treble, a weeknight DJ for an Atlanta pop station, was used to addressing an audience. An audience she'd be late for if she didn't get moving.

Although she would be in-studio tonight and not doing a remote broadcast at one of the clubs she occasionally visited, she stopped long enough to run a brush through the dark ringlets that spilled past her shoulder blades and to apply her favorite dark red lip gloss. Even if her listeners couldn't see her, it helped her get into character for "Trouble J," one of the most popular non-commuting show hosts in the city. While the best air-time was in the mornings and afternoons, when most of the working crowd was stuck in gridlock on I-75, I-85 or the 285 loop around Atlanta, Treble held damn good ratings for her period and liked the late hours that allowed her to sleep in on weekdays and leave her weekends free for a social life. Not, she reflected as she headed toward the parking garage, that she'd had much of one lately.

The last guy to ask her out had been a producer on one of the station's other shows, and she wasn't interested in merging her professional life with her personal life. The producer aside, she'd been subtly discouraging men for several months. She had been busy booking extra personal appearances for her off-hours, making the most of her minor celebrity status. The additional funds deposited into her savings account were the start of a down payment. Maybe it was the almost-thirty part of her, but when spring had bloomed, she'd actually been sorry she didn't have a real house to subject to seasonal cleaning, and a yard to enjoy instead of a railed-in concrete balcony.

It was time she found a home of her own—a paradoxically domestic wish for a woman who would be on the air from seven-thirty to midnight playing rock songs interspersed with risqué commentary. Well, risqué within proper FCC guidelines, of course. No matter how grown up she was or where she moved, there was always *someone* who'd disapprove of her.

And in Joyous, Tennessee? Possibly hundreds of someones.

So what? Outside of ratings, she never cared what

strangers thought. Witness "Trusty," the eyesore of a car parked among other residents' vehicles. If cars were status symbols, what did the hatchback say about her? *That you take risks.* It had been used when she purchased it during college, and couldn't possibly have much life left in it. Still, now that it was paid off, she wanted to get her financing approved for a house before taking on new monthly bills.

But her rebellious attitude and antistatus-symbol car aside, opinions in Joyous would carry more weight than most. Maybe she was sensitive because some of the criticism from the town's citizens would be deserved. After all, she had been something of a hellion, sneaking out to meet Rich Danner her sophomore year, trying to use a fake ID to get into Duke's bar and "borrowing" her stepfather's car to attend a rock concert two counties over after Harrison had refused to let her go with friends. The fall of her junior year, there had also been that period of indiscriminate and outrageous flirting. Everyone had heard about Rich dumping her before he left for college. She'd tried to hide her broken heart with drawled comments and suggestive smiles directed at any boy in range—even a cute chemistry teacher.

Despite the exaggerated gossip, she hadn't meant to cause breakups between other classmates or steal anyone's boyfriend. She *certainly* hadn't planned for anything to ever happen with the chemistry teacher, no matter what the nervous guidance counselor had told Harrison in a meeting about Treble's "acting out" for attention. The memory of Harrison Breckfield's icy condemnation as he'd walked Treble to his car was enough to make her shiver even now. Harrison didn't believe his wife's death was any excuse for misbehavior. He'd pointed out savagely that *Charity* had lost a mother, too, yet continued to be a perfectly respectable daughter. Even if Treble had known how to articulate her unspoken insecurities, pride probably would have kept her from asking if Harrison had ever loved Treble, the born troublemaker, as he did his own child.

He had been the adult in the situation. Couldn't he have reached out to his stepdaughter just once and assured her of her place in his home? Still, were bitter memories of Harrison not being there for Treble a valid reason not to be there for Charity now?

On Saturday, Treble's only scheduled appearance was at a mall grand opening midafternoon. *Let's just hope I don't blow the small stipend I'm getting on cute shoes before I even leave the premises.* Ah, retail therapy. Thank God for clearance sales and outlet stores.

A coworker from the station had recently invited her to do some outlet shopping near the Georgia-Tennessee border—Treble's enjoyment over her finds had been marred by the guilt of being less than an hour and a half from the pregnant sister she hadn't seen in four years. Treble knew she'd been a disappointment as a daughter, but did that mean she was doomed to be a bad sister, too?

Stop it. She refused to spend a sunny June morning cooped up in her apartment, agonizing over Charity's recent request. At the very least, Treble could agonize by the pool.

After loading this morning's juice cup and cereal bowl into the dishwasher, Treble changed into a fuchsia-striped bikini.

"You're so lucky," Charity had said back when she'd

been selecting bridesmaid dresses. "You can pull off *any* color. I have to stay within three main hues or look so washed out I scare people."

Untrue. Charity looked like an angel, a beautifully blond vision of their mother. Petite, fine-boned with flawless porcelain skin. Treble took after her biological father, the first of many men who'd been unable to commit to her. When she'd tracked him down after leaving Joyous, she'd been surprised at how handsome he still was. But the dimpled persona and rich drawl were just superficial niceties.

Treble had inherited his height, dark hair, bold features and almond eyes. *And his tendency to run away?* No, her leaving Joyous had been best for everyone, not an act of cowardice. Trouble J was audacious and unafraid.

She packed a tote bag bearing the station's call letters with a towel, SPF protection, a black pen and a Sudoku book—one of the assistants at the station got her hooked on the puzzles—then hurried toward the front door. Fresh air would do her a world of good.

Outside, the warmth embraced her. Though the sun would be punishing in large doses, she looked forward to stretching out for a little while like a relaxed feline basking in the rays. Treble had barely situated herself in a poolside lounge chair when she heard her name called. She peered over the top of her sunglasses at the smiling Latina woman in a one-piece suit coming through the gate.

"Hey, Alana." Treble waved, then waited for her friend to come closer so that they weren't yelling over the commotion of kids splashing in the pool.

Alana Torres was a fellow tenant and friend. Sometimes Treble got the woman passes into clubs where Treble was broadcasting. Both of them were fans of high-octane action films, and they went to a lot of movies together when they were mutually between boyfriends. The curvy bank teller, however, had been seeing an airline pilot since February.

"Haven't seen much of you lately," Treble said as her friend dragged a chair closer across the concrete. "But seeing you now, you look incredible. *Muy caliente.*"

The woman lowered her dark eyes but smiled proudly. "Thanks. I haven't entirely adjusted to the new haircut." Since they'd known each other, Alana had worn her thick black hair long, but had had about six inches taken off recently.

"It's sophisticated." Treble put her hands behind her and lifted her own hair off her neck. "And probably a lot cooler."

"My high school reunion is this month. I know it's shallow, but I'm determined to look hot. Chubby girl's prerogative."

"I doubt you were ever as chubby as you felt, and you've already lost—what, fifteen pounds?"

"Twelve."

"Promise me you won't drop so much that you turn bony, okay?"

Alana laughed as she opened her sunblock. The citrus scent was strong, but preferable to the chlorine from the water. "Yeah, *that's* likely to happen, given the way I'm addicted to the bakery across the street from the bank. Whoever invented soup in a loaf of bread was a diabolical genius."

To Alana, baked goods equaled what cute shoes were to Treble—an irresistible vice.

Glancing around, Alana lowered her voice. "Thank goodness Greg has such stamina and creativity when it comes to helping me burn calories."

"You mean his suggestions are more fun than jogging?" Treble grinned. "No, seriously, I'm asking. It's been so long that I barely remember what it's like to… burn calories."

Alana returned her smile. "Your listeners would never believe you. I heard some of the advice you gave your callers last night and, girl, where *do* you get those naughty ideas?"

"Repressed sexual energy. It leads to a rich fantasy life."

"You had a great show. I know you tease that your main concern is boosting the ratings, but I think you enjoy helping people. You're a generous soul."

Yeah, so generous she wasn't even bothering to examine her schedule for the possibility of lending physical and moral support to her only sibling. Treble heaved a sigh.

"Don't tell me work's not going well?" Alana asked, misinterpreting her friend's brief frown.

"It's not the radio thing, it's… You know the expression 'you can't go home again'? Let's just say I always clung to that as kind of a guarantee."

"Okay. And…?"

"Someone I really care about wants me to take a few weeks out of my life and go home. I think I'd rather have my show canceled."

Alana winced. "*That* awful?"

"Hard to say. I've managed to avoid finding out for the past four years and was tipsy for part of my last long weekend there." Her behavior had fuelled the fires of gossip.

While she wasn't proud that she'd had too much to drink at Charity's wedding, she didn't feel she should have to apologize, either. The person with the real right to be annoyed was the bride, who had been so starry-eyed over Bill anyway, she wouldn't have noticed if Treble had set herself on fire at the rehearsal dinner. In fact, one of the underaged bridesmaids had downed four glasses of champagne at the reception and thrown up in a topiary, garnering nothing but an off-color joke and some pitying "Guess she learned the hard way" comments. Treble, on the other hand, had been a legally drinking adult who neither table-danced nor drove anywhere while under the influence. Couldn't a girl nurse a broken heart with a few festive libations without, the next day, her stepfather acting as though an intervention was in order? It was as if he held her to a high standard of behavior, then watched her, waiting for her to screw up.

Harrison had financed the open bar in the first place! Why was it no one minded when weathered, old farmhand Bobby Charles Picoult got buzzed on draft beer and started loudly guffawing at the same anecdotes he'd been telling since Treble first moved to Joyous as a girl? *Because Bobby Charles is local color. You're an outsider.* Even though Treble had moved to Joyous right before kindergarten, by the time she'd left, she'd felt completely out of place. She doubted anyone besides her sister had been sorry to see her go. Even poor Charity had probably been relieved at the decrease in tension at home.

"A few weeks is a long time," Alana pointed out loyally. "Do you have that much vacation? Whoever asked should completely understand if you say no."

"Charity would understand. It's not in her to whine or hold a grudge." The thought made denying the request even more difficult somehow.

Well, Alana's right, a few weeks is *a substantial chunk of time.* Weren't first babies often overdue? There'd been a woman at the station who'd seemed pregnant for, like, a year; by the end of it, she'd been miserable, the size of a house and threatening violent death to anyone stupid enough to ask, "Still haven't had that kid?" Treble couldn't imagine sitting around her sister's house waiting for an unknown date.

"I know what you mean about not wanting to go back," Alana said. "I skipped my five-year reunion. I told myself it was because I was busy that weekend and most of the people I cared to keep in touch with, I already was. But that was just rationalizing. At the time, I'd been interning for a company, making less than minimum wage and sharing a closet-sized apartment with three other girls, but that job was supposed to lead to a great full-time position. Until the corporation declared bankruptcy and cut their losses, me included."

Treble shot her friend a sympathetic look. Interning had been crucial to getting Treble's foot in the door at the station, and she would have been devastated if no job had materialized. She loved having her own show, loved her listeners and the relative freedom of sharing her opinion over the airwaves.

"In high school," Alana continued, "I was one of those socially acceptable nerds. Chubby and awkward, never with an actual date to a dance, but smart enough that I had my own niche with the other straight-A geeks.

So when the reunion rolled around and I was minus a job and plus the college 'freshman fifteen' I never lost… It's frustrating how the least healthy food is usually the cheapest. I felt like a total failure."

"You're not! Corporate America has many problems, none of them a reflection on your abilities. Also, you're gorgeous."

"Now, maybe. And it's sickening how much I want other people to see that. I've asked myself a dozen times why I even care what they think."

"Ever come up with an answer?" Treble's comparatively small graduating class held an annual reunion in conjunction with the town's July festival. She'd never once been tempted to attend.

"I don't know." Alana shifted on her lounger. "I think for most of us, adolescence is when we were the most insecure and vulnerable. Maybe when we're around the people who knew us then, we think they can see those insecurities. Or maybe their presence brings back all our vulnerabilities the way catching an old song on the radio can lead to visceral déjà vu."

Tell me about it. When Treble had helped deejay parties in college, there were one or two songs with such negative personal connotations that she tried never to play them. Then there was music that to this day made her feel good all over. Particularly the U2 song that had been on the radio her junior year at university when Brady McCall had…

"Something funny?" Alana asked. "You sure are grinning."

"Um, it's nothing."

"Liar."

"Ask me about it next time you invite me over for peach daiquiris."

"It's a date." Alana scowled. "I'm going to hate it when you finally find your dream home and move out of the complex."

"Hey, I'm looking in the metro area! Aren't you spending half your time at Greg's place anyway?"

"More like three quarters. So I guess I'm being a tad hypocritical about hating to see you leave. How *is* the house hunt going?"

"It's on hiatus until I've saved up more. Nothing I saw was quite right anyway. Even the ones that didn't need so many repairs felt…off. During a walk-through, I told the agent it's like the perfect pair of shoes—occasionally I see some that are adorable, match an outfit I have exactly, but when I slide them on, they're not comfortable. They're just not me."

"Maybe homes are something you have to break in, like boots?"

"Maybe. But when it's worth the blisters, you know. No sense in my shelling out my life savings for something that's wrong. I want a place that's *mine,* one where I belong." Although the only place where she'd truly felt that sense of belonging was at the station, her employers would frown on her sleeping in the studio, but, at least there, they liked Trouble.

Some of the people in her past would never like her, never approve of her, but avoiding them wouldn't change that. What if visiting Joyous was not only a chance to help Charity but an opportunity for Treble to return on her own terms? She wasn't expecting citizens to be thrilled to see her or her stepfather to applaud her job as a titillating radio host, but perhaps once she looked them all in the eyes and knew for sure that their opinion didn't matter, memories of the past would lose their mythical power over her. She'd be free to visit her bouncing baby niece without dreading the homecoming.

On her next birthday, Treble would be thirty. Wasn't that grown up enough to stop letting Joyous be some geographical boogeyman in her life? Maybe once she'd slayed the demons of her one-time home, she could return to Atlanta and start building a home that was truly hers.

Chapter Two

"Trusty, you move your chassis now," Treble instructed the car, "or I swear I'm renaming you!" *Traitorous Pile of Junk* had a nice ring to it.

As warnings went, hers lacked oomph, but she didn't want to threaten dismantling in case that invited even worse vehicular karma. The air conditioner had sputtered and died before she cleared north Georgia, blowing only warm air until she gave up and rolled down the windows. Then the fuel light had come on, alarming her. She should have had a full tank of gas…unless there was a leak? Not even wanting to contemplate that, she'd been thrilled when the light turned off by itself. Maybe the gas had just been sloshing around as she drove through mountainous territory and temporarily confused the monitoring mechanism.

Most recently, the "check engine" light had begun

flashing. Concerned, she'd pulled onto a wide shoulder alongside fenced meadows to give Trusty a chance to cool down. After all, Treble rarely drove for this long at a stretch; the car might simply be overworked. Treble's sensible plan had backfired, however, now that the hatchback wouldn't start again. Turning the key only produced a grating sound that made Treble want to get out and kick something.

"This is the thanks I get for assuring Charity you're roadworthy?" she asked the vehicle in exasperation.

Her sister had been *ecstatic* when Treble called Monday afternoon to say she was making the trip to Joyous. Treble had accumulated some vacation time at the station and almost never called in sick. All she'd had to do was explain to her manager that her pregnant younger sister was experiencing complications, and the father of four had been happy to help her schedule some replacement talent.

"It's a nice way for up-and-comers to get experience and start building a name," he'd reminded her. "We can also do a week of 'best of' clips where we replay interviews of favorite guests or phone segments. You go take care of your sister—just don't get too 'down-home' on us. We need you full of sass and attitude when you get back."

"Don't worry," she'd assured him. "I am all attitude."

"I can't believe you're really coming!" Charity had squealed when she heard the news.

Neither can I, Treble had thought. "I should be in Wednesday afternoon. Or evening. I'm not what you call an early riser."

"We'll be watching for you. What are you driving these days?"

"Same car as always."

There had been a brief pause before Charity said, "Maybe you should look into flights."

Ridiculous. The nearest airport to Joyous was in Chattanooga. By the time Treble drove to Hartsfield—two hours early to allow for security and long check-in lines—caught her plane in Atlanta, deboarded in Chattanooga and met Charity's husband for the ride to Joyous, it would have been just as quick to drive straight there. Besides, while Treble had talked herself into making this journey, keeping a getaway car at her disposal was mandatory.

"So much for being a reliable escape plan," she growled at her motionless hatchback. She hadn't expected a triumphant return, but she would have preferred something less embarrassing than being dragged into town limits by a tow truck.

Picking up her cell phone, she said a quick prayer that she could get a decent signal out here. She exhaled a whoosh of relief when the call to her sister's house went through.

"Hello?"

"Hey, Charity. It's Treble. I don't suppose Bill's there?" Bill worked in the office of a milk plant for Breckfield Dairy Farms and Creamery, but he'd been keeping sporadic hours to look after his wife. *One of the perks of the CEO being your father-in-law.* "I have a car question for him."

"He and Dad went to look at some heifers one county over, but they'll be back by dinner. Just how urgent is this question?"

Treble wondered how long it would be before any

other drivers came down the two-lane road. "Oh…fairly urgent."

"I knew it!" Charity's voice took on a breathless, panicked rhythm. "That darn car. It's crapped out on you, hasn't it?"

As much as she would have liked to assure her sister otherwise, there was no escaping the reality of the situation. "Pretty much. But maybe we can save the I-told-you-so's until after we've rounded up a mechanic?"

"Well, that would be Ronnie over at Carter and Sons, but Carter closes for a late lunch every day from two to three. How far away are you?" Charity listened, did some mental calculations, then decided, "I could have Doc Caldwell come get you. Ronnie can go back with the tow truck later, but there's no sense in you just waiting on the side of the road."

"Who is Doc Caldwell, and what makes you think he's available smack-dab in the middle of the day on Wednesday?"

"A friend and sometimes fishing buddy of Dad's. He's Doc Monaghan's replacement, moved to town right after Bill and I found out I was pregnant."

Doc Monaghan had been the general practitioner in Joyous who'd told Treble's mom that she was pregnant with Charity and later diagnosed Treble's tonsillitis. He had to have been nearing seventy by the time Charity got married, so it was about time the town brought in someone else. Hopefully this Doc Caldwell still had a few good years left in him before retirement.

"As far as his schedule," Charity continued, "he told Bill he didn't have many appointments and could check in on me. I keep promising these men I won't do anything more strenuous than get up to pee, but apparently they don't believe me. I'd just as soon sic the doctor on you as have company show up when I'd rather be napping. Afternoons hit me hardest."

Treble laughed. "If asking him to come get me will gain you a little peace, I suppose you should do it."

Ten minutes later, Charity called back to say the man was on his way.

"Sorry I didn't have any distinctive landmarks to give him," Treble said, looking around at a whole lot of nothing. Wildflowers dotted the roadside, and bales of hay had been spaced across the meadow for unseen cows. Some people might find the pastoral scene beneath the blue sky and cotton-ball clouds soothing, but the charm had worn off, leaving Treble antsy for air-conditioning and antihistamine.

"Don't worry," Charity said. "He knows that if he sees Peggy's Pancake House he's gone too far. How many brunettes stranded inside old hatchbacks do you think he's going to pass between here and there?"

"Good point." So Treble settled into her car, which she was thinking of having compressed into a doorstop, and waited. She considered turning on the radio to help kill time, but taxing the battery was probably a bad idea.

To keep from screaming in boredom or thinking much about the inevitable moment she saw her stepfather tonight, she pulled out her omnipresent Sudoku book, but she couldn't concentrate. Instead, she grabbed a small manicure kit from her duffel bag. Her fingernails were looking ragged and could use some attention.

She'd finished applying a second coat of metallic blue polish when a pickup truck rounded a bend up ahead and came toward her in the opposite lane. The scuffed white Chevy veered onto the grassy shoulder across the road and parked. From her position, Treble could tell it was a man driving, but between distance, dusty windows and the billed cap he wore, any other details were obscured.

Wondering if this was her stepfather's buddy or just a random soul stopping to offer assistance, Treble watched with unabashed curiosity. The truck door opened and a pair of long, denim-encased legs unfolded. In addition to the jeans, the stranger wore a green polo shirt, the short sleeves loosely molding nice shoulders and revealing equally nice forearms. She climbed out of her car, experiencing a tingle of prurient appreciation over the man's chiseled profile as he looked both ways for nonexistent traffic. The cautious habit made her grin, and she was still smiling as he reached her. As he got closer, she realized he was taller than her five foot ten by at least three inches.

Hellooo, Good-Looking Samaritan.

Beneath the Tennessee Vols cap he wore, he had thick brown hair and a fantastic face. Not blandly attractive in the urbane "metrosexual" way as some of her guy friends back in Atlanta, but rugged. Though he couldn't be much older than Treble, there was a lot of character in the intriguing planes and angles of his face, the slashes bracketing sensual lips where dimples might appear when he smiled, the deep, deep blue eyes.

Charity had sky-blue eyes, nearly pastel. This man's were dark like the ocean with serious potential for undercurrents that could suck a girl in without her realizing. Or protesting.

"Treble?"

Her body warmed when he said her name, making her feel silly. "You know me?" Had they gone to school together in Joyous? With her somewhat public antics, there were plenty of people who might recognize her before she recognized them, but she imagined this guy would have left an impression even as a teen.

"No, I haven't had the pleasure." He shoved the cap back on his head, that blue gaze sliding over her in assessment. "Keith Caldwell. Charity sent me."

Treble was dimly aware of gaping. This broad-shouldered man with the piercing gaze and large hands, currently resting with thumbs hooked in his front pockets, was Doc Caldwell? Women in Joyous must be forming lines down Main Street just to get their temperatures checked—though a fever in the good doctor's presence seemed a foregone conclusion.

His brain on autopilot, Keith extended a hand toward the woman in front of him. "Nice to meet you."

There was a framed wedding picture on Charity and Bill's mantel that included Treble, but the flesh-and-blood version looked less like the satin-clad demure brunette in the back row of a bridal party and more like the wild-child stories he'd heard since moving to Joyous. He'd never asked Harrison or Charity to expound on the gossip about the "ungrateful stepdaughter" and her unlawful habits of shoplifting and grand theft auto. Keith knew what it was like not to want to discuss a painful family past or self-destructive siblings.

"I'd shake your hand," Treble drawled, "but I just painted my nails." She waggled her fingers near her face long enough for him to notice the flash of blue, a color choice that made him think momentarily of frostbite.

He almost laughed at the irony since everything else about this woman said *hot*.

She wore a cropped black T-shirt, with sleeves so short it was almost a tank top, and denim shorts. While her outfit wasn't unduly revealing for June, she definitely showed a tantalizing amount of supple skin. There was even a light sheen of sweat across her rosy cheeks. Whether she'd wanted her hair off her neck because it was cooler or she just customarily wore it up, she'd pulled the wavy mass into a haphazard topknot with a sparkly black barrette. Several strands fell free, however, giving her a look that was arrestingly bold when combined with her full lips, high forehead and the tiny cleft in her chin. Each detail from the almost indefinably exotic shape of her dark eyes to the sliver of bared skin at her midriff suggested she was a girl who liked to color outside the lines.

Or was he projecting based on speculation?

"You about done looking?" Treble asked, her tone amused.

Keith's face warmed. He felt as awkward as a teenager caught ogling a hot substitute teacher. "Sorry. Guess I was surprised. For sisters, you and Charity don't look alike."

Treble's eyes narrowed. "Half sisters. I'm sure as a doctor you understand how having different fathers leads to very different genetic makeup."

Which part was she touchy about, Charity or the father situation? Harrison certainly looked tense whenever someone made mention of his stepdaughter. The last thing the older man needed right now was more tension, although that was something the family would have to sort out themselves.

For now, best to change the subject to something that

didn't make her glare daggers. "What all do we need to grab out of your car before we lock it up and go?"

"I have a couple of suitcases in the trunk." She turned on her heel and headed toward the back of the vehicle.

Keith wished he could realistically offer to help get the car started, but his specialty was fixing people, not automobiles. He'd leave the mechanical maintenance to the professionals. Treble hefted two bright red suitcases, and he reached to take them from her.

She frowned, not letting go. "I'm able-bodied, Dr. Caldwell."

"And so gracious," he said mildly. "Why do I feel like we got off to a bad start?"

Silently, she handed over the cases, then ran a hand through her hair as if she'd forgotten it was pulled back, further dislodging ringlets that fell into her face. "Sorry. It's been a stressful day."

"Well, don't worry. Ronnie will take care of your car, for sure."

Treble laughed dryly. She followed him to the truck, strangely rigid for a woman with blue fingernails and carefree curls. There was more on her mind than automotive problems, but he didn't pry. She didn't owe him explanations in return for the ride. In fact, Keith frequently sought out chances to do favors for Harrison Breckfield and Charity.

Keith had first seen moving to Joyous as an escape— from the double loss he'd suffered in Savannah, from the chaos of working in an Atlanta E.R.—but it had become more than that. With the endorsement of the town's leading citizen, Keith had gradually become a true part of the community. He had a brand-new life and was aware of how much he owed to Harrison's support.

When you were replacing a town institution like Doc Monaghan, people didn't warm to you right away. Some old-timers didn't cotton to the idea of progress and had repeatedly stressed the way Monaghan had done things. Meanwhile, husbands and fathers expressed discomfort—and occasional outrage—at the thought of Keith examining their wives and adolescent daughters. A few people had actually chosen to drive to the GP in nearby Devlin rather than visit "that young newcomer."

Harrison Breckfield, however, had been propelled into the downtown clinic five months ago when he'd experienced chest pains. After a brief subsequent stay at the county hospital, Harrison had taken Keith under his wing. He'd invited the younger man to dinner, given him a tour of the original Breckfield Dairy—part of a Southeastern empire with its own line of milk, yogurts, cottage cheese and desserts—and made it clear to the townspeople the new doctor was to be trusted and accepted. Following that first dinner at Harrison's gigantic house, office appointments had doubled and other invitations had gradually trickled in. Keith loved this town, its slow rhythm and the way he'd been accepted here. Though it would be crass to think of them as replacements for the sister who drowned or the father who later died, Harrison, Charity and her husband were the closest thing to family Keith had found since his mom remarried while he was away at college. If only Keith could pay back the older man's generosity by getting Harrison to take his heart problems more seriously....

Temporarily lost in thought, Keith hadn't realized how quiet it was in the cab of the truck.

"Um, Keith? Is it cool with you if I turn on the radio?"

"Of course. Sorry, I'm usually more companionable than this, I was just thinking about…a patient."

"Stumped by a medical mystery?" she asked. "I occasionally tape episodes of *House*."

He laughed. "Nothing that dramatic. And only a really talented actor can pull off that bedside manner. The people of Joyous expect someone more traditional."

"You got that right," she muttered, a scowl darkening her face. But then she forced a smile and reached for the radio dials. A twangy ballad about a redneck Romeo seeking his honky-tonk Juliet spilled from the speakers.

"Yeesh." She punched the buttons quickly.

"Not a fan of country music?" he asked. There were a few other options in this neck of the woods, but not many.

"My view on music mirrors my philosophy on men," she told him with a mischievous glance. "I don't have just one type, but I am selective. That song was bad on many levels. Ah. This is more like it." She'd landed on a classic rock station for the opening chords of a late-seventies hit.

Keith smiled as he turned up the volume. "This one's a little before your time, isn't it?"

"Baby, I'm *timeless.*" She flashed him a grin that nearly had him skidding off the road.

It occurred to him that, since moving to Joyous, he'd been subjected to a much different male-female dynamic than he'd known in his twenties. Lately, potential romances involved aging couples with single daughters inviting him to Sunday dinner or available women bringing him frozen casseroles and gelatin molds. Treble hadn't meant anything by her throwaway comment, but there was a lot to be said for a brazen smile and baby-doll T-shirt over a strawberry gelatin salad.

Not that Keith would ever do more than appreciate from a cautious distance the smile that belonged to the notorious prodigal stepdaughter of Harrison Breckfield. As appealing as she might be, the woman had *trouble* written all over her, and that was the last thing Keith needed in his new life.

Chapter Three

By the time they'd rolled into town on picturesque streets flanked by storefronts and pink flowering crepe myrtles, Treble was so tense she felt as if her neck muscles might actually shatter. If Keith had noticed, he hadn't commented. About all he'd done was occasionally bob his head in an endearing manner along to guitar riffs and drum solos. Maybe he was oblivious to her stress, but weren't doctors trained to be observant? She'd *flinched* when they'd passed the town limits sign.

Technically it read Welcome To Joyous, Home of Famous Breckfield Ice Cream, but judging from her suddenly clammy palms and the unpleasant way her stomach had flipped, it might as well have proclaimed, Abandon Hope All Ye Who Enter Here. *Get a grip, girlfriend. Nothing scares you, remember?* Well, except low ratings and spiders. She was only human.

A fan had asked her once if she ever worried about losing her train of thought or not knowing just the right comeback. Treble could say she truly wasn't too worried about that. Saying something that got her called into the boss's office the next morning was possible, but speechlessness? Unlike her. In fact, in times of nervous crisis, she usually talked *more,* relying on her radio persona until she felt balanced again.

She relied on chatting now. "Will you be taking me straight to my sister's or are we going to the garage first?"

"Your call."

"I do like an accommodating man."

He shot her a quick look with those too-dark blue eyes. A shiver—the good kind—rippled through her.

"Penny for your thoughts," she said.

The corner of his mouth quirked. "Doctors make decent money, even out here. I can afford to keep this to myself."

"Spoilsport. Do you need to rush back to the practice?" she asked. "I missed lunch and owe you for the ride. I could buy us some barbecue."

"Not necessary. This was a favor for Charity. But if you're hungry, I'll stop and eat with you."

A favor for Charity. There'd been a protective note in his voice. If her sister weren't so happily married, Treble might have entertained a twinge of envy. As it was, she found herself curious.

"So…you're pretty good friends with my family?"

"Yes, ma'am."

She waited for him to elaborate before realizing he'd completed the thought and showed no signs of voicing another. Treble was nothing if not hardheaded, a trait her mother had remarked upon often. "How did you meet them?"

"In a town this size? I've met most everyone."

She already knew he wasn't as talkative by nature as she was, but now she got the distinct impression he was actually stonewalling her. Did he not want to discuss her family? It wasn't as if she were a stranger nosing around for Breckfield secret recipes, for crying out loud. She was making small talk. Okay, and prying a little, too, but they were *her* family.

Maybe she should tackle his instead. "Do you have relatives in the area?"

"No." His jaw tightened in punctuation.

Well, she was just batting a thousand. By the time they parked in front of Adam's Ribs, her appetite was no longer her top concern. What had Keith heard about her? Charity wouldn't have said anything bad, not purposefully, but the doctor was a friend of Harrison's. Had her stepfather disparaged her? Was he glad she'd done the sisterly thing by coming home, or did he wish she was still in another state? Treble told herself she didn't personally care, she just didn't want any latent tension or awkward moments upsetting Charity this late in a complicated pregnancy.

Whatever bad karma was responsible for her defunct car apparently hadn't finished toying with her. Feeling borderline apprehensive already, the *last* person she needed to see the second she stepped into the smoke-scented restaurant was Rich Danner. *Now you know that's not true, Treb. It could have been Mitchell Reyes...* But her mind immediately shied away from that memory and the pain associated with it. Rich Danner was bad enough.

He'd been a high school senior, two years older than her, the year her mother had been killed by a drunk driver. Treble had desperately needed solace and felt outside the circle of grief Harrison Breckfield shared with his younger natural daughter. Blindly adoring, Treble had turned to Rich.

More than a decade later and he was still good-looking, she noted dispassionately. Was there no justice in the world? Ex-boyfriends who casually took your virginity, then moved on to college and older girls, were supposed to go bald and develop a paunch. It should be a law of physics. Rich's black hair was close-cropped, but showed no signs of male pattern baldness. His body was as lean as ever.

Rich had been enjoying a plate of the best spareribs in the state, but looked up as if he'd felt her watching. For a second he was frozen with surprise. Then his lips curved into a slow, meaningful grin. As if he was remembering the "good times" they'd shared.

Good times that had ended one muggy August night. "It wouldn't be fair of me to ask you to wait until we can be together again," he'd cooed with persuasive and patently false caring. "I'm moving on, and you'll be here with football games and high school dances you shouldn't be cheated out of. There will be plenty of guys your age who want to go out with you." Yeah, especially after Rich shot off his mouth about how willing she'd been in the backseat of his dad's Cadillac.

Looking away from Rich, she whirled around so quickly she almost collided with Keith, Treble conjured a bright smile and equally bright tone. "It's been forever since I ate here. What do you recommend?"

"I'm fond of the pulled pork sandwich." He raised an

eyebrow. "I would have you pegged as a woman who liked to decide her own order without advice."

Pouting prettily, she wagged a finger at him. "Shame on you, judging so quickly. Wouldn't it be more fun to get to know me? I don't bite. Well, rarely."

He studied her, looking unimpressed. "Are you always so…flirtatious with virtual strangers?"

Embarrassment warmed her cheeks, but she refused to get defensive. "That was just joking around, Doc. If I decide to flirt with you, trust me, you'll know." Irritating man. She hadn't been coming on to him. She'd been anxious after his responses—make that *non*responses—about her family, and seeing Rich had been the toxic icing on the cake. Would it have killed Keith to smile back at her? Surely a guy who looked like this had some experience bantering with women.

"If you decide to flirt," he said blandly, "give me a heads up so I can be elsewhere. I prefer genuine to calculated feminine wiles."

No wonder the man was good friends with Harrison. Two like-minded judgmental sticks-in-the-mud.

A gangly teenager with minor acne and major amounts of musky aftershave cleared his throat, making it clear Keith and Treble were blocking the entrance. The doctor mumbled an apology and steered her away with his hand on her elbow. His touch was gentle but seared her skin nonetheless.

She jerked her arm away, then sighed inwardly. Now she probably looked petulant on top of everything else. What if she approached the situation as she would a caller she had inadvertently offended? Debate and sassy comebacks were good for the show, but there was a line she didn't cross when it came to antagonizing listeners. Why not just try the direct approach?

"Sorry if I was snippy there for a moment." Unwilling to discuss the family part of how difficult coming home was, particularly when she had a feeling Keith was already prejudiced on the subject, she gave him the other half of the truth. "There's an ex-boyfriend of mine in here."

She gave Keith credit for not turning to scope the ex in question, which Alana would have done immediately. Then again, Alana was a friend with a vested interest in Treble; Keith most likely didn't care.

"Bad breakup?" he guessed.

With aching, unwanted clarity, she remembered crying all night over the one-two punch of losing her mother, then her first love. She'd gone behind Harrison's back and against his wishes to see Rich; learning that her stepfather had been correct in his assessment had only made her angrier. How could Harrison be so perceptive when it came to a teenage boy he barely knew yet remain so blind about how much Treble needed him?

She swallowed. "Bad enough. I wasn't trying to use you to make him jealous or anything. I haven't even thought about him in years. It was just disorienting, walking through the door and... Sometimes we're not prepared to come face-to-face with our past, you know?"

"Yeah." He glanced away, but not before she saw the sudden intensity in his eyes.

Her earlier annoyance faded into curiosity. She knew what *her* issues were. What lurked in Dr. Caldwell's past that he'd rather not face?

* * *

Lunch with Treble reminded Keith of his first-year labs in med school. Part of him had enjoyed the challenge while the rest of him was edgy because he'd sometimes second-guessed whether he knew what the hell he was doing.

Treble's earlier moment of vulnerability had startled him, leaving him to wonder if he'd imagined it as she effortlessly dazzled the young man working the register. By the time they left the counter with their food, Keith concluded that his companion was as unpredictable as she was gorgeous, which was saying something. The more moods he watched play across that expressive face, the more the full impact of her beauty hit him. Did she know men were watching her as she sauntered across the room?

Of course she does. She paints her fingernails blue and carries bright red luggage. This is not a woman who hides from attention. And yet she'd seemed sincerely nervous about running into some long-ago flame. From her reaction, Keith guessed the guy must have dumped her. Had this ex been the jealous type and didn't like others checking out Treble? Or maybe he'd been intimidated by her. Or—

"Well, well, well. Looks like Trouble's back in town." A man stopped next to Treble's chair. "Time's been good to you, darlin'."

"Certainly better than you ever were," she returned sweetly.

Or maybe the guy who dumped her was just a jerk, Keith concluded. He didn't know Rich Danner very well except that the landscaper had moved back to Joyous about two months ago, apparently licking his wounds from a divorce. He'd remarked to Keith that they were the most eligible bachelors in town. *"Us and Jason McDeere, but he's raising a toddler, which puts us ahead in desirability. 'Course there's plenty of fillies to go around for all three of us."*

Now, Rich was turning green eyes full of apology toward the "filly" he'd let get away. "Don't be like that, Treb. I was a kid. Teenagers make bad romantic decisions."

She reached for her sandwich. "I couldn't agree more."

Keith grinned at her implication, but the diss had obviously sailed over Rich's head.

"I knew you'd understand. How about I join you, and we can reminisce about what good times we had before I screwed up?"

"Actually," Keith interjected, his impulsive words surprising him, "I kind of wanted Treble all to myself for another few minutes before we have to leave. She was fascinating me with stories about her job as a DJ in Atlanta."

Treble's eyebrows shot up, but she played along. Truthfully, they'd never once discussed what she did for a living, but Charity had mentioned it. Whereas Harrison rarely spoke of his stepdaughter, Charity was effusively proud of her older sister, her naked affection almost masking her disappointment when Treble missed yet another holiday or birthday at home.

"Sure, buddy." Rich held his hands in front of him and gave a quick nod of male understanding. "I get it. But, Treble, we'll have to catch up some other time."

When they were alone again, Treble said, "Thank

you. I don't *need* a man to rescue me, but I'm not gonna look a gift horse in the mouth, either."

"Does everyone born in Tennessee compare people to livestock?"

"What?" Lines of confusion furrowed her brow.

"Never mind. And you're welcome," he added. "That guy can get on my nerves."

She nodded, taking a big bite of her sandwich and letting out a moan of pleasure. "God, I forgot how great Tennessee barbecue is. I mean, I knew I loved it, but this… This is better than sex."

He squeezed his own sandwich and barbecue sauce ran down his fingers.

If she'd noticed, he would have been embarrassed, but she seemed oblivious, lost in enjoyment of her food. Some of the women in town would have fainted—blushed, at the very least—at having the word *sex* tossed casually into meal conversation, but Treble clearly thought nothing of it.

She washed down her food with a swallow of soda. "Earlier, you said people 'born in Tennessee.' So you're not a native?"

"Nope. Charity first mentioned you when she heard I'd moved here from Atlanta. I went to med school and interned there. Grew up in Savannah."

A city steeped in rich tradition and history, Savannah seemed like a good place for ghosts. He preferred to leave his there. In the E.R. of a major Atlanta hospital, he'd found himself dealing with too many reminders, too much trauma. He'd become a doctor because he wanted to save people, but if he'd stayed where he was, he was the one who'd wind up needing saving. So he'd found salvation in the relatively peaceful town of

Joyous. He had the practice, real friends. Of course, Charity tutted that he'd be even happier once he found a girlfriend.

"It's not as if there aren't willing women," she'd teased, threatening to count the number of foil-covered casseroles in his freezer.

He'd considered deflecting her interest in setting him up by suggesting she encourage her dad to date instead—Harrison needed something in his life besides control of the dairy business and grueling work-weeks. But even though it had been a long time since Charity's mother died, Keith didn't push the idea of a replacement romance. Losing family was hard, and Charity had mentioned how much she'd been missing her mom lately.

"I suppose you think it's pitiful that I called my sister and begged her to come be with me?" Charity had asked.

"Of course not." The only thing Keith hadn't understood was why Bill and Harrison had been so shocked Treble agreed. If Keith's older sister were still alive, there wasn't anything he wouldn't do for her.

"Keith." Treble's voice was soft, but persistently inquisitive. "Are you okay?"

He met her eyes, not sure what to make of the woman. Her gaze was filled with what seemed like empathy, hardly the selfish person she'd been painted as in unflattering gossip. He understood better than most the value of a fresh start. Maybe Treble had changed, maybe she'd returned not only to help her sister but to earn her stepfather's forgiveness for whatever youthful transgressions were in her past.

"I'm fine," he assured her, "but a lousy lunch date, huh?"

"Well, you won't be winning any awards for witty conversation, but you're easy on the eyes, so it balances out." Leaning forward, she lowered her voice conspiratorially. "You *do* know there's a blonde in the corner who's been checking you out, don't you?"

His gaze darted in the direction she'd subtly indicated, and he spotted elementary school receptionist Dinah Perkins having lunch with two other women. When Dinah caught him noticing, she smiled and offered a small finger wave. Moments later, she and her girlfriends huddled into hushed conversation. Either they wanted to know who the stranger was sitting with Dr. Caldwell, or they already knew and, like Rich Danner, were intrigued by Trouble—er, Treble's—return to Tennessee.

"Friend of yours?" Treble asked Keith.

"Just a friend," he stressed.

How long had it been since he'd had a girlfriend? Med school and his stint at the hospital had been hectic, and since moving here he'd been…cautious. There'd been a few dates and a nice weekend when a female friend had come to visit, but if his love life hadn't completely flatlined, its prognosis wasn't rosy, either. Eventually, he wanted to find the right woman to make his fresh start complete, but now that he was fitting in, he didn't want to jeopardize that with social missteps. Citizens gathered round their own, and if Keith broke up with a local girl, he risked becoming an outsider again. Maybe he was overanalyzing, but he hadn't felt at home anywhere in a long time.

It wasn't something he was willing to lose.

"About done?" he asked Treble.

She nodded. "I've taken up enough of your day. If you can swing me by the garage so I can give the mechanic my keys, you'll be rid of me soon."

Standing, she leaned over to grab a couple of napkins and clean off the table. He found himself looking straight into a tempting view of her cleavage. *Stop ogling Harrison's daughter!* But forcing himself to turn away was damn difficult.

In one short afternoon, Treble had had more of an effect on him physically than any of the women he'd met in town. Maybe it helped that she had a body that was sinfully perfect, making him think of fallen angels, but he was a doctor. He'd seen lots of bodies, many of them undressed.

The sooner he delivered her to Charity's, the better.

With the "downtown" area covering only a half-dozen blocks, it didn't take them long to reach Carter and Sons. Keith had just pulled up to the garage when a mechanic in dusty blue coveralls emerged from one of the open bay doors.

"That's Ronnie," he told Treble. "She'll have your car working better than when you drove it away from the dealership."

"She?"

There was no need for him to answer since Ronnie was removing her cap. Sleek red-gold hair fell to her shoulders.

"Huh," Treble grunted. "You know, before you came to get me, I was expecting 'Doc Caldwell' to be a good bit older. And Ronnie's *definitely* not what I anticipated. Lots of surprises for such a sleepy little town."

Sleepy? A twinge of foreboding rippled through him

as he regarded the woman seated in his truck. He'd watched her varied reactions to Joyous—apprehension over arriving, sassy rebuffs to an ex-boyfriend, nearly sensual enjoyment of good barbecue—but now he wondered how the town would react to her. Treble James looked like a wake-up call waiting to happen.

Chapter Four

Treble stepped down from the truck, shaking her head. She'd always teased Charity over her affection for routine. "Don't you ever want to mix things up a little?" she'd asked her younger sister.

"Nope," Charity had maintained. "Predictability suits me just fine."

At the moment, Treble could use a few less surprises herself. "You're the mechanic?"

The woman nodded. She was shorter than Treble, their height difference exaggerated by the mechanic's flat-soled sneakers. Her clear jade eyes were lovely, but Treble wondered if men looked past the freckles bridging her nose and the shapeless, grease-stained overalls to notice.

"Ronnie Carter." The redhead extended a hand, noticed some black smudges near her fingertips and winced, dropping her arm to her side. "Technically, Veronica. No one calls me that. My brothers use 'Red,' but only to make me crazy."

Keith came around the side of the truck to stand with Treble. At his renewed nearness, her body hummed— it was like static electricity she couldn't control. *Try harder.* The good doctor probably wouldn't appreciate it if she drifted closer and stuck to his clothes.

"Afternoon, Ronnie," he said. "Treble had some car trouble outside town, and I assured her you were the best in the state at taking care of the problem."

"Flatterer." Ronnie grinned at him, but then her eyes widened and she swung her gaze back to Treble. "Good Lord. You're Treble Breckfield, aren't you?"

"James. Treble James." The distance she put between herself and her stepfather's name was automatic, although at least Harrison Breckfield attempted to stand by his responsibilities. More than she could say for her biological father. "I'm Charity Breckfield's sister. Er, Charity Sumner's."

"Wow. My brother Devin was crazy in love with you in high school." Ronnie nodded thoughtfully. "I can see why."

Treble couldn't remember Devin but hoped she wasn't awful to him.

"Daniel warned him that a guy two years younger didn't have a shot." Ronnie's tone was matter-of-fact, not vengeful on her brother's behalf. Good thing. A mechanic wielding a grudge was not someone you wanted tinkering with your engine.

Treble searched her memory for Carter brothers and finally landed on a name, though she couldn't put a face with it. "Are you related to William Carter? He was in my grade. Salutatorian, I think?" Her high school graduation ceremony was a blur, mostly occupied by plans to leave that summer. Despite the times she'd been sent to the principal's office for behavior problems, she'd kept her grades up and aced her SATs—college had represented her ticket out of town.

"Yeah, Will was the bookish one," Ronnie confirmed. "Though you wouldn't know it to look at him—he's as hulking as the other two. He went to university in North Carolina and settled there. The rest of us stayed," she said wistfully. Gifted mechanic or not, Ronnie didn't sound one hundred percent satisfied with her life.

Well, who is? Treble ignored the impulse to draw out the conversation and brainstorm solutions; this wasn't a radio broadcast. "So, Ronnie, are you as good with cars as I keep hearing?"

"No. Better." The woman's confident smile completely endeared her to Treble.

They chatted for a few minutes about where Trusty was parked, what the escalating symptoms had been before the vehicle died altogether, and where Treble could be reached.

"I'll call you this evening at your sister's," Ronnie said after she'd filled out some paperwork and taken Treble's keys. "I doubt I'll have fixed anything yet, but I should at least have an idea of the problem."

Moments later, Treble and Keith were back in the truck and en route to Charity's house. Charity had issued several invitations to visit over the years, and Treble might have been quicker to accept any of them if her sister had moved more than four miles away from the Breckfield family manor. Treble wondered if she could ever step inside the ancestral home—built on profits of the century-old dairy—without immediately thinking that it seemed cold. She'd been four the first time she'd visited, once her mother and Harrison were seeing each other, and it had seemed large and drafty. Like the haunted houses in scary stories. It hadn't improved her opinion that the place was full of antiques and Breckfield heirlooms that she was admonished not to touch.

At least Mom warmed it for a while. With her gone, the place had become positively glacial, full of long, mournful silence and, as Treble grew more rebellious in her teenage years, even colder arguments and chilly words.

"Hey." Keith's voice was amused. "I've seen people in hospital waiting rooms less nervous than you. Your car's in great hands with Ronnie."

"Hmm?" Treble followed his sidelong gaze to where she'd been drumming her fingers on the passenger side windowsill. "Oh, no, I..." On second thought, it suited her fine if he attributed her apprehension to vehicular woes and not her dubious homecoming.

"You what?" Keith prompted.

"I'm sure Ronnie's terrific. I guess I'm anxious because I know the car's on its last legs. Or tires, as the case may be. I need it to hold out until I find a house, get approved for financing and close." The goal warmed her from the inside, and she smiled at the plans she couldn't wait to start making. Decorating, furnishing, even landscaping. "My apartment's become a bit claustrophobic over the past year."

Keith nodded. "For me, the city got claustrophobic. A mentor of mine knew Doc Monaghan and let me know he was looking for a replacement. I'd never even heard of this place, but as soon as I moved… It's like I could finally breathe again."

She chuckled wryly.

"Guess that was corny," he said, sounding more guarded.

"No. No, I was laughing at the irony. I feel free in Atlanta, whereas here I would suffocate." Under expectations, the watchful eyes of nosy neighbors, the weight of the past.

"To each his own, right?"

"Exactly. To each her own." Because her natural inclination was to fill dead air, when it became clear conversation had lagged, she turned back toward him. "So, did you always know you wanted to be a doctor?"

He stiffened, so imperceptibly she wouldn't have noticed if her body weren't bizarrely attuned to his. "It… seemed right for me."

She hadn't expected his profession to be a sore subject. Yikes, she'd promised her boss she wouldn't lose her edge out here in the sticks, yet only a few hours in, she was already floundering her way through awkward chats.

"What about you?" Keith returned. "You always know you wanted to be a radio host? Charity makes it sound fascinating."

Treble smiled self-consciously. "It probably seems more glamorous than it is because she's lived in the same place her whole life and works for her dad." The girl should have been named *Patience;* Treble would have snapped by now.

"You mean she's easily impressed because she's a local yokel?" Keith's tone was deceptively mild, his delivery belying the disapproval of his words.

"I didn't mean it quite like that. I adore Charity."

He slanted her a look. "Yeah. I could tell you two are close."

Was he being sincere? Had Charity painted a rosy picture of their sibling relationship? *Which would be like her.* Or was he being sarcastic, passively condemning Treble for not being a better big sister? He didn't have that right.

I swear I'm better with people than this.

Well, not all people. Definitely not her stepfather. Or her actual father. Sometimes not even with her sister. But, normally, she was very popular with people who didn't know her well.

It was being back in this town that was messing with her head. By the time she'd left here, she'd been full of misery and anger, feeling unloved and paradoxically going out of her way to be unlovable. She hoped for all their sakes that Charity had that baby on time and not a single day late.

"Just about there," Keith said, apparently seeing— and misreading—her impatience.

She nodded, the cloudless sky outside her window vast. "I recognized this particular spot of nothing."

Joyous had undoubtedly grown some over the years, but the town moved at a slower pace than the rest of the world, still relatively untouched by urban sprawl. Pastures and trees that had been there since before she was born existed today, and even though there were few landmarks on this last stretch before they turned onto the dirt road that would lead to Breckfield property, she could have found her way from here blindfolded. Having not been home in so long, the familiarity was unexpected. There were some blocks in Atlanta where new

gyms grew overnight as if having sprung from magic
seeds and, if you blinked, the restaurant you were used
to driving past could be replaced entirely by a shopping
center without you ever noticing the construction crews.

As promised, they reached Charity and Bill's place
a few seconds later. Keith took a left on Willy Wooten
Drive—a mud strip probably no more than twenty feet
long, named for a guy who'd once built a house there—
and quickly encountered a paved fork. One finger of
asphalt snaked its way up the hill and led to her stepfather's house. Another jogged a shorter distance to a
well-kept yard and honest-to-God white picket fence.
Treble didn't need to see the cheery *Sumner* stenciled on
the mailbox to know this must be where Charity lived.

If Harrison Breckfield had ever run for mayor, he
would have won by a landslide. So many townspeople
were employed by or in some way affiliated with the
dairy that the Breckfield family held a prominent position in the community. Yet Treble couldn't help wondering why Harrison had never proposed that the town pave
Willy Wooten or even offered to have it done himself—
especially now that his pregnant daughter had to drive
over it in all manner of weather conditions. His own
vehicles must have jostled over the years as he plowed
through puddles and potholes, but something about that
very specific concrete, starting precisely at the Breckfield property and not one inch sooner, personified the
man. He had clear boundaries. He stayed unswervingly
within them and expected others to do the same.

There were both a garage and carport to the side, but
Keith parked more casually in the curve of the circu-
lar driveway, right out front. The house was predom-
inantly brick, although it had a cottage-style facade

bordered by a railed-in wooden porch. Treble imagined Bill and Charity sitting in the double swing, discussing baby names and drinking cold lemonade. Of course, she could just as easily imagine Charity in the picturesque little house, singing as woodland animals helped her clean and making seven beds for seven little men.

Treble hadn't finished climbing down from the passenger side of the truck when the screen door clattered and her sister appeared on the front porch. In deference to her current medical condition, Charity didn't try to navigate the stairs and greet them in the yard. Still, her enthusiasm was evident even from several yards away.

"You made it!" she called to Treble.

"Thanks to your friend Dr. Caldwell." Treble really was grateful to the man for riding to her rescue, even if their short time together had been…charged.

"Well, come in, come in. I have some iced tea freshly brewed," Charity told both of them. She placed a hand over her distended belly. "Decaf, of course."

Treble turned to collect her luggage, only to find that Keith had grabbed both suitcases and slung her duffel bag over his shoulder.

"You should at least let me get one of them," she chided.

He half shrugged as he passed, repeating her words from their first meeting. "I'm able-bodied."

I'll say. Her gaze slid down from where his thick hair lay rumpled against his collar to his jeans.

She followed him up the stairs. Charity had stepped aside to make room for Keith and the baggage he carried, but as soon as Treble cleared the top step, the blonde swooped in for a hug. The sideways angle, not to mention the bulk of Treble's unborn niece, made the embrace a little awkward but it was appreciated none-theless. Treble couldn't quite hook her arm around her sister so settled for patting her on the arm in greeting.

"Thank you for coming," Charity said softly, still not letting go. "Thank you, thank you, thank you."

"You're welcome," Treble said. "In triplicate. But, about my needing to breathe?"

Charity laughed, stepped back. "Guess I always was the hugger in the family."

Well, it sure as hell hadn't been Treble or the aloof Harrison Breckfield. "Like Mom. You have a lot in common with her." As soon as tears began welling in Charity's eyes, Treble wished she'd said something else. She struggled to lighten the moment. "Although, now that I think about it, that bone-crushing grip might have come from Harrison. Imagine the tackles you could have made if you'd played football!"

Harrison had been a college linebacker for the Ten-nessee Vols. At six foot three with steel-gray eyes, he was as formidable off the field as he'd reputedly been on it. Maybe Treble should have been smarter than to try making end runs around him, but she'd been sixteen. In theory, she was older and wiser now, but she was also a grown-up no longer seeking her stepdad's approval. She was who she was, and she refused to make apologies to him if she liked her music loud and her heels high.

"Where'd I lose you ladies to?" Keith asked, stick-ing his head out onto the porch. He'd obviously set the bags down somewhere inside.

Charity sniffled. "Sorry. Just exchanging sisterly greetings."

Keith glanced at the woman's obviously teary expression, then shot Treble a look that bordered on accusatory. *Two minutes and you already made her cry?*

"We're coming," Treble said brightly. As soon as he retreated, she told Charity, "I hope I didn't upset you. You warned me you were thinking about Mom a lot, and I didn't mean to say anything that made you miss her more. I know I'm a poor substitute for her being here right now."

Charity squeezed her hand. "It's wonderful that you're here. And I'm touched that you think I'm like her. Don't worry about the waterworks. It's the hormones. Honestly, all I do these days is cry—and eat Breckfield banana ice cream. Sometimes I cry *while* I'm eating the ice cream."

Treble laughed, glad they were on less sentimental ground as they joined Keith in the cool, aromatic house. Charity's air-conditioning bill must be a fortune, but the low temperature felt heavenly after driving in the heat for much of the day. Equally divine was the scent of spices and meat cooking. Treble had never been all that proficient in the kitchen, but she thought she smelled thyme and rosemary, underscored by sautéed onions. A little garlic? As her eyes adjusted to the comparative dimness of the living room, she stood still, breathing in the tantalizing scent. An archway at the far end led into a modest kitchen. Treble saw maroon laminate flooring and gold appliances.

"You." Keith took Charity by the hand, steering her toward a rose-and-cream sofa. A rocker upholstered in matching fabric sat by the large picture window in the room, a wicker basket full of knitting supplies and remote controls tucked next to the chair. "Off your feet. Then explain to me how you whip up one of your gourmet dinners while adhering to your OB's advice. Don't make me call Dr. Whalen because you know she will kick your butt. Metaphorically speaking."

Much as Treble wasn't ordinarily a fan of men chastising grown women over their choices, she had to admit this was no time for Charity to be rolling out the welcome wagon. "He's right. Well, I wouldn't know about the doctor, but definitely the dinner part. Don't you dare try to cook just because I'm visiting. You and this baby are what's important."

Leaning back against the couch, Charity shook her head, her honey-blond ponytail swishing. "Boy, you guys impress easily. I promise I wasn't slaving over a stove. I gave Bill some basic instructions for what to throw in the Crock-Pot, then stood long enough to season it myself. Honestly, the most strenuous thing I've done today was lift a pepper grinder. I spent hours in the rocking chair with my feet up, watching television, dozing and talking briefly on the cordless phone to both of you. Those are all approved activities, aren't they?" The impish grin she shot Keith made her look so young it was hard to believe she was going to be a parent soon.

He sat on the couch next to her. "If I overreacted, I did it because I care."

"I know," Charity said fondly. "You're a good friend. You will join us for dinner, won't you?"

"Um…" Keith darted a look toward Treble, who shifted her weight from foot to foot and tried to ignore feeling out of place. "I should check in at the clinic."

Charity laughed. "Well, I wasn't planning on eating dinner in the middle of the afternoon. Come back tonight. Bill and Dad said they'd be back by six, so I'll have dinner on the table around six thirty."

Treble cleared her throat. "You'll do no such thing."

"All right," Charity amended. "*Someone* will have dinner on the table around six thirty."

"Won't I be intruding on a family get-together?" Keith asked.

"Don't be ridiculous." Charity swatted him on the arm with all the force of a two-pound kitten batting string. She'd always been diminutive in height and build and, in some ways, her protruding beach ball of a stomach highlighted that; it was comically disproportional in comparison to the rest of her. "You're like family. The more the merrier! Right, Treb?"

"Right. Sure." Merry? Not the word Treble would have used to describe an evening with her stepfather, but rumor had it Keith actually enjoyed the man's company.

It probably helped that when *Keith* spent time with Harrison, the conversation wasn't laced with disapproval and derision over his dating life and career choice.

"I gotta say, Keith, I'm disappointed that you won't find enough time in your schedule to at least *go* on a date." Charity put her hands on her hips, but given her reclining position, it wasn't as effective a stance as it could have been.

When he'd returned this evening, Keith had turned the sofa that served as a divider between the two rooms so that it faced the kitchen. It was a more comfortable choice than the four chairs at the small oval table—besides, the spindly-legged seats didn't look sturdy enough for a woman in her final weeks of pregnancy. Tonight they'd eat in the dining room. For now, Treble was tear-

ing and washing lettuce leaves while Keith sliced veg-
etables for the salad.

She was glad *she* wasn't the one wielding the knife
or her occasional glances at Keith, who was standing
a foot away by the kitchen counter, could have been
disastrous. He'd obviously showered before changing
into a starched white button-down shirt and dark jeans,
because the ends of his hair had still been damp when
he'd arrived, filling the small room with the scent of
soap and sandalwood cologne. *And I thought the beef
stew smelled delicious.*

Keith could definitely make a girl's mouth water. In
fact, according to Charity, that's exactly what he did.
Girls throughout town were lusting after him, although
Charity had put it more discreetly as the two sisters
chatted over tea this afternoon.

"If I thought he was happy as a single bachelor, I
wouldn't nag him about finding someone," Charity
had said. "But, honestly, I'm not convinced he's happy.
We're friends, but there's a lot he still doesn't tell me."

"Not for a lack of your asking, I'm sure," Treble
had teased.

"I think he's lonely."

Since Keith had ignored Charity's previous statement, his only response being a rhythmic *chop chop
chop,* she pressed on. "I know your occupation is important to you, to the town, but do you really want your
career to be the be-all and end-all of your existence?"

Treble stole another covert glance at the dark-haired
doctor. He could have his pick of women in Joyous. Was
he simply a loner by choice? The way he'd chatted with
Charity earlier made that seem unlikely. Though he
couldn't discuss any medical cases, he still had lots of

funny anecdotes about patients and their families, especially kids. His genuine smile when he spoke about them, compounded with his willingly coming here tonight to have dinner with a pregnant woman and her family, made him seem like a people person.

"Enough," Keith warned his hostess, brandishing a carrot menacingly in her direction. "You have to at least feed me before interrogating me."

"I thought I might be able to wear you down easier on an empty stomach," Charity said. "You know, weaker state and all that. But now that you mention food…if Dad and Bill aren't ready to eat soon, we're digging in without them. I'm famished."

Treble grinned at her sister's newfound appetite, thinking about the snacks Charity had downed earlier. Healthy snacks granted, but plentiful.

Charity cocked her head, listening. "I don't hear the water running anymore, so maybe Bill's done with his shower. That just leaves Dad." Bill had come through the kitchen door shortly after Keith arrived. He'd spared a nod for the doctor before smiling in Treble's direction.

"I'd hug you, but I smell like cow." Then he'd sent his wife a glance of such sheer adoration that it had almost been too intimate to watch. "Hey, gorgeous. How are you and that daughter of ours?"

Beaming back at him, Charity had assured him she and the baby were doing great. "But clean up fast," she'd warned. "This kid is getting hungry again."

By the time Treble was scooping all the salad ingredients into a large pottery bowl and Keith had his head stuck in the refrigerator to find Charity's homemade dressing, Bill padded into the living room clean and nicely dressed, but barefoot beneath his khaki slacks. A man with calloused hands but a soft smile, he was solid, short and just the right height for Charity. He kissed his wife, giving her the greeting he'd postponed when he was gritty and malodorous. He rested his forehead against hers, his sandy hair a few shades darker than her blond. They were a well-matched couple.

Treble hoped that the listeners who periodically called her show, wistful for this kind of love, found what they were looking for, but she suspected it was more elusive than movie producers and greeting card companies would have the public believe.

As Bill entered the kitchen to see what he could do to help, Treble noticed his soapy, fresh scent was similar to the way Keith had smelled when he walked in the door. Recalling her visceral overreaction to the doctor, she mentally smacked herself in the forehead. So the man bathed—it took more than basic hygiene to impress her.

"Treble?" Keith's voice directly behind her made her jump. "What are you doing?"

Trying not to imagine you in the shower. "Um, tossing salad?"

He peered over her shoulder at the nearly mangled lettuce. "Interesting technique you have there."

Her face warmed. "Would you believe I learned it on one of those Food Network cooking shows?"

He laughed, the sound as rich as dark chocolate and just as addictive. "No, but you get points for creativity."

"Yeah, I always did have an imagination." She turned slightly as she said it, and their gazes collided. It wouldn't have mattered except that he was just so close. Not crowding her or being overly familiar, just there, his body near enough for her to melt with its heat, his indigo eyes—

"I take it Harrison hasn't called?" Bill's voice broke the spell, and Treble seized the opportunity to scoot away from Keith while she had the good sense to do so. Her brother-in-law was staring down at the wristwatch Treble knew had been an engraved anniversary present from Charity. "He said he'd be here by six thirty."

"It's just that now," Charity said. "Let's set the table, and the timing will probably work out perfectly."

They did, but it didn't.

Bill sat on the edge of the couch. "We should go ahead and get you fed, sweetheart. Treble, you wouldn't recognize her when she gets hungry. The woman turns mean."

Keith scoffed. "Mean? Charity? You must have her confused with some other tiny blonde who has a Napoleon complex."

"I do not," Charity protested, glaring up at him with twinkling eyes.

"You're a bossy nag," Keith retorted with a grin. "If I'd known the dinner invitation was just another excuse to needle me about dating…"

Treble took a seat at the kitchen table, a safe distance from the doctor, and smirked at her sister. "He's right, you know. She used to play 'school' with all her adorable stuffed animals and collectible dolls, and she was very strict. She's the only person I know who's ever given detention to a teddy bear."

The men laughed, but Charity sniffed daintily. "Well, I wanted the best for Mr. Snuggles and he was never going to get anywhere in life if he didn't do his homework." She wagged her finger at Keith. "I only want what's best for you, too."

"So, what did we decide about waiting for Harrison?"

Treble interjected. Funny how much she wanted to help Keith avoid the subject of his love life. Normally, she made a living off of commenting on people's love lives or asking them to do so.

Charity frowned. "I'm sure he wouldn't mind us starting without him, but…this is a special occasion. Bill, if you'll please freshen up my tea, I can wait a few more minutes to eat." She extended her empty glass.

As Bill pressed the automatic ice maker, the refrigerator performed noisy variations of a churning grind, the sounds mirroring Treble's stomach. She knew why Charity was so intent on this dinner, it would be the first time since the weekend Charity was married that the two sisters and Harrison had sat down for a meal together. But the night hadn't truly started and already the déjà vu had her insides in knots. After her mother's car accident, Harrison dove into work. In retrospect, she understood that had probably been his coping mechanism, but that didn't excuse him for being late to meals or letting the girls eat with the housekeeper, Joan, while he had a sandwich in his study. Treble couldn't truly say whether her initial stunts—shoplifting cosmetics, stealing Harrison's car—were because she was trying to get his attention or because she was just so angry.

Charity, living up to her name, had always been more understanding, the family peacemaker. She'd been content with the moments of absent affection her father managed to give, the pats on the head in passing even if he wasn't sitting down and asking about their day the way their mother had. Maybe if he'd looked at Treble the way he did his own daughter, *she* would have been content, too. What she usually got, though, were reminders not to talk back to her teachers and admonishments to change into shirts that weren't so revealing.

Not that I'm bitter, Treble thought with a wry smile. Well, she was, but at least she had a sense of humor about it.

Charity sipped her sweet tea. "Oh, I almost forgot! Treble, I had Bill pick up a bottle of wine for you at the store. Could I get one of you strapping men to open it for us?" She glanced to Treble, her expression apologetic. "You usually drink white, don't you? The selection in Joyous isn't all that sophisticated, but—"

"I'm sure whatever Bill found will be fine," Treble said. She would have been okay without a glass, but refusing seemed inhospitable. Bill was more a beer man than wine drinker, and it was a sure bet Charity didn't plan to have any; Treble couldn't let it go to waste. Of course, she didn't intend to drink a whole bottle, either, so hopefully her stepfather and Keith would have some. Bill disappeared into the dining room, hunting through the china cabinet while Charity called out likely locations for the corkscrew they obviously never used.

Treble caught Keith's gaze. "Join me for a drink?"

He took longer than necessary to answer, and she wondered what he'd been thinking. "Sure." Turning, he opened a cabinet and reached for the wineglasses on the top shelf. It wasn't the first time he'd known without asking where something was kept. He seemed at home here.

Home. During the afternoon, Treble had had ample opportunity to study her surroundings, not so much the floor plan and the furniture as the personal touches that made the place uniquely Bill and Charity's. This was what Treble wanted for herself, this…sanctuary.

Because Bill was out of the room and Keith was wiping the infrequently used wineglasses with a paper towel, Treble was the only one whose hands were free when a quick knock sounded against the kitchen door.

"That must be Dad!" Charity looked giddy. "Treb, will you answer the door?"

"Of course." Taking a deep breath and reminding herself this night was important to her little sister, Treble twisted the knob.

In the glow of the back porch light, Harrison Breckfield looked down on her. "Hello, Treble."

"Harrison." She swung the door wide and stepped out of the way.

"I understand you had some difficulty with the trip?" he asked as he entered the kitchen. His once black hair was now as gray as his eyes, yet that only made him look distinguished. It was something else—indefinable in his face, in his carriage—that made him look as though he'd aged.

"Nothing insurmountable," she said. Come to think of it, she hadn't heard from Ronnie the mechanic yet. Was no news good news...or silent foreshadowing that expensive parts needed to be specially ordered?

Harrison nodded absently. "It was good of Dr. Caldwell to leave his practice for the afternoon and bail you out."

Would it have killed him to say "help you out"? It wasn't as though she'd called from the county jail. One could argue that it was just an expression, but Harrison never *just* said anything. "Yes, I'm very grateful to the doctor."

Harrison stopped to greet Keith, and the younger man clapped him on the shoulder and leaned in to say something the rest of them couldn't overhear. Then Harrison shook hands with his son-in-law, who'd successfully found the corkscrew and opened a chilled chardonnay, before crossing to his daughter.

"Smells wonderful in here. I hope you haven't been waiting on me?"

"Not at all," Charity lied. "We were just enjoying some cocktails before dinner."

Harrison glanced over his shoulder in time to see Treble accept a glass of wine. He frowned at her, no doubt thinking of Charity's wedding.

Looking him dead in the eye, she tilted her glass and took a hefty swallow. He shook his head in disgust.

Truthfully, Treble might have been annoyed if she allowed herself to dwell on the moment. What was it about the man's low expectations that goaded her into wanting to say stuff like, "Could you all excuse me for a minute—I think I left my bong in Keith's truck?"

You know the answer to that. Maybe they'd never had the warm fuzzy step-bond that would earn them a biopic on the Hallmark Channel, but deep down, she'd at least respected the way Harrison lived up to his responsibilities. He might not love her, but he'd tried to do right by her. Until spring break of her senior year, when he'd walked in on Treble and dairy worker Mitchell Reyes. Instead of asking what had been going on or even acknowledging the uncharacteristically grateful way Treble flew to his side, Harrison had simply concluded that his flirtatious, rule-breaking stepdaughter had once again caused trouble that reflected badly on the family. But that was a long time ago.

Right now, Treble's only concern was getting through this dinner.

Chapter Five

Bill and Harrison, seated opposite each other at the antique walnut table, talked at length about the day they'd had and their decision to add another large-animal vet to the dairy farm's permanent staff. Even though it was the kind of conversation Treble had grown up around, she couldn't intelligently contribute. Then again, with home-cooked food of this caliber, keeping quiet and enjoying the meal wasn't a hardship.

Her well-meaning sister, however, had other ideas. She cleared her throat gently and, judging from Bill's slight double take, Treble wouldn't be surprised if Charity had poked him in the thigh, too. "All this talk about work, and what I really want to hear about is Treble's job! I know you were already involved in radio last time you were here, but to have your own show? We're all so proud of you!"

Seated as the dubious guest of honor at the head of the table, Treble smiled. "Thanks, Charity. It was very gratifying to get my own slot. The station manager displays a lot of trust in me, and that means as much as the callers who check in and let me know they like what I'm doing."

"Reaching all those people. It's very impressive." Charity turned to her father, adopting the reproachful tone she'd used when Mr. Snuggles hadn't lived up to his potential in stuffed animal class. "Isn't it, Daddy?"

With a sigh, Harrison leaned forward so that he could better see Treble around Keith. "What exactly do you do on this show? Mainly play records or is it more like talk radio?"

Keith chuckled. "Harrison, I think there are only about ten people left in the country who still own 'records.' One day I'll introduce you to this modern marvel called a compact disc."

"Fine, disrespect your elders. I'll have you know all that walking to school uphill both ways in the snow made me the determined, successful man I am today."

Treble froze, stunned by the exchange and the genuine humor in her stepfather's eyes. The man adored and indulged Charity, but even with her, he'd rarely joked. Had he mellowed with age? Four years was a long time. Maybe he wasn't exactly the person she remembered.

"Actually, it's a little of both," she explained. "I play music and take requests for songs, but do a lot of interaction with the audience, too. A lot of nights, we'll form a theme. I'll try to find songs that match up somehow with the topic we're discussing."

"What kind of topics?" Charity asked, looking both

genuinely interested and pleased by the way things were going.

"It varies, but my trademark has become relationship stuff. Dating advice, commiserating, popular—"

"*You* give dating advice?" her stepfather asked incredulously.

"I..." Treble trailed off, aware that all eyes were on her. This conversation would have been easier if she were in a booth somewhere with her familiar headset. "I've never made false claims to be an expert in the field. My listeners understand that I'm more like a moderator. People call in to share their experiences and perspectives, and I keep things moving, provide food for thought, color commentary. Last week, this woman called in complaining that her boyfriend—" *Uh-oh.* Probably not the best example for this group.

Harrison raised his eyebrows, waiting.

There was a pause while Treble tried to think of a less risqué anecdote. She hated the uncertainty churning inside her. Her job was terrific; she worked hard and received steady e-mails from grateful listeners who enjoyed her show.

She squared her shoulders. "Well, they were having a problem in their love life and some of my other listeners were able to offer constructive solutions for not only the woman who called, but also anyone else out there experiencing the same problem, who might have been too shy to seek advice."

Harrison's ruddy complexion had turned blotchy. "By love life, you mean their sexual relationship?"

"Yes, I do."

Out of the corner of her eye, Treble saw Charity open her mouth, no doubt to rescue them. But her stepfather was already speaking again before anyone had a chance to diffuse the tension rolling in like a low-pressure front.

"This is what you've chosen to do with a college degree? Make your living by discussing sex with the entire city of Atlanta?"

"It's not like I'm *having* sex with them," she snapped.

There was a squeak from Charity's end of the table, and the sound helped dispel some of Treble's temper. In spite of herself, she found the humor in her stepfather's words. If the entire population of Atlanta actually tuned in to her show, her station manager would name all his future children after her. And possibly rename the first four.

She focused on sounding calm rather than defensive. "Male-female relationships aren't something to be ashamed of. Most healthy adults have a sex drive. Isn't that a medical fact, Doctor?"

Keith whipped his head toward her. Though she wouldn't classify his strained expression as outright hostile, he clearly didn't appreciate being dragged into the discussion. Was he going to back her up or agree with Harrison that her job was distasteful?

Charity seized the opportunity created by Keith's hesitation. "Did everyone leave room for dessert?"

Obligingly, Bill sprung out of his seat. "I could go for a bowl of ice cream. Keith?"

The man pushed his chair away from the table. "I'll help you scoop."

Charity glanced between her father and sister, her baby-blue gaze equal parts crestfallen and beseeching. "I have three flavors of Breckfield ice cream and some store-bought chocolate chip cookies."

That they could no doubt wash down with a nice cold glass of Breckfield milk. Possibly the only way Treble could be *more* of a misfit in this family was if, on top of everything else, she were lactose intolerant, too.

Keith kept his gaze lowered as he finished his dessert. No offense to the man seated next to him or the many hundreds of employees who made the ice cream possible, but Keith barely tasted the Neapolitan he'd selected from Charity's freezer. Normally, whenever Charity asked him to dinner, he accepted her offer automatically. His fondness of the family aside, her food beat the hell out of whatever he microwaved at home. After tonight, however, he might think twice about future invitations.

Previous experience had braced him for Charity's habitual hassling about his lack of a romantic life, but he hadn't been sufficiently prepared for working with Treble in that warm, cramped kitchen.

They'd spent a fair amount of time in his truck this afternoon, but that had been static. This evening, they'd bumped into each other more than once or simultaneously reached for the same drawer. She'd changed from her travel clothes into faded jeans and a bright pink shirt with a satiny collar. Whenever she brushed by him, he caught a whiff of something appealingly spicy. Almost cinnamon, but not quite. It didn't smell like perfume, but maybe a body lotion? It somehow made him think of baked apples and sex, *not* a normal combination for him.

But he had a feeling Treble James and "normal" rarely co-existed. Look what had happened to tonight's dinner. Usually Bill and Harrison talked business for a few minutes until Charity complained, then redirected conversation with either plans for the baby or mild local gossip. The men would praise her on another wonderful meal and the evening would conclude peacefully. Tonight had been so tense Keith had the urge to whip out a blood pressure cuff and make sure Harrison's readings were still in a safe range.

With his bowl empty, Keith glanced up to make his farewells. "Charity, thank you for having me, but I should head on. No need for you to get up, I can show myself out. Wait—Treble, walk me to my truck? Couldn't hurt to double-check and make sure you didn't forget anything. Wallet, sunglasses, whatever."

Her amber eyes narrowed. He pretended not to notice as he bid Harrison and Bill goodbye.

As already evidenced, Treble didn't have a problem speaking her mind. The second they hit the front porch, she turned to him in the dark. "So, why did you really want me to come with you?"

He sighed, formulating his words as he preceded her down the stairs.

"You're not denying an ulterior motive," she observed when they reached the yard. "So I was right?"

"You are. I'm just trying to figure out a way to say this without getting my head taken off."

Her face was inscrutable, the light shining from the house windows and the moon not enough to illuminate her expression. "If it makes you feel any better, I haven't decapitated anyone in days. Practically weeks."

"Maybe we could just drop the wordplay and get to it?" He'd unconsciously adopted the stern, authoritative tone he took when giving patients advice he knew they weren't going to like. "While I don't want to exaggerate your sister's condition, I'm sure you can understand why it's not a good idea to upset a pregnant woman, especially one this close to term."

"This is about dinner tonight," she said. It wasn't a question.

"And the rest of your visit. You and Harrison seem to…agitate each other."

Her voice fell surprisingly quiet, nearly inaudible beneath the buzz of summer insects. "Yet I don't see *him* out here getting this little reprimand."

Keith leaned against his truck. "Don't you think you should cut him some slack?"

"I'm sorry, were we at the same dinner?"

"Try to see it from his perspective." Keith didn't object to what Treble did for a living—although for his own sanity, he preferred not to think about her discussing sex in that throaty drawl of hers. Understandably, Harrison held more old-fashioned views. "What dad wants to think of his daughter as sexually active, much less giving other people instructions on how to do it?"

"It's not…*he's* not…many of my shows have nothing to do with that. And I've given reminders about abstinence, not letting yourself be pressured, or at least being safe. Don't you think he knows how Charity got pregnant?"

"Charity doesn't have your history," Keith said, his brain catching up to his mouth about a second too late. *Crap.* He couldn't believe he'd blurted that.

So much for finesse. Maybe it had been too long since he'd had a conversation with a woman that didn't start with "How long have you been having these symptoms?" Well, he talked to Charity, but she was more like a— Not letting himself think "sister," he was almost relieved when Treble lit into him.

"What the hell do you know about my 'history,' Doc?"

Having opened Pandora's box himself, he figured he might as well brazen through the aftermath. "Bits and pieces that I've heard in town. Petty theft, sneaking out at night, trying to get into a bar even though the fake ID was ridiculously amateur, not to mention at least half the people there knew exactly who you were and that you were only sixteen. Is it true you got some poor slob fired from the dairy after he made out in a barn with you?" If Harrison had been judgmental with her, he was probably reacting to her track record.

Treble's breath left her in a whoosh. She even leaned forward as if her abdomen hurt. Then she straightened. "You really think I took a leave of absence from a job I love just to drive a state over and deliberately stir up trouble with a pregnant woman and an old man?"

"No." Keith tilted his head back, wondering how a man with precious little family left had ended up embroiled in this particular family drama. "But I do worry that you just can't help yourself."

Staring upward, Treble watched the ceiling fan in the guest bedroom rattle through its repeated orbit. On this slow setting, it didn't do much to cool things down— despite the air-conditioning, she'd felt overheated ever since her little chat with Dr. Caldwell. But on the higher settings, the fan shook so much she had visions of the entire thing crashing down on her.

Was she like the fan, just moving in meaningless circles? As a successful adult, the mistakes of her past should be behind her. But they'd felt as close as ever tonight over dinner. If there'd been a camera in the room, the whole thing could have been aired on Court TV. Did Harrison really have the right to put her life on trial?

The bigger question was, why did she still let it get to her so much?

She tried to imagine a caller with this problem. What would Trouble J say? *If you live your life to please other people, odds are no one will end up happy. Do your best to be comfortable in your own skin without obsessing about what other people think.* That went double for interfering doctors who doled out opinions after less than a day of acquaintance.

Sighing in the dark, she admitted that she wasn't even that angry at Keith. Well, she had been—she glanced at the oversize blue numbers on the digital clock—four hours ago. But he'd been speaking out of loyalty to Harrison and, more importantly, genuine concern for Charity. Treble's sister had been quiet after dinner. *Too quiet,* as they said in old movies.

Harrison had left almost immediately after Keith's departure. Bill had glanced between the two women as though he wanted to say something but couldn't for the life of him figure out what. Then, he'd suggested he clean the dishes so the two sisters could catch up. Treble had lifted a jigsaw puzzle Charity had started onto the coffee table, so her sister could work on it from the couch while Treble sat on the floor. The expression in Charity's blue eyes had been so fragile, so precariously close to tears, that Treble abandoned her plan to talk about dinner, but Charity hadn't responded to any of the other conversational gambits, either.

Living in an apartment complex, Treble had grown

used to filtering out footsteps and thumps, so it took her a moment to realize someone was moving around in the house. When light spilled down the hallway, she acted on impulse and got out of bed.

The center of the house was bracketed by the living room and kitchen on one end and the master suite that included Bill and Charity's room and bathroom on the other. In the middle were the dining room, a small bedroom for guests and an identical room that was in early throes of being decorated for a nursery. Treble had been surprised earlier, given Charity's enthusiasm for having her daughter, that the nursery wasn't farther along.

"Well, we've registered for a lot of stuff," Charity had said, "and the baby showers usually come in the last trimester. I'm so excited that you'll be here for the one next week!"

Additionally, Treble had picked up the vibe that maybe Charity had been nervous to commit to the nursery too soon. Just in case.

She blinked, adjusting to the overhead light of the kitchen. As she suspected, her sister sat at the table.

"Hey." Charity looked up from the gallon of ice cream and bowl next to it, her expression sheepish. "Did I wake you?"

"No, I couldn't sleep."

"Me, either. So I thought I'd come have a snack." She gestured with her spoon. "I know ice cream's junk food, but technically, I didn't eat mine after dinner."

Treble sank into one of the empty chairs. "I noticed."

"Want some Butter Butter?"

One of Breckfield's signature flavors, vanilla with peanut butter and butterscotch ripples. The ads claimed

Doesn't Get Much Better than Butter Butter. "Thanks, but I don't think so."

Charity sighed. "Yeah, if I had your figure to protect, I'd be wary of hitting the ice cream like this, too. Since I'm the size of a full-grown hippo, I've decided to just give up the ghost."

"Oh, stop. You can't be any bigger than, say, an *adolescent* hippo." Relief washed through her when Charity laughed.

Treble could remember Charity's first day of school. No one in her family had seemed nervous. Their mom had already been through kindergarten angst once, Charity had been dying to get on that school bus every day like her big sister, and Harrison had assumed in that arrogantly Breckfield way that his daughter was so gifted that of *course* she would excel. As it happened, he'd been right. Still, Treble, an experienced and worldly twelve-year-old, was wise enough in the ways of playground bullies and lunchtime seating that she worried on her sister's behalf. She'd looked at the cherubic blonde in her pristine pink jumper and vowed to punch—or possibly shove, if the offender were too young to justifiably hit—anyone who hurt her baby sister. *I just wanted to protect her.*

A lot had changed, but not that. At one point after her mother's death, Treble had experienced a blip of resentment toward the sister Harrison so easily loved, who still had a clearly defined place in the world. But then it had occurred to her that, in a way, Charity was the only piece of Mom she had left.

"Charity, I'm sorry I screwed up tonight."

Her sister put down her spoon. "No. I pushed. I should have known better."

"Than to prompt him into talking about my job or to ask me here in the first place?" Treble swallowed, wishing she hadn't felt compelled to ask the question. She wasn't sure she wanted to hear the answer, especially since she still didn't have a getaway car. *I have got to call Ronnie first thing in the morning.*

"I'm *glad* you're here," Charity said firmly, her tone brooking no further doubt. "I practically coerced you into it, remember?"

"Yeah, but this could be one of those cases of be careful what you wish for."

"Treb. Honestly, I want you here. For my baby's birth, for the showers…for the free manual labor wallpapering the nursery."

"Ah. The truth comes out." Treble grinned, feeling more relaxed than she'd been during the hours of tossing and turning in bed. "I should put that in the freezer for you before it melts. Unless you were going to eat another bowl?"

"Nah, I'd better call it quits. You've inspired me to maintain my adolescent hippo figure."

Standing, Treble reached for the gallon. She paused. "You know I love you, right?"

Charity's eyes shimmered, then spilled over as a few tears rolled down her cheek. "I know."

Wow. That had to be some kind of speed record for going from fine to crying.

"Hormones!"

Treble didn't know if the word was supposed to serve as a reminder for why her sister was so emotional right now, or if Charity were cursing the reason she was so volatile. Either way, Treble decided to be tactful and moved to the refrigerator to give her sister a moment to pull herself together.

Charity caught her off guard by blurting, "Dad loves you, too."

All evidence to the contrary. Treble bit her tongue. Hard.

"He does," Charity insisted.

"Well." Treble spoke slowly, carefully, not turning around. "If he didn't, you couldn't blame him. I was a hellacious handful."

"You were a teenager," Charity countered. "A grieving one, at that. If puberty hormones aren't quite the roller-coaster ride of pregnancy hormones, they're at least darn close. All girls at that age are—"

"Charity, what's the worst trouble you ever got into during high school?" Treble asked over her shoulder.

"I'm a freak of nature, bad example. A square peg." Her cheeks reddened. "I always wanted to be bolder, like you."

"Don't be crazy. You have this great little house and a husband who adores you."

"Yeah, but I had this English teacher I loathed."

"You never loathe anyone," Treble said, sitting next to her sister and swiping a taste of the Butter Butter pooling at the bottom of the bowl. "You're the nice sister."

Charity stuck her button nose in the air. "I can loathe people just as well as anyone! This guy I loathed with the burning fire of a thousand suns."

Treble choked on a laugh.

"Honestly. He was so pretentious, analyzed litera-ture to death, sapping out everything I actually *enjoyed* about it. The thing is, I didn't even agree with most of his interpretations, but I regurgitated what he said on essay tests because I knew it would get me an A. Just once, I wanted to take a stand, tell him he was full of it in front of the whole class. You would have."

"Babe, I'm not a solid role model."

"I don't know about that. You're funny, independent, interesting. You're your own person."

"It can get a little lonely being your own person," Treble admitted quietly.

Charity straightened, her eyes going from dim, as she recalled her past "failings," to the bright intensity of a zealot with a mission. "You're lonely?"

"No. I mean, sometimes, sure, who isn't? But no. Charity! Look at me, I'm content with my life. Very content." Treble realized she was babbling, but couldn't help herself. She had a bad feeling she knew what was coming.

"Bill knows some single guys—"

"Dairy guys. *Not* that there's anything wrong with that, but let's face it, my time in town is limited. I have a job and a house hunt to get back to after this baby's born."

Charity's face fell. "I guess you're right. I know you can't stay...but I'd love it if you could visit more often."

"I will," Treble promised, meaning it.

No matter how difficult dinner had been, Joyous had more going for it than she remembered. The chance to hang out with Charity, the meditative effect of this charming little house, a female mechanic Treble could easily imagine befriending, some of the best barbecue in the Southeast. *And the best-looking town doctor in the Southeast?* Maybe, but Keith Caldwell's sex appeal had no relevance in her life. She might not even see him much for the rest of her visit.

By the time she finally went to bed and dozed off, she still hadn't decided whether never seeing Keith again would be a good thing or a bad one.

Chapter Six

"Morning, Doc Caldwell. Sleep well?"

"Morning, Velma." *And, no.*

Anytime Velma Hoskins encountered someone else before eight in the morning, she asked them if they'd slept well. His receptionist was a firm believer in rest being a key to good health. "I don't drink coffee after noon," Velma would tell anyone who'd listen. "Don't want to interfere with the suggested eight hours, you know. My late mama, God keep her, swore by eight hours every night and frequent napping. She lived to ninety-five." At which age she'd died peacefully, in her sleep.

Keith was all for the medical benefits of getting enough rest, but he sometimes wondered if Mama Hoskins's fanatical devotion to sleep and napping stemmed from having eight children. If he had that many kids running around the house, he'd be counting the hours until afternoon naps and bedtime, too. Nevertheless, maybe he should get to bed early tonight to make up for last night's restlessness. He'd been alternately haunted by the musical sound of Treble's voice when she was having fun and the flat hurt when she'd asked if he thought she was here only to cause trouble.

He cleared his throat, leaning on the desk behind the reception window. "Who do we have coming in today?"

Velma lifted the purple glasses that hung from a chain around her neck. "A couple of routine checkups midmorning, and Maggie Cline called at seven o'clock this morning. I told her we could squeeze her in if she'd get here by eight thirty."

He nodded. "This appointment's for Nathan?"

"Poor little guy has another ear infection."

Actually, probably the same one. Keith didn't think he'd quite managed to get rid of it, as it was proving resistant to antibiotics. With some altering of the original prescription, the right medicine could hopefully knock it out. He wanted to keep *all* the kids who came to see him healthy, but he knew Maggie especially panicked when anything seemed wrong with Nathan.

Loss did that, made you hypersensitive to losing anyone else.

Maggie was a widow whose husband had died in a factory accident the year before Keith moved here. The entire town had rallied around her and her toddler. Because of a generous insurance policy and the money her late husband's company paid after the accident, she was now one of the most wealthy citizens in Joyous. She'd told Keith once that every time she wrote a check, she wished she could return the money and get her husband back. In the past few months, however, she'd mentioned the man less and less.

"I think Maggie is finally finding her footing," he told Velma. "She and Nathan seem more steady every time I see them."

"You just be careful you don't see her and Nathan too often," Velma said, pulling out a handful of manila folders from the patient file drawer.

"Excuse me?"

She jabbed a skinny finger at him. "That girl's sweet on you."

"Maggie? Maggie Cline? I don't think so."

Velma was an astute woman who'd lived in Joyous her entire fifty-eight years, so she didn't miss much. But even insightful town icons had an off day.

She snorted. "Look here, whippersnapper, I'm a woman more than twenty years your senior, and I was married twice. *You're* a clueless male—no offense— who's hardly been on a date since you got here. Which one of us do you think has a better grasp of the situation?"

"Well, when you put it like that," he said sarcastically. It didn't bode well for his authority around here that his only full-time employee called him a whippersnapper. He hoped it didn't catch on with the three part-time nurses.

"I've read about this. Don't remember what it's called, but I know I've read about it. She loved her husband, and he took real good care of her and Nathan. Then Nathan got so sick in the spring, and *you* helped take care of him. It doesn't hurt that you're good-looking as all get-out and she was probably getting to where she's ready to dip her toes back in the dating pool, anyway."

"Transference," Keith supplied. "Is that the term you're looking for?"

"Yeah. Now, personally, I have no objection to you dating, so long as you run off with me eventually." It was a long-standing joke between them. Her voice sobered, full of compassion for Maggie. "But if you don't have any romantic interest in her, you don't want her or that boy to get falsely attached."

As a result of the unexpected conversation with Velma, he found that his smile of greeting for Maggie and Nathan twenty minutes later was nervous. He scanned the young widow's face, but the only emotion he saw was an antsy desire to get her son better.

"Hey, buddy." He lifted Nathan onto the freshly rolled white paper covering the exam table. "Can I take a look in your ear? I lost a shoe and think it might be in there."

Giggling, the towheaded child turned his head so that Keith could flash the otoscope into his left ear.

When the visit was over, Keith escorted them up front. Nathan pawed through Velma's selection of bright round stickers while Keith wrote out a new prescription.

"Thank you," Maggie said. "I don't know what this town would have done if you hadn't come along. Doc Monaghan was fantastic, but we all understood he needed to retire. I know there are other towns close by with capable doctors, but if you're already losing time from work to take the trip or you're like me, with a sick kid you're desperate to have seen…"

Keith doffed an imaginary cowboy hat. "Just doing my job, ma'am."

"Ahem."

He turned to catch his receptionist giving him the evil eye. She hadn't thought he was flirting with Maggie, had she? Had *Maggie* thought he was flirting?

The single mom fluffed the ends of her shoulder-length auburn hair with her fingers, shooting a befuddled glance at Velma before looking back at him. "As grateful as we are to have someone like you on the job, Dr. Caldwell, I hope you still have time to get out and have fun. Like Days of Joy?"

He hadn't been here for last year's fun, but the annual Joyous festival held the first week of July was supposedly a major social happening in these parts. Craft booths that drew both consumers and vendors from a range of counties, fair rides, competitions with final rankings in all age groups at the award ceremony, fireworks, cook-offs and a parade that featured the mayor waving from the back of a white convertible and an appearance by Bonnie the Breckfield cow. In addition to Breckfield, many local businesses sponsored teams, displays, free samples and games. As a result, most of the town was scheduled to close at noon on festival days.

"I'm looking forward to it," Keith said.

"Oh, good." Maggie let out her breath. "Festival's one of my favorite times of year. I'll have several jars of homemade jelly in the canned goods tasting—wish me luck. And, of course, you know about the big dance. Will you be attending?"

"I, ah…" Behind him, Velma's telepathic *I told you so* was deafening. He rubbed an ear. "I really can't say. But if I don't see you there, I hope you have a nice time. Thinking about going with anyone special?" Clumsily done, but it was the gentlest way he could think of to dissuade her before she got out the invitation she appeared to be working toward. Damn, he *was* a clueless male.

Maggie's disappointed gaze dropped to the floor. "I suppose not. After all, I already have a pretty special guy in my life." She shot a wistful glance at her son, took his chubby hand and told Velma and Keith to have a nice day.

On the way out, she looked again at her son, rather sadly, but then smiled and ruffled his hair as he pointed to the plane flying overhead. Keith watched him through the large window that was part of the storefront between Claudette's Beauty Salon to the left and the town's newspaper office on the right—it was hard to say which of those two locations got all the local news first. If she typed as fast as she could curl, cheerfully nosy Claudette could freelance for the *Joyous Journal-Report*. This building, with its trio of businesses, was located on the most trafficked street in town. Across the way was the library. At one end was the Bestest Bakery and Sandwich Shoppe, at the other a feed and supply store frequented by all the farmers and ranchers in the area. While spreads like the Breckfields' were the exception, there were plenty of small farms, parcels of property that had been passed down throughout generations where families supplemented other incomes with fresh produce sales or birthday party pony rides. Keith himself had bought three acres at a good price, even though it was more space than he needed. Right now, he lived at the front of the clearing in a forty-year-old house that boasted no central air—window units only— a gas stove with cranky disregard for pilot lights and unpredictable plumbing. All part of its quirky charm.

The aging two-bedroom was a temporary situation. Eventually he'd get more ambitious with the land and have a house built. *For whom?* Himself? Himself and a wife? Kids? As he'd told Maggie, he really couldn't say.

He cast another look through the window, but Maggie and her son were no longer on the sidewalk. They'd probably gone around to the back, where the majority of parking was available. He sensed Velma following his gaze. "She didn't think I was disinterested because of Nathan, did she? Because he's a great kid."

"Her dating choices will probably be more limited because she's already a mommy," Velma said noncommittally. "But I hope she and Nathan find the right man."

"I'm not that man."

"'Course not. You and *I* were destined to be together."

He grinned over his shoulder as she retrieved the number of an insurance office from her Rolodex. "I don't know what I did to deserve you."

"I choose to take that as a compliment," she informed him.

Wanting to grab a cup of coffee before his nine o'clock appointment, he left Velma to her work.

When would it be time to find out whether or not he could be anyone's right man? Pushing aside personal relationships had been almost necessary during med school, then his insane hours at a hospital and being the newcomer in town…but he'd settled in now. His mother had made her own fresh start back in Savannah, including a round-faced husband who sold cars and doted on her. Keith was genuinely happy for them, but he didn't know her second husband very well and he'd allowed his demanding hours to become an easy excuse for not visiting often. Though he loved his mom, Savannah would never feel like home to him again. It was part of who he'd been before Gail's drowning, which seemed surreal now, like looking back at someone else's life.

His father's coronary just two months after Gail's death had been like a shot of Novocain to the heart. Keith had become numb, channeling his energy into school. As an intern, he'd mastered the detachment doctors needed in order to survive their profession; inevitably, not all emergency room patients could be saved. Over the past few years, however, he'd realized it wasn't so much detachment as deferral. Rather than risk any more pain, he'd put off feeling anything for anyone. How long could he have existed like that without losing part of himself for good? The lazy pace in Joyous had taken away his excuse for working himself into exhausted oblivion, giving him a better look at what his life had become. Until now, he'd kept people at a distance, but here, he'd needed help integrating in the community, and the resulting friendship with Harrison and Charity had thawed his defenses.

With the icy numbness wearing away, he was more aware of the empty spaces he'd ignored. *Charity's right*…though he had no plans of telling her so. The woman would waste no time lining up dates for every night of July and half of August. He didn't need to pick out rings or anything, just someone nice he could have dinner with. Unbidden, Treble's strong features and sassy smile flashed through his mind. *Anyone but her.*

What he needed was a local girl who would mesh with his calm new life here in Joyous. Treble would be gone soon, causing who-knows-what kind of discord in the meantime. Besides, what possible interest could she have in him after their last encounter? He'd felt drawn to protect Charity and her father, wishing yet again that Harrison would be honest with his family about his heart condition, but Keith hadn't planned to hurt Treble's feelings.

Trying to push aside the picture of her lush mouth and the equally disturbing wounded expression in her eyes last night, Keith refocused. He would start slowly, maybe a cup of coffee with someone who worked nearby or actually setting foot inside Guthrie's and asking someone to dance. Letting himself spend any more time thinking about Treble was the opposite of starting slow—it was the emotional equivalent of throwing himself on the freeway in a sports car with no brakes or air bags.

Treble's Thursday and Friday were idyllic, not counting the unwelcome news that she needed a new carburetor. "I'd recommend getting a rebuilt one," Ronnie had said. "Why pay for a new one when this car, despite the magic I plan to work on it, doesn't have many years left in it anyway?" Although the automotive diagnosis was grim, Treble was enjoying her stay more than she'd expected. Bill was easygoing and likable, if not the most exciting man in the world, but Charity made up for that, her pregnancy hormones and occasional moodiness prompting her to say some unpredictable and frequently hilarious things.

Having been cooped up in the house, Charity was thrilled to have company, and they had a lot to catch up on. Charity told her all about their cousin's comically disastrous wedding, Treble shared some of her best nightclub stories, and on Friday, Charity's friend Lola Ann brought sandwiches for all three of them.

"So, you're the radio star?" the brunette asked as she unpacked a white paper bag onto the coffee table. "I've been looking forward to meeting you. You're something of a legend around here." Lola Ann's father worked at the tractor dealership and the family had come here two years after Treble's departure.

"Lola Ann!" Charity glared from her higher perch on the couch.

But Treble was unfazed. "I'll just bet. I gave the local gossips plenty to wag their tongues about." She wasn't surprised Lola Ann had gathered an earful, but it did startle her to know that recent citizen Keith Caldwell had heard so much about her exploits. Even if some of his information was flawed. "Still, you'd think people would have more to talk about by now."

"Nope," Lola Ann said cheerfully, exposing dimples on either side of her grin. "I mean, there's the occasional scandal or good news or noteworthy crop issue, but it's a sleepy town. During the lulls, people fall back on old topics. The fact that Charity and your father are so loved in this town keeps you relevant."

Stepfather. Treble couldn't help the mental correction, though she managed not to say it out loud.

"Can we eat now?" Charity looked annoyed, although personally, Treble found the candid librarian endearing.

Charity's best friend, Penny Paulson, was a woman Treble remembered from their girlhood and Charity's wedding. She taught middle school and, now off for the summer, was currently enjoying a two-week cruise with her husband, a town deputy. They'd scheduled the trip so that she'd be back for the baby shower and well ahead of the due date.

Lola Ann passed around the sandwiches. "Hope turkey is okay with everyone. Mac sliced it while I was waiting, and he baked the sourdough rye fresh this morning."

Treble took a bite and was suitably impressed. The special horseradish dressing on the sandwich cleared the sinuses nicely without being too hot to enjoy. *Mom always said the food tasted better here.* She'd claimed it was the country air.

Treble only remembered bits and pieces of her early childhood in Chattanooga. Her mom had worked at a local tourist attraction, both giving tours and taking shifts in the gift shop. Treble had been left home one Saturday with her father and woke up early from her nap, coming into the living room to find him kissing another woman. She remembered feeling guilt after he left, thinking that if she'd just stayed in her room… Six months later, he'd come back, apologetic, swearing to do better by both of them, but then he'd left in the middle of the night. Treble's mother hadn't said much about it, but Treble suspected he'd taken any cash that was in the house with him. Not long after, Treble's mom had applied for a job with Breckfield, giving tours at the dairy and promising Treble all the ice cream she could eat.

Although Charity and Harrison both knew Treble had planned to track down her father when she left here, neither had ever asked how the reunion went. Which was just as well. There'd been sporadic birthday cards from him growing up, but apparently he'd meant for that to be the extent of their father-daughter relationship. She should have kept it at that.

"Treble? You don't like your sandwich?" Lola Ann was peering at her, her mouth pursed in disappointment.

"Oh, no, the sandwich is wonderful. Truly. I just thought about something my mom said. She always thought the food here tasted better than anywhere else."

Charity smiled. "I remember. I don't have much of a basis for comparison, not being a big traveler. What do you think, Treb?"

"Well, there are some *great* restaurants in Atlanta— I'll take you if you come visit me—but the food in Joyous can definitely hold its own."

After that, Treble made a concerted effort to keep the chatter going, but the pervasive, nostalgic melancholy lingered after Lola Ann had to leave.

"She seemed nice," Treble commented to her sister. "I mean, it stood to reason that as a friend of yours she would be, but she seemed to actually like me. Whatever stories she's heard didn't scare her off too badly."

Charity laughed, closing her eyes as she rested her head on the back of the couch. "Lola's passion in life is books and she likes larger-than-life people. They remind her of her favorite characters. Besides, she's lived here long enough to know gossip gets embellished with time. No one should be judged based on whispers about what happened ten, twelve or twenty years ago."

"Tell that to—"

"Who?" Charity's eyes popped open. "My dad?"

"I was going to say Dr. Caldwell. Honestly," she amended, "I hadn't planned to say it at all but caught myself too late."

"What do you mean about Keith?"

Treble refused to bring up the lecture he gave her by his truck the other night; it would feel too much like tattling. Besides, he'd genuinely been looking out for Charity, and she could respect that. "Nothing. Just a gut feeling. I'm not sure he likes me much. To be fair, he didn't see me at my best the other night."

"I think he likes you fine. I know dinner was…tense. But before that, you made him laugh. He has a great laugh."

"Oh, yeah."

"Aha!" Charity straightened, looking pleased with herself. "Liked his laugh, did you?"

And a lot of his other attributes. "I was simply agreeing with you," Treble said. "Don't read too much into it."

"Are you sure? Because watching you two work together, there appeared to be some *looks*."

Drat, she'd thought she'd been sneaky enough not to get caught. "The summer heat has clouded your thinking. Want me to turn the oscillating fan back on?"

"This has nothing to do with heat. At least, not the kind from the sun."

Treble stood, although she didn't really have any clear purpose or destination. "Charity, I'm warning you, drop it. I know you want the good doctor to date, and that's between you and him—or him and whatever woman he ends up dating—but leave me out of it."

Charity arched a pale eyebrow. "You don't threaten a pregnant woman."

Treble had to laugh at her sister's imperious tone. Maybe Keith was on to something with that Napoleon complex theory. "Let's just change the subject, pregnant woman. You guys decided on a name yet for that baby girl of yours?"

"No. There are just too many to choose from, plenty we like but no combination we love yet. We discussed

naming her for someone in the family—Mom, maybe—
but that didn't fit exactly right, either. There are so
many people who've been important to us. Besides,
we'd rather she have her own identity and never feel
as if she's supposed to be living up to someone else."

Treble, named for a maternal great-grandmother
she'd never met, smiled at the gentle fierceness in Charity's voice. "You and Bill are going to make good parents."

"Thank you. As tiring and occasionally alarming
as this pregnancy has been, I know deep down *this*
is the easy part. It's only going to get harder once she
pops out."

Treble grimaced as she walked toward the window.
She preferred not to think about the "popping out" details. "You look tired now. Why don't you go lie down,
so you're rested enough to visit with Bill when he gets
home tonight?" Charity had admitted on the phone that
afternoons were hardest but had skipped a nap yesterday, probably feeling obligated to entertain her sister.

"What about you? I made you drive all the way here
from Georgia, murdered your car in the process and
now I'm just going to make you sit in my living room
while I sleep?"

It was a gorgeous day. If it weren't so hot, she would
go for a run. "Don't feel bad about the car. Trusty would
have died anyway. At least here, there's a mechanic
who comes highly recommended and won't gouge the
price. And I can keep myself busy. I can brainstorm
notes for future shows, do Sudoku or put in a movie.
You're the one who's watched every DVD in the house
three times, not me."

"They occasionally put one of those Sudoku puzzles in the paper. What are they, exactly?"

Treble went and got a book and a pen, happy to show Charity another way to kill time while she was couch-ridden.

Her sister balked at the numbers. "How many math skills do I need for this? Because being pregnant has a way of Swiss-cheesing your brain."

"It's not about math. It's about patterns. Sometimes it helps to glance at the grid without really concentrating and you'll find something you weren't actually looking for. You have to make the numbers line up in exactly the right places so they don't repeat. Here, I'll show you."

Fifteen minutes later, they'd completed a puzzle labeled "moderate" in difficulty, but Charity was actively yawning.

Treble set down her pen. "All right, now I'm going to *insist* you take a nap. And if you're still worried about my having something to do, give me a task. You know I'm looking forward to helping in the nursery. Or maybe I could grab some groceries so it's one less thing Bill has to do when he could be spending time with you?" Sometime between now and next Thursday evening, she needed to go into town anyway; she hadn't yet bought a shower gift.

"You're sure you don't mind running errands?"

"As long as you don't mind me taking your car."

Charity put together a short list, and Treble made sure her cell phone was charged so her sister could get in touch with her.

"I think that's everything," Charity said. "You shouldn't have any trouble refilling my prescription for prenatal vitamins, but have the pharmacist call me if there's a problem. Those are the sandals you're going out in?"

Treble glanced down at the lilac open-toed mules she wore with her short-sleeved, square-necked retro peasant blouse, modernized by the funky print of the sheer fabric, and white shorts. "Yeah. What's wrong with them?"

"Nothing, as long as you can walk without killing yourself." Charity sounded awestruck. "I'd never make it ten steps without toppling over."

They weren't *that* high. Charity should see the six-inch heels. "I've had practice."

"Okay, but if you end up with a broken ankle, we'll be bed-rest buddies. Can you grab me my purse?"

It was hanging on the doorknob of the coat closet just inside the house. Treble carried it over to the couch.

"Thanks." Charity dug out her car keys, then startled her sister with a surprisingly accurate and irreverent impression of Harrison Breckfield. "Here are the keys to the car, young lady. I'll expect it back without a scratch and you home by dinner."

Treble laughed. "Brat."

In the garage, Treble found her sister's sensible and economic American-made compact. Probably got exceptional mileage and safety ratings, although secretly, she thought it didn't have a tenth of Trusty's individuality. She climbed inside, and as soon as she'd turned the key in the ignition, classic music rolled from the speakers. Mozart. Or Beethoven, maybe. She wasn't an authority on musicians prior to the nineteen hundreds. Grimacing, she punched radio buttons until she found the station they'd listened to in Keith's truck. A Rolling Stones tune filled the inside of the small four-door. *That's more like it.*

As she backed out of the garage, a shrill beeping started, making her jump.

Simultaneously tapping the brake and glancing back at the dashboard to see where she possibly could have screwed up already, she noticed a flashing red seat-belt symbol. "Give me a second," she told the car. "I was getting to that part."

It kept blinking at her and blaring as if skeptical she'd had any intention of following proper regulations. Yeesh. A car with a censorious attitude. She was calling Ronnie this afternoon for an update on Trusty.

On the other hand, not three minutes down the road, the air-conditioning had fully kicked in, cool currents circling her in a way she hadn't realized possible with the sun shining through the windshield. So there were at least one or two perks to being a rule-abiding conformist. Who knew?

Chapter Seven

For someone who'd sat bumper to bumper in Atlanta traffic, navigating the streets of Joyous was refreshingly simple. Even though a few buildings had changed and the years away had left a few blanks in her memory, there was no real chance of Treble getting lost in town. Traveling on the more winding, rural roads that weren't painstakingly marked might be a different story, but "downtown," four main roads formed a square. All the smaller side streets fed back into it eventually.

The drugstore was exactly where it had always been, although the pizzeria next to it was new. Brand-new, according to the Grand Opening A-frame sign sitting on the sidewalk amid a profusion of colorful potted flowers. After driving the length of the picturesque street, she found an available spot. She parallel parked, relieved when the rusty skill proved sufficient. Though

Charity had been kidding with her whole "back by sundown, paint job unscathed" warning, Treble would die of mortification if she got into a fender bender.

In the shade of awnings and roof overhangs, the fresh air and short stroll were pleasant. She'd hit the pharmacy first in case they needed time to fill the prescription. She could always swing by for the pills after running her other few errands. The jovial, mustached man behind the counter, however, assured her he'd have everything ready for her in just a minute.

"Anything for Miss Charity. You say you were her cousin?"

"Half sister," Treble corrected.

"Hmm. Can't rightly say I remember you."

There was a sniff behind Treble, and she turned to find an austere middle-aged woman wearing a navy knit top and a plastic badge that proclaimed her the manager. Even without the name tag, Treble would have known Midge Moore immediately. She'd been a thirtysomething cashier with a pinched expression the last time Treble had seen her. In the interim years, she'd cut her graying hair into a bob that ended exactly at her jawline but otherwise looked exactly the same.

"I remember her," Midge told the pharmacist. "I remember her *perfectly* well. If she makes a move toward the cosmetics aisle, call security!"

The man frowned. "Security? But we—"

"Just page me on the walkie!" Midge stalked off, darting one last suspicious glance at Treble.

I really should apologize for stealing the makeup. Not that Midge had given her much of an opportunity. And acting as though Treble needed to be escorted through the store so that someone could keep an eye on her seemed over-the-top.

Treble faced the perplexed pharmacist. "Don't worry, I promise not to rush the counter and steal all the good drugs."

His eyes widened. "I'll just get you Miss Charity's vitamins so you can go."

Okay. Not a situation where humor was helpful.

Moments later, Treble was back out on the sunny sidewalk, this time feeling like a notorious felon. *Incredibly sexist.* She happened to know one of the men Charity said worked for the sheriff's department used to indulge in weekend cow-tipping, and the current elementary school principal had pulled more than his share of false fire alarms to shorten boring class periods. Then again, maybe misspent youth gave him a foundation for relating to the current pupils.

A wolf whistle directly behind her stopped her in her tracks, and she pivoted. If that were Rich Danner, she— "Bear!"

Technically, the man with the emerald eyes and broad grin on his face was named Teddy, but he'd been six feet tall by his freshman year in high school. The coaching staff tried to recruit him for basketball and, after he'd filled out more, for football. Bear had confided to Treble once during detention that he wasn't much of a team player. He was a decent guy, though, only ever in trouble when he lost his temper on another's behalf. When someone wrote Treble's number and a rather predictable limerick on the wall of the boy's bathroom, Bear had offered to draw and quarter the culprit if he were ever caught.

"Trouble J!" He swept her into a bone-crushing hug

that lifted her off the concrete. "I heard you were in town, but had to see it for myself."

Hearing her radio name caught her off guard. "You know about my show?"

He nodded as he set her back down. "Went to a Braves game once in post-season playoffs. Drivin' in, a buddy and I saw your picture on a station billboard. I don't think I ever did convince him that I knew you, but we listened to your show every night I was in town."

She was touched. "You should have called in and said hi!"

The big man in his appliance repair outfit—probably specially made—blushed six shades of red. "Nah, I couldn't do that. Interrupt you at work? Besides, you might not have remembered me."

"Trust me, Bear, I—"

Behind them, a man cleared his throat. They were obviously in his way. She had to admit, Bear was tough to pass on the sidewalk. They both turned to apologize, but her words froze in her throat when she found herself face-to-face with Keith Caldwell.

"Sorry, Doc," Bear said. "I was just renewin' my acquaintance with Trouble here. She's something else."

Keith's gaze went from her eyes to the hot-pink toes peeking out from her mules and back up. "Certainly is."

"Aren't you supposed to be at work?" she asked, flustered by running into him in the middle of the afternoon. She adjusted her tone. "I mean, are you just on a break or are you off to rescue yet another damsel on the side of the road?"

He chuckled, his eyes crinkling slightly at the corners. *Definitely a nice laugh.* "Late lunch. So many patients come in during the noon hour that I wait until things slow down to grab a bite. Thought I'd check out our newest restaurant."

"How was it?" she asked.

Leaning forward, he advised in a low voice, "I'd stick with the barbecue place and the sandwich shop, personally. Unless you consider grease an acceptable food group."

Bear shook his head. "This place has been five different eateries in the last six months, none of them good. I wish they'd scrap the restaurant idea and use the space to sell fishing supplies or hardware. Somethin' useful."

The doctor cocked his head, studying Bear and Treble. "So, the two of you are old friends?"

"Oh, Trouble and I go way back." Bear squeezed her shoulder. "I told her in the ninth grade that if she ever needed someone's kneecaps broken, I was her man."

"I see." Keith took an almost imperceptible step backward.

"Offer still stands, by the way," Bear told Treble conversationally. "What's a decade or two between old friends? Speakin' of which, I guess this'll be the first year we see you at the reunion! Festival days are right around the corner."

She hadn't thought that far ahead. "I don't know." Not everyone from her graduating class held the same place of affection in her heart as Bear.

"Well, you think about it! Meanwhile, I was plannin' to duck into the drugstore before getting back to work. Summer's our busiest time. People get darn cranky about their freezers and window units breaking down in this heat."

Treble nodded. "I'll look for you if I'm at the festival."

Bear flashed a grin. "I ain't hard to spot in a crowd."

His departure left a rather large void. She turned back to the man last seen blaming her for the awkward family dinner and jeopardizing her sister's health.

Keith exhaled. "I should be going, too."

"Yeah. I promised Charity I'd take care of some stuff for her. So...'bye."

He snapped his fingers. "I didn't ask. Did you get any news on your car?"

"Talked to Ronnie yesterday. The prognosis wasn't great, but treatable. She's tracking down a carburetor, hopefully one I can afford. I should have Trusty back next week."

He grinned. "You call your car Trusty?"

"You're mocking me because I named my car?"

"I just find that particular name ironic, considering how we met."

He had a point.

"Have a nice day," he told her.

"You, too."

They both turned, obviously headed in the same direction. *Naturally.* She could just ignore him and keep walking, but she'd feel stupid pretending he wasn't there for the next couple of blocks.

"I parked Charity's car down that way, but if you'd rather, I'll just stop and do some shopping." She punctuated her teasing comment by jerking a thumb to the storefront behind her, not bothering to turn.

Keith's lips quirked into a grin so wicked her knees went weak.

Half-afraid to look, she glanced over her shoulder at the pawnshop window that inexplicably featured an array of handcuffs. Rather than get embarrassed, she just went with it. "Yep, a girl can't have too many pairs of handcuffs. You never know where you might misplace them."

"I could make a crack about that, but my kneecaps and I are terrified of Bear."

She laughed.

He lifted a hand as if to touch her face, but dropped his arm quickly back to his side. "It's nice to see you smile. I figured that after what I said the other night—"

"About how if I didn't watch my mouth I'd be the ruination of my family and put my sister in the hospital? I've forgiven you." More or less. It helped that he'd been trying to look out for the person she'd always been most protective of.

"Really? I'm surprised you're taking it so well."

"Even bad girls have their reasonable moments," she informed him, leaving him to ponder that as she sauntered toward her car.

It took him only a couple of strides to catch up with her. "You need a trained medical professional walking with you," he said. "Catch one of those heels in a sidewalk crack, you're gonna require X-rays."

"You don't like my shoes? They're one of my favorite pairs."

"I *shouldn't* like your shoes. You know what repeated wear of heels like that can do to your knees and feet? But…"

"But?"

His gaze went to her legs, and her body tingled as if he'd actually slid his hands over her thigh. "But," he said softly, meeting her eyes again. There was no need for him to finish the sentence out loud. Words would only be redundant, and she couldn't imagine the mere syllables that would accurately capture the heat in his gaze.

Treble's lips parted. She should say something to end the moment, but she couldn't think when he had that expression on his face. If she didn't stop staring, she really would trip and break something. *Like your heart?* Stupid, out-of-the-blue thought, but at least it got her moving again.

They fell into step. After a few seconds, she convinced herself she'd exaggerated the connection.

"So," Keith began. "This festival? I've never been, but it seems to be a big deal around here."

"Yeah. Have they recruited you for judging? It's normally town 'dignitaries' who officiate over the tastings, livestock prizes, Little Miss Joyous."

"No. Being a newcomer, I doubt I'm eligible for that kind of honor."

Something in his voice surprised her. She tilted her head. "You don't still consider yourself an outsider?" As far as she could tell, he fit in better in six months than she had after years. And not just with the town.

"*Outsider's* too strong. This is my home now, but I'm still proving myself." It took a self-confident man to admit something like that so casually. "Roots in this town go far back."

"*Everything* in this town goes way back," she muttered. Midge Moore's disapproving scowl flashed in her mind.

"They should ask you to judge," he said.

"That your idea of a joke?"

"No, my idea of a joke is the one about the guy who comes into the clinic and says, 'Doctor, it hurts when I move my arm like this, what can I do?'"

She rolled her eyes. The punch line "Don't move your arm like that" was older than she was. "You're hilarious. Really. I should have you on my show sometime."

"That's why you should be one of the judges, because you have your own show. Local girl goes off to become a minor celebrity and comes back to serve as guest judge in the town festival? The *Joyous Journal-Report* could do a whole article."

"You just have this all planned out, huh?" Not used to driving Charity's car, she almost passed it, but stopped when Keith slowed, recognizing the vehicle before she did.

"Well, I work next to the newspaper office. I'm always afraid that if there's a slow news day, they'll canvas the neighborhood looking for story suggestions."

"You yourself pointed out that I'm not remembered fondly," she said, her tone souring despite her noblest intentions. "So I'm sure you'll understand if I don't get asked to participate in the town's most time-honored traditions."

Keith looked down. "About that. I didn't mean to hurl all that stuff at you the other night. And I didn't mean to make it sound as if you're the talk of the town. Those are snippets I've picked up here and there over the past few months because people know I'm a friend of Harrison's."

Somehow, between Keith's joking and admiring her legs, she'd temporarily forgotten that he and her stepfather were close. "It's okay. Most of the talk about me is my own fault." What wasn't her fault, she'd been blamed for anyway.

He paused, then offered her a conciliatory smile. "Guess everyone's past is complicated, right?"

"Including yours?"

"Yeah."

She waited a moment, the silence confirming her hunch that the conversation was over. "See you 'round, Doc," she said, unlocking the car door.

"See you, Trou—Treble."

The rest of her afternoon went smoothly, with no one threatening to sic security guards on her or unintentionally breaking her ribs with enthusiastic hugs. She ran out of time to find Charity a gift, but that earned her an extra day or so to think of ideas. The worst of the day's heat was dissolving into shadows and welcome breezes by the time she steered the car back into the garage.

Charity was awake, seated on the couch and frowning at a Sudoku square when Treble joined her in the living room.

"Hey," Treble said.

"Hey, yourself. I hate you for getting me hooked on this. I messed one up but couldn't figure out where the mistake was and just tore it out of the book."

Treble laughed. "That's happened to me plenty of times. I'm going to get a drink. Want something?"

"Yes, please. Lemonade, if there's any left in there. You have a good time in town?" she said as an afterthought.

Treble paused in the kitchen, recalling the surprise of seeing Keith Caldwell and the much greater surprise of how his smile had made her body flush with pleasure, the unexpected, intense kind that sent tingles up her spine. "You know, I really did." She carried the drinks into the other room. "I can see why you like the doctor so much."

"You saw Keith?" Charity's eyes widened. "You saw

Keith and had a really good time. Sounds like there's more to this story I should hear."

Treble rolled her eyes at her sister's excited tone. "Well, we were both in the drugstore, our eyes met and we were overcome. I dragged him off to the condom aisle where I had my way with him. What kind of story were you expecting? We ran into each other on the street, and he was very pleasant. So maybe I was wrong about him not liking me."

Charity sighed. "Your first story was better. I'll bet Keith's really good in…the condom aisle."

"Charity!"

"Sorry. My condition. Sex is off-limits, and my fantasy life is going berserk."

"Drink your iced beverage and cool down, hormone girl." Meanwhile, Treble would do the same. Because if she weren't careful, Keith Caldwell could start making appearances in *her* fantasy life, too.

When and if she decided to end the drought her love life had become, it was not going to include a close friend of her family's or, for that matter, anyone else in Joyous. This town had already been the scene of some of her worst choices and mistakes. While she wouldn't bend over backward to become a demure and respectable citizen, she wasn't looking to repeat history, either. Not even Trouble J was that reckless.

Chapter Eight

Keith watched the first rays of light glisten orange across the embankment, making the trees glow. He forced himself to appreciate the view, even though he'd never again enjoy being out on the water as much as he once had. It would be a little while before the sun hit the lake, which was why he was wearing a thick, long-sleeved T-shirt beneath his life jacket on this last Saturday in June.

"I never realized how peaceful this time of day is," he remarked to Harrison. "That could be because I'm normally *asleep* at this hour."

Harrison chuckled. "Whiner. On a farm, this is practically midday."

"Thank God I didn't grow up on a farm," Keith groused good-naturedly as Harrison handed over the blue plastic tackle box. "What am I looking for in here?"

"The crank bait. Like mine." Harrison held up the lure he'd used, at a safe distance. Keith had treated several emergency fishing wounds and had no desire to be on the receiving end of one.

Truthfully he wasn't much of a fisher, but he'd been trying to get his friend to relax more. Despite the rural setting, Harrison Breckfield was as much a stressed-out workaholic as any Armani-suited CEO in New York, Chicago or Dallas. He was letting a lifetime of being hale and hearty convince him that he was immune to health concerns, but it didn't work that way. Just because he rarely caught a cold or had the stomach flu didn't mean he wasn't a prime candidate for heart failure. While Keith loved some of the local food, the people in Joyous were awfully quick to deep-fry everything from catfish to corn on the cob to Oreo cookies.

So when Harrison proposed going out on the lake to do some bass fishing, Keith had accepted. The man needed more recreation, less salt.

"Do you actually expect to catch anything?" Keith asked, competent enough with rod and reel to cast the line without ending up in the water himself. "Or do you just like being out here?"

Harrison snorted derisively. "Son, I don't need fishing gear to be out on the lake. That's what I have the boat for. I plan to take home some bass. 'Course, that would hold even more appeal if Joan were still with me."

Joan McMillan, Keith knew, was not Harrison's late wife but the longtime housekeeper who had shocked and irritated her employer when she quit two years ago. Now she worked part-time at the town's only retirement home.

"That woman could cook fish like no one's business," Harrison said. "She could cook damn near anything."

Too bad she no longer worked for him. From what Keith had heard about her stubbornly nurturing disposition, he could have enlisted the lady's help to make sure Harrison followed certain dietary regulations. Keith could give him medical advice until he turned blue in the face, but whether or not Harrison chose to take it—or admit to his family the extent of his condition and hand over some of his workload—was beyond Keith's control.

Harrison stared out across the water, talking as much to himself as to Keith. "House is so empty with just me in it. Maybe I should just ask Charity and Bill if they want it, although she seems to love that little place of theirs. And I'm not sure where I'd go after all this time."

Goading him because he knew it would chase away the melancholy, Keith suggested, "You could move into the old folks' home downtown. Probably get some of Joan's cooking that way."

"Old, hell! I ought to shove you right into this lake. I'm in my prime."

"As your friend, I applaud the sentiment. As your doctor, I'll remind you that if you want to keep feeling that way, you have to take care of yourself. You want to be there to watch your grandchild grow up, don't you?"

Harrison looked startled hearing it in those terms. Keith probably shouldn't have been so blunt—it wasn't as though the man were dying—but having lost his own dad to heart failure, Keith rationalized it was better to alarm Harrison a little than risk Charity losing another parent when it could have been prevented.

"Playing hardball, son?"

"I play to win," Keith said with an unrepentant grin.

"I don't know why I put up with you," Harrison grunted. "You're too much like me."

"I'll take that as a compliment, sir."

"Just be careful you don't get to be *too* much like me. You know how Charity's always after you to date?"

"About that. I—"

"She has a point. You don't want to wind up alone in a house that's too big."

"You're not alone. You have friends and family. Two…" Two loving daughters? One? One and a half? "If you're not entirely content with the way your life is turning out, seems to me the proactive thing to do is make some changes. Maybe Treble's visit is the opportunity to do that."

The man's bushy eyebrows rose, angling closer together. "Gutsy move, bringing her up."

"Charity shouldn't have to—she has enough to think about in her condition. And the other night at dinner it looked like you and Treble are too obstinate to work it out yourselves without a nudge." When Keith had first heard that the prodigal stepdaughter was returning, he had worried no good could come of it. He'd come to realize, though, that in his loyalty to the Breckfields, he'd oversimplified the situation.

Despite his initial reservations, Treble's being here might benefit Charity, and it provided an opportunity for Harrison to resolve issues that clearly troubled him. Though their dinner had proven that time around Treble sent Harrison's blood pressure into the red zone, maybe it would be healthier in the long run for Harrison and his stepdaughter to address past conflicts instead of continuing to let them fester.

"You were pretty rough on her the other night," Keith said. Harrison was responsible for the employment of so many people in this town, including his son-in-law, that few people said anything that could be construed as criticism. *He can't fire me.* Besides, the man needed to hear the truth from someone he respected.

"I don't see as how that's any of your business," Harrison retorted.

"But my dating is *your* concern?"

Harrison stared him down, unwilling to bend. "I know you're smart, getting through medical school and all that, but some things you won't understand until you're a parent. That girl— You wouldn't believe the nights she kept me awake, worried about where she was or when she would be home or what the hell I was going to do with her. Nothing worked. I felt like everything she did was to spite me. I won't let her go to some rock concert; she steals my car and then grows up to get a job playing rock music. I take her to the dairy her senior year to give her some part-time hours and try to instill a work ethic, and end up having to fire a man over it. Family man, too. The guy had a wife and new baby at home, and I walked into a barn to find Treble in his arms."

Keith was surprised at how annoying the image of Treble kissing someone was. Someone other than himself, anyway—that mental picture had stolen into his mind more than once. "She was in error, but shouldn't the adult married male have pushed her away?"

"Why do you think I fired him? Of course he was dead wrong. But he wasn't the first older guy she flirted with, and he was sleep-deprived and making bad decisions already. My point is, she shouldn't have put herself in harm's way, constantly teasing men."

Had Treble ever noticed her stepfather's gruff concern for her well-being, or had she only seen the overlying disapproval?

"Yet here she is now with this sex talk show," Harrison continued, "so she obviously didn't learn her lesson."

"I didn't get the impression that it's a show about sex; callers just sometimes bring up male-female relationships. That's not uncommon, and what passes for scandalous here would barely raise eyebrows in Atlanta."

Harrison grunted, recasting his line. "Surprises me, the way you're defending her. You barely know the girl." Then his eyes narrowed, taking Keith's measure. "Something going on there?"

"What do you mean, 'going on'?" Keith echoed, recognizing it as a lame stall tactic. "Don't be ridiculous. As you said, we just met. I empathized with her, is all, knowing how hard it is to lose a parent and how that can mess you up."

"Charity lost her mama and still managed to make decisions that weren't based on antagonizing and shocking others. *You* lost family and went on to become a doctor." Harrison held up his hand, warding off any further argument. "Why don't we just agree to disagree and enjoy our fishing, son?" In other words, he'd closed the topic and Treble was hereby off-limits.

Funny, that's just what Keith had told himself as he walked back to his office yesterday afternoon. There'd been a moment, when Treble looked into his eyes, when he'd had the insane impulse to kiss her there on the street in front of anyone who cared to watch. *Talk about off-limits.*

She'd been right the other night about healthy adults having certain…needs. He'd ignored his far too long, which didn't mean he was going to go out on the prowl and seduce the first woman who crossed his path. He had self-control, and he had goals. Somewhere out there was a local girl he could laugh with and make plans with, come home to after a long day, a girl who'd understand when his schedule unraveled due to a patient emergency.

Tonight, he'd make his first real step in finding her.

Treble's shoulders were sore, but the sense of satisfaction she felt more than made up for it.

"Looks good," Bill said, standing in the doorway of the nursery. He'd just screwed in the cute switch plate that matched the curtains and wallpaper. The décor was a modified teddy-bear-picnic theme. On a background of the palest pink, there were scenes of four stuffed-animal friends, including an absolutely adorable flop-eared rabbit, who was lying on a blanket and having tea while watching the clouds. Each of the four animals was featured on the curtain, and the teddy bear held the place of honor on the switch plate. "Should we wake Charity up so she can see it?"

They'd started work on the room after an early lunch—Bill had painted the bottom halves of the walls weeks ago, but that still left wallpapering the top and the trim work. Charity had been eager to see the results of their labor but had fallen asleep for an afternoon nap.

"No, let her rest," Treble said. "The baby's room isn't going anywhere."

He grinned. "That's what I thought. Just wanted to get a second opinion in case she fusses about it. I could use a cold beer, how about you?"

"Lead the way." Cold beer followed by a hot shower sounded like heaven.

They crept past his snoring wife into the sun-filled kitchen, golden with the afternoon.

"It's a nice place you guys have here," Treble said as she sat down. Would Bill hear the wistful note in her voice, or was it evident only to her?

He retrieved two bottles from the fridge. "I think so. Maybe when the baby gets older, or if we decide to have more kids, we'll need a bigger place, but right now…it's perfect."

Treble accepted the frosty bottle he handed to her, smiling inwardly at the way he'd removed the cap first. The last few guys she'd dated had been missing the chivalry gene and she forgot that some men possessed it. She sipped her beer, trying to remember when she'd felt so relaxed. If someone had told her a few weeks ago that she could feel as comfortable in her sister's kitchen in Joyous, Tennessee, as she normally did inside her broadcasting booth, she never would have believed them.

"I'm glad Charity talked me into coming here," she said aloud.

"Me, too. She's different when you're here," Bill said. "Braver. She's tried not to show it much, but she's been worried since they diagnosed the previa. I think she feels bolder with you as inspiration."

Treble glanced away. "I'm happy to make myself useful. That first night, my being here seemed…"

Bill shook his head. "As much as I respect Harrison, he can be a hard man. When I proposed to Charity some people made snide remarks about my taking the fast track to the top of the company. But—"

"He makes you work twice as hard as anyone else for half the praise?" she guessed. Bill was below several Breckfield cousins in the chain of command, but she knew her stepfather well enough to know that whatever position Bill held, he'd earned it.

"It's not that bad." Bill swallowed more of his beer, then allowed a wry smile. "Most days, it's not that bad."

"Bill? Treb?" Charity's sleep-slurred voice reached them as she pulled herself into a sitting position, her tousled blond hair just visible over the top of the couch.

Treble stood. "Sleeping Beauty wakes! We have a surprise for you."

"Ooh, I like surprises."

Bill helped his wife to her feet, and Treble followed the couple down the hallway to the nursery.

"Oh. You guys. It's…" Tears welled up in Charity's eyes. "It's just…"

When it became clear that full-on happy sobbing would ensue, Bill pulled her into his arms. Treble took that as her cue to leave, knowing this was a special parenting moment and husband and wife should be alone. Happy to take a shower, Treble scrubbed away bits of wallpaper paste and the primary paint colors they'd used on the trim to brighten the doorway, closet frame and baseboards. By the time Treble toweled off, she'd decided that maybe she could find something to do by herself for the night. She'd been underfoot for every meal since she got here, and since she planned to be here at least a couple weeks more, it might be nice to get out of Bill and Charity's way.

She pulled on a pair of shorts and the black T-shirt she normally layered over a turtleneck when she attended a hockey game, then passed Bill in the hallway as he headed to the back of the house for his chance to clean up.

Charity arched an eyebrow when she saw her sister. "'Puck You'?"

Treble shrugged, running a comb through her long, damp hair. "I go to a lot of Atlanta Thrashers games. Hey, what would you think about my hitting the town tonight? Don't worry, I'd change first."

Charity laughed. "Well, it's Joyous, so there's not much town to hit. You going stir-crazy here?"

"It's not that. I just thought you two might like an evening to do whatever it is boring married couples do." Treble grinned as she heckled her sister.

"Wish we could, but the doctor gave us strict orders."

"I hear conversation can be nice," Treble said sympathetically.

"Talk, talk, talk." Charity made a face. "I miss action."

"And they call *me* the wild child."

"Take my car, stay out all hours. You'll have to be wild enough for the both of us."

Treble smirked. "Haven't I always been?"

There were essentially three after-hours hot spots in Joyous—with a peripheral fourth in the form of a bowling alley just across the county line. The first was King Cinema, the town's movie theater. There were only two screens, though, so movies sold out quickly and were often behind the times compared to what the rest of the world had already seen. According to Charity, there'd been talk of trying to reopen an old drive-in, but too many parents recalled their own teenage outings; the idea had stalled out indefinitely in town council.

Possibly the seediest place in town was the bar. Technically the name was Duke's, but there were no signs outside that denoted the ramshackle building as such. It was reputed to be a dim, smoky place with décor limited to a single pool table. Treble had tried to glimpse the inside of the building once; from what she'd heard about the owner, he wasn't judgmental enough to care if an ID was valid. But it was a bar for serious drinkers, not troublemaking underage girls, and the no-neck bouncer—a man who would make Bear look slight— had blocked her at the doorway, his phone call to Harrison Breckfield adding insult to injury.

Blinking away memories of the stony ride home, Treble focused on the third social venue and her destination this evening, Guthrie Dance Hall. She'd been there plenty of times. The first thing a person saw upon entry was the wooden dance floor, a stage serving as its backdrop. To the right were picnic tables—long, scarred, unadorned wooden planks affixed to equally unsightly benches. Rustic surroundings notwithstanding, the establishment's cheeseburgers and home fries or chicken-fried steak with gravy could transport a diner straight to nirvana. There was also a ratty foosball game that she assumed would still be there, and a quarter billiards table. Patrons didn't have to be twenty-one to enter the hall, but they were supposed to stay on the right half of the glorified barn. On the left side was a bar with a wide range of beers on tap and a dartboard, where more than one yahoo in a cowboy hat had injured a buddy through drinking and darting.

Judging from the number of vehicles—mostly American-made trucks—crammed into the parking lot, Treble suspected both halves of the hall were equally busy tonight. Classmates from her high school had come to Guthrie after prom, girls in taffeta dresses swirling in a colorful kaleidoscope across the sawdust on the floor. Everything from birthday parties to wedding receptions were held here, publicly inviting comment and participation from the entire town. It wasn't the kind of place where a back room was available for private rental. Not counting the kitchen and restrooms, there was no back room. *What you see is what you get.*

The thought made Treble smile as she got out of her sister's car. Guthrie was one of the few town institutions she'd truly enjoyed while she lived here. She had a dim recollection of Harrison Breckfield taking some of his top staff from the dairy here one night. Maybe they'd been celebrating someone's anniversary of employment or having a small retirement party for someone. She remembered Charity, customarily angelic in her stroller, and herself sitting on one of the benches drinking a chocolate milk shake, the kind that was so gloriously thick that drinking it through a straw was nearly impossible. They'd looked on as Harrison and their mother shared a slow dance on the floor.

It wasn't a stretch to envision that as Charity and Bill's life just a few years from now—Bill out with fellow Breckfield employees, perpetually infatuated with his own wife, the two of them doting parents of a cherubic toddler. The last thing Treble would have expected to feel was jealously knifing through her, but there it was anyway. She wasn't even sure which part she envied.

The smile of unabashed appreciation the guy at the door flashed her went a long way toward restoring her spirits. He handed her change from a ten-dollar bill and made her feel younger than she was when he winked at her. Good-looking kid with the devil twinkling in his eyes, but he couldn't be any older than twenty-four.

"Have fun," he told her, letting his fingers brush hers more than necessary.

She grinned, shaking her head. "I always do."

While country music would never be her favorite style, she couldn't deny the toe-tapping appeal of the song the band was playing. She cut across the edge of the floor, navigating dancers to make her way to the formerly forbidden left side. Looked a lot like the right, with the addition of a few more neon signs and brewery logos.

She took her place beside a redheaded woman ordering a drink from the bartender, idly surveying the crowd as she waited her turn. Awash in déjà vu, she wondered how many of the faces surrounding her belonged to people she actually *knew* and how many merely reminded her of people she'd known once upon a time. Everything about being here was both familiar and foreign.

The redhead's voice was legitimately recognizable, though, catching Treble's attention.

"Ronnie?"

The mechanic turned, looking beautiful but uncomfortable in a skirt and eye shadow. "Hey, Treble. Car troubles driving you to drink?"

Treble laughed. "Something like that. I almost didn't recognize you. You must have way more patience than me to French braid your hair like that."

It was gorgeous, the plaiting bringing out different highlights and her rich color.

"I can't take credit. A friend did it for me. Lola Ann convinced me that wearing my garage cap was not acceptable attire for a girls' night out."

"Lola Ann from the library?" It was a small town; how many Lola Anns could there possibly be?

"That's the one. Lola Ann Whitford. It was my turn to buy a round, so she's freshening up her lipstick."

"She's nice. Met her the other day at my sister's."

Ronnie scanned the crowd. "Are you here with Charity?"

"No, she's on bed rest. I thought she and her husband might appreciate the evening without me underfoot."

"That's right. I forgot about her being on bed rest. Hope she and the baby are doing well. This is going to sound completely insensitive, but I'm a little envious that you were able to come without siblings in tow."

Treble studied the younger woman's frustrated expression. "Your brothers?"

"That's Danny over there, bookkeeper for my dad's garage and technically the only 'son' at Carter and Sons, kicking Joe Stubb's butt at darts." She jerked her thumb at a good-looking auburn-haired man in his midthirties whose attention seemed equally divided between the bull's-eye and his kid sister. "And that's Devin."

Seated farther down the bar, a second attractive, jeans-clad man in a plaid shirt scowled at a guy who'd been ogling Ronnie. Treble smothered a laugh. It was the Good Ole Boy Secret Service. She imagined that if any male worked up the courage to make a move on the pretty mechanic, one brother would contact the other through a walkie-talkie. *Hostile approaching. Swarm, swarm!*

"Your brothers spend their Saturday nights stalking you?" she asked, trying to keep her amusement at bay.

"Danny's married, but my niece Ashley goes away to horse-riding camp every summer. This year, Danny's wife volunteered to help there. They get home tomorrow night, so he's currently as free as he is overprotective."

Having once been caught violently off guard by a man's unwanted attentions, Treble thought the way Ronnie's brothers looked out for her was sweet. In a cloying, crazy-making, uncalled-for kind of way. After all, there were dozens of people in the establishment who knew Ronnie and would come to her side if some Neanderthal hassled her.

"Devin," Ronnie continued, "is the total opposite of married. He dumped his last girlfriend for telling him she loved him. Or, technically, because she expected him to say it back. It's been a few weeks, so I was hoping he'd get back in the game, busy himself tonight with single ladies, but he seems content to sit at the bar swapping jokes with his buddies and making sure no man comes within ten feet of me unless it's to ask a question about tire rotation. The truth is, I've gotten used to it, but…"

Treble waited, but Ronnie seemed too distracted to finish the sentence. She was staring past Treble, her green eyes vivid with yearning. Resisting the urge to be obvious and turn to check out whomever Ronnie was checking out, Treble instead said, "Ronnie? I get the impression there's someone you'd like to dance with."

The woman tensed, then shrugged. "Not that he'll ever notice me. Even if he did, the infamous Carter brothers would probably have him calf-roped before he got within ten feet. They both participated in 4-H rodeo when they were younger."

"No rule that says a woman has to *wait* to be noticed," Treble said. "Go make him notice you. It looks like things are getting intense with Danny's dart game."

"Which leaves Devin."

"I could help you sneak away," Treble offered. "I have lots of experience." In her teens, sneaking out had included a tree outside her window. She'd overheard an exasperated Joan, the family housekeeper, admonish Harrison that he should just have the oak cut down. Treble had wondered at the time if her stepfather secretly hoped she'd leave one night and not come back, thereby freeing him of his duty to raise his late wife's child.

"You'd do that for me?" Ronnie asked.

"Do you have any moral objections to my flirting with your brother for a few minutes to distract him?"

"None. If he can't get it through his head that I'm a grown woman and not a fourteen-year-old who needs a chaperone, he deserves what—oh, hey, Lola Ann!"

The brunette, shorter than most of the crowd around them, squeezed by a man trying to talk a slim woman into dancing. "Treble! When did you get here?" Lola Ann's bright smile was welcoming.

"Just a few minutes ago. Nice to see you again."

Ronnie leaned forward, her voice conspiratorial. "Treble's going to help me try to get a few minutes of Jason's time."

"Thank goodness," Lola Ann said. "You can't keep carrying a torch for that boy and never talk to him. You don't do something soon, I'm planning to take an ad out in the *Journal-Report* letting him know how you feel."

"Not unless you want your car mysteriously dismantled and sold for scrap metal," Ronnie retorted. "Besides, this isn't just about Jason. My dim-witted brothers need to understand they aren't my wardens. It would serve them right if I asked Jason to coffee over at Bestest Bakery and slipped out of here completely, but I wouldn't abandon you like that on girls' night."

Lola Ann bit her lip. "You can make it up to me later."

"Seriously?" Ronnie blushed at the thought of actually leaving with the aforementioned Jason. Treble had no idea which man in the room he was, but she had a hunch he was cute. "Treble, you'd better go do your thing before I lose my nerve."

"What thing is that?" Lola asked.

"She's going to use her feminine wiles on Devin, and I'll sneak out while he's melting into a little pile of goo."

Lola's Ann expression dimmed a few watts, her dimples disappearing. "Oh."

Ronnie cocked her head. "What? It's foolproof. I mean *look* at her."

Lola Ann did as directed, the last bit of welcome in her expression turning to resignation. "Yeah."

Uh-oh. "Maybe it's not a very good idea," Treble backpedaled. Suddenly she didn't think Ronnie was the only one harboring a crush from afar. "I don't have to—"

"What? You're not backing out on me now, are you?" Ronnie squeezed her hand. "Maybe I can work out some kind of discount on your car repairs?"

Treble couldn't help laughing. "No. While I don't mind flirting with a cute guy for a good cause, flirting for financial gain seems ooky. I appreciate the thought, though."

"Then you'll still help me out?" Ronnie pressed.

"Go ahead, Treb," Lola Ann said listlessly.

"But don't you—"

"It's fine," Lola Ann said, a note of panicked enthusiasm in her voice as her eyes met Treble's. Why didn't she want her friend to know she had a thing for Devin?

"Okay," Treble told them both, turning with a sigh.

Devin was discussing baseball with another man when she approached, monitoring his sister with an occasional glance. His eyes widened with interest as Treble wandered into his field of vision.

"Hi," she said. She turned to the other guy. "Am I interrupting your conversation?"

The man lifted his drink from the bar in a small salute. "Pretty ladies are never interruptions, ma'am."

"Oh, good. Because I was hoping to catch up with Devin here. Ronnie reminded me that we went to school together."

Devin leaned back on his bar stool, smiling lazily. "We were both in the same building during the same hours, but I don't rightly think you can say we were there 'together.' If Ronnie hadn't mentioned me, would you even have known who I was? You only had eyes for Rich Danner, as I recall."

Though she nearly grimaced at the reminder of Rich and her ill-advised feelings for him, she knew Devin was being kind. Half the town had believed she'd been trying to seduce every man she ran across, from high school teachers to married dairy workers. Shaking off the past like dirt from her boots, she summoned a smile.

"That was a long time ago, and things change. For the better."

"Yeah, I've grown up a bit since high school," he said, confident in his own appeal. Why shouldn't he be? He was a great-looking guy. Yet the way he smiled at her now didn't have a fraction of the impact as merely standing on the sidewalk next to Keith Caldwell did yesterday.

"You dance as good as you look?" she challenged.

He laughed. "Guess there's one way to find out." Taking her hand, he led her through the throng toward the floor.

The band was playing a fast tune with lots of exuberant fiddle. Treble enjoyed dancing at clubs, but she was a little rusty on classic western footwork. So it was a relief that Devin mostly wanted to spin her in tight circles. She didn't have to worry about following his steps, she merely had to hold on and laugh at the sensation of whirling beneath the multicolored track lighting and hope she didn't throw up.

She meant to check covertly and discover whether or not Ronnie had left the building or was back in her previous corner with Lola Ann, but Treble was too dizzy to focus on the crowd. Her heartbeat was racing and her cheeks felt flushed when the song came to an end. Everyone, including her dance partner, stopped to clap, and she stumbled slightly.

"Easy there," a male voice said near her ear, his hands coming to her hips to steady her.

The scent of Keith's cologne did nothing to slow her pulse. How had it become so familiar in such a short time? His thumb grazed the ribbon of skin bared between her sleeveless white shirt and her jeans. Sensation rioted through her midsection, starting where his flesh met hers, such a small spark to ignite a conflagration of awareness.

She tried to catch her breath as she turned toward him. "Hey."

His lips quirked in greeting, but the expression in his eyes was more complicated than a simple smile. "Hey, yourself. I keep bumping into you in the arms of other men."

"Devin did me the honor of a dance." She fanned herself, smiling at her partner. "You could've warned me you were hell on wheels."

Ronnie's brother flashed a grin. "You looked like you could handle it. Evening, Doc Caldwell," he added with a nod.

"How's it going, Dev? That rash clear up for you?"

"Uh, yeah. The foot cream worked as promised." He shifted his weight. "Thanks for the dance, Treble."

The music had slowed, and now the three of them were standing in the way of couples swaying around them.

"Thank *you*," she said, meaning it. "That was fun."

"You find me later if you want to do it again," he told her. Then he scowled in Keith's direction, his single syllable of farewell as sharp as a bowie knife. "Doc."

Treble waited until the man had merged into the crowd before she tucked her middle finger against her thumb and flicked Keith on the arm. "That was mean."

He rubbed the spot, trying to look indignant. "I'll say."

"I meant *you*. 'How's the rash?'" she mimicked, her hands on her hips.

"I care about his well-being." Keith gave up trying to

sound convincing halfway through the sentence, then pinched the bridge of his nose. "You're right. It was immature. It was unprofessional, although technically he asked for the advice at the grocery store and not at the clinic. I just... Watching the two of you spin around, I suddenly felt old and stuffy. As young and self-assured as Dev is, I'm sure he'll bounce back from my momentary lapse of manners."

She arched an eyebrow, gazing in the direction Devin had gone. "He's not *that* young."

"It wouldn't be nice to toy with his affections," Keith said. "He'll be crushed when you leave."

Since she had no interest in anything other than dancing with Devin, she wasn't sure why she felt compelled to play devil's advocate. "You're jumping to the conclusion that he'd get attached. How do you know he even wants something more than a quick fling?"

Keith startled her by brushing her cheek with his fingertips. "Whatever he *thinks* he wants, you'd have a lasting effect."

She froze, surprised by the quiet sincerity that had crept into their bickering. Keith stood motionless, as well, neither coming closer nor dropping his hand. From behind, a teenage boy and his date jostled the town doctor.

The boy drew himself up to his full height, which was still about five inches shorter than Keith. "Dude, dance or get off the floor."

"He has a point," Treble said, glad her chuckle didn't sound as nervous as she inexplicably felt. Now was the perfect time to go, maybe find Lola Ann.

"Absolutely." Keith closed his warm fingers over hers. "We should be dancing."

"What? I—"

He placed her hand on his shoulder, then slid his own to her waist. The nearby whisper of "one, two, three" from a young dancer trying to keep count with a waltz drifted to her. Treble and Keith, however, weren't doing anything so formal. Were her feet even moving? In his embrace, her thoughts had become as formless and fleeting as the atmospheric puffs of smoke from an ancient fog machine. Her blood felt thick and too hot in her veins, and she experienced a completely different kind of dizzy than she had earlier with Devin.

Deciding conversation was beyond her current abilities, she simply let herself dance. The slow, steady pull of the music encouraged her to let go of conscious deliberation and fall into instinctive movement. When would she ever again have the chance to twine her arms around Keith's neck, find out for herself if his thick hair was silky or coarse across her fingertips? *Silky.* She felt rather than heard him suck in a breath when her fingers trailed across the nape of his neck. Had he tugged her closer, or had her body swayed toward him of its own volition? Sandalwood and sawdust and the less definable male scent of him swirled together in a surprisingly heady combination.

Entering the hall tonight, a place where she'd danced away numerous adolescent nights, had been like stepping through a door to her past. She recalled once waiting for her date to buy a soda and overhearing other high school girls discuss how the end of a date was the most apprehensive moment. "You never know if there's going to be a kiss," one had said. Treble had thought at the time that when you were wracked with uncertainty, the best solution was just to seize the moment. Take matters in your own hands and end the wondering.

So when Keith's gaze dropped from her eyes to her mouth and she felt that same fluttering against her ribs she'd experienced with him yesterday—when, against all reason, it had seemed he might kiss her—she followed her own long-ago advice. While the brown demi-boots she wore tonight didn't have a particularly high heel, she was still plenty tall enough to reach up and touch her lips to his. Especially since, at the last second, he lowered his head and met her halfway.

Chapter Nine

An electric current shot through Keith. A tiny, removed fraction of himself couldn't believe he was kissing Treble James. The rest of him just wanted to deepen the kiss and make it last the duration of the night.

His hands were caught in the loose curls of her hair, holding her close as he explored her mouth, learning its taste and dips and curves. She slid her tongue along his, and he wanted to groan with tortured pleasure. But for the second time in the span of one song, other dancers bumped them, jarring Keith back to reality. He jerked his head back, pulling away quickly enough to catch Treble's dazed expression. Even though she'd instigated the kiss, she looked as surprised as he'd been.

He cleared his throat as music gradually replaced the sound of his own heartbeat in his ears. "We should... leave the floor." They were a menace. People couldn't just stop in the middle of a dancing area like that, inviting collisions. *And gossip.*

How many people had witnessed his moment of temporary insanity?

"Sure." Treble's gaze had become guarded, but she met his eyes. "I could use a bottle of water, anyway."

They wound their way through the tangle of bodies, Keith wincing inwardly at all the good-natured hellos he was receiving. He hadn't realized just how many people in Joyous he knew until joining them for a rare night out in the town's most popular Saturday destination. Had he lost his mind? He'd come here tonight wanting to look for the woman Charity, Velma, Harrison and his own intuition told him his life lacked, and instead of asking some nice local girl to dance, he'd ended up making out with Treble.

Okay, it had only been a short kiss, but that mollified neither his inflamed libido nor his misgivings.

"Evening, Doc Caldwell." Jack, the bartender, offered a bemused smile. "Don't usually see you in here."

Keith darted an involuntary glance at Treble, and Jack followed the doctor's gaze, his eyes widening behind wire-rimmed glasses.

"Can I get you and your lady friend a drink?"

Fighting the juvenile urge to disavow any acquaintance whatsoever with Treble, Keith asked for two waters.

"On the house," Jack said, handing them two chilled plastic bottles slippery with condensation.

Treble took hers. "You're a very popular man, Doc. Must have cured a cold or set a broken bone for just about everyone in the county."

"Not really." He twisted the lid off his bottle. "But it sure does feel like it tonight, doesn't it?"

"So, educate me on how this works for people like you. Do we just pretend the kiss never happened?"

He choked, coughing and spluttering but mercifully managing not to spit water on his date. Er, lady friend.

"Because when you dragged me off the dance floor," she continued in the same deceptively mild tone, "I got the impression that maybe I was supposed to apologize or something."

"No." His ego didn't want her to say she was sorry for kissing him.

"Good. Because, if I'm not mistaken, you were thinking about kissing me, too."

Oh, he'd been thinking about it. He'd been thinking about it as he pulled her toward him on the dance floor and noticed the glimmer of her lip gloss—chocolate-flavored, apparently. He'd thought about it yesterday when she grinned up at him during their encounter in town.

"Thinking isn't the same as doing, Treble."

She raked him with a scathing gaze. "Tell me about it."

He blinked, feeling as though the tables had been turned with no warning. "Now you make it sound as though I should apologize. For what, utilizing self-control?" Right up until that second when he'd seen what was coming, thought *hell, yes* and bent into the kiss like a man rushing to his own doom.

Treble shrugged. "We should just agree to disagree. What one person might call restraint, another could call repression. Not reaching for something you want could as easily be cowardice as control."

She was calling him a coward? His temper boiled, at

war with the banked but still-heated urge to touch her again. Proving his self-control, he kept his tone civil. "Do you goad your listeners, too?"

Instead of firing a glib response, she thought it over. "Sometimes. When I think I have a good point they need to hear."

He opened his mouth to challenge her, demanding to know if she could *take* advice as easily as she dished it to others. But then he realized he couldn't fault her for speaking her mind, not when he'd done exactly that the other night. He'd hauled her out of Charity's to criticize her behavior, yet she'd forgiven him because what he'd said at least held a nugget of sound advice. Or at least honest intentions.

"You remind me of another outspoken woman I knew once." His words stunned him. He hadn't meant to say anything of the sort, but his sister would have liked Treble. Both women exasperated him while earning his grudging admiration at the same time.

"Is that a flattering comparison?"

His smile felt tight on his face, a mask that might not hold. "Difficult to say."

She glanced around. "I had planned to find Lola Ann Whitford after my dance with Devin. I'd better go do that. Thanks for the water."

Keith would rather have been thanked for the dance—or their brief, searing kiss. He used his few inches of superior height to help her scan the crowd. "Lola Ann's over by the dartboard, with Ronnie."

"Ronnie's still here? Nuts." Treble swished the remaining water around in her bottle somewhat violently.

"Problem with Ronnie?"

"What? Of course not. It's just that I was trying to

help her out with something earlier, and I guess it didn't work. I'm really on a roll this evening." She muttered the last bit almost to herself, then recovered. "Take care, Doc."

He nodded, absently curious about the favor Treble had tried to do for the mechanic she'd only met days ago. Watching her angle her hips to thread through the growing number of people in the hall, he thought to himself that Ronnie was lucky. He wouldn't mind having a woman like Treble on his side. Whatever else could be said about the fearlessly irritating woman, she was passionate, loyal and bold.

Because he'd yet to look away from her, he saw Rich Danner approach Treble, staggering slightly. The draft beer in his hand probably wasn't his first. Keith leaned forward as though trying to catch their conversation, which was stupid. Even a few feet closer, he wouldn't have been able to hear them over the din of people chatting and the band belting out a Southern-rock standard.

Still, Keith didn't need the exact words to follow the conversation. Treble's body had tensed almost imperceptibly when the ex-boyfriend reached her side, but in profile, she appeared to maintain her smile as he spoke. She shook her head, gesturing toward the back wall where Ronnie was throwing darts. Whatever Rich said next erased her smile, and Keith found himself moving forward at the same time Treble did, instinct and an uncharacteristic flare of possessiveness spurring him into motion.

While Keith muscled through the crowd, Treble didn't get very far. Rich had grabbed her shoulder and continued to plead his case. The second time she jerked her arm in an effort to dislodge him, Keith saw red. He lunged and clasped his fingers around Rich's shoulder.

"Let go of her now." Keith's voice was low.

Rich glanced around, his eyes jittery. "What's your problem? I'm just convincing an old flame to dance."

"Let go."

"Sure. Sure, man." The man slid his hand off of Treble. "We were just chatting about old times, Doc. No hard feelings."

Keith didn't trust himself to look at Treble. Would she even appreciate his interference? But her scowling at him was the least of his worries. If she was furious with Rich, it would further fuel Keith's anger with the man. And there was a strict no-fighting rule at Guthrie's.

Reflexively, his fingers tightened on Rich. "Have Jack call you a cab. Go home, and sleep it off."

Rich frowned. "Evening's young."

"Your evening is over."

Rich glanced down at the doctor's hand, looking for a moment as though his own temper was riled. Then he met Keith's eyes. Whatever he saw there penetrated his buzz. "Okay, Doc."

Only then did Keith release him and turn to Treble. Her eyes, unnaturally wide in her pale face, shot through him like twin cannonballs to the gut. She looked shaken. Where was the righteous indignation he'd expected? Frankly, he wouldn't have been surprised if she'd drop-kicked Rich before Keith had a chance to reach them. Yet he hadn't been able to stop himself from coming to her aid.

"You all right, Treb?" It took effort not to snap out the words, switching gears from annoyance with Rich to concern.

"Yeah. Not the first time a guy's asked me to dance and didn't want to take no for an answer." She folded her arms over her chest, the bottle of water peeking up around an elbow, and glared at Rich. "But it had better be the last time you ask."

He nodded, sheepish now. "You know I didn't mean anything by it."

"I don't care." She was standing straighter now, more self-possessed than she had been a moment ago. "Don't ever touch me again."

"You clear on that?" Keith double-checked, only partially satisfied when the man nodded again, then shuffled off posthaste in the direction of the bar.

"Wow," Treble breathed when they were alone. "For a second, I thought you might actually hit him."

Adult skeletons were made up of 206 bones; for a nanosecond, Keith had contemplated breaking all of Rich's. "I'm a physician. Violence is against our creed."

"Right. Well, thank you." The way she avoided his gaze when she said it bothered him. He wanted to see in her eyes that the unpleasant encounter hadn't done any real harm. When she did glance back at him, it was with a dismissive expression. "Would you mind following him? It's for the greater good that we make sure he orders that cab and not another drink."

"Agreed." He almost asked her again if she was okay, but he would have felt like a mothering idiot. It had been a brief moment and was over now. Besides, if she weren't okay, he doubted she'd admit it. They locked gazes for another moment, but then she turned and began walking in the opposite direction.

At the bar, Rich was living up to his promise of calling it a night. He was slumped on a bar stool, cradling a chipped white mug in his hands. The coffee smelled a lot better than he did.

"Taxi's on its way," Rich muttered when he noticed Keith. "But it'll take a while."

Keith nodded. There was one family-owned cab company in Joyous, with two brothers driving old sedans that Ronnie kept in good shape for them. A rural area like this wasn't exactly a hub for public transportation.

"I really am sorry about earlier," the man added, his eyes bleary and his tone defeated.

"I'm not the one you should apologize to." Although he wasn't sure Treble would be interested in hearing anything her ex-boyfriend had to say. The last glare she'd sent him was sharper than anything being thrown at the dartboard.

Rich dragged a hand over his face. "I just miss her so much."

Keith frowned. "I can see why, but that was years ago. Treble's moved on."

"Huh?" His head pitched to the side as he stared up at Keith. "Not Treble. My wife. Ex-wife. I came here tonight because it's too damn lonely at home and I had too damn many beers feeling sorry for myself. Thought Treble could help take my mind off my problems, you know? She was always real good at that."

Keith's finger clenched in an involuntary fist. He didn't know if the man had meant his words in a lewd way or not, but Treble shouldn't be anyone's second choice. And Keith didn't like hearing Rich talk about her, no matter the meaning. "Give up ladies until you're coping better with the divorce. Beer, too, while you're at it."

"Dang, Doc." Rich said something else, but Keith wasn't paying attention. In his peripheral vision, he'd caught Treble heading toward the front door. Her stride was too quick to be casual, and her head was ducked in a way that didn't jibe with her innate boldness. Was she okay?

It's none of your business. She said she was fine. But that wasn't enough to lay to rest the protective instincts that had been aroused. With another glance at Rich, who appeared to be sobering up, Keith followed Treble out the door.

The night air, though sultry, was considerably cooler than the packed hall. Treble dragged in a lungful of oxygen, trying to stifle the last of the threatening hysteria as she crossed the pavement. She was being an idiot—recognizing that fact was why she'd done an about-face as soon as Keith was distracted and left instead of joining Ronnie and Lola Ann. She'd prefer no one else get a glimpse of her in idiot mode. Rich Danner wouldn't have hurt her. The room had been full, and he'd been wobbly enough that she could have taken him out with a few choice Tae Bo moves. Still, as nostalgic as this evening had made her, there were parts of her teen years she'd rather not relive.

It was Mitchell's hand she remembered on her bare shoulder, not Rich's. The former dairy worker's face had been hard with lust. He hadn't wanted her, he'd merely wanted to prove something. She was surprised and appalled that the memory still had any effect on her. After all, they'd been interrupted before the intent she'd seen in the man's hungry gaze and set jaw could become a reality.

She remembered in slow-motion clarity how *relieved* she'd been to see Harrison Breckfield, emotion prompting the spontaneous "Dad!" she'd never used before or since. But he'd showed no signs of hearing her, too busy drawing his own conclusions about her swollen lips. Then he'd turned to her with an expression that made Mitchell's look kind by comparison.

"He's a married man, Treble, with a new baby at home. Even for you, this is... Get out and go home. Now."

She learned later that he'd fired Mitchell with a hefty severance package. Harrison blamed her for making "a good man lose his job." He probably held her responsible for Mitchell's wife leaving a few months later, but as far as Treble could tell, the woman was well quit of her husband.

"Treble?"

She jumped, her heart in her throat when she faced Keith. She jabbed her car keys in his direction as she spoke, punctuating her sentences. "Don't sneak up on me! You're a doctor. Isn't too much adrenaline at once dangerous?"

"Sorry." He peered at her, a vertical line of concentration forming between his brows. He looked like a guy trying to decipher a sign in a foreign language.

Bad enough that she'd overreacted inside when Rich grabbed her, but now she was making a habit of it. *Pathetic.* "Don't be. I guess I'm just jumpy tonight. I'm two screams away from being one of those blondes in a horror movie who shrieks at her own shadow but goes down into the scary basement anyway."

He laughed. "I'm having trouble picturing that."

"Well, it's a more convincing image when you're

eating overbuttered popcorn." She stopped at Charity's car, propping her hip against the hood. "You should be inside, Doc. That's where all the fun is."

He cast a look over his shoulder; the hall was the only building visible in the dark. From the outside, beneath the milky spill of parking lot lights and thousands of stars, it looked smaller somehow. "I'm pacing myself. Tonight was my first time here."

"You're kidding? You've been in Joyous *how* long?"

He shrugged. "Doctors stay busy. And I'm not much of a dancer."

Her mind flashed to the way his body had felt flirting in close distance with hers, his hands splayed over the denim seams of her jeans. "That's not the way I remember it."

"What about you?" he challenged, leaning on the bumper. "Why are you leaving so early?"

She averted her gaze, watching a sizable cricket hop its way across the asphalt. "I've had about all the fun I can stand for tonight."

"You're not letting Rich run you off?"

"Not exactly. He's harmless. Annoying but harmless. He just…dredged up some memories."

Keith didn't say anything, assessing her silently. Treble had never done well with silence. At home, it had meant disapproval. On-air, it meant she wasn't doing her job. In her own thoughts, it formed a void where self-doubt could rush in.

Hell with it. It wasn't as if half the town didn't already know she and Mitchell had been kissing in that barn. Why not give someone the accurate version? "When I was in high school, after Rich and I broke up and he was kind enough to further my already tainted reputation, one of the guys who worked at the dairy caught me off guard."

Next to her, Keith stiffened, immobile but exuding leashed tension just below the surface. It was like energy being flash-frozen. "How off guard?"

"Not enough to require therapy, but bad enough that Harrison was scandalized when he walked in on us." She kept her tone flippant. "He assumed I'd been playing modern-day Lolita and leading the guy astray. Hard to blame him, really, all things considered."

Keith digested this information. "It wasn't your fault."

"I didn't try very hard to convince him of that. That first second, I was too numb to realize what he thought. Then I was stung and stubborn and... Doesn't matter now."

"Seems like it matters to you."

"You're wrong." Harrison had made up his mind about her a long time ago, and she'd certainly demonstrated over the past decade that she didn't need his presence in her life.

It shouldn't matter what Keith thought, either, but she found herself wondering what he made of her admission. Physicians were trained to analyze situations with scientific detachment, weren't they? Maybe his logical deduction was that a teenage girl who'd run around town with reckless disregard for the rules, earning attention through outrageous flirting, deserved whatever consequences she brought down on herself.

She straightened. "I should go. I didn't tell Charity how late I'd be, and I don't want them to worry."

Keith raised an eyebrow. "You live in Atlanta without having to answer anyone. You really think Charity's going to be concerned about you loose on the wild streets of Joyous at the ominous hour of nine p.m.?"

Okay, put that way, it had definitely been one of her flimsier excuses.

Come to think of it, she didn't have a lot of practice making excuses. Normally she just put herself out there without defending her words or actions knowing people were going to form their own impressions, regardless.

Keith stood, facing her. "I said earlier you reminded me of someone—my older sister, Gail. I used to admire her, the way she seized the day. Full speed ahead and damn the torpedoes."

"Used to?"

"She drowned. It's not something I talk about much." He looked down at his hands, splayed wide across his thighs. "I was with her. Gail was such a strong swimmer, Dad used to call her part mermaid. She challenged me to a race, but an undertow advisory had been posted. When I was younger, I was fascinated by her bravery in bending the rules, even egged her on with dares. But by that summer, I'd realized some of her behavior was just plain self-destructive. I told her not to be an idiot and that I was leaving. I thought maybe she'd come with me, calling me a chicken all the way up the beach, or that the lifeguard would notice her and yell at her to get out of the water, but... Dad died two months later. Heart failure, officially. His heart wasn't healthy enough to withstand the shock and the stress of losing his baby."

"That's awful." Her chest constricted in sympathy. She knew all too well how difficult it was to lose a parent. And coming on the heels of already burying a beloved sibling? Unimaginable.

"Once he passed away, I started blaming Gail. If she

hadn't been such a daredevil, if her hobbies had been stuff like stamp-collecting, she would still be here, and so might he. The more I missed her, the less angry I felt. I was able to remember her many good qualities instead of just the one that pissed me off and got her killed. I started blaming *myself* instead. I beat myself up for not talking her out of a quick swim, for not being able to reach her when it became clear she was struggling. But eventually I realized that no amount of blame could change what had already happened."

Treble had heard all kinds of personal information when people called into her show, but Keith confiding in her was a far more unexpected intimacy. "Why are you telling me this, Doc?"

"I don't know." He shoved his hands in his pockets. "You said it doesn't matter what Harrison thinks of you, but it matters what *you* think. Maybe I wondered whether there are things in your past you're blaming yourself for, things that weren't your fault."

"Well. Thanks for the psychoanalysis, but I didn't think that was your specialty." She'd made it all the way to the driver's side door when her conscience gave her a swift, pointy-toed kick in the ass. "I'm sorry, Keith. That was... You're really not getting me at my best to-night, are you?"

His teeth flashed white in the soft darkness around them. "It wasn't all bad."

Was he thinking of their kiss? Warmth spread through her until she recalled what she'd said to him afterward. "I gave you a hard time for not reaching for what you want when a wiser woman would have ap-plauded you for being a gentleman. I temporarily let myself forget that there are other guys who—"

"No. There's a big difference between reaching for something and trying to take it by force, Treble. You had a point. People afraid of taking any risks at all miss out on a lot of the rewards." He came closer. "In keeping with that theme, are you free for breakfast tomorrow?"

"You're asking me out?" Her breath caught.

Who would have guessed the town doctor had a thing for mouthy women who tottered around in unhealthy shoes and nearly caused bar brawls? Maybe he'd picked up a fever of some kind from one of his patients. Fever was known to cause delusional behavior.

"Not exactly," Keith clarified. "More like I'm asking you in. Harrison and I have this Sunday brunch tradition. The first time, I came to his house to check…well, that's not important. Tomorrow morning I could pick you up on my way. Do you want to join us?"

That sounded as cozy as falling face-first into a beehive. "You, me and Harrison?" The doc was *definitely* delusional.

"We just agreed that sometimes people have to gamble, step out of their comfort zones."

"This isn't one of those times." The words *Harrison and I have this Sunday brunch tradition* were curdling in her stomach like sour milk.

It was one thing for Harrison to have a great relationship with Charity; she was his flesh and blood. Treble had accepted that she and the old man would never be so close. But that Harrison had a more fatherly relationship with even Keith… The day Treble turned twenty-two, she'd returned to her college apartment and found a message from her roommate that Charity had phoned. When Treble called home that night, Harrison answered. As soon as he heard her voice, he'd said,

"I'll get your sister for you." He hadn't even wished her happy birthday.

"I know Harrison Breckfield is a friend to you, Doc, but you didn't have to grow up with him." Cringing, she realized Keith's own father had died before watching his son become the compassionate doctor he was now. "I'm not trying to be selfish, but I think it's best for everyone if I don't go."

"A few days ago I would have thought the same thing. I was wrong about you, Treble. Don't you think you and Harrison could be wrong about each other?"

Tears pricked the back of her eyelids, making her feel foolish. "I don't think it's about right or wrong. Some people just… Look, I'll think about what you said. Maybe I can join the two of you for breakfast some other time."

"All right." When she opened the car door, Keith placed his hands over the window, leaning forward to impart a few final words for her to mull over on the ride. "But remember, we rarely have as much time as we expect."

Chapter Ten

"Treble? You do realize that you just agreed Cinnamolicious would be a good name for your niece?"

"Sure, it has a nice ring to it." Treble stared through the lacy kitchen curtains and across the backyard. Belatedly, her sister's words registered, causing Treble to drop a mug into the sinkful of warm suds. "Wait. What the heck kind of name is Cinnamolicious?"

Propped in one chair with her feet up on another, Charity grinned. "A malicious one?"

Treble flicked a handful of water at her. "Next time, *I* get to run into town for groceries and Bill can stay here to groan at your puns."

"At least the groaning means you heard me. Honestly, you looked a million miles away."

Just up the road, actually. Was Keith still at Harrison's, or was brunch over by now? Would the doctor tell the other man he'd invited Treble to join them? She hoped not. Her stepfather would probably view her not showing up as another failure. Which would make him a hypocrite because she'd bet her down payment that Harrison would be relieved not to have her there. She hoped Keith never mentioned it to Charity, either. Treble's sister had never been subtle about her wish to have a whole, happy Rockwellian family. Why let the young woman in her overemotional state get her hopes up about something that had been a spur-of-the-moment invitation Keith himself had probably thought better of within the hour?

With a sigh, Treble allowed herself to think of the other question that had been circling her mind all morning like the wash water swirling down the drain. If Keith's invitation had been for a true breakfast date, just the two of them, would she have accepted?

The jangle of the telephone interrupted her thoughts, and Charity picked up the cordless she kept close to her at all times. "Hello? Hey. What are you doing working on a Sunday?" Charity asked, her voice full of affectionate reprimand.

Harrison, maybe? Lord knows he worked unrelenting hours. Or…Treble's heart rate accelerated, the sun streaming through the glass suddenly hotter than it had felt seconds ago. Perhaps Keith was on the phone.

"Yeah, she's right here," Charity said.

Treble turned with raised eyebrows, not even trying to disguise her eavesdropping. "For me?" she mouthed.

Charity nodded but didn't offer any clues as to who the caller was. Instead, she angled her head suddenly as if she didn't want Treble to know about this part of the conversation. Treble reached for a dish towel so she could dry her hands. Meanwhile, Charity's eyes were growing as wide and round as the frying pan they'd used to make pancakes.

"You're kidding! No, she neglected to mention anything like that."

This didn't sound good. "Charity, is it for me? Give me the phone."

But Charity merely switched hands, moving the cordless farther away from her sister. "You're sure? It's not like—"

"Charity!" When her sister looked up with the world's worst expression of feigned innocence, Treble huffed out an impatient breath. "Did they or did they not call to talk to me?"

Charity's shoulders sagged in defeat. "I guess I should give Treble the phone. What? You're sure you don't want to talk to her now? I thought— Well, okay. Yeah, I can give her the message." With one punch of her index finger, Charity maddeningly tapped the red Talk light, disconnecting the call.

Treble took a seat. "Did you just hijack my phone call?"

"Is there something you maybe neglected to mention about last night's excursion to Guthrie Hall?" Charity asked, her expression completely blank.

Oh, yikes. Treble had actually omitted several details about her evening. For starters, given Charity's overzealous interest in Treble's running into Keith the other day, she could just imagine Charity's reaction to the news that they'd danced last night. And then kissed. And then spent a good ten minutes sitting on the hood of Charity's car exchanging confidences. Treble also hadn't mentioned drunken Rich Danner hitting on her, only to be chased off by the town doctor with murder in his eyes.

"Nothing, ah, comes to mind." Treble was such a patently *bad* liar that she was shocked to this day Harrison hadn't been able to see that she was telling the truth that afternoon with Mitchell. Or would have told the truth if her stepfather had given her half a chance to explain. Instead, he'd merely frozen her out. Again.

Charity pursed her lips. "Well, that was Ronnie on the phone. She said that your car should be ready by midweek. And that she appreciates your help?" There was a pause, as Charity obviously hoped for more information.

If Charity didn't know about Ronnie's crush on this Jason guy, Treble wouldn't be the one to tell her. Relief ebbed through her. "That's all? She just wanted to tell me about Trusty and say thanks?"

"No. There was also the part where she said rather apologetically that she wouldn't have 'dangled you in front of' her brother if she'd known you were involved with Doc Caldwell."

"I'm not *involved* with anyone. You know that. The doctor and I danced only once. I think it might have been a slow dance. Maybe she saw us and drew the wrong conclusion."

"Actually, she seemed to be basing her conclusion on—and I quote—'that kiss half the women in town were talking about after church.'"

So not only was the gossip grapevine alive and well in Joyous, Tennessee, Treble was once again on the tip of everyone's tongue. The adage must be true—the more things changed, the more they stayed the same.

* * *

Charity's childhood friend, Penny Paulson, arrived late Wednesday afternoon to help set up everything for the baby shower. Officially, she was the hostess, but given the guest of honor's limited movement, the party would be at Charity and Bill's house.

Treble was in the process of relocating dining room chairs to the living room to provide more seating. "How many women are we expecting?"

Penny, tanned from her cruise, looked up from the cooler of party trays she was unpacking and chortled. "Now, see, once the party starts, you'd have to give me your passy because you said *expecting*."

Since none of Treble's close friends had kids, Mommy slang was foreign to her ear. It took her a minute to realize that *passy* referred to the pacifier she wore around her neck on a shiny green piece of curling ribbon.

Charity, directing from the couch, wore a pacifier on yellow ribbon because it matched the daisy print on her maternity dress. "There will be eight guests."

"Nine total," Penny chirped, "including the glowing mommy-to-be."

Treble waited until the other woman made another trip out to her car before asking, "Remind me, was she always this chipper, or did she just really have a good time on that cruise?"

Charity giggled. "A little of both. Confidentially, she and her husband went through a rocky few months last fall. They've been working on getting their marriage back on track, and the long cruise was part of that. I don't think we could wipe that smile off her face with two rags and a bucket of bleach. But, under normal circumstances, she does have a naturally sunny disposition. We're a lot alike."

They were. Both lifelong friends were bighearted, glass-half-full optimists married to their high school sweethearts, but Penny took cheerful to a whole new level—one Treble hadn't realized could be reached without pharmaceutical help. *Speaking of help.*

"I'll go see if there's anything left in the trunk I can carry for her."

This got another laugh from Charity. "How could there be? Her car isn't *that* big."

So far, Treble and Penny had brought in two coolers of food, a cooler with ice and soft drinks, banners and pink and white balloons that now hung all over the living room and an enormous pink-wrapped gift topped with a silver bow the size of Treble's head.

"What do you think's in the box?" Treble asked as she crossed the living room toward the front of the house.

"It could be the bassinet we registered for, in its unassembled state. Or a big-screen TV."

"I'm sure Bill would vote for the latter," Treble teased. Her brother-in-law planned to grab dinner with a couple of guys from the dairy tonight since his home would be an estrogen extravaganza for the next couple of hours.

She pushed the screen door open and stepped onto the porch. Penny stood by her car, but she wasn't unloading packages. Instead, she was talking to an attractive black woman with close-cropped hair and cheekbones that supermodels would covet.

"Treble, have you met Keisha Lewis? She'll be having her own shower before she knows it!"

Keisha beamed, her hand going to her still-flat belly in the same reflexive gesture Charity made about ten times a day. "I'm four months along with my first. Charity's promised to lie to me and tell me delivery's a piece of cake."

Treble grinned. "Nice to meet you. And congratulations."

Penny hefted the last of her party supplies, and Treble offered to carry Keisha's gift inside.

"It's a Johnny Jump Up," Keisha whispered as they took the porch steps.

More terminology that wasn't part of Treble's everyday life—wasn't "Johnny Jump Up" a drinking song she'd heard in a pub during her month with an Irish charmer?

Keisha was taste-testing Penny's ginger-ale-and-sherbet punch when another car came down the driveway. Treble opened the door to admit two women. The strawberry-blonde with great taste in shoes introduced herself as Heather Lynn Jacob. Not to be confused with her slender companion Heather, a woman who offset her pale lavender sundress with funky sunglasses and the most unruly mop of auburn curls Treble had ever seen. Next came Fawn, a teacher like Penny, but for a much younger grade. Lola Ann walked in as Treble was handing out pacifier necklaces and name tags shaped like diaper pins.

That left only one arrival. At the knock on the door, Treble swallowed, knowing who was on the other side. After Treble's mother had been killed, Joan McMillan had been the most maternal figure in the girls' lives. However, Treble had resented her presence at the time, the warm hugs offered in lieu of her mom's, the scrumptious hot meals designed to help the girls forget their father wouldn't be home in time for dinner. She'd last seen Joan at Charity's wedding when the woman had still worked for Harrison, and while the woman had always been more loving than her stepfather, her disapproval had been equally evident.

Wonder if she's heard the latest rumors, Treble thought as she opened the door. She'd overheard her brother-in-law on the phone last night and, as far as she could tell, Harrison was suggesting Bill not let Treble run amok while she was staying under the Sumner roof. To his credit, Bill hadn't even mentioned the conversation to her. Charity seemed not at all worried about her reputation, although she was annoyed that Treble wouldn't share any details about her night on the town. Charity had expressed skepticism over Treble's official statement: "It was a one-time thing, a quick kiss at the end of a dance that got exaggerated by people who clearly need to get lives."

Joan McMillan, standing on the porch in periwinkle slacks and a white polo shirt with periwinkle embroidering on the collar, looked so much the way Treble remembered that she swore she could smell baking bread and Joan's signature spaghetti sauce.

"You haven't changed a bit," Treble breathed, slightly startled. It was like a memory walking up to you on the street.

The woman's green eyes crinkled at the corners behind her bifocals. "What a polite liar you turned out to be. Not what I expected. On either count."

Not knowing entirely how to take the older woman's words, Treble decided on amusement. Joan had always had a paradoxical expression, a mischievous smile on her matronly features. The truth was, Treble might have really liked the other woman if it hadn't been so tempting to tell Joan all the things she wanted to tell her mother—about who the cutest boys were at school, the classes Treble actually looked forward to, the colleges she wanted to attend. It had been easier to dismiss Joan along with Harrison and the annoying "I know how you must feel" high school guidance counselor than to bond with the housekeeper and feel guilty about it. As an adult with more than a decade of perspective, Treble knew her mother would have *wanted* Treble to have some adult allies, people who cared for the daughters she'd left behind. That knowledge only made Treble feel more awkward over the bad attitude she'd displayed on more than one occasion.

"You going to let me in?" Joan asked gently. "Or should I just hand over the present and get out of here?"

Treble blinked. "I'm sorry. I guess I was—"

"Reliving old memories? It's like that for me, too. I ran into Charity at the grocery store when she was about six months along. She was reaching for the same brand of cookies she always loved as a little girl and it was surreal, the woman she is overlapping the child I adored."

Treble waved Joan in. "At least one of us was adorable. I probably just gave you gray hairs."

Joan smiled, running a hand through the chin-length hair that had been all-white since Treble was in high school. "Nature took care of that for you, dear. But maybe you helped me get a jump start on the high blood pressure...not that I mind having an excuse to routinely visit Doc Caldwell."

The knowing expression when she said his name

made it clear that, yep, she'd heard the latest rumors about Treble.

"It was just a dance," she blurted before she could stop herself.

Joan's laugh trilled over top the conversation of the other women crowded into the living room and kitchen. "I didn't ask, dear. You're a grown woman."

You're a grown woman. She'd said it almost... proudly. Treble swallowed a lump of emotion. She'd told herself dozens of times that it didn't matter what people from her past thought of her; now she knew that was a lie. The understated approval in Joan's voice warmed her soul.

"Thank you."

Pausing just long enough to squeeze Treble's hand, Joan walked into the room to greet Charity. Treble used the moment to compose herself, then turned to hear the rules to Penny's "buzzword" game and how the woman who'd collected the most of her opponent's pacifiers by the end of the shower would take home a door prize.

"Charity shouldn't be eligible," one of the Heathers teased. "She's already getting a pile of loot."

True. The coffee table was completely hidden beneath pastel-colored boxes and gift bags.

"I think we should open presents first," Penny said. "We need to free up the table space for food and games!"

Charity grinned. "Works for me."

Treble was designated note-taker, writing down everyone's contribution so that Charity could write the appropriate thank-you letters. As Charity predicted, the gift from Penny was a bassinet. Joan had hand-knitted an absolutely gorgeous baby blanket. Fawn had put together a breast-feeding supply kit, which gave Treble pause. Other than the prerequisite breasts, she hadn't realized a woman needed supplies. She did her best not to contemplate how some of the more complicated apparatuses worked. There were a couple of outfits so cute that Treble momentarily wanted a baby of her own to dress until she came to her senses and remembered that she could buy tons of clothes for her niece without worrying about how she was going to put the kid through college.

"That one's from me," Treble said when Charity finally got to the plainly wrapped flat box.

The practical part of the gift was a hundred-dollar gift certificate to the town's only store devoted to infants—that way, Charity and Bill could put it toward anything they didn't get or use it for ongoing needs like diapers and crib sheets. The sentimental part was a cherrywood rectangular frame with four square cutouts in various sizes.

"Treble!" Charity pressed a hand to her trembling lips.

"The empty square is for Baby Sumner," Treble said lamely, once again surprising herself with how choked up she felt. Maybe Charity's hormones were contagious?

Inside the frame, there was a baby picture of Treble—she was diaper-clad and crawling away from the camera, laughing over her shoulder—one of Charity, angelic even at a week old, and a black-and-white photo of their mom at six months old. Both girls had been given small cedar boxes of their mother's keepsakes after her funeral, and Treble had found the photo in hers.

Charity sniffed. "So do I waddle over there to give you a hug, or—"

"I'll come to you." Treble stood, then wove her way between the rearranged chairs that crowded the room. As she leaned down to embrace her sister, she whispered, "You gotta stop the waterworks, or I'm going to cry, too."

"Nonsense," Charity returned. "You're made of stronger stuff than me."

Really? Because Treble thought it took a certain amount of inner strength to make a relationship last as long as Charity and Bill had and to face the uncertainties of motherhood. Treble hadn't even invested emotionally in a pet. Maybe once she got her own place, she'd get a cat. Better yet, a hamster. Start small.

Penny clapped her hands together, making Treble think two weeks aboard a cruise was definitely too long. The woman seemed to think she was the activities director responsible for keeping them all on schedule. "Okay, ladies, what's say we eat? Charity, you stay there, honey, and I'll fix a plate for you."

Charity nudged Treble. "You'd better get in line. That covered plate Joan brought in was her homemade apple pecan bars. They'll go fast."

Did Charity want a moment to herself? This was quite a crowd for a woman who'd been mostly housebound for the past month. Treble obligingly took a place in line, ending up between the redheaded Heathers.

The one wearing the great lime-green kitten-heel slides laughed self-consciously as she picked up a paper plate. "I need these extra calories like I need a hole in the head."

"Oh, live a little," the other Heather said playfully.

Easy advice to give, Treble noted, when you were built like a stick figure. The observation prompted a self-admonishment not to sound dismissive the next time Alana mentioned her weight. Though her friend back in Atlanta was definitely not fat, the woman had to work harder on her figure than Treble did.

"So, Treble," Keisha asked from the other side of the kitchen table, "do you know most everyone from when you lived here?"

She shook her head. "Just Penny and Joan. Lola Ann moved here after I left, and since Charity and I were so many grades apart, there were a lot of classmates of hers I never had the chance to meet."

Keisha nodded. "My husband and I are fairly new to the area ourselves, but we just love it here."

The Heather with darker hair made a face. "I've lived here my whole life, but my sister and I were home-schooled, so I didn't really start meeting people until I moved out."

"Now she works for the town paper!" Heather Lynn interjected. "I love my job at the local florist, but it must be exciting to be a reporter."

"Oh, you're with the *Joyous Journal-Report?*" Treble asked. "Keith mentioned that's right next to his office."

The immediate silence that followed as speculative gazes turned toward her served as an unspoken *whoops*. Why on earth had she gone and mentioned the doctor? The women had lulled her into a false sense of security by their seeming ignorance of any gossip concerning Treble.

"You mean Doc Caldwell?" A smile flirted at the edges of Heather's lips. "Yeah, passing him on occasional mornings and evenings is one of the perks of working at the paper. I'm not so much a reporter as glorified fact-checker, part-time photographer and horoscope writer."

Treble latched on to the conversational rope, glad the woman had turned the subject back to her job. "Oh, are you an astrologer?"

"No, a single parent. I fill in here and there, occasionally taking an extra duty in exchange for a salary bonus."

"That can't be easy," Treble said, "juggling your job responsibilities and kids." Her stepfather hadn't even had the financial worries most parents would, but other challenges had certainly defined their household.

Heather scooped some pasta salad onto her plate. "I put together a support group for a little while—single parents in Joyous. Me, Becca Gibbons, CJ Sanchez, Maggie Cline, Jason McDeere—"

Heather Lynn sighed dreamily and Keisha fanned herself.

"—But it just didn't last," Heather said. "Because we were already so stretched to spend whatever time we have with our kids that it was difficult to find even more to spend with one another."

"That," Heather Lynn said, "and all the women in the group were lusting after Jason, which could have caused tension eventually."

"True." The other Heather laughed. "He's a babe."

Hmm. Could this Jason possibly be the man who attention Ronnie wanted last night? Treble tried to catch Lola Ann's gaze, but the brunette kept her eyes averted, giving the ham-and-Swiss finger sandwiches her undivided attention.

"The job *I* want to hear about," Fawn said, "is Treble's. I hear you're practically famous in Atlanta. You must miss being there."

Treble studied the other woman. The skinny blonde was nearly as tall as Treble, but her shoulders hunched slightly as if she was uncomfortable with her height. She wore a black sweater, even though Sunday would be the first of July, and didn't smile much. Few of her smiles so far had actually reached her brown eyes, anyway. *She doesn't like me.* The woman looked vaguely familiar, though Treble couldn't connect her with any specific incident.

"Famous is a stretch, but I like my job," Treble said neutrally.

"You give dating advice, right?" Fawn pressed, dousing her few leaves of spinach salad with buttermilk dressing. "So I guess you date a lot."

Picking up on the faint note of disapproval lurking in the woman's voice, Treble thought it was a shame Harrison abstained from the company of women. Even though she was probably half his age, Fawn seemed like a great match for him.

"Is that true?" Lola Ann piped up, conveniently forgetting the ham long enough to acknowledge Treble's presence. "You give women pointers?"

"Ah…sometimes. I'm not actually an expert—"

"You must know what you're talking about to get your own show," Keisha protested kindly as she returned to the living room with her plate.

There were murmurs of agreement and several simultaneous questions that Treble couldn't answer as quickly as they were asked.

She glanced at the Heather behind her. "I should get out of your way so I'm not holding up the line." But once they were all settled in the living room with their food, the ladies, even Penny, continued to express interest in Treble's job.

"I was going to play this game where we all wrote down a piece of mothering advice on a slip of paper and then have Charity guess who it was from," the hostess said. "Now I'm wondering if we should all write anonymous questions for Treble about relationships and let her answer them."

Oh, no. Trying to sound as polite as possible, Treble demurred, "I wouldn't want to upstage the mother-to-be at her own shower."

Charity sat back, interlocking her hands over her stomach and somehow reminding Treble of Brando in *The Godfather.* "Not at all. You know how happy I was when they gave you your own slot. You should favor us with a small sample of your show, since we only get like four stations out here in the sticks."

Treble wet her lips. "But on my show, the dynamic comes from people calling in. It's not that a listener poses a problem and I solve it for them. I normally ask my audience for their input, too. It's more a…discussion than anything else."

"Still." Lola Ann sounded wistful. "I'll bet you've learned more about relationships than most women ever do. Like how to get a guy who just sees you as his—as a platonic acquaintance, to notice you?"

To Treble, that problem was easier addressed than her trying to see a certain doctor as only a platonic acquaintance. "Well, eye contact is a small but simple start. I think, especially if a woman likes a guy, her tendency is to look away nervously. Meet his gaze head-on. Ask him personal questions, not the type that will motivate him to get a restraining order, but if he's someone you know from work and you only ever discuss job stuff, make it a point to ask him about something else. Or you could tell him about yourself, but asking conveys an interest. It's flattering without being over-the-top."

Penny exhaled audibly, muttering almost to herself. "There's such a thing as having him notice you *too* much."

Keisha, seated closest to the hostess, widened her eyes. "Penny Paulson, don't tell me there's trouble in paradise!"

"Yeah," Lola Ann echoed. "You've been floating around town for the past couple of days like a newly-wed."

Penny blushed. "Don't get me wrong, y'all. I'm very happy, and I'm a lucky woman. It's just that…well, most of you know Bert and I went through a bumpy patch. Now that everything's all better, he's trying so hard *not* to take me for granted that we're rarely apart. It was nice on the cruise, doing all that stuff as a twosome, but—"

"He's smothering you?" Keisha guessed. "That's how my husband's been ever since he found out I was pregnant. He's thrilled, but he also acts like I'm so delicate I can't be left alone."

Charity laughed. "Wait until the hormones kick in. Bill was suffocating me—in the sweetest way possible—but after a few really big mood swings, I think he's afraid of me now. That gained me some alone time."

Penny grinned ruefully. "I'd like to find some solution that doesn't involve terrorizing him."

"You could always drop some nice hints that it's not taking you for granted to have separate hobbies," Treble suggested. She *had* picked up lots of ideas and an informed viewpoint from her listeners, but at the same time, she felt like something of a fraud in this living room. Most of these women were in stable, happy relationships. Her helping them was akin to a blind shopping consultant telling customers what outfits looked best on them. "Let him know it would be okay if he and his buddies had poker night at your place. Work Sudoku puzzles or cross-stitch while he watches a game on TV. Buy him a certificate for a round of golf for his birthday. You don't want to push him away now that the two of you are so close, just make it clear that you have interests of your own and encourage him to find some, too."

"I'm impressed," Penny said.

Heather laughed. "Ever think about doing an advice column on personal relationships, Treb? The *Journal-Report* could use some modernizing."

Fawn sat back in her chair, her eyes brooding. Whatever motivation she'd had for bringing up Treble's talk show, it apparently hadn't played out in the way she'd hoped. She forced a smile. "Goodness, Joan, are you suddenly feeling as out of place as I am, being another single gal?"

Joan's answering smile was somehow both tight *and* gracious. "It's a baby shower, Fawn, dear. Traditionally when women gather at these events, relationships and families do come up."

Treble bit her lip, figuring a "you go, girl" wouldn't be appropriate.

As if feeling Treble's gaze on her, Joan turned. "I always knew you were a bright girl. Good to see you're putting it to good use and helping people."

Shifting in her seat, Treble admitted, "It's more about entertainment than bona fide help."

The former Breckfield housekeeper arched a snow-white brow. "Since when is entertaining people *not* helpful in today's stressful world? Well, girls, it was delightful seeing you all, but I volunteered to cover a dinner shift at the home tonight. They're so under-staffed there. I hope we raise some cash at the festival."

Treble thought about jokingly suggesting they put together a kissing booth, but the last thing she needed to be introducing as a topic was kissing. Besides, what-ever poor souls they rounded up to work the booth might end up having to lock lips with losers like Rich Danner. No, small-stakes bingo was probably a better way to go.

"If there's something I can do to help with the festi-val," Treble heard herself say, "call me. You have Char-ity's number?"

Joan paused, her smile slow and achingly maternal. "I do. And you'll be hearing from me."

They hugged, and if it was a little awkward, it was also…nice. Treble regretted not taking the woman up on the comfort she'd offered so many years ago. When Treble got back to Atlanta, she should make it a point to stay in touch with the older woman.

Joan sat on the couch hugging Charity goodbye, too. "I'm sorry to leave before the motherly advice game, although technically speaking, I never had kids of my own. But if I were going to give a new mom advice it would be this—love your child unconditionally. You'll have to discipline them at times and will disagree with them, too, but never act as if love is something that can be revoked as a punishment." Even though she was speaking to Charity, Joan glanced at Treble.

Treble walked the woman to the front door, curious

about the vehemence she'd heard in her tone. "Joan, why did you quit working for Harrison after all these years?"

"You know he can be difficult."

An understatement, Treble thought but held her tongue.

"He's a good man, but really seeing what's right in front of him is not one of his strong points." Joan's eyes had taken on an unfocused look, but then she blinked. "I should be going, or I'll be late. Talk to you soon!"

After that, they played a game where everyone supplied random nouns, adjectives, locations and verbs. Penny then used the words to fill in the blanks in a birth scenario.

"If I'm in labor for ninety-nine hours," Charity said, "I'll hurt someone. I didn't mind the part about the doctor being Patrick Dempsey, though."

Heather Lynn, who had contributed that particular actor's name, sighed. "That smile!"

Fawn and Keisha announced that they both had to be going, but everyone else stayed for a few more of Penny's party activities. Finally, Heather stood, saying she'd promised to help with her daughter's troop float for the Days of Joy parade.

The other Heather eyed her. "You look too skinny to have had a kid."

"Thanks, but I wouldn't mind a few more curves. It's hard to feel like a hot mama when I have to shop in the training bra section."

Heather Lynn propped her chin on her fists, her expression dubious. "I felt a lot more like a hot mama before I was a mama. I don't think I'll ever again have the body I had before the boys." She darted an apologetic glance at Charity. "Oops, sorry. I'm not trying to sound negative about being a mommy."

"It's okay," Charity said. "But, for what it's worth, I think you're being too hard on yourself."

"That's what Ray says, too," Heather Lynn admitted. "But *he* hasn't gone up two sizes in the last eighteen months. Sophie, who works with me, said I should get some really hot lingerie to wear in the bedroom and re-ignite my confidence, but I felt like an overweight centerfold for a low-budget men's magazine."

Treble shook her head. "It's not just about trying to be sexy for him behind closed doors. Find clothes that make *you* feel good. Turn a few heads!" Though she didn't know what Heather had looked like before, she knew the woman wasn't built much differently than Alana after her recent weight loss. The main difference was in how they carried themselves.

"Maybe you're right," Heather Lynn said hopefully. "Maybe I've just made bad fashion choices that are making it worse."

"Did you pick out those?" Treble asked, gesturing toward the woman's cute green shoes.

"Yeah."

"Then you have fantastic fashion sense in there somewhere. Meant to tell you earlier I love those slides."

The woman's eyes were now positively bright with enthusiasm. "Would…would you like to go shopping with me sometime?"

"You bet. No one's ever had to twist my arm to get me in a store."

When it was down to just Treble and Penny cleaning, with the guest of honor resting her head on the couch and surveying her haul, Charity said, "You turned out to be quite the popular lady, Treb. Joan saying she'd call you, Heather Lynn inviting you shopping, the other Heather asking if she could do a short blurb about you in the paper."

"Yeah. Your friends were really nice. Except…" Treble shoved empty plates and crumpled napkins into a black trash bag, searching for the tact that had never been her strong point.

"Except?" Charity prompted.

"I'm not sure Fawn liked me much."

Charity and Penny exchanged glances, then Charity said, "I think her older sister blames you for a breakup back in high school. Not to mention Fawn is close friends with Dinah Perkins."

Treble sighed, feeling tired. "What did I do to Dinah?" *Talk about past sins coming home to roost.*

"Dinah's been determined to get Doc Caldwell out on a date since he moved to town," Penny put in. "She's not happy about you dancing with the doctor at Guthrie's."

"But that was just a dance," Treble protested. "It was practically—" *Nothing?* She found herself saying that about Keith a lot. Running into him in town had been "nothing." That one brief kiss had meant "nothing." So how was it all these nothings were adding up into a niggling, inescapable something? She thought about him every day and steered conversation toward him whenever she thought she could do so without Charity noticing the deliberate maneuvers. Yet now that Treble knew bits and pieces of his past, she was even more curious about how it had shaped him, how, instead of becoming bitter and angry about his loss—twin emotions she remembered all too well—he'd become a person devoted to helping others.

Penny leaned her arms on the kitchen counter, peering around the corner at them. "Just how interested are you in getting involved?"

Treble blushed, even though the reaction made her feel juvenile. "I'm not. Whatever you might have heard, it was just a dance."

Penny's mouth fell open, but then mirth pealed out of her in unguarded laughter. "I meant in the *festival*. You mentioned getting involved with the festival."

"Oh." Treble's fading blush took on new life, her cheeks so hot that her face was probably a radioactive red. "Right. The festival. Is there something you need?" *Please say yes. Please say* anything *that doesn't have to do with the fool I just made of myself.*

"Actually…" Penny trailed off, her grin feline. "Local PTAs are sponsoring cakewalks and various games on the midway, but I've been put in charge of coming up with an idea to raise money for the middle school library. We need more books, and some of the reference materials are close to being obsolete. I had an idea this week, but need a very special person to volunteer. A gutsy person, comfortable with talking to crowds."

Treble shrugged. "Sounds right up my alley. I'd love to help." Plus, it was for a worthy cause and would give her another avenue for keeping busy while they all awaited the baby's birth.

Penny's smile widened. "Wonderful! Oh, and by any chance, did you happen to bring your bathing suit with you?"

Chapter Eleven

All week, Keith had thought about seeing Treble, then immediately produced reasons why that was a bad idea. Monday morning, Velma had greeted him not by asking how he'd slept the night before but inquiring whether he'd had a good time at Guthrie Dance Hall Saturday. "A friend of my pinochle partner's granddaughter said you were having a *really* good time—danced with a tall brunette, kissed her and left with her."

This revelation had startled Keith. Anyone who'd happened to glance their way at the right moment could have noticed the kiss, but it hadn't occurred to him that people would think he left with Treble. After she drove away, he hadn't had any lingering enthusiasm for his original plan of finding a nice hometown girl who might like to have lunch with him at the sandwich shop or catch a movie sometime at the King Cinema.

"We left separately," he'd told the receptionist, even though it struck him as distantly ridiculous that a thirty-four-year-old man was explaining himself to an employee.

Velma had insisted it made "no never mind" to her. "I just wanted to double-check that this won't interfere with our eventual mad elopement."

Avoiding Treble was driving him mad. Normally he spoke to Bill or Charity about once a week. Now he was avoiding them by association—a fact Bill subtly pointed out when the two men ran into each other Thursday during a busy lunch hour at Adam's Ribs. *Enough*.

So he sat parked in front of the Sumner house on Thursday afternoon, his truck the only vehicle in sight. Was Charity's car in the garage? He hadn't called first, although he assumed Treble was here. For all Keith knew, she'd driven off to Chattanooga to spend the day at the aquarium there. Only one way to find out, he told himself, popping the door open.

As he climbed the stairs, he saw that behind the screen door, the front door was open, suggesting someone was home. Then he saw her, shadowed in the comparatively dim interior. She sat on the couch, her long legs crossed on the cushions, her dark hair spilling loose over the tank top she wore as she stared at a book. From what he could see in profile, she was either nibbling the end of a pen or sucking on a lollipop. He hoped it was the former; he wasn't sure he could get through an intelligent conversation watching her do the latter.

"Knock, knock," he said, loudly enough for his voice to carry through the thin pane of glass lowered on the door in deference to air-conditioning.

Treble's head jerked up, dropping her pen to the carpet. She stood, stretching as she did so, as if she'd been sitting in that position for a while, and Keith drank in her body's lithe movements. Her grace was almost liquid.

He concentrated on not blatantly ogling when she opened the door for him. "Hi."

The hello she offered him in reply was filled with surprise. "I heard a vehicle drive up a few minutes ago, but assumed Bill and Charity were back. They're at the OB's this afternoon."

"I ran into Bill at lunch, and he mentioned her appointment with Dr. Whalen. He also mentioned that you guys were nearly finished with the nursery and that I should come see it."

Treble sat on the edge of a sofa cushion, her elbows resting atop casually parted knees. "So you thought you'd take a look when they weren't here?"

"I wanted to see you," he said simply. "Is this a bad time?"

"No." Her face softened. "And it is nice to see you. Charity mentioned she's used to talking to you pretty regularly, that you make a point to at least call and ask about her pregnancy. Since she hasn't heard from you at all since Saturday night, I was afraid—"

"You thought I was avoiding her because of you." He walked to the couch. "Can I have a seat?"

She nodded, though he detected a new tension in her posture when he joined her.

He kept proper distance, but his body hummed at the proximity nonetheless. This might be the first time he'd seen her barefoot or completely without makeup. Despite her skill with cosmetics and the way her lips had shone when he'd seen her Saturday, seeing her like this had an even greater effect because it felt more intimate.

"You look nice," he said impulsively.

She regarded her cotton tank top and jeans that were worn at the knees and frayed at the hems, clearly skeptical. "Thanks."

Past experience with women suggested that opening with a compliment was a good icebreaker, but maybe not. For one thing, his past experience didn't leave him feeling prepared for someone like Treble. Someone who was audacious by turns but couldn't quite hide the flashes of vulnerability in her eyes. Someone he'd expected to be self-centered, although he'd overheard Ronnie saying something about a "favor" in the sandwich shop and when he'd seen Heather on her way into the newspaper office this morning, she'd made a point of mentioning how smart and helpful Treble was.

"She really made an impression on us at Charity's shower yesterday," the auburn-haired woman said approvingly.

"Yeah, she tends to do that," he'd replied, bemused.

Had Heather mentioned it because she knew he was friends with Charity, or because she'd heard the buzz that he was involved romantically with Treble? Ironic that half the town thought they were carrying on a passionate affair when they sat here now, at opposite sides of the couch like two nervous high school freshmen on a first date.

Treble stood suddenly. "You want anything to drink? Sweet tea, lemonade, ice water? We made cinnamon rolls for breakfast and there are a few left."

"Lemonade would be fine," he told her, following her into the kitchen.

Her hand hovered over the cellophane-wrapped plate as though she couldn't decide whether to take a roll for herself or not. She glanced back at him, her voice low. "I'm sorry I wasn't able to join you for breakfast on Sunday."

"Really?" He found that hard to believe, considering how adamantly she hadn't wanted to be there, yet she didn't seem like someone who would utter insincere words in the name of being polite.

A sassy smile stole across her face. "Well, I vacillate between being sorry and being relieved. Right now, it's sorry."

He grinned back at her, encouraged. "Maybe this Sunday, then."

"Ah...I'm not sure that's a good idea," she said over her shoulder, pulling glasses from the cabinet.

"Guess that 'sorry' was short-lived."

"Well, I get the impression Harrison isn't too pleased with me at the moment. Even less pleased than usual," she added sardonically.

"I'd think he would be proud of you. Bill says you've been a big help to Charity, and half the women I talk to seem to be singing your praises suddenly."

"They are?" She beamed like a premed student who'd aced her MCAT. Then she sobered. "I guess Harrison heard from the other half, the one that saw me with you Saturday."

He laughed. "Oh, you mean our torrid romance? My receptionist asked me about it first thing this week."

"And that doesn't bother you?" She leaned against the refrigerator, crossing her arms as she regarded him. "I had you pegged as someone who would care about his reputation in the community."

"Since when has being favored by a beautiful woman hurt a guy's reputation?" he wanted to know.

Her lips tilted up into a lazy half smile. "Very smooth, Doc."

He dipped his head in modest acknowledgment. "Even if Harrison has heard some twice-removed rumor, he knows me. He can't possibly think we're…" Images of what Keith and Treble could "possibly" be doing suddenly halted his capacity for speech.

She broke through his momentary fantasies with her flat tone. "Right, because he has such a track record of giving people the benefit of the doubt."

Crap, he was moving further from his goal instead of closer to it. Some time since that first dinner, where he'd witnessed how Harrison and Treble brought out each other's negative qualities, it had become irrationally important for him to help mend the rift that wasn't technically any of his business. Maybe Treble's barely concealed hurt had gotten under his skin as much as the glint in her eyes and the shape of her mouth. Or maybe it was penance—Keith had been prepared to dislike her on sight for any difficulty she'd caused his mentor, but he'd conveniently let himself forget there were two sides to every story. Maybe it was simply that after so many years without a father in his life, he thought it was a shame this father-and-daughter pair who obviously shared certain traits, stubbornness chief among them, were estranged.

"I wanted to talk to you about Harrison," he said.

Her eyebrows rose. "Haven't we already had this conversation?"

"When I said I wanted to see you today, it was the absolute truth. But I also wanted to discuss something with you without Charity around. She has enough to worry about with the pregnancy."

The faintly mocking challenge in her expression faded away. "Worry? Is there something wrong with Harrison?"

Keith knew he was wobbling on a fine line here. As Harrison's doctor, he couldn't divulge medical specifics to Treble. "Not wrong, per se. I'm speaking now only as a family friend, nothing more." *Liar.*

"Okay."

"Harrison is used to being the head of a company, the patriarch of his family and, in some ways, this town. I don't think he knows how to slow down without feeling weak. He's still taking out-of-town trips to visit other plants and distributors when he could send someone else—Bill or even another Breckfield employee. He works himself too hard."

She laughed, the short sound bitter. "From what I've seen, he's the picture of relaxation. Sunday brunches? Dinner over here last week?"

"I'm afraid, though, that becoming a grandfather is going to make him feel old and that he'll try too hard to prove he isn't less than he was. It would be great if someone…inside the family could convince him there's more to life than work."

"Then you should talk to someone inside the family," she retorted. "Maybe you didn't notice, but as far as that man is concerned, I'm so *outside,* I practically had to apply for a passport to come here."

He rubbed his temples, wishing he could give her more details about Harrison's cardiac episodes in the past few months. Would that make a difference in her stance? Frustration with Harrison filled him. The man wanted to stay in denial about his health realities, and he was keeping his daughters in the dark to do so. "All right. I said my piece, it's up to you whether or not you want to listen."

She straightened, dropping her arms to her side. "Hey, it's not like I don't hear you. There are just some things I can't change." After a moment, she added, "Not by myself anyway."

A valid point—Harrison had to meet her halfway, and until Keith was certain the old man would bend a little, maybe it was unfair of him to push Treble toward any acts of reconciliation.

"I shouldn't be meddling," he admitted. "I'm not generally a meddler. Keeping a professional distance is one of the things they start preaching as soon as you hit med school."

"Yeah, but from patients, right? That's not the same as interacting with friends."

True, but emotional detachment could be difficult to turn on and off with the flick of an internal switch, especially if you'd grown comfortable with the rest of the world being on the other side of an invisible buffer. There were reasons he hadn't had a girlfriend in a long time.

He took a step toward Treble. "And are we friends?"

She regarded him softly. "I—"

The phone shrilled in the kitchen, and they exchanged startled glances.

"Should get that," she finished, tacking a different ending on her sentence. "Hello? This is she." Whatever Treble heard took her by surprise because her face furrowed into perplexed lines he wanted to smooth away with his touch. "Yes, I definitely have experience at that...I suppose I could. I'll talk it over with my sister and call you back tonight. But, tentatively, yes."

Keith smiled inwardly at the thought of her being "tentative" about anything.

She found the magnetic pad and attached pen Charity kept on the refrigerator and jotted down a phone number before hanging up. "Now it's just getting weird. You came over to talk to me, and I've had more calls here today than Charity. When I start getting mail at this address, I'll know it's time to leave."

He chuckled, although the reminder of her eventual departure stabbed his insides like a small fleck of glass in the foot, too small to be seen but plenty sharp to cause discomfort whenever stepped upon.

"Shoot, I came in here ages ago for lemonade and never got around to pouring it." She opened the fridge and pulled out a blue glass pitcher. "That call was from the receptionist at the nursing home. Apparently Joan mentioned me as a possible disc jockey for the big festival dance. The guy they'd planned to use cancelled this morning because his daughter's softball team qualified for some kind of out-of-state tournament."

"So you'll be at the dance?" he asked, truly interested in attending for the first time.

"Maybe." Turning away from him, she poured lemonade into their glasses. "I've already volunteered to help with a booth for the school library, and I want to help Charity out around here as much as I can."

"I'm sure she doesn't just expect you to sit in her living room, waiting to be needed," he said reasonably. "You should come to the dance, even if you don't end up playing DJ."

She sipped her lemonade, watching him over the rim of her glass. "Will you be there?"

"I was undecided," he admitted, "but the idea is growing on me."

Setting her drink down for a moment, she offered him the other one. His fingers brushed hers, and tiny bubbles of heightened sensory awareness fizzed through his veins. For just that moment that they touched, the underlying smell of cinnamon in the kitchen seemed stronger, Treble's smile brighter, the soft sound of her breathing more audible. And then she pulled her hand back, and the world dimmed a little. So what would it be like when she retreated to Atlanta—the sun going dark in the sky?

He shook his head—mentally, at least—such fanciful thoughts unlike him as a man of medicine. "Any word on Trusty?"

Treble passed him, the sway of her hips beckoning him to follow her like the illumination of a lighthouse offering salvation to a storm-drenched sailor. "Actually, that's who called earlier. Ronnie. She said the car's ready to pick up, but by the time she phoned, Bill and Charity had already left. I need someone to drop me off so that I can drive myself back here."

"I can take you," he volunteered. "We could just finish our lemonade, then go."

"You wouldn't mind?" she asked. "If you have the afternoon off, I'm surprised you didn't have other things you wanted to do with your time."

"Velma will call my pager if there's an emergency," he said, resuming his place on the couch. "I work strange hours sometimes, people phoning late at night because of scares they don't want to drive all the way to the county hospital to have treated. But because I put in some of that evening and weekend time, no one complains when I leave the clinic early every once in a while. Besides, I'm the one who picked you up. Not taking you back to Ronnie's would be like only doing half the job. Isn't follow-through as important as the initial act?"

Treble opened her mouth as if to say something, then lowered her gaze, fidgeting with a slim book that sat on the cushion next to her.

He studied the title, surprised to see the familiar word. "Sudoku? Someone left one in the waiting room right after I first moved here. Now I go through a couple a day." It was part of his routine, like someone else's cup of coffee or morning paper or Sunday crossword.

"Same here." She grinned. "Well, not the waiting room part, but it helps kill downtime at the station."

"Huh." *Go figure.*

"What?"

"Nothing. I just didn't imagine you having a hobby that was so…"

"Logic-based? Quasi-intellectual?"

"Sedate," he said hurriedly, sensing that he'd been on the verge of inadvertently offending her. He scooted closer to her. "Do you do the ones with just numbers, or letters, too?"

She tossed her hair. "Depends on my mood. I like to mix things up. Traditional vertical and horizontal, diagonal variations, irregular grids. You?"

"I'm more of a purist. The alternatives get to be a bit convoluted for me."

"Don't you like a challenge, Doc?"

The teasing gleam in her eyes prompted an answering wickedness in his own tone. "I'm here, aren't I?"

"Yes, you are." Just like that, her gaze shifted from playful to thoughtful, proving once again why time alone with Treble was not for faint-hearted men.

Though Keith wouldn't call her difficult, he couldn't truthfully call her predictable either. Was that why she was so memorable, because he never fully knew what to expect from her but looked forward to each new discovery?

When she spoke, her husky voice was nearly a whisper. "You're staring."

"I'm admiring."

"You shouldn't look at me like that," she said, her tone more beguiling than admonishing.

"Like what? Like I want to kiss you again?" No sense in pretending otherwise. He wasn't enough of an actor to hide the desire in his expression, and saw no point in trying. It had been Treble herself who suggested he practice reaching for what he wanted. And while it might not be logical or even in the best interests of his well-being, he certainly wanted her. He'd tried all week to ignore that basic fact, but all it had done was delay the moment he'd ended up on her doorstep. On this couch, with her bare feet inches away.

Treble wet her lips in a reflexive gesture that heated his blood. Scientifically, he knew about pheromones, testosterone and chemicals like oxytocin. Hormones and standard physiological responses to arousal. But right now, he wasn't an M.D., just a man. All his brain could currently process was that she had tasted like sinful nirvana the last time they'd kissed, and he'd craved her ever since.

He cupped her face with his hands, holding her gently in place. Not because he had any fear that she would turn away—if he thought she wouldn't welcome his kiss, he would never have leaned toward her. Quite the contrary, he didn't want her to initiate their kiss this time. *He* wanted the credit, or the blame, depending on one's viewpoint. Mostly, he just wanted her.

It was a deep, sliding kiss, her tongue meeting his in bold, unabashed strokes. She was tart and sweet and citrusy, paradoxically evocative of cool refreshment even as she stoked an insatiable fever. Their bodies mimicked the explorations of their mouths as they angled in different positions, coming into closer contact. She had one hand palmed against his chest, making him wish his shirt would just dissolve and leave them skin to skin. Her other hand was restless, one moment caressing his shoulder, the next dropping to his thigh as she leaned into him with a small *mmm* of satisfaction. She'd slid her arm up and around his neck so that there was more room for the softness of her body to nestle into his, and her pliant warmth left him taut with need.

Had he ever held a woman who made him feel like this? Had there ever been a woman before Treble? Her mouth melded to his. She was, in this fleeting heartbeat of time, his universe, the intoxicating air he happily breathed. Which was probably why he neither heard the transmission of Bill's old truck, the doors shutting, or even Charity's substantial weight on the creaky porch stairs. Keith remained happily oblivious to those warnings until voices sounded directly outside the screen.

He and Treble sprang apart in the same unison they'd come together, so she must have heard the returning couple, as well. Keith recalled the way he'd been able to see Treble through the screen before she'd realized he was here. Had Bill and Charity glimpsed them making out like a pair of teens who'd sneaked down to the basement for a few minutes of unsupervised groping?

Too bad the small Sumner house didn't have a basement.

He glanced at Treble, their gazes meeting in a fusion of frustration, amusement and chagrin. The door opened and Charity called hello to both of them, but he couldn't tear his gaze from Treble. With her flushed cheeks and rumpled hair, the way her lips were still breathlessly parted, Keith couldn't imagine how anyone past puberty could miss what had been going on here.

Charity confirmed that suspicion when she stopped suddenly, arms akimbo, her eyes widening. Bill stood behind his wife, looking from Keith to Treble, then back again. Although the man was someone Keith considered a friend, right now his protective, steely-eyed expression held a hint of "Boy, I know places in this county where they'd never find the body."

While her husband glowered in silent warning, Charity found her voice. "Nice to see two of my favorite people. And what have *you two* been up to this afternoon?"

Keith swallowed. "Um…Sudoku?"

Bill's eyebrows shot up, his sotto voce question not quite sotto enough as he asked his wife, "Is that dirty?"

Chapter Twelve

Now what? Treble watched Keith cross in front of his pickup, after gallantly opening and closing her door for her. She'd been the one to remember Keith's offer of taking her to pick up the car, and she'd immediately blurted that they were just on their way out. Even though they'd been seated on the couch…and she hadn't even been wearing shoes.

At least my fib was better than his. In this case, Treble refused to feel guilty for the deception. If Charity knew the truth, she was likely to launch into a victorious I-told-you-so jig, the female version of an athlete's touchdown dance, and that couldn't be good for the baby.

By the time Treble had escaped to her room to grab shoes, she'd realized she hadn't asked about the OB appointment. Keith beat her to it. When Treble returned, Charity had confirmed that the previa had not resolved itself, as some cases did, and that Dr. Whalen had scheduled a Cesarean at the county hospital for July ninth. Bill had held her hand, offering silent support, as Charity assured them that she wasn't too upset.

"We knew it was looking like we'd have to do a C-section," she'd said, managing to sound more matter-of-fact than she probably felt. "All I need to make me happy is a safe delivery and healthy baby."

It was then that Treble had offered to stay home, and pick up her car tomorrow, but Charity had shaken her blond head.

"No, I think I'll just rest." Her grin had been sly. "You two kids run along."

Embarrassed after all her insistence that Guthrie Hall had been "just a kiss," Treble could barely look at Keith as he started the truck. Wasn't there some saying about two being a coincidence and three forming a pattern? Did the brief seconds where they'd stopped for air make today count as several kisses or one prolonged, rapturous encounter?

She'd think about that later, when watching his hand work the gearshift wasn't making her think about how that same hand had felt tracing her collarbone. There was not a single thing about his appearance or build that could be characterized as *delicate,* but perhaps because of his profession, he had a surprisingly gentle touch. Or, more accurately, a very precise touch. Soft at times, applying heady pressure at others. Damn, what it must feel like for those hands to slide down over a woman's body.

"You can turn those vents toward you," Keith said, indicating the air-conditioning slats in the center of the dashboard. "Or I can turn it up a notch. You look hot."

"Are you being sincere or cocky?" Her temperature had nothing to do with the sun.

He flashed a movie star smile at her. "Little of both."

She chuckled, appreciating his humor even if it was the tiniest bit at her expense. "So, you're telling me *you* don't need those air vents aimed at you?"

"Honey, nothing short of ice water is going to cool me down right now."

She blinked. "Why, Doc Caldwell, I'm shocked at you."

His laugh was deep and masculine, an audible aphrodisiac. "To tell you the truth, I am, too." Whatever else he was, he certainly didn't sound remorseful.

Good thing, too. If he'd been surly or apologetic about what had probably been the best kiss of her life, she might have had to kick him in the shin. "I suppose I've corrupted you."

"You don't know me well enough to make that determination," he said, dropping his voice to a comically mysterious tone. "Wait until you hear my dark secrets...."

For the rest of the ride, he regaled her with an embellished tale of a med school prank. He'd mostly let himself get talked into acting as the lookout for some buddies, but the humor in the story was more in the way he told it than the act itself.

"Could you have been kicked out for that?" she asked.

"Probably not," he admitted. "First-time offenders and all, but there would have been some kind of disciplinary action if we'd been caught. The whole time I was keeping watch for my friends, I was grumbling in my head about how angry I was going to be if they got me in trouble. But when I got back to my apartment—it was about three in the morning by then and I was sleep deprived between working and studying—I had this stupid moment where I almost called Gail to tell her about it. Of course, I immediately realized I couldn't call her, but I knew it was the kind of thing she'd get a kick out of. It was the first time I'd felt close to her since she died. Maybe even the first time I'd felt connected to anyone. I acted put-upon, but those guys did me a favor including me. I wasn't really *that* close a friend for them to trust with their scheme."

Treble leaned her arm against the window, enjoying his profile. "People don't have to know you very well or very long to see you're the kind of person who can be relied on."

"Thank you." He cut his eyes toward her for a single second. "The same seems to be true about you. Pitching in with this festival, suspending your life to be here because Charity was frightened."

"She and the baby will be okay, won't she?" Treble told herself *she* wasn't frightened—Charity would get through this fine—but she wouldn't mind hearing her amateur diagnosis confirmed by a medical professional.

He reached over to squeeze her hand. "Charity's been very careful to play it safe, and Dr. Whalen is fantastic. I've known many pregnant mothers with more severe cases who left the hospital with happy, healthy infants."

She swallowed, nodding her gratitude at his words. Impulsively, she flipped her palm upward, lacing her fingers with his. A mile down the road, she felt oddly shy. When two people were kissing, they were aroused—if they were doing it right—but holding hands was a calmer, more thoughtful intimacy. Though one of the simplest, most innocent touches, something even sixth graders with crushes could indulge in, a person couldn't just say they'd been temporarily caught up in the moment.

Pulling her hand free, she simultaneously reached for the radio dial and asked, "Mind if I turn on some music?"

"Knock yourself out," he said affably.

But she was disgusted with herself for manufacturing an excuse to pull away. So once she'd settled on a station she liked, she found his hand again, cramming her fingers between his.

Keith grinned.

Soon, the Carter and Sons garage came into view, and Keith retrieved his hand to shift into Park. She was relieved to have the contact broken without feeling like a coward for having been the one to break it. An older man with a crooked nose and Ronnie's green eyes met them outside one of the bays.

"Mr. Carter?" Treble asked. "I came by to pick up my hatchback."

He nodded. "Ronnie's got that relic purring like a kitten. Go on inside, and she can go over the invoice with you."

The office was a small multiroom area that had probably been a single room they'd divided with cubicle walls. A large brown air-conditioning window unit kept the place reasonably cool, considering the outside heat index, but chugged along at such a high volume, Treble was surprised Ronnie had been able to hear her during any of their phone conversations about the car.

Ronnie sat behind a small, scarred desk, an amalgam of the two identities Treble had seen up until now—the grease-stained, overall-wearing mechanic and young woman in skirt and makeup at Guthrie Dance Hall. Today, Ronnie wore jeans and a pink T-shirt with a line drawing of a vintage convertible. Her hair spilled in a sunset-colored ponytail through the back of the billed cap sporting the garage's logo.

"Hey, Treb!" Ronnie smirked. "Doc Caldwell."

She's assuming we're a couple. Treble was no longer sure what the hell they were. "Hey, Ronnie. I hear you have my four-wheeled beast tamed into a kitten?"

Fifteen minutes later, keys and payment had been exchanged. Ronnie asked Treble to drive the car around the block and verify that it was running well before she officially took the vehicle home.

"We pride ourselves on customer satisfaction," Ronnie said, once Treble assured her that Trusty was running like new. "Word of mouth is really important for the business."

"Well, I'll try to recommend you to as many people as possible before I leave town," Treble promised.

Ronnie scowled. "Now that you actually have a method of transportation for getting home, how long will you stay?"

"You're stuck with me for at least another week or so. Charity's current due date is July ninth, so I'll probably be here at least a couple of days past that." Part of her hated that she wouldn't be staying long after her niece was born, but a leave of absence only bought so much time. Besides, Charity was surrounded by loved ones here who could help. Treble's main function had been emotional support during an uncertain time. And Treble was glad they'd had this warm, lazy time together before Charity's life was temporarily taken over by bonding with the baby, needing to feed her daughter every four hours and change a diaper every four minutes.

Ronnie's goodbye was cut short as another customer drove onto the lot, his car emitting a high-pitched whistle from the vicinity of the tailpipe. "Sounds like someone is having some exhaust problems. I'll see you at the festival, Treble?"

She nodded, flexing her fingers in a quick wave. "I'll definitely be there."

"Well." Even though he could have dropped her off and left, Keith had stayed while she test-drove Trusty and chatted with Ronnie. Now they both stood awkwardly next to where her car was parked. "I guess I'll let you get back to Bill and Charity."

"Thank you again for bringing me over," she said. "Bill would have, but I hate for Charity to be alone at the house for long this close to her due date."

"No problem. I enjoyed the company. Thank *you* for listening to my med school stories and pretending they were interesting," he said with a grin.

She laughed. "You underestimate yourself. You're fun to talk to."

"Fun." He repeated the word as if tasting it on his tongue like an exotic spice.

He opened her door for her, and she nearly told him "see you at the festival." That became the official town farewell in the days leading up to Sunday's kickoff parade and the six days of activities that followed. Instead, when Treble spoke, what she heard was, "Come over for dinner tomorrow night? If you're free. I know Charity and Bill would be delighted to have you over, and you never did see the nursery."

A slow smile broke across his face. "That's right. I never did, did I?"

"So you'll join us?"

"I will." He brushed his knuckles down the curve of her cheek. "I'll see you tomorrow."

She nodded wordlessly. It wasn't that she couldn't find her voice, she just didn't trust it. She'd already surprised herself by asking him on what some might call a date. Heaven only knew what less restrained invitations she might make if she weren't careful.

Since she was the one responsible for a guest coming to dinner, Treble offered to cook, which worked out nicely since she ended up with a lot of nervous energy to burn. *I blame Charity.* The woman had kept up a running commentary the entire time she'd snapped fresh green beans, which would soon be sautéed with almond slivers.

"Because when you think about it, you hold the record for the most dates Keith's been on since he moved here," the pregnant commentator was saying.

"How do you figure we've been on *any* dates?" Treble asked, despite her best intentions not to engage. Maybe if she ignored her sister and just kept stirring at the stove, the blonde would move on to some other topic.

"Well, you took him to lunch less than an hour after coming to town. And paid, no less. Around here, that's an extremely modern, Cosmo-girl thing to do."

Treble ground her teeth. "It was a thank-you for rescuing me from the middle of nowhere."

"And then you guys had dinner again that night."

Yeah, with the entire family and followed by a lovely

chat outside about how she was potentially evil and how Harrison potentially had his head up his own posterior.

"The biggie, of course, was Guthrie Hall."

"We went separately. We left separately." Treble should have imbibed the white wine instead of pouring it into the pot in front of her.

"Right, sure. I know. And anything that happened in between was an 'isolated incident.'"

"Using air quotes like that is a legitimate reason for me to spit in your bowl of risotto." Worse than the air quotes or Charity's smug smile was that—dammit—she had a point. While Treble had to take her sister's word for it that Keith hadn't spent much recreational time with any other single woman, Treble knew that *she* hadn't spent this much time with a man. Coworkers and significant others of friend's didn't count.

What am I doing? Treble didn't try to live her life by following a lot of rules, but contrary to what anyone might think, she didn't go out of her way to create chaos for herself, either. She and Keith were like the numbers in the puzzles she liked to work. Each one had a certain, correct location. If you stuck it in the wrong place, you could throw off everything else. Treble knew where she belonged, not just the geographic area where her job, friends and house-search took place, but the *world* in which she belonged, her personal attitudes and philosophies. Keith was a different sort of person, at home with the fishbowl atmosphere in Joyous, comfortable with interactions and personal interactions that would leave her squirming. Just look at their job descriptions—she frequently worked alone; with the exception of a producer and a few guests, her audience was separated by space and phone lines, and there was a measure of anonymity afforded by her on-air persona. Keith, however, was known so well in town that people noticed when he spent ten seconds kissing a girl in a crowded hall on Saturday night. Sometimes the only thing that separated him from his professional "audience" was a paper gown.

And despite all that, she'd invited him here tonight. *For dinner. He's a friend of the family.* He'd become a friend of hers.

A friend who kissed really, really well.

"Do you honestly have to stir that stuff so much, or are you just manic?" Charity asked irreverently.

Treble shot her a look.

"I figured since you were already planning to spit in mine, I might as well just say whatever," her sister said cheerfully.

"Good risotto takes a lot of stirring." She hoped it would be good. The side dish, which called for two kinds of cheese, olives and sun-dried tomatoes, sounded promising, and she'd been cheered to discover the local grocery store did in fact carry arborio rice.

"You want me to call Bill in here to take over for you while you change?"

"Change?" Treble's voice came out with a squeak she didn't recognize. She cast a glance down over the casual pink-and-white striped blouse she wore untucked over a short denim skirt. "I was planning to wear this. What's wrong with— You're messing with me, aren't you?"

"Sorry. I've gone through all the books and movies in the house. I take my entertainment where I can find it."

"Just so you know, the next time you ask for a favor that involves my trekking here from Atlanta, I'm going to laugh long and hard, then hang up on you."

"Liar," Charity said cheerfully. "Hey, what do you think about Shelby?"

Although Treble wasn't opposed to the non sequitur, she couldn't for the life of her remember meeting a Shelby since she'd come to town. "Which one was Shelby? I'm sure I have an opinion, but I can't put a face with the name."

Charity laughed. "Well, I could show you yesterday's sonogram pictures again if it would help. Bill and I were talking about names last night, and I thought Shelby sounded kind of nice."

"Shelby Sumner. Not bad."

"I really like 'Faith,' but come on…with Charity for a mother? She'd have to have a sister named Hope, and Bill would probably need to legally change his name to Valor or something."

They continued to discuss potential baby names as Treble finished up the risotto dish, green beans and chicken breasts. The timing worked out surprisingly well with everything finished mere minutes before Keith was expected.

"I'll be right back," Treble said, pivoting toward the hallway.

"If you're thinking about changing, I was just kidding earlier. Besides, you don't have time."

"I was not planning to change," Treble called back. But maybe it wouldn't hurt to apply fresh lipstick and make sure the heat in the kitchen hadn't frizzed her hair into some sort of beast from a B horror movie.

As she stood at the mirror in the hall bathroom, running a pick through her hair, Bill appeared just outside the doorway.

"Is Keith here already?"

Her brother-in-law shook his head. "No, but thanks for inviting him. Charity was so quiet on the ride back from Dr. Whalen's yesterday, but she's been chipper as a squirrel in springtime since you told us you'd asked him over. She's been after him to date on occasion and remarked that you could stand to meet a good man, so this is…what do you call those happy coincidences when everything meshes?"

"Serendipity?"

He snapped his fingers. "Exactly."

"Bill. You know I want Charity to be happy, so I'm glad if I did anything to improve her mood. But she's… being unrealistic, isn't she? Keith Caldwell is great, and I'm sure he'll find a terrific woman." Treble's jaw clenched involuntarily, but she tried to keep her tone as breezy as possible. "He and I are just friends, though. I'll be out of here in about two weeks."

Bill shrugged. "When it comes to stuff like this, I just listen to her. Hell, when we fell in love, she was barely fourteen. Plenty of people told her our relationship wasn't going to last through high school, much less make it to the altar."

"Well, that's different." Her voice softened. "You and Charity are perfect together."

"Exactly," he said again. "My wife has great instincts about love."

"This isn't love," she corrected, but he was already ambling down the hall.

So she repeated it to her reflection just to make her point. What she felt for Keith was nowhere *near* love. They barely knew each other. Yes, she was attracted to Keith and respected him, appreciated his loyalty and dedication, empathized with his past, enjoyed laughing with him and trusted him. She looked forward to being with him, experienced fluttery quivers of excitement when she thought about seeing him tonight, and his kisses made her knees go liquid, along with other parts of her body, but...

Frowning at herself, she tried to remember the point of her mental meanderings. Hadn't she been going somewhere with this?

"Treble? Keith's here," Charity called out in a sing-song voice.

Even though she was a nearly thirty-year-old woman and she'd been expecting his arrival, her pulse picked up to a kicky tempo that put a slight spring in her step as she exited the bathroom. As she approached the voices in the kitchen she thought, *oh, right.* Now she remembered her point she'd been trying to make: she was in no danger of falling for Keith. Of course, she'd probably do a better job of convincing others of that if Treble were more sure of it herself.

Dinner was a blast, as far removed from that first time they'd sat around the table together as late-night talk show hosts were from early-morning news anchors. The easy, spiteful explanation was to note that the chief difference in tonight's meal was Harrison's absence, but Treble resisted the oversimplification. Not only had she and Keith gotten to know each other better since her arrival, her overall attitude had shifted from defensive to admitting that Joyous possessed its own charm.

"The food was incredible," Keith told her with a smile. "If I'd known you could cook like that, I would have encouraged you to enter some of the competitions next week. Especially since you were right, and I *was* asked to judge a few of them."

Charity laughed. "Oh, between the library fund-raising booth, an interview for the *Journal-Report* and being the DJ for next Saturday's dance, I think Treble's already got her hands full, festival-wise. Dr. Whalen cleared me to go for one day if I sit at the Breckfield booth with my feet up, oscillated fans going and sip plenty of water. I'm really looking forward to it!"

Treble pressed her lips together. She hadn't heard much about the Breckfield booth. Since she'd been in Joyous, they hadn't seen much of Harrison, and while Charity might feel comfortable to tease or push in other areas, she'd more or less dropped the subject of her father. And Treble hadn't mentioned Keith's cryptic words to her, about Harrison perhaps not being as healthy as he would have his underlings believe. If his condition was anything serious, hopefully Keith would let Charity know after the baby was born.

Bill reached over to rub his wife's arm. "You look tuckered out."

"I am." She closed her eyes, smiling. "Carry me to bed?"

"Sure thing, sweetheart. Soon as I get that system of pulleys installed in the house."

Without opening her eyes, she swatted her hand in his general direction, making contact only with air. Bill grabbed her fingers and pressed a kiss to their tips.

"I'll take care of the dishes," Treble reminded them. "Bill, you just get your wife to bed."

Charity peered at them from one eye, looking like an impish Cyclops. "Yeah, come on, Bill, honey. I'll teach you how to play Sudoku."

It was good to know that as siblings got older, they matured beyond the childish musical taunt of "Sittin' in a Tree, K-I-S-S-I-N-G," but still retained enough of a bond to find new ways to needle each other.

Despite all the teasing back and forth throughout dinner, Charity really did seem tired, faint purplish shadows appearing under her eyes as the evening progressed. When she stood to tell Keith good-night, she was barely stifling her yawns.

"Want some help with the dishes?" Keith offered once they were alone.

"That would be nice, thanks." Not that she minded tackling the plates and pans by herself, but she didn't want to see him go just yet.

They worked in companionable efficiency, him washing—she laughed when he snapped on a glove, prepared for him to hold out one hand and bark "Scrub brush!"—and her drying. At intervals, she talked about other recipes she enjoyed making and the roommate who'd tried to teach her to cook, and he described a card one of his pediatric patients had made him. Other times, they lapsed into silence and just let the house settle around them. If she'd been alone instead of orbiting in Keith's personal perimeter, would the random creaks, the sudden motor of the refrigerator running over top of the sound of the breeze outside, the rising and falling symphony of insects and bullfrogs seem so cozy?

"It sounds so different here," she said, closing her eyes to isolate her hearing. "I grew up with these same noises every summer, but it's been a long time. Now I'm used to traffic and apartment sounds. There was this one couple that lived in my complex for a few months, I swear they—" She broke off suddenly, deciding that the story that usually got laughs at parties or with co-workers was bad conversational fodder with Keith. It's not that she thought he'd disapprove, it was that she thought she knew how he'd look at her as she described the couple's lusty activities. And if the look in his eyes turned into anything like the expression he'd had this afternoon, she'd be too tempted to give him a live demonstration of what had been going on in the apartment next to hers.

"Well, they were noisy," she concluded weakly.

Keith grinned, drawing his own conclusions. "Squeaky mattress springs?"

"Among other things."

"We're done with the dishes," he noted.

"Mmm." Which meant he would be going…unless she asked him to stay. For what? To watch a movie? To make out on the couch? She thought of Bill and Charity just down the hall and how often Charity got up in the middle of the night for all manner of pregnancy-related reasons—water, cravings, heartburn medicine, late-night television when she couldn't sleep after weird dreams or going to the bathroom for the tenth time.

No, it was best if Keith went home.

"Thank you for coming over tonight," she told him. It had been the first time she'd seen him by her own deliberate choice, not through an accident or car failure or anyone else instigating it.

"My pleasure. And not just because the food was so good." He held a hand out to her, intent clear in his eyes. "Walk me outside? The stars are supposed to be incredible tonight."

She laughed out loud, belatedly bringing a hand to her mouth to stifle the sound. "It's been overcast all afternoon and they predicted a cloudy night with scattered showers."

"All right." His grin widened as he closed the gap between them and interlocked his fingers with hers. "Walk me out on the porch so I can kiss you goodnight the way I want to without anyone overhearing or walking in on us?"

She smiled up at him. "Okay, you talked me into it."

Chapter Thirteen

Though more than three-quarters of the town had turned out on various curbs, sidewalks and lawns, waiting for the parade to start, Treble spotted Keith in the crowd immediately. His height helped, even though at the moment he was stooped somewhat, talking to a toddler with pigtails whose hands and face were sticky blue from the cotton candy she held. Whatever the kid had said, Keith grinned in return, broadly enough that an indentation deepened next to his cockeyed smile. From the side, he looked like a young Dennis Quaid.

Treble continued watching as Keith tousled the girl's hair and straightened. She knew that his job required a certain proficiency with kids, but he seemed to genuinely enjoy them. *He'll make a good dad.* Whoa.

The thought, so random and futuristic, made her blink.

Whenever she next visited Joyous, would he already be involved with the woman who might one day have his kids? Treble couldn't claim to like that idea, but there were too many men in the world who had children but didn't do right by them—her own biological father included.

So even though the image of Keith kissing another woman the way he'd been kissing *her* every time they'd found themselves alone together since Thursday twisted her guts into painful knots, she hoped he did settle down and have a family. He deserved it. He'd lost so much of his own family. He explained to her, over an impromptu late picnic lunch from the sandwich shop yesterday, that he and his mother kept in touch but weren't really close. Love didn't always translate into comfortable affection.

"I withdrew after Gail and Dad died," he admitted to Treble at the table they'd shared in a deserted back corner of the town's smallest park, unadorned by new playground equipment or decorative fountains for kids to splash in. "Mom was proud of my scholastic success and becoming a doctor, but I left her in Savannah by herself. When I visited, we didn't know how to talk to each other with ghosts floating around between us. She met this guy who makes her smile, and I'm glad for them. But when I try to stay too long…it's like I suck the joy out of their being together."

Treble had empathized, but encouraged him to give it another try next time he had a long weekend. "After all, I thought this trip home was going to be a disaster of epic proportions."

"And…?" he'd prompted, leaning closer.

She'd met him halfway. "And not so much," she'd murmured against his lips.

"What are you smiling about?" Keith asked.

Treble started. "Did you sprint through the crowd? You were way over there with that cute little girl just a minute ago. How'd I miss your getting here?"

"You were daydreaming. About something good?"

She peered through her lashes. "Ask me when we're alone."

"I like the sound of that."

Unzipping the oversize purse she wore on her shoulder, she pulled out a surprisingly compact video camera.

"What is that for?" Keith wanted to know.

"Charity. Even though she got permission to sit in the booth later this week, she's not supposed to overdo, and with this heat and crowd… It's the first Days of Joy parade she's missed in years, and Bill wants to test out the recorder they got so they can document the baby's first smile and crawling, et cetera. So I'm out here to film for them." She turned the lens toward him, learning the buttons. "Say something brilliant, and I'll record it for posterity."

"No pressure."

"You're a doctor. Don't you guys have to be geniuses whenever the situation calls for it?"

"You seem to have a romanticized image of my career."

"Blame television."

He laughed. "Maybe you should read more books."

Moments later, air horns sounded and members of the high school marching band broke into song, announcing that the parade had officially started. It was only about forty-five minutes long, which amused Treble since she knew some people came out more than an hour in advance to get a good seat. After the parade,

Adam's Rib catered a huge barbecue and the rest of the day was spent erecting booths and registering contestants for the competitions that would take place all week.

"Want to grab lunch with me?" Keith asked her.

"I'd love to, but I actually have to find Penny Paulson and get some information about the booth I'll be working on Tuesday and Wednesday." She packed the recorder back in its case. "I promised Charity I'd bring back some barbecue and watch the tape with her so it's sort of like being here."

"All right. I'll look for the middle school booth and see you later this week." When he first leaned toward her, she didn't immediately realize his intent.

As soon as it registered—*duh*—that he meant to kiss her, she took an involuntary step backward. It was a reflexive movement, not premeditated, but she could tell by his stung expression that he wasn't happy about it. "Keith. I...there are so many people around."

He glanced pointedly to his left, then to his right. "Yeah. And most of them are more concerned with getting some of that barbecue than my giving you a quick peck goodbye. I know it's a family audience, I wasn't shooting for anything R-rated."

She fidgeted, seeing two girls she'd gone to high school with who'd been happy to spread rumors about her when Rich dumped her and, in contrast, catching Lola Ann's friendly wave in her peripheral vision. On the curb immediately opposite her across the street, two grizzled men she recognized as working for the dairy chatted with each other. "There are people around," she repeated dully.

Now Keith was the one to take a step back. "You

embarrassed to be seen with me? As I recall, you're the one who kissed me at the dance hall."

She was a grown woman, yet after that one kiss at Guthrie, people had practically fallen all over themselves to tattle to Harrison and Charity. While Treble was no longer trying to convince herself there was "nothing" going on with Keith, neither was she eager to foster her sister's hope that this was an actual, lasting relationship. Once Treble was gone, Keith would eventually want a real relationship. Despite whatever jokes he'd made the other day about a beautiful woman only enhancing his reputation, that wasn't quite true. Some of the proper local girls, the ones who knew more than three recipes and would make good mothers, would have definite opinions about him kissing Trouble James. Men who saw her kissing Keith would form smirking opinions, as well. She hadn't been in town long, hadn't known the doctor before this—was she reinforcing whatever odes had been composed to her on bathroom walls?

"Treble, what is this really about?"

"I don't know." Her primary reason for being in Joyous was to help Charity, but it had seemed like a good secondary goal to prove to herself once and for all that other people's opinions didn't matter. So *why* did they suddenly seem to matter so much? As a teenager, her attitude had been "screw 'em," and when people assumed the worst about her, she'd simply lived up to their low opinions. She was more mature and less adversarial now, which was a good thing, she assumed, but that progress had left her without a clear sense of how to carry herself.

Not only wasn't she the same person she'd been

twelve years ago, she didn't even feel like the same person she'd been two weeks ago. Getting to know Keith, watching Charity's excitement over becoming a mom, living under the same roof as a happily married couple day in and day out…*it's all clouded your judgment. You're becoming a sap.*

Confusion and irritation sharpened her tone. "Look, you and I both know what we have isn't going anywhere, so I don't particularly want to advertise it. I'm sorry if that wounds your ego."

His eyes narrowed. "Fine. If you'll excuse me, I'm going to get something to eat."

The thought of food turned her stomach, but she held fast to the edges of her composure as she inclined her head. "Enjoy your lunch."

The minute he walked away from her, she wanted to call him back. And *that's* what was wrong. Because even though her statement may have come out bitchy, it was still true. They had no future together, and she was only just starting to realize how much driving away in her newly tuned-up car and no longer seeing Keith Caldwell on a regular basis was going to hurt. Not the quick, sharp sting of a shot, but a lasting, indefinable ache that she didn't think aspirin, ice cream or new shoes would heal.

On Tuesday, Keith smiled and shook hands and had his picture taken with various cook-off contestants, but mostly he wished he were back at the clinic. He'd worked a full morning, treating a broken thumb for one of the construction volunteers, a bee sting, a sinus infection, a concussion and a case of dehydration.

"Hey, Doc Caldwell." A woman in a red sundress

passed him with a smile, and it took a moment for his brain to catch up to the spark of recognition.

"Afternoon, Heather Lynn." He wondered if he would have placed Heather Lynn Jacob without seeing her two boys, who'd both been in to see him during the spring. Their mom looked different today, although maybe that was the less harried effect of her not carting around sick kids to the doctor and pharmacy. "You look nice."

Her pleasure at his words blossomed in her pale cheeks, and she smiled shyly. "Why, thank you. Charity's sister, Treble, took me shopping yesterday. She helped me pick this out."

Of course she did. He sighed—hearing the woman's name mentioned didn't exactly further his campaign to keep from thinking about her. Now that he took another look at the gently clinging dress, more a design of the fabric than a revealing cut, he could easily see it appealing to Treble, although he had to admit, she had a good eye for what worked on the florist.

Heather Lynn fluffed her hair. "I didn't think strawberry-blondes were supposed to wear red, in case it clashed or something, but Treble helped me see things differently."

"Yeah. She does that." He glanced down, including Heather Lynn's sons in his smile. "You all have a nice time at the festival today."

Waving, he watched them walk away. Then he glanced up and froze. Standing a few yards away, near a clown twisting balloons into poodles and swans for waiting children, was Treble, staring across the distance with an unreadable expression in her dark eyes.

What should he do? Walking away without acknowledging her would be stupid, petty. They'd already made eye contact, but they hadn't parted on the best of terms. Still, despite his ire with her—that tiny step she'd taken in the opposite direction when he'd tried to kiss her had made him feel publicly rejected—could he fault her logic? He had no idea how to define what was between them, so at least in part, he could understand why she didn't want half the town taking it upon themselves to assign their own definitions. Especially since Treble had grown up here, been labeled the stepdaughter of a town magnate. The surviving daughter of a deceased mother. The troublemaker in her class.

When she continued to meet his gaze, her body language softening, he crossed the space between them.

"Hey." If he reached out and caught a long tendril of her hair in his fingers, would that be too public a display of affection?

"Hi." Her smile was fleeting, regretful. "You still mad?"

"Yeah." He found his own smile. "But I'm not entirely sure why."

"Well, if you need a reason, it's been commonly held that I'm a pain in the butt."

"Being a pain doesn't make you wrong." He took a verbal leap of faith, blurting out the words before he could suppress them. "I'll miss you when you go. If I thought I could get away with it, I'd tamper with Trusty's engine, but everyone would immediately suspect foul play because Ronnie's handiwork has never failed."

"Thank you." Treble's tremulous voice matched her bright eyes.

He lowered his gaze, for the first time noticing her

bizarre attire. "Is that a *poncho* you're wearing?" He glanced up to the clear, cloudless azure sky, wondering if she knew something he didn't.

"Uh…yeah." She hitched up the duffel bag that hung by a black strap on her shoulder. He recognized the bag as one he'd carried inside for her that first day they'd met. She'd become such a vivid presence in his life so quickly, it was funny to think that not long ago he hadn't even known her. "I guess it's a rain slicker Bill never uses. He and Charity let me borrow it to throw over my—we never talked about what I'll be doing for Penny's middle school booth, did we?"

"Well, hello, Keith." A honeyed, feminine drawl, thick with generations of Tennessee, interrupted, keeping Keith from asking Treble for more details.

He turned, the friendly public smile he'd been offering earlier back in place, a bit more sincere now that he'd seen Treble. If nothing had truly been resolved between them, at least the worst of the tension had eased, like a bad storm passing on, replacing the howling, destructive winds with only steady rain.

"Hi, Dinah." His smile tightened slightly when he saw the blond receptionist. Not long after he'd moved to town, she'd pursued him aggressively with cobblers and corn bread and baked lasagna. "You know Treble James?"

"Oh, sure," Dinah said, even though she didn't spare a glance for the woman at his side. She kept her gaze fixated on Keith. "How are you doing today?"

"Fine, great. Getting ready to judge some of the handmade quilts that were entered this year and the first-round dessert cook-offs."

Treble touched his arm. "Speaking of which…I'm due at Penny's booth. See you later?"

"Of course." He smiled at her, almost laughing at his own impulse to kiss her goodbye. She certainly wouldn't appreciate the gesture, and it wasn't as if they'd be apart for long. He turned back to Dinah, blinking at how close she was. Maybe it wasn't so much that she'd invaded his personal space as how large her eyes were, still fixed expectantly on him. When he'd been a kid, he and Gail had tossed some sandwich crusts to pigeons at the end of a meal, and suddenly the birds had descended in droves, hopping closer with dark eyes and sharp beaks. Something about the small blonde in front of him struck him as very birdlike.

"I didn't compete in the cook-offs this year," Dinah said. "Usually I enter the fresh bread category. I've always loved the smell of baking bread, find it so comforting. Did you have a favorite comfort food growing up?"

He was half-afraid to answer, fearing that if he said, for instance, chicken soup, he'd find a steaming vat of it on his front porch one day soon. "Dinah, I hate to run, but judge duties call."

In fact, his responsibilities as a festival "official" kept him legitimately busy for the next couple of hours. It was nearly three o'clock when he asked a popcorn vendor if he could point the way toward the middle school library booth.

The older man grinned beneath his bushy white mustache and pointed down the lane. "Go toward the big crafts tent, but take a left at the funnel cakes—if you get to the portable restrooms, you missed the turn. Once you're on the next row, just look for the huge crowd."

As it turned out, "crowd" was not an exaggeration. There was quite an assortment of people, many of whom were hooting and whistling from the back as a guy in a backward ball cap, past age to shave but probably not old enough to buy beer, stood at a duct-taped line on the ground. A small tin pail of baseballs sat in front of him, and a shapely girl waited to his left. Though Keith couldn't see the guy's expression as he turned toward the young woman, he heard his boast that he would win a teddy bear for her.

Then a voice Keith knew well carried out over the crowd, teasing, but with enough playful lilt in her tone to keep it from sounding spiteful. "Honey, if he misses the target, maybe *you* can buy a bucket and win a bear for him. Remember, all proceeds go to a good cause!"

Even though Keith had an idea of what he was going to see when he turned toward the sound of that voice, his body was unprepared for the sight of Treble sitting atop a narrow platform. Her dark hair was dripping in wet ringlets down her back, and the creamy, long-legged body that drove him to distraction bared but for a few brightly striped scraps of—pink? purple?—nylon Lycra. His throat went dry, the blood draining from his head. Every time he'd cupped the nape of her neck or ran his hands down her spine, he'd wanted to explore further. To see for himself the lush curves beneath her clothes. Well, in part, he'd gotten his wish.

He just hadn't expected it to be in front of the greater population of Joyous, Tennessee.

Treble wondered how long Keith had been standing in the crowd—his perfect stillness distinguishing him from the teenage boys who jostled one another, the moms who fished in their purses for cash and the dads who shifted under the weight of preschoolers atop their shoulders—before she noticed him. She met his eyes, and the swell of heat from his gaze practically evaporated the droplets of water that clung to her shoulders and arrowed in slick beads down her collarbone toward her cleavage. Her breath caught. Though she distantly registered the thud of the ball hitting the target, for the first time, she was unprepared for the fall.

The water wasn't cold, just cool enough to be bracing, and she came up, half spluttering, half laughing. All things considered, she preferred this to other volunteer duties. Some poor guy was walking around in what had to be a sweltering-hot Seth the Safety Squirrel costume, handing out brochures on campfire protocol, hiking first aid, and poison ivy and sumac identification.

Treble flipped wet hair out of her face, and called graciously, "Let's hear it for our second winner of the day. Nice throw, buddy."

She'd been surprised that Penny set the throwing line so far back, but the other woman had laughed. "Gotta make 'em work for it, right?" The first guy to dunk her had been spurred on by his ego and the crowd, actually going through two buckets of balls before he accomplished it.

Penny leaned over the counter at the small covered booth adjacent to the tank. "Okay, just a few more takers, then we'll let our mermaid here have a short break."

One of the guys in the audience let out a good-natured boo, another called out his offer to run and fetch her anything she wanted. "Soda, corn dog, the keys to my Chevy?" Laughter rippled around him.

Treble darted a glance to where Keith still stood, to

see if he were one of those smiling. Nope. His expression was intense, making her feel so momentarily exposed that she almost looked down to make sure her bikini top wasn't floating on the surface of the water. She tried to push aside her awareness of him long enough to goad passersby into lobbing a few tosses her way. A few took her up on the invitation, but no one else dunked her before Penny declared the booth closed for business until three-thirty.

Penny reached the gated side of the booth, towel in hand. It had been hanging on a hook just outside the splash zone, next to the poncho Treble had wriggled out of two hours ago. "You're *such* a good sport for doing this. We really appreciate it."

Treble smiled as she climbed down. "No problem. But if you see my brother-in-law in the crowd wielding a video camera, please tell him taping is against our policy."

"You need anything? Hot chocolate? Well, they probably aren't selling that at a summer festival," Penny said to herself, "but I'm sure we could find you some coffee."

"I'm fine, really. I've only been in twice."

"If you're not cold, would you mind maybe walking around in that bathing suit?" Penny grinned at her. "It would be *excellent* advertising."

Treble's laugh faded when she saw Keith standing past Penny's shoulder. "I'll be back in fifteen minutes, okay, Penny?"

"So this is how you're raising money for more books, huh?" Keith said softly when she reached his side.

She shrugged, pulling the towel around her. "Well, we weren't all invited to taste desserts."

"Did you buy that bathing suit just for this?" he asked. "I heard you were shopping yesterday."

He knew about her road trip to the mall with Heather Lynn? Not that it particularly mattered, but she suspected you couldn't sneeze at one end of town without someone at the opposite end saying, "Bless you."

"No, this is just my bathing suit. Penny asked if I'd happened to bring one with me, and I had. Whenever I travel in the summer, I take it just in case."

"So you didn't specifically get the bikini to help make—sorry—a splash here? That's just what you walk around in at the pool or beach."

"Yeah." It wasn't really all that revealing, as far as two-piece bathing suits went, she only seemed nearly naked because everyone else was in shorts or skirts and, in a few cases, jeans. "Are you okay?"

"My vision's gone all spotty. Don't you worry about sunburn?"

"It's all right, Doc. I slathered my entire body with sunscreen, promise."

"Little dots in front of my eyes," he said. "And you're doing this again tomorrow?"

"Yeah." She still wasn't sure if he approved, but he didn't sound mad.

His gaze met hers, suddenly more focused and a lot more wicked. "Can I help with the sunscreen?"

Chapter Fourteen

"Come on, come on, come on," Charity chanted, adorably impatient in her red, white and blue maternity shirt. Her earrings were red outlines of large stars. "Why am I the only one ready to go?"

Treble exchanged wry glances with Bill. "She was like this as a kid, too, always antsy for the school bus to come in the morning."

Charity glared. "You'd be excited, too, if the warden gave you a day pass! It truly is Independence Day."

Treble appreciated her sister's enthusiasm—she herself never liked to feel caged—but was glad Dr. Whalen had been playing it safe during Charity's last trimester. In some cases, the OB might not be quite as conservative, but Bill and Charity lived a good drive from the nearest hospital, and no one wanted her sister to take any unnecessary risks. Still, getting permission to sit at a booth today and watch the fireworks over town square tonight had done wonders for Charity's morale.

"Maybe we'll name our daughter Liberty," Charity said as Bill helped her down the stairs.

"Can her middle name be Belle?" he teased as they walked toward the truck.

Treble was helping them carry a blanket and cooler, but would follow in her own car in case they wanted to come home at different times. Flashing back to yesterday evening, when Keith had stolen a soft, hot kiss from her between booths featuring rustic interior decorating pieces and handcrafted Amish dolls, Treble thought about how the night could have ended differently.

She could have sworn, as he nuzzled the side of her neck, he'd murmured that he wanted her. Even if he hadn't put it in words, the sentiment was there. A sentiment she wholeheartedly returned. It had occurred to her that even though she was bunking with her sister, Keith had his own place. Was she brave—or foolhardy enough—to ask to see it?

Her conjecture had remained exactly that, however, because some guy trying to impress his girlfriend with shenanigans at the rock-climbing demo had managed to break his arm. Keith's medical skills had been needed, and Treble had used the reprieve to go home and let her hormones cool. Only the thought of seeing him again today was already warming her.

"Or July," Charity said as Bill opened the passenger door for her. "July can be a name. Maybe too specific. Summer?"

Treble snorted. "Summer Sumner?"

"Oops." Charity grimaced. "I forgot that, for a minute."

Bill gaped. "You *forgot* our family name?"

"I always thought Autumn was a pretty name," Treble offered.

"For a girl born in the middle of summer?" Charity asked.

Treble shrugged. "Why not? Dare to be different. No rule saying she has to be a conformist right from the womb, is there?"

Charity laughed. "We'll see you at the festival. Drive safe."

Treble gave a jaunty salute. She'd been in the car about ten minutes when her cell phone rang, and she wondered if Charity had forgotten anything back at the house. "Hello?"

"Hi." Keith's voice was as tangible a caress as any touch, and her body reacted accordingly.

"It's nice to hear from you," she said, catching sight of her own moony smile in the rearview mirror.

"Well, we didn't get a chance to say a proper goodbye last night."

"How's that kid doing?" she asked.

"His arm should heal with no problem. His pride was plenty injured, but his girlfriend fussing over him seemed to help. Or maybe it was just the pain medication kicking in. Look, I know you're driving, so I don't want to keep you. But…any plans after today's aquatic performance?"

"Same as the rest of the town's, I reckon." Had she just said *reckon?* It wasn't a word she recalled ever using on-air. "Watching the fireworks."

"Want to watch them together? You, me, a blanket and a bottle of chardonnay?"

"See, that poor schmo wanting to impress his date

could use some pointers from you," she said. "It sounds perfect."

"Great. I'll be the one with the chilled wine and wandering hands."

She laughed, delighted by his flirtatious tone. Lord, had she ever actually thought the doctor was *stuffy?* "I'll be the one with wet hair and willing lips."

Because so many people wanted to find a good spot for the fireworks or had pre-show dinner plans, the crowd broke earlier Wednesday evening than it had the day before, which suited Treble just fine.

Penny checked her watch. "We'll give it ten more minutes, then close shop. Sound all right?"

"Fine by me." Treble flashed a smile. *I have a hot date tonight.* Keith was meeting her here shortly.

The refrain of a country song trilled from inside Penny's open purse behind the counter, and she bent to answer her cell phone. "Hello. Charity? What's wrong, sweetie?"

Treble's heart lurched to her throat. Oh, God. Had today been too much excitement for her sister? Was something wrong with the baby? *Calm down.* If anything had happened to Charity, wouldn't Bill be the one calling?

"Yeah, she's still here," Penny said. "What—?" There was an interminable pause as Treble imagined the worst, then Penny nodded. "All right, I'll let her know."

"What is it?" Treble asked, her fingers gripping the edge of her platform seat.

"Charity called from the Breckfield booth she's been helping with today. She and Harrison argued. Apparently, a couple of guys were…" Penny lowered her gaze guiltily. "This is my fault. Some guy made a ribald comment about you that Harrison overheard. I don't think he approves of the way we're raising money for the library."

"Don't worry about it, Pen. His disapproval is nothing new."

"Well, I guess he's coming over here. Why don't we go ahead and shut the booth down?"

"No," Treble said calmly. "This was a two-day stint on my part, and I want to bring in as much revenue as possible." There was another woman who'd work the booth tomorrow and a man who'd volunteered for Friday.

Penny winced as if she'd glimpsed a furious fork of lightning and was cowering in anticipation of the boom and tremble of thunder. She didn't have long to wait.

Harrison Breckfield stalked toward the booth with the stride of a powerful, fit man, though his mottled face gave him an unhealthy appearance.

Treble spoke before he could. "A bucket of balls for five dollars. We're closing soon, so you'll have to hurry if you want to take a shot."

He looked appalled by the suggestion—although maybe she was misreading him; after all, he'd looked pretty appalled already. "Come down from there and put on some clothes."

"Well, I have an outfit in my duffel bag, but I was saving it for the fireworks. It's not really appropriate for the dunking booth."

"You call that appropriate?" He gestured vaguely toward her bathing suit but wouldn't lower his eyes from her face as if just the sight of the bikini would sully him. "Do you know what people are saying about you?"

"I'm not sure," she bit out the words. "What day is it, Wednesday? Today would be Elvis rumors, right?"

"I don't know why I bother trying to talk to you."

She laughed harshly. "*When?* When have you tried to talk to me?" Certainly not after her mom died. Or in any of the condescending lectures over her many failings and outrageous behavior—shouldn't talking involve two-way participation? He hadn't wanted to hear what she had to say. Even during her weeks here in Joyous, their direct interaction had been limited to that one disastrous dinner.

"Harrison."

Both of them turned, surprised at Keith's firm voice. He didn't look happy, but as he was the only one in their little triangle not vibrating with angry emotion, he was pretty calm in comparison.

"I think you should go sit down somewhere, take a few deep breaths," Keith advised.

The older man's eyes narrowed. "I warned you that there were some things you were going to have to stay out of. Charity and I live here, make our home here. I don't appreciate her waltzing in just long enough to make a scene."

Keith glanced around. There was still no crowd at the booth, but other vendors were watching with un-abashed curiosity. Those that caught the exact words exchanged would no doubt repeat it for the benefit of others; those who didn't catch what was said would speculate. "Harrison, as far as I can tell, you're the one making the scene."

Her stepfather's already red face now looked posi-tively apoplectic. Treble's heart hurt. She knew that Harrison had been a friend to Keith, and it had never been her desire to cause trouble between them. Maybe he was right that first night they'd met. Maybe she just couldn't help it. Tears pricked her eyes, the hot, salty drops far more unpleasant than the tank of water she'd fallen into a dozen times today.

"All *Treble* is doing," Keith continued, still in that even but unyielding tone, "is helping the library raise money. You support the cause, right?"

"That's not the point!" Harrison whirled on the doctor. "A school counselor warned me once that Treble was desperate for attention, but you'd think she would have outgrown it by now. Tons of people are here today raising money, yet my stepdaughter seems to be the only one half-naked." He turned back to Treble. "I wanted to punch those two roughnecks who were exchanging sleazy comments about you, but how can I protect you if you insist on putting yourself on display?"

Protect her? Treble blinked, surprised that one of the town's most honorable citizens had considered decking anyone on her behalf. As happy as she'd been to see him in the barn that one afternoon, when the intent look in Mitchell Reyes' eyes had genuinely alarmed her, it wasn't protection she'd wanted from her stepfather.

Before she could sort through her thoughts, a female voice interrupted. Joan approached her former employer, taking his arm. "Don't be an old fool. I asked Treble myself to get involved in this year's festival."

"But look at her," the man said, though his anger was faltering now. He seemed more sad than anything else. How ironic to actually have something in common.

"No, Harry." Joan's voice wasn't unkind, but it was stern. Treble had heard exactly that tone many times. "You look at her. She's a grown woman, and you can't keep judging her based on the actions of a sixteen-year-old kid who needed more parental guidance."

"I…" Harrison Breckfield blinked, looking for a moment lost in the streets of his own hometown. Looking very much his age and every bit as miserable as Treble currently felt. "I did the best I could."

Was he talking to her, apologizing in some oblique way? Or merely defending himself to Joan?

As the twosome moved away and people stopped paying attention—or at least, stopped blatantly rubbernecking—Treble shivered.

"Let's get you out of there," Keith said from the other side of the protective cage. He sprung the latch and held his hand out to her.

She slid down into his waiting arms. "I should get my towel. I'm still damp."

Not even bothering to respond, he pulled her against him in a fierce hug. Witnesses no doubt saw their embrace—would remark upon it later—and she found she honestly didn't give a damn.

"You stood up for me," she muttered against his shirt.

He angled back so that he could meet her gaze. "Of course I did." He made it sound unremarkable. Maybe for him it was. After all, he'd ridden to her rescue when she'd been a total stranger, stranded. He'd nearly decked Rich Danner on her behalf even though, as a physician, "violence was against his creed."

For Treble, however, his unflinching defense of her brought fresh tears to her eyes. Her own father hadn't wanted her. Some of the men she'd dated could barely be bothered to remember to call her, much less stand up for her. "Thank you."

"You're welcome." He leaned toward her, then hesitated, his eyes seeking permission that she granted with a nod. Then he kissed her.

And Treble's heart squeezed with something that felt very much like love.

By the time Treble had changed into her blouse and shorts and was situated on a cotton blanket next to Keith, she'd recovered her composure. So she and Harrison had fought—that wasn't news. She wanted to hold on to the glow of Keith and Joan being there for her and forget the rest entirely.

During the last moments of fading light, Keith wrestled with a corkscrew, trying to open the bottle of wine he'd supplied as promised. "I didn't even know they made disposable plastic wineglasses until yesterday," he said.

She hid a laugh, watching him. "They *also* make wine with twist-off caps."

He sent her a wry smile. "Nothing but the best for you."

Despite the number of people present to watch the Fourth of July display, Treble felt nicely isolated with her date for the evening. Everyone was on their own island, the growing dark casting an illusion of privacy even while the steady rush of conversation, the pockets of laughter and the homey aroma of fried chicken over the lighter scent of honeysuckle, provided the feel of community. For a split second, Treble experienced a frisson of déjà vu. This was how she felt sometimes on-air. As if she and her listeners were all in it together, a faceless community of people she couldn't see and didn't always know but who were important to her nonetheless.

Her cell phone jangled, and she flashed Keith a look of apology. "I know it's rude to leave it on during a date—"

"You're talking to a doctor," he said mildly. "I'm not bothered."

"Thanks." She kept it on in case Charity had any news or requests. And it was her sister's voice she heard, shaky, on the other end of the phone.

"Treb? I know we passed each other earlier, but I didn't want to ask in front of Keith. Are you all right? I heard it got ugly."

Treble sighed. If it pained her that Keith had been dragged into an argument on her behalf, it upset her even more that Charity had been involved. Harrison could stalk her down to yell at her if he wanted, but he never should have breathed a word about his displeasure in front of his very pregnant daughter, who'd always preferred the image of him as loving benefactor.

"Don't worry," Treble said. "You know how everything gets exaggerated in this town."

"Yeah."

"Are *you* okay?"

"I've been better, but yes, I'll be fine."

"Enjoy the fireworks, then go home and get some rest."

Charity laughed, sounding more herself. "You're turning into a regular mother hen."

"Good night, brat. Oh, Charity?" Treble cupped her hand around her mouth and turned her head to the side to whisper, "Don't wait up for me tonight."

Once she was off the phone, she accepted a glass of wine. "Keith? I'm sure you know that even a little bit of alcohol can alter a person's reflexes and response times.

Maybe I shouldn't drive myself all the way back out to Bill and Charity's tonight."

Keith's eyes were as dark as the night around them. "Do you need a lift?" he asked haltingly, hopefully.

She took a deep breath. "I was thinking...more along the lines of a place to stay?"

Setting down his glass, he leaned in to capture her mouth in a searing kiss she felt down to her toes. As she brushed her tongue against his, a high-pitched whistle erupted overhead in a series of pops, and brilliant blazes of white and violet and green filled the sky.

"It's not much to look at," Keith warned as he parked the car in his driveway, his tone endearing.

"That's all right," Treble assured him breathlessly. Her body still thrummed, not from the tremor of fireworks that had shaken the ground below but from the impact of Keith's periodic kisses throughout the night. She wasn't here to criticize his decorating choices.

He took her hand, guiding her over a sidewalk that was broken in several places. Then they were at his front door, and Keith slid his key in the lock. Treble took a deep breath, part of her still surprised that she was going through with this. She already knew how she would feel driving back to Atlanta, so why compound the inevitable ache?

He left her standing on the welcome mat as he braved the dark room to provide light for them. He'd leaned over a lamp, and the low-wattage bulb threw his chiseled profile into shadowed relief. Her heart flipped over beneath her breast, a somersault that left her giddy and distantly queasy at the same time.

Why compound the ache? The answers were so clear.

One, because she'd never wanted another man like this. *Two,* because how much worse would that ache be if she didn't at least let them have these few cherished moments before she was gone? She'd regret leaving here without making love to this man, and it wasn't as if abstaining from tonight would make her not miss him later.

"You look sad," he said simply.

"No. Not sad. It's been a wonderful night."

He lifted a brow as he came toward her, neither of them commenting on the evening's inauspicious beginning. All that mattered to Treble now was how it would end.

"I probably should have warned you that the house isn't air-conditioned. At least not very well." His smile turned boyish. "But I was afraid you might change your mind about coming over. Can I get you anything?"

She clasped his hands. "Just you."

Their mouths met in a tangle of pent-up desire they'd both tried fruitlessly to deny. Maybe because they'd wanted this for days or because they were too aware their time left together was easily measured in days, their exploration of each other was bold, purposeful. Perhaps later there'd be time to enjoy each other slowly. Right now, neither had the patience.

A spiral of liquid heat unfurled within Treble, delirious sensations rolling through her as he trailed his kisses from her lips to her throat, into the vee of her blouse. His fingers were just ahead of him, skimming the buttons free of their holes and exposing the lace edging of her bra. Her breasts felt pleasantly heavy, full, ready to be freed to his touch. He pushed aside the front panels of her blouse, and the fabric slipped down over her arms and to the floor.

His own shirt wasn't as effortless to remove, but she made up for any lack of finesse with her unabashed appreciation of the muscles in his chest. The man was as beautiful as he claimed her to be.

He ran his index finger over the lacy scalloping, tracing a straight line down over the silky cup. "Nice."

Her body tightened in response to the light touch. She hitched her thumb under a bra strap, her tone husky. "It's part of a matched set." Managing a deftness that surprised her, she unbuttoned her shorts and let them fall. Would another woman have been more modest, coy? *Pointless.* He'd seen her in a bikini for the past two days, and coyness wouldn't have darkened his eyes to their current, aroused indigo shade.

Taking her by the hand, he led her into the bedroom. He didn't bother to turn on the light, but illumination spilled in from the living room. She only glimpsed fleeting impressions—quality furniture, walls that needed fresh paint, little personal decoration, but sheets that felt cool and soft against her sensitized skin as he lowered her to the mattress. His fingers had already found the clasp on her front-closure bra, and she arched up toward him as he kissed her breasts, drawing one nipple into his mouth and wringing a cry from the back of her throat. The way he touched her was far more intoxicating and potent than the wine they'd shared earlier.

By the time she pressed one hand against his shoulder and whispered for him to roll back, she'd ceased thinking in words, only in scents and tastes and sensations, free-form and inarticulate. She straddled him, helping him roll the condom down, poised to take him inside her body. He was already in her heart.

She sank down slowly, by excruciating degrees, until he filled her. *"Oh."*

"Treble." He cupped her face, lifting up to kiss her before falling back to the pillow, his hands moving to her hips. He held on to her, stroking her, letting her set the pace.

Riotous, rapturous need coiled deep inside her, tightening until her movements became less controlled, frantic. Keith rolled with her, braced above her, his eyes locked with hers as pleasure burst within her. She let her eyes close then, forgetting to breathe, offering her body up to his as he continued to move, finding his own pleasure. She pulled him down on her, holding him tightly.

At first his attempted words were little more than pants, but he managed to get out a short sentence. "I'll squash you."

"Impossible. I'm floating." She was weightless, limp with satisfaction. Either she drifted to sleep or her mind simply wandered in perfect relaxation.

Keith stirred long moments later. "Thirsty?"

"Water, yes," she said gratefully. By the time he returned, she'd realized she was also sticky with perspiration. Before the memorable interlude in his bed, she'd spent most of the day outside. "Can I ask you a favor?"

He smiled. "Right about now, you could probably ask me for anything."

"Use of your shower?" She set the water glass down next to the alarm clock on the nightstand. "You could join me."

"That's not a 'favor,' that's you granting wishes."

He warned that the water took a few minutes to get

hot, but they managed to stay pleasantly occupied until tufts of steam billowed over the glass door of the shower stall. He reached in to adjust the temperature, then stood back to let her precede him.

"Ladies first."

"Very chivalrous."

"Not particularly. I was admiring your butt." He stood behind her, lifting her hair atop her head with one hand and leaning down to kiss her neck. At the last minute, when she could feel his breath warming her skin, he froze. "You have a *tattoo?*"

It wasn't easily visible, often mingling with dark tendrils even when she wore her hair up. But it was there, below the base of her skull. "It's a treble clef."

He traced the graceful scrolling curves of the symbol as water cascaded down over them. "I can't believe I just made love to a woman with a tattoo."

She stiffened. "Is that a problem?"

"Not remotely. It's just that I was thinking I'd gotten a pretty good look at your body." He slid his hands down over her rib cage as he caught her earlobe between his teeth. "You have any more surprises?"

"None that I can think of…but feel free to take your time looking."

Chapter Fifteen

A jarring sound pulled Treble from the peaceful cocoon of sleep. She awoke in stages of confusion, noting that her surroundings were dark and unfamiliar. The night came back to her in a hazy flood of images and sensual memories. Where was Keith?

"It's just the phone," he said quietly. Now that she had an idea of where to look for him, she saw him silhouetted in the moonlight, tugging on a pair of jeans, his smile rueful. "I told you doctors get calls at strange hours."

She sat up, pulling the sheet around her and watching him head into the lamp-lit living room. The ringing stopped immediately. There was always something ominous about late-night phone calls. Maybe when Keith returned, he'd tell her it was just a wrong number and they could make love again, use the most of their hours togeth—

"Treble?" He hastened back to her, his demeanor so apologetic that she knew bad news was imminent. "It's for you."

Even before she'd said hello into the receiver, Keith busied himself gathering up her discarded clothes. An unpleasant buzzing filled her head, and dread choked her.

"Treble? This is Harrison. Charity's being prepped for the operating room and Bill's with her. They wanted me to find you. We left a voice mail on your cell phone."

It was on, but she must have slept through the ring. Or had she been in the shower with Keith? Shame tweaked her. It was as if everything he'd ever said about her was true. Charity had needed her, and she'd been…

"Is she okay?" Treble found her voice. "The baby?"

"She woke up bleeding heavily, so Bill rushed her to the hospital. The doctors say she's in pre-term labor. They're going to go ahead and do a C-section. Keith can get you here?"

Squeezing the phone in bloodless fingers, she nodded.

"Treble?"

"Y-yes. We're on the way."

Keith had finished lacing up his sneakers and was carrying her blouse and shorts toward her. He stopped short. "You're shivering. Here, wait."

She didn't turn her head, still staring at the disconnected phone as if it might offer more information, reassurance, but she heard the muted squeak of a drawer sliding open.

"Wear this." He handed her a sweatshirt, which she pulled over her head.

The fabric swallowed her, the fleecy warmth distantly comforting. Her body felt better, but inside she felt untouchably cold.

"Let's get you to the hospital." He helped her stand.

He was good in a crisis, she noted inanely. Right. Of course he was. He was a doctor, he'd seen plenty of crises. Hell, he'd endured several of his own. "Do you think she'll be okay?"

"The baby's nearly full-term," he said calmingly. "Charity's safely at the hospital, where they're all doing what's best for her. By the time we get you there, you'll probably be an aunt."

She tried to visualize Charity, smiling and holding a baby, the only palatable conclusion. During the drive, time stopped meaning anything, passing in slow drip-drops of impatient worry and frustration that they couldn't safely go any faster, then moving in a mindless blur as Treble sat numbly in the passenger seat. Finally, they were there, and Keith was ushering her inside the too-bright maternity ward. It was the middle of the night, technically morning, when the world should be asleep and peaceful, but the activity here was restless. Nurses passing with clipboards and medications, pregnant women breathing *whew-whoo-whew* in wheelchairs, family members pacing or demanding answers or merely handing each other cups of coffee. Treble registered her surroundings in fits and starts, barely recalling the parking lot but focusing on strange specifics like the yellow cartoon kitty cats one nurse wore on her scrubs.

They found Harrison in a small alcove on an operating floor. He truly looked aged enough to be a grandfather. He didn't get up from the blue padded chair when he saw them approach. "No news yet," he told them. His eyes flicked to Treble's, then away.

How must he view the scene? In her haste to get here, she hadn't even bothered with a bra under the thick sweatshirt. She'd rolled up the sleeves, but the shirt itself fell practically to the hem of her shorts. The outfit doubtless looked ridiculous with her sandals. The distorted reflection in the nearby vending machine reminded her that she hadn't combed her hair after the shower earlier. Tangled strands fell across her face, but she brushed them away impatiently. Given the hour, she couldn't possibly be the only person who'd just rolled out of bed.

But it was unfortunate that she stood in front of her stepfather having just rolled out of Keith's bed. Before Keith had been her lover, he'd been Harrison's friend, and his action probably seemed like a defection to the older man. One she'd caused.

This was a small area—Harrison had chosen to be apart from the larger waiting lounge with its magazines and corner television and numerous chairs—and Treble eschewed the only remaining chairs, which were to her stepfather's left and right. Were she and Keith supposed to sit on either side of the man? Instead, she sagged against Keith, grateful for the arm he wrapped around her.

"Treble!" Bill's voice down the corridor reenergized her, and she straightened, whipping her head around to search his expression. He had circles under his eyes, but the eyes themselves were bright with excitement. "I'm a dad. Harrison, you're a granddad! Brooke Elisabeth Sumner is five pounds, six ounces. Missed being a Fourth of July baby by a few hours, so it's just as well that we didn't go with the name Liberty. She's small but beautiful. Like her mom."

"And Charity?" Treble and Harrison asked in unison.

"She's fine. Tired. They're stitching her up now, but she hung in there. She was real—" Bill's voice broke, and Keith clapped him on the shoulder. They all waited, stranded in myriad emotional reactions to the events of the night. Bill pulled himself together, then looked at Treble and Harrison. "Charity was so worried that maybe she should have stayed home today, like this happened because she went to see fireworks. But the doctor said it could have just as easily happened if she'd stayed home in bed all day. It was just time. Nothing *caused* this."

Treble swallowed, thinking about how Charity had sounded upset on the phone earlier and the chaos that seemed to plague Treble's family when she was around them. "Thank you," she told her brother-in-law. For the first time since the phone rang, she felt a smile blossom on her face. "And congratulations."

She'd convinced Keith that he should go home and get at least another hour of sleep—he'd have patients tomorrow that needed him, and after glimpsing her absolutely gorgeous, albeit bald and wrinkly, niece, Treble's admiration for doctors ran deeper than ever.

"You're sure you don't want to ride back with me?" he'd asked.

Even though she knew logically that she wasn't currently needed here—and could come back when Charity and Brooke were awake—she couldn't bring herself to leave just yet. "I want to stay. I know it's stupid sitting out here, but I want to stay for just a while longer."

"I'll take her home," Harrison had said.

When she'd glanced toward him, he'd returned her stare stoically, giving nothing away. Once they were all agreed, Keith pressed a platonic kiss to her forehead and left. The hospital cafeteria started serving breakfast at five, and Bill joined them there, too keyed up to sleep in the uncomfortable chair at his wife's bedside. He hadn't wanted to be away from her long, and by five thirty, Treble was leaving the hospital with her stepfather.

"Thank you for calling me tonight," she said once they were in the car, even though she knew he'd only been acting on Charity's behalf.

"I'm just glad I was able to track you down." His gaze flicked to her. "That didn't…I meant nothing derogatory. I know how much Charity wanted you to be there to see the baby."

She'd avoided the man for years, and it certainly hadn't improved their relationship. Why not finally meet trouble head-on? "It bothers you that I was with Keith?"

"He's a good man. He deserves to be happy."

"Deserves better than me, you mean."

"Dammit, girl. I know I'm a pigheaded old coot—Joan's certainly repeated it ad nauseam, but it doesn't help that you're always looking for a fight! I meant what I said. Keith deserves to be happy. *You* deserve to be happy. I'm not trying to judge—"

She snorted. "You've always seemed more than willing to judge me, even when your view of the situation was skewed. Years ago, at the dairy, just yesterday at the dunking booth."

"I apologize for losing my temper yesterday. Joan read me the riot act. For years, she tried to tell me I wasn't handling the situation with you right, but I thought she was too softhearted. Lately Charity's been taking little jabs, too, and then even Keith who barely kn—" He broke off, realizing that obviously Keith knew her quite well in some respects.

Treble, torn between wanting to defend her burgeoning relationship with the doctor and knowing that relationship didn't actually have a future, merely stared out the window at the thin fingers of light slowly starting to reach across the landscape.

Harrison sighed. "It's a dangerous thing, falling for someone. Not everyone gets the fairy-tale ending, though I like to think Bill and Charity will prove an exception."

"Charity always was exceptional," Treble agreed with a tired smile.

A look of affection passed over his face at the mention of his daughter, but the worry he'd been expressing quickly returned. "I'm sorry I didn't do whatever it was I needed to do differently for you. When Meg died, I felt like part of me was yanked out. The best part."

She could identify with his grief, but it didn't change the fact that she'd needed him. No matter how forgiving she *wanted* to be, years of resentment didn't magically melt away.

"*My* loss was unavoidable," he continued. "Nothing I could have done, no check I could have written, could have changed the outcome of your mother's car crash. But now I know how painful it is to lose someone who has your heart. I'd hate for you or Keith to feel that pain in another week. You've both already had to say goodbye to important people in your lives."

His tone was so melancholy, the loss he'd experienced still evident. Did he regret falling in love with his late wife? Treble could have asked, but she was afraid to hear the answer. Instead, she turned the topic from the past to the future. "You said…if you could have done things differently with me? Do them differently with Brooke. I know how important Breckfield Dairy is to this family and this town, but slow down a little. Look at your priorities and enjoy your granddaughter."

He said nothing for so long that she almost didn't hear his, "Okay." It was slow and rusty, like hinges on a door that hadn't been opened in years.

All in all, fairly impressive for their very first talk.

Having now attended his first ever Days of Joy festival, Keith could definitely say the week had been memorable. It was hard to believe that now, it was over. Or would be after tonight's dance.

A portable dance floor that looked like wood but wasn't took up most of the space inside the large, elegant tent. Or maybe *canopy* was a more accurate term, he thought. This made him think more of wedding receptions than the circus, not that he'd attended either in the past few years. To the side of the floor were tables, many with citronella candles in the center. Box fans blew at each entrance, creating a nice breeze, and strands of tiny lights had been woven throughout the interior. The festival dance committee had done a lovely job.

Keith particularly approved of their choice in DJs.

When he'd walked in, Treble had been composing an on-the-spot poem to congratulate a couple on their thirtieth anniversary, then she'd reminded everyone that she took requests. But by the time he reached the table set up with her CDs and equipment, she was no longer addressing the crowd, merely humming with the music, her body swaying. There was a chair behind the table, but she'd chosen to stand.

"Hi," he told her, wondering if she could tell, even from that short word, how much he'd missed her. They'd seen each other in passing since he dropped her off at the hospital in the predawn hours of Thursday morning, but they hadn't had more than five or ten minutes alone. Most of their conversation had been about the new mommy and her beautiful baby, very little had been spared to reference what had happened between Keith and Treble. Absolutely nothing had been said about when she would leave.

She smiled. "Hi, stranger."

"I'm glad you decided to come tonight. With Charity still at the hospital, I thought you might change your mind."

"It was Charity who convinced me to come. That room is tiny, and there's nothing they really need me for. I just like to hold Brooke."

"Dr. Whalen still thinks they'll go home on Monday?"

Treble hesitated, then nodded. When she spoke, her voice was too high, too thin. Full of false cheer. "Then the new family will be back home, and I'll just be underfoot during their bonding time."

A bright edge of panic flared within him, even though he'd known this was coming. "Actually, I'm sure they'd appreciate the help with the new baby."

"Maybe, but my landlord would also appreciate rent. And I'd appreciate the station not giving my job to whatever great new talent has been filling in for me." She wouldn't meet his eyes. "It's time for me to go, Keith."

Keith. It made him think of the way she'd said his name in the shower, her body soapy and sweaty and clinging to his, her voice throaty with sensual bliss. Reluctantly, he blinked the image away.

"Hey, you two!" Joan McMillan joined them, grinning with the energy of a much younger woman. "Treble, you're doing such a great job tonight. I knew you would! You ever want a job livening up radio broadcasts around Joyous, you give Bud Petro a call. Now, can I request something slow and outdated for the golden oldies among the crowd? You'll never believe who agreed to dance with me."

Treble and Keith both followed her sly gaze, and Keith saw Harrison Breckfield, overdressed in a buttondown shirt and navy blazer. The man raised one hand, offering them all a nervous wave. With a laugh, Keith bent to kiss Joan's cheek.

The woman beamed. "My, whatever on earth was that for?"

"Because I think you're good for him," Keith said. He knew Harrison had been alone a long time and on some level found that preferable, but even though this was just a dance and nothing more, Keith thought Joan McMillan might be just what the old man's heart needed. Besides—he stole another glance at Treble, who was smiling at her stepfather—one never could tell what would come of a simple dance.

"What about you?" he asked, when Joan had returned to Harrison's side. "Can you break long enough for a turn around the floor?"

Treble sighed. "I should stay here. But I'm glad to see so many people dancing tonight. Look…"

He did as directed, not sure why she was grinning

so broadly at the sight of Lola Ann and Devin Carter walking toward the floor. Keith was more concerned with Dinah Perkins, who'd just edged into his line of vision, along with her friend Fawn.

"Okay, now you *have* to dance with me," he pleaded. "I'm being stalked. Every time I turned around at the festival, Dinah was there, staring at me, asking all kinds of weird questions." She'd been wild-eyed and breathy, reminding him of a college kid he'd seen once who'd accidentally doubled the dosage of her already strong prescription.

Sure enough, here came Dinah and Fawn, although the latter hung back at the last minute so that her friend could talk to Keith.

"You look nice," the blonde began. "The black shirt is great on you."

"Thank you." Then she asked about his favorite color, volunteering that hers was green, and he wondered if there would be a quiz later. Treble, he noted, was no help at all. She'd ducked her head and seemed to be making studious inventory of the available music. It wasn't until Dinah drifted back into the crowd that he realized Treble's shoulders were shaking with silent laughter.

"Let me in on the joke?" he asked.

"It's my fault." She glanced up, her eyes dancing merrily. "The random questions and the way she keeps trying to hold your gaze? I gave some advice at Charity's shower on, um, how to catch a man's attention."

"You told her to stalk me?"

"Of course not. She wasn't even there. I was talking to Lola Ann, but Fawn was there. I think she passed along my suggestions, but something got lost in translation."

"Well, dance with me. Help me show the interested ladies of Joyous that I'm off the market." The cajoling statement was out of his mouth before he could take it back.

Treble froze.

Damn. He wanted to hold her, not scare her away. But it seemed as though the more he tried to pull her to him, savor the last of their time together, the more she distanced herself with frequently impersonal smiles and little reminders that her home was in Atlanta.

"Off the market?" she repeated neutrally.

If it were up to him, yes. He'd lived in that house for six months and the night he'd spent in it with her was the first time it had truly felt like home. Charity had been right all this time about something missing from his life, only it had been Charity's sister who'd finally helped him see it. He loved laughing with Treble, dancing with her, arguing with her, telling her about his patients, telling her about his past—something he'd never been very comfortable discussing, but she had enough baggage of her own to understand. Whereas so many here saw him as Doc Caldwell, which in a way was as much a persona as her radio personality, she knew Keith.

"For tonight, at least," he evaded, "there's only one woman I'm interested in."

"I can't." She swallowed, making her tone more casual. "I can't be your date tonight. I'm working. You should ask Ronnie to dance. She looks lovely and is standing alone—she'll protect you from Dinah."

Nobody there would have minded if Treble excused herself from behind the DJ table and danced one song with him, and they both knew that. Still, he pressed. "What about after the dance? Could I see you then?"

For a moment, he didn't think she'd meet his gaze, but then she did, looking straight into his eyes. Despite the resolve she projected, he saw the wistful regret, the longing, in those dark depths. "I have packing to do."

"I…should let you get back to work then." Somewhat blindly, he stumbled toward Ronnie, his head and heart reeling. He wound up dancing with the mechanic three times that night, waltzed with Joan and Heather Lynn Jacob once each—Heather Lynn seemed delighted by her husband's scowl, even though the man had said he didn't mind her dancing with the doc—and even let Velma Hoskins show him a few moves. But while he tried his best to be good company for the people of Joyous, his focus was elsewhere.

Watching Harrison and Joan talking in a corner and Rich Danner cradle a mug of coffee in his hands, Keith smiled, a bittersweet moment. Now that Treble had come to town, would Joyous ever be quite the same?

Would he?

The funny thing was, he didn't want to be the same man he'd been before he met Treble James. And he'd tell her that if he thought it would make a difference… or if he thought she'd want to hear it.

Chapter Sixteen

It had been easier this way, Treble thought, leaving from the hospital with its bustle and sterilized rooms instead of saying goodbye at Charity's place, where she'd grown closer to her sister than she'd expected. They'd dutifully loved each other over the years, but she thought they had a better understanding of each other now.

Charity sniffled, propped upright in her hospital bed and looking rumpled but healthy in the robe Bill had brought her from home, Brooke sleeping in her arms. "You really have to go?"

Treble's laugh was a raw scrape against the inside of her throat. "If I don't now, I might never."

Charity met her eyes. "Would that be so bad? Honestly? If you think Brooke's adorable now, just wait until she stops sleeping and crying for fourteen hours out of the day. And instead of buying some house in Atlanta, you could build exactly what you want here. The family owns a ton of land. You're part of the family. Little radio stations out in these parts would probably love to have someone with your exp—"

"Sweetheart," Bill interrupted softly from the cramped chair that had served as his bed since Brooke was born. Treble stayed here during the day so that he could go home and stretch out on an actual bed, but by this time tomorrow, they'd all be back home.

"Was I babbling?" his wife asked.

He smiled. "Why don't you let me take the baby so Treble can give you a hug?"

Though her emotions were running fierce, Treble kept the hug gentle. Charity said the incision still hurt when she laughed or sneezed or moved very fast.

"You are going to make a *great* mother," Treble whispered. "You're intuitive. You've been right about so many things. Brooke is blessed to have a mom like you."

"And an aunt like you. Promise me you'll come visit."

"Cross my heart." Joyous was no longer a town of ghosts. Treble found she could even be in a room with Harrison without all the old phantom hurt and blame and mutual anger flaring to life.

No, the only thing that would haunt her now was the memory of Keith Caldwell. Would it be difficult to avoid him on her much shorter visits to Joyous in the future? If she could go back and do things differently, would she have avoided him on this trip? She hadn't realized it was possible to give your heart so completely to someone in such a relatively short period of time.

Bill looped one solid arm around her shoulders, pulling her into a brief hug that included the baby. "Drive careful."

"I will. You take care of your two girls," she said.

"That's what I'm here for." His easy acceptance of that role—provider, protector, emotional support—reminding her again of Keith. Two good-hearted men who would never intentionally disappoint or abandon.

But there were hundreds of ways to let someone down or hurt them unintentionally, and she needed to get a grip. It was getting to where even the cabinet of medical supplies could remind her of Keith, for crying out loud. *Well, he is a doctor.*

"If you wanted to stay just a little longer," Charity said, "Dad was planning to stop by."

"That's okay. He came over to your house early this morning to say goodbye." Before his traditional Sunday brunch with Keith, she assumed. She hadn't asked. If it hurt this much to *think* his name, she knew she wasn't ready to say it.

In less than half an hour, she was on the road, on her way home. *Home.* Her throat tightened, and she turned up the speaker volume, hoping the CD she'd popped in could blast away her blues. It would be good to be back in her apartment. Her small apartment with no view of the stars amid downtown lights and smog, her lonely apartment where there was no ice cream in the refrigerator for late-night snacking or even a cat for company. *So buy some ice cream. Get a cat.* She'd call Alana when she got home, catch up…although her friend was more than likely at Greg's.

Absorbed in her thoughts, Treble didn't notice the pickup truck gaining speed on the road behind her until the horn blared. She jumped, her gaze shooting to her rearview mirror. *Keith?* Her heart pounded, absurdly happy, although she tried to tell herself some of it was the adrenaline of him startling her. She pulled over to the wide, grassy shoulder, her sense of irony prompting a chuckle at the bucolic scenery. This wasn't where they'd first met, but it looked similar enough. She unfastened her seat belt, but hadn't yet climbed out of her car when he slammed his own door and approached at a jog.

Her eyes devoured him. He looked good…but furious. Standing in the wedge of space between her open door and the vehicle itself, he ducked his head toward her, eyes blazing.

"You *left* without saying *goodbye,*" he admonished, his tone accusatory and unforgiving. "If Harrison hadn't mentioned he'd seen you this morning, I wouldn't have even caught you in time. You weren't going to tell me?"

She swallowed. "I told you last night. At the dance. I didn't think there was anything else to say—you knew I was leaving."

"Soon!" He straightened, threw his hands up. "I knew you were leaving soon, but I didn't realize you were dashing out of town first thing this morning."

"Well. Then…" She swallowed again. Darn him for chasing her down; she'd tried to spare them this kind of scene. "I suppose it's fortuitous Harrison mentioned I was headed out." Darn *him,* too, for that matter. "Now we have a chance to exchange formal goodbyes."

"I don't want to." Keith's expression was mutinous. Under other circumstances, she would have smiled. Who looked like the rebel now?

"Then why are you here?" she asked tiredly.

"Because we need to talk. I would have driven all

the way to Atlanta if I had to, but there's something I need to tell you. I love you, Treble."

Her heart stopped. "Wh-what?" He'd seemed so angry, so contemptuous of the way she was running off, that the last thing she'd expected was a declaration like that.

"You heard me. I love you." He crouched next to her. "You needed to know."

Why? So she could miss him even more? This conversation was a mistake, just something for them to regret later. *Really?* The knowing voice in her head sounded a little like Charity's. *Do you regret making love to him?* No, she didn't. She'd felt too vulnerable to repeat the experience before leaving town, but she wouldn't undo it for anything in the world.

"I love you, too." She was probably a fool for telling him, but better an honest fool than a gutless coward.

He trapped her face in his hands then, kissing her soundly, repeating with his actions what he'd already put into words. She tasted tears and realized she was crying even as she kissed him back.

"Now what?" she asked when they stopped momentarily, their foreheads resting together.

"Now...I look for a job as a doctor in some suburb outside Atlanta," he improvised.

Oh, my God. "You're kidding? You wouldn't seriously do that?" She sat up, shaken to the core that he would even consider uprooting himself for her. "Keith, you haven't known me a full month. You can't *move.*"

His gaze was somber. "Life is short. You and I have both unexpectedly lost people we loved. So, I could spend the next few months in Joyous, being miserable without you and writing thoughtful lists with Pro and Con columns, or…I could be with you."

"You make it sound simple."

"Geography's not the hard part. It's all the other pieces of relationships that will get complicated."

"Like the fighting over who gets to sleep on which side of the bed?"

He laughed. "Of course not. *I* get the left side."

She bit her lip. "Keith, people need you here. I'm sure there are thousands of doctors in all the suburbs surrounding metro Atlanta. And you love Joyous."

"I do. But I didn't realize that when I came here, I was looking for something. I found a hint of it when Harrison and Charity befriended me. I got more of it when the people in this town began to slowly make me one of their own. But where I really discovered it—discovered myself—is with you. I want to be with you, Treble."

She wanted that, too, her heart full to bursting even though her head told her they were both crazy. But life was short, precious, and even more precious was finding a person who made you feel like this, saw your flaws and accepted you anyway. Stood up for you, stood beside you, helped you face your fears and demons and become a better person for it.

"Let's be together here," she said impulsively. "In Joyous." Never before had that name seemed so appropriate.

He recoiled, searching her face. "You can't be serious?"

"I've worked so hard to create my own community on-air, a family of sorts, but I already have one." She grinned. "Maybe *this* community could use a little shaking up."

He took her hand, standing and tugged her out of the car and into his arms. "This community would be lucky to have you."

His lips teased hers, coaxing arousal and optimism, the belief that sometimes people *did* get the fairy-tale ending, if they were willing to reach for what they wanted and work hard to keep it.

"Mmm." She sighed against his mouth, feeling it was only fair to warn him between kisses, "I can be difficult, stubborn sometimes…"

He nipped her bottom lip. "Just sometimes?"

"And impatient with small-town propriety. I could cause…trouble for you, even without…meaning—"

He deepened the kiss just long enough to silence her disclaimers. Then, when she'd completely forgotten what she was saying anyway, he pulled away and winked at her. "A little trouble is exactly what was missing from my life."

She grinned. "Well, then I'm your woman."

"That's what I've been trying to tell you." He angled in for another kiss, this one promising to be hot enough to scandalize anyone driving by, but she supposed they'd have to get used to it. Trouble was here to stay.

* * * * *

MARIE FERRARELLA

Marie Ferrarella, a *USA TODAY* bestselling and
RITA® Award–winning author, has written more than
two hundred books for Silhouette and Harlequin,
some under the name of Marie Nicole. Her
romances are beloved by fans worldwide. Visit her
website at www.marieferrarella.com.

Look for more books from Marie Ferrarella in
Harlequin American Romance—the ultimate
destination for romance the all-American way! There
are four new Harlequin American Romance titles
available every month. Check one out today!

MONTANA SHERIFF
Marie Ferrarella

To
Kathleen Scheibling,
who apparently likes
cowboys as much as I do.
Thank you.

Chapter One

Cole James blinked. As he did, he expected the image to fade away.

This wouldn't be the first time that his eyes—aided and abetted by his heart—had played tricks on him.

In the beginning, when Veronica McCloud had initially left Redemption—and him—a little more than six years ago, he kept seeing her all the time. He'd see her walking down Main Street, or standing in line at the movie theater they used to go to regularly, or passing by the sheriff's office which had, these last four years, all but become his second home.

He couldn't begin to count the number of times he'd thought he saw her peering in the window, a funny little half smile on her lips, the one that always used to make his heart stop. But when he'd bolt from his chair to chase after her, or run across the street in pursuit, ready to call out her name, he'd discover that it was someone else who just happened to look like Ronnie.

The worst times were when there turned out to be no one there at all, just his memory, torturing him.

Eventually, his "sightings" of Ronnie became less frequent. Whole days and then even whole weeks would go by without him even *thinking* that he saw Veronica McCloud, the woman who had, for all intents and purposes, tap-danced on his heart and then deliberately disappeared from his life six summers ago.

Sheriff Cole James frowned as he watched the woman across the street walking toward the wooden building in the middle of the block: Ed Haney's Livestock Feed Emporium.

She wasn't disappearing.

Instead, she looked as if she had every intention of walking into the store. Just like Ronnie used to when her dad sent her into town.

The funny thing about this particular mirage was that all the other times, when he thought he saw Ronnie, she looked pretty much the way she had that last night by the lake.

The night that would forever be imprinted on his soul.

Her golden-blond hair would be flowing loose about her shoulders, that soft, cream-colored cotton peasant blouse dipping down low, making him all but swallow his tongue.

Each and every time he thought he saw Ronnie, she would be that green-eyed hellion, part eternal female, part feisty tomboy. The woman who could instantly make him weak in the knees with just one look.

But this time, the mirage—Ronnie—looked different.

This time, she looked a lot like the picture she'd once showed him of her late mother, Margaret, when she'd been a young woman. The photograph was taken just after she'd married Ronnie's dad, Amos.

Old image or new, why wasn't she vanishing the way she always did? he wondered impatiently.

Damn it all to hell, Cole silently swore. Lifting his Stetson, he dragged a hand through his dark chestnut, almost black, hair. Exasperation zigzagged through him.

He wasn't going to go and check it out. He wasn't. The people in town looked up to him. They depended on him for guidance. It went without saying that the sheriff of Redemption, a pocket-size town fifty miles north of Helena in the proud state of Montana, wasn't supposed to be given to having hallucinations. Leastwise, not without smoking something—which he hadn't done except for that one time when he was fifteen. He did take the occasional shot of whiskey, but only when the weather turned bitter cold, and never more than one. And even then, it was to warm himself up more than for any other reason.

He didn't need anything to warm him up now, even though it was September and this year the temperature was already dropping down at night into regions that tried a hearty man's soul. Just thinking of Ronnie, even after all this time, more than sufficiently warmed him up, thank you very much.

Cole bit off the rough edge of a curse. The next minute, he was making a U-turn at the end of the block. Telling himself he now officially qualified as the town idiot, he turned his truck around and slowly drove along the length of the street until his vehicle was parallel to the Livestock Feed Emporium.

The mirage had definitely gone inside.

Cole stopped the truck and squinted, looking in through the store's huge bay window. From where he sat, his hallucination was talking to the store's owner, Ed Haney. And Ed answered the hallucination.

Cole pushed back his black Stetson with his thumb and blinked again. Nothing changed. Either he was having one hell of a daydream or—

The word hung in midair, refusing to gather any more words around it. Refusing to allow him to even finish his thought.

Or.

He *couldn't* finish his thought.

Because it wasn't true. He *knew* that, knew it as sure as he knew his own name.

Veronica McCloud had left that summer six years ago. Left Redemption and left him. Left after they had enjoyed possibly the best night of their lives—certainly the best night of *his* life. And not once, not *once* had she come back to visit, or just to talk or even to throw rocks at him. She hadn't come back at all.

She never wrote, never called, never sent carrier pigeons with messages attached to their tiny little ankles. Never tried to get in contact with him in any way at all. Half a dozen times he'd set out to see her father or her older brother, Wayne, to ask them for her address or her phone number, just about any way at all to get in contact with her. But each time he set out, he never quite completed his journey.

His pride just wouldn't let him.

After all, *he* hadn't left her, *she* had left him. And if she hadn't wanted to stay gone, to remain missing from his life, well, hell, she knew where to find him. He had the same phone number, the same address, the same *everything* he'd always had. None of that had ever changed, not since they were kids together, growing up in each other's shadows.

Back then, Ronnie had been a rough and tumble tomboy, more agile and skilled at being a boy than any of the boys in town. Partially, he'd always suspected, to curry her father's attention and favor. And she'd always been a type A competitor.

In any event, they'd been each other's best friends almost from the moment of birth. And they shared everything. They bolstered each other, supported each other and just enjoyed being kids in an area of the country that was still relatively uncomplicated by the demands of progress.

Everyone in Redemption knew everyone else by their first name. The people of the town were always ready to lend support through the hard times and especially ready to rejoice during the good times.

Sure the twenty-first century had brought some changes to the town, but not all that much. Certainly not enough to make him want to be anywhere else but right where he was.

But not Ronnie. For Ronnie it was different. Once she hit her teens, Ronnie started talking about someday wanting to go someplace where "the possibilities were endless and the buildings stretch up against the sky. Someplace where I don't have to be stuck on the ranch all the time if I don't want to be."

At the time, he'd thought it was just talk. Or at least, he'd hoped so.

But then she started to talk about it more and more. Her big dream was to go to college, to get that all-important piece of paper that called her a graduate and allowed her to "make something of myself."

As if she wasn't good enough.

That was around when they began having arguments, *real* arguments, not just squabbles and differences of opinion about things like who had the faster horse—he did—or who was the better rider—she was.

Moreover, Ronnie wanted him to come with her. She wanted him to go to college, too, and "become someone"—as if he couldn't be anything without holding that four-year degree in his hand.

But all he wanted to be was a rancher, like his father, and she, well, she didn't want to live on a ranch her whole life. Didn't want to be a rancher's wife and certainly didn't want to live and die in Redemption without "leaving her mark" on the world, whatever that meant.

He'd thought after that huge blowup they'd had that last night at the lake—and especially after the way that they'd made up—that the argument had finally been settled once and for all.

To his great satisfaction.

Apparently, he'd been wrong because when he woke up that morning at the lake, she wasn't there beside him the way she had been when they'd fallen asleep.

She wasn't anywhere.

Suddenly uneasy, afraid something had happened to her, he still pulled together his courage and went to her house just in case she'd decided to go home. When he asked to see her, Amos McCloud had looked at him for a long, awful moment, then said he'd just missed her. She and Wayne had just left. Her older brother was driving her to the next town. From there she was taking the train to Great Falls. There was an airport in Great Falls. And planes that would take her away from here.

Away from him.

Remembering all that created the same pang in his heart that had gripped him that terrible morning.

"Hey, Sheriff, you gonna sit in your truck idlin' like that all morning?"

The sharply voiced question came from directly behind him. Wally Perkins was sticking his head out of his dark green pickup truck and he looked none too happy about the fact that the sheriff's truck had stopped moving and was blocking his way.

Wally knew that he could always pull his vehicle around him, Cole thought, but it didn't seem exactly right, seeing as how he represented the law and all.

"Sorry, Wally. Got lost in my own thoughts," Cole murmured the apology.

With that, he pulled his truck headfirst into the first parking spot he could. It was in front of the next building, just one door down from the Emporium.

Cole cut off his engine and sat in the truck a moment longer.

If he had any sense at all, he silently told himself, he'd start the vehicle up again, go back to his office and work on this month's monthly report. A report that was tedious given that there was actually very little to report. Crime in this small town of three thousand strong involved nuisance disturbances and not much else.

Of course, there was that horrible accident two weeks ago involving Amos McCloud and his son, Wayne, and a trucker who had been driving cross-country, but that wasn't a crime, either, not in the sense that all those prime-time TV programs liked to highlight. His investigation had shown that inclement weather and bad brakes had been to blame for the truck suddenly jackknifing. Amos had seen the accident happening but it had been too late. He couldn't stop his own truck in time.

Lucky for Wayne and Amos, Cole had been driving by or there might not have been anything left of the two men except for bits of cinders. Racing from his own truck, a sense of urgency sending huge amounts of adrenaline through his body, he'd managed to get first Amos and then Wayne out. The latter had been brutal. The cab of the truck had folded like a metal accordion, trapping Wayne in its metal embrace. He'd worked like the devil to get Wayne free and had succeeded just seconds before the whole damn truck exploded.

Fortunately, no one had died at the scene. But the jury was still out about the final count. The trucker and Amos had been pretty banged up, but Wayne had been unconscious when he was taken to the hospital in Helena.

He still was.

Was that why she was here? Cole wondered suddenly, straightening in his seat. Had Ronnie come back because of the accident? He might have tried to contact her about the accident himself if he'd known how to find her, but she'd done a good job of disappearing from his life.

"Damn it, she's not here any more than she was all those other times you thought you saw her," he declared angrily, upbraiding himself.

If he got out of the truck and went into the Emporium

to investigate, he would feel like a damn idiot once he proved to himself that she wasn't really there.

More than likely, it'd turn out to be some other woman. Or maybe nobody at all.

But if he didn't go in, if he went back to his one-story, 1800-square-foot office, and tried to get some work done, this was going to eat at him all day. He knew that. *Especially* since he hadn't imagined seeing her in a while now. Almost a whole month had gone by without a so-called "Ronnie sighting."

It had begun to give him real hope. He was beginning to think he was finally, *finally* over her. For real this time. Not the way he'd thought before, the time he'd gotten engaged to Cyndy Foster at the diner.

Getting engaged to Cyndy had just been a desperate act on his part to force himself to move on. Except that he really couldn't. Not then. And when he caught himself almost calling Cyndy Ronnie one night, he knew it wouldn't be fair to Cyndy to go through with the wedding.

So he'd called it off and tried to explain to Cyndy that he thought she deserved better than spending her life with a man who was only half there. He'd hoped she'd take it well, the way he'd meant it. But she didn't. His ears had stung for a week from the riot act she'd read him at the top of her lungs. Not that he hadn't deserved it.

From that point on, he dedicated himself to the job of being town sheriff and saw to it that he was a dutiful son, as well. Cole figured he'd either eventually work Ronnie out of his system, or become a confirmed bachelor.

These last few months, he'd begun to think that he

was finally coming around, accepting what his life had become.

A lot he knew, Cole thought sarcastically. If he was on the road to being "cured," what the hell was he doing having another damn hallucination?

Only one way to battle this, he decided, and that was to walk in, see who Ed was really talking to and be done with all this racing pulse nonsense.

With that, Cole pulled his key out of the truck's ignition.

Tucking the key into the breast pocket of his shirt, he shifted in his seat and opened the driver's side door. He got out and walked the short distance to the Livestock Feed Emporium. Cole deliberately avoided glancing in through the window, giving himself a moment to prepare for the inevitable disappointment.

He opened the door to the store. The same tiny silver bell, somewhat tarnished now, that had hung there for fifty years, announcing the arrival or departure of a customer, sounded now, heralding his crossing the store's threshold.

Cole's deep blue eyes swept over the rustic store with its polished, heavily scuffed old wooden floors. Ed took pride in the fact that the store looked exactly the way it had back in his grandfather's day when Josiah Haney opened the Emporium's doors for the first time. The only actual concession that had been made to modern times was when the original cash register had finally given up the ghost. Ed had been forced to replace it with a computerized register since manual ones were nowhere to be found anymore.

The air had turned blue for more than a week until Ed had finally learned—thanks to the efforts of his incredibly patient grandson—how to operate the "dang infernal machine."

The store was empty. Even Ed didn't seem to be around. The man was probably in the back, getting something—

Okay, Cole thought, relieved and disappointed at the same time, the way he always was when a mirage faded. She wasn't here.

It had been just his imagination, just the way it always was. Just the way—

And then he heard it. Just as he turned back toward the door to leave, he heard it.

Heard her.

He froze, unable to move, unable to breathe, as the sound of her voice pierced his consciousness. Skewered his soul.

Taunted him.

Almost afraid to look, Cole forced himself to turn around again. When he did, he was just in time to see the owner turning a corner and walking down an aisle. He was returning to his counter at the front of the store.

He was also talking to someone. A visible someone. He was talking to a woman.

And that woman was Ronnie.

Ed Haney's round face appeared almost cherubic as he continued conferring. He seemed to be beaming as he bobbed his head with its ten wisps of hair up and down.

Ronnie McCloud returned the shop owner's smile. "I'll tell Dad you were asking after him."

Ed was doing more than just asking after the rancher's health and he wanted her to be clear about that. "Tell Amos that if there's anything I can do to help, anything at all, he shouldn't let that damn pride of his get in the way. All he has to do is say the word. I want to help. We all do," Ed emphasized, then said in a conspiratorial voice, "There was really no need for you to have to come back here, although I have to say it surely is a pleasure seeing you again, Veronica. You've become one beautiful young woman, and if I was twenty years younger—well, no need to elaborate." He chuckled. "You get my meaning."

Veronica McCloud laughed. "Yes, I do." He was teasing her. But he meant the other thing, the part about offering his help. Edwin Haney, a man she had grown up knowing, was a man of integrity—even if he did remind her a little of Humpty Dumpty. He meant what he said. About himself and about the others. The one thing she could never fault this town for was indifference.

The citizens of Redemption were anything *but* indifferent. So much so that at times they seemed to be into everybody else's business. A private person didn't stand a chance in Redemption. The people wore you down, had you spilling your innermost secrets before you could ever think to stop yourself.

She knew they meant it in the very best possible way, but when she'd been younger, she felt that it was an invasion, a violation of her rights. She'd wanted to be her own person, someone who made up her mind without the benefit of committee input or an ongoing, running commentary.

She wanted more than Redemption had to offer.

Even so, she had to admit, especially at a trying time like this, it was nice to know that there were people her father could count on. God knew he was going to need them once she left and went back home again, she thought. Her *new* home, she emphasized, since *this* had been home once.

"Hi, Sheriff, what can I do for you?" Ed's voice broke into her thoughts as he addressed someone just behind her.

Ronnie smiled. The sheriff. That would be Paul Royce. He had to be, what? Seventy now? Older?

Remembering the gregarious man's jovial countenance, Ronnie turned around, a greeting at the ready on her smiling lips.

The greeting froze.

She wasn't looking up at Sheriff Paul Royce and his shining coal-black eyes. She found herself looking directly into the new sheriff's blue ones. And suddenly wishing, with all her heart, that she was somewhere else. *Anywhere* else.

But she wasn't.

She was right here, looking into deep blue eyes she used to find hypnotic, her mind a complete, utter useless blank.

"Hello, Ronnie."

Chapter Two

As she was driving to Redemption, Ronnie had told herself that she would have more time before she had to face him. Instead, Cole had appeared out of the blue, and she was *so* not ready for their paths to cross.

Who was she kidding? There wasn't enough time in the world for her to prepare for this first meeting after so much time had passed.

And, damn it, Cole wasn't helping any. Not looking the way he did. This harsh land had a terrible habit of taking its toll on people, on its men as well as its women. So why wasn't he worn-out looking?

Why wasn't Cole at least growing the beginnings of a gut like so many other men who were barely thirty years old?

Heaven knew that her father looked like he was coming up on eighty instead of being in his early sixties.

And the last time she'd seen her older brother, Wayne, the land had already begun to leave its stamp on him, tanning his skin—especially his face—the way that tanners cured leather.

Not that there weren't any changes with Cole. But those changes only seemed to be for the better. Cole had lost that pretty boy look he'd once had—although his eyelashes appeared to be as long as ever. But now there was the look of a man about him, rather than a boy. A lean, muscular man whose facial features had somehow gone from sweet to chiseled.

In either case, his face still made her heart skip a beat before launching into double time.

No, that hadn't changed any no matter how much she'd tried to convince herself that it would.

Oh, but so many other things *had* changed. Her whole world had changed and it wasn't because she'd gone on to college, or gotten a business degree, or now worked in one of the larger, more prestigious advertising firms in Seattle. It also had nothing to do with her carefully decorated high-rise apartment in the shadow of the Space Needle and everything to do with the little boy who lived in it with her.

Christopher, the little boy she hadn't wanted to bring to Redemption with her, but knew she had to. Leaving her son behind with the woman who looked after him every day after kindergarten was not an option. Oh, Naomi had even volunteered to have him stay with her for the duration, saying she would be more than happy to do it. Heaven knew that the woman was very good with Christopher and Christopher liked Naomi. But there was no way she was going to leave her son behind, especially since she really wasn't sure exactly how long she would be gone.

The occasional overnight trips that her company sent her on were one thing. Christopher thought of it as "camping out" when he stayed at Naomi's house. But an open-ended trip like this one promised to be was something else entirely. So she had brought the five-year-old with her, hoping that his presence would somehow help to rally her father's alarmingly low spirits.

Meanwhile, Ronnie was struggling to do her best and ignore the stress that having Christopher here with her in Redemption inadvertently generated.

The one thing she clung to was that the boy looked like her.

And not like his father.

Forcing a smile to her lips, Ronnie waited half a beat while the rest of the surrounding area pulled itself out of the encroaching darkness and slowly came back into focus.

She couldn't wait until her knees came back from their semiliquid state. If she took too long to respond, Cole would be able to see the effect he still had on her. And that was the very last thing in the world she wanted.

It was bad enough that he probably suspected as much. She didn't want to confirm the impression.

So she forced a smile to her lips and returned his greeting. "Hello, Cole."

Her eyes slid down to take in the shiny piece of metal pinned to the khaki-colored, long-sleeved shirt that Cole wore. Had her father mentioned this development to her in one of his visits to Seattle? She couldn't remember but she really didn't think so. She would have remembered if he had.

In a rare display of sensitivity, her father went out of his way to avoid all references to Cole whenever they talked. He never even asked if Cole was the father of his grandson. Amos McCloud was a firm believer that everyone was entitled to their privacy. It was basically a policy of don't ask, don't tell. She didn't ask and her father didn't tell—even though there were times when she *ached* to know what Cole was doing these days.

She still didn't ask. Because if her father had said that Cole had gotten married, or worse, gotten married and started a family, the news would have sliced through her heart like the sharp blade of a cutlass. No, not knowing anything was the far better way for her to go.

But that had left her entirely unprepared for this first encounter.

Ronnie struggled against the feeling that her soul was suddenly completely exposed.

"So, you're the town sheriff now," she acknowledged pleasantly, silently congratulating herself on being able to mask all the feelings that rushed to the surface. "When did that happen?"

Cole's reply was sparsely worded. Just long enough to get the answer across. "Four years ago. The old sheriff got sick. Decided he needed to be someplace warmer. Nobody would take the job, so I did." He punctuated the final sentence with a careless half shrug.

She could feel every one of his movements echoing inside of her. *Get a grip, Ronnie, or you're going to blow this.*

"He's being modest," Ed told her, cutting in. "The whole town took a vote when Paul left and just about everyone cast their ballot for Cole here. Couldn't ask for a better sheriff, either," Ed said, beaming his approval in the town's choice. "Painfully honest, this boy. Won't even take a cup of coffee when it's offered to him at the diner without paying for it." Ed chuckled as he shook his head, his wide waist undulating ever so slightly as he did so. "Gives graft a bad name, Cole does." And then the Emporium owner sobered just a shade. "We're all lucky to have him here."

Ronnie looked at Cole for a long moment. She could see why Ed and the other citizens of Redemption would feel that way. Something about Cole exuded strength.

That had always been the case.

Having him in a position of authority allowed people to sleep better at night, she imagined. He made them feel safe. She had certainly felt that way when she was with him. Right up until the end. But then, the threat had come from her own feelings at that point, not from him.

"Where else would he be?" she asked quietly. She'd meant her question to have a touch of humor in it, but it had come out deadly serious. "He never wanted to be anyplace but here."

To the outside observer, the comment seemed to be addressed to the shop owner. But her eyes never left Cole's.

His eyes were still hypnotic, she thought. Even after all this time, they hadn't lost their ability to pull her in. To make her long for things that just didn't have a prayer of working out.

In the end, that last turbulent summer where they seemed to argue all the time, it came down to a matter of the irresistible force meeting the immovable object.

She wanted him to leave Redemption, to test his wings and fly away with her, and he wanted her to stay with him. Wanted her to start a life with him in earnest.

So, he had stayed and she had gone.

But not before taking a part of Cole James along with her.

And that, along with the radio silence that followed, was something she knew Cole would never forgive her for. There wasn't any point in thinking about it, or any of her reasons—good reasons—for having done what she had.

Forcing herself to look away, Ronnie turned her attention back to Ed. "So, you'll deliver the order to the ranch today?" she asked, referring to the items she had just paid for.

"I'll get on it right away," Ed promised. "You'll have it by this afternoon." He beamed at her, his brown eyes regarding her kindly. "Nice seeing you again, Veronica. You do your father proud."

Ronnie inclined her head, feeling a little embarrassed by the compliment. "Family does what it has to do," was all she said, deflecting any further words of praise.

Right now, all she wanted to do was get back into her car and drive away. Quickly. Before her knees melted away altogether.

Cole surprised her by asking, "Mind if I walk you out?"

The words sounded so formal, so stilted. So unlike anything that had ever been exchanged between them before, even going back to the time when they were kids. She couldn't remember a time when they hadn't known one another.

And now, now they were just strangers, feeling awkward in each other's presence.

Strangers with a past.

If she wanted to get through this with her sanity intact, she would have to treat Cole James the way she treated a client. Politely, competently, but always with preset boundaries.

Never once had she mixed business with her private life. Mainly because her private life was all about Christopher.

"Of course not," she finally replied. "I wouldn't want to say no to the sheriff."

This time the smile that rose to her lips came of its own accord. The idea of Cole being the sheriff of the town they had grown up in just didn't seem real to her. It was more like something they would pretend in one of their elaborate games.

Cole opened the door for her and held it. The bell just above the door rang softly, ushering them out.

She barely heard it, listening instead to the sound of her heart pounding.

Breathe, Ronnie, breathe. You knew he was going to be around.

The thing was, she'd expected him to be on his ranch. Which cut the chances of running into him down rather drastically.

"What happened to you being a rancher?" she asked him.

"Town needed a sheriff," Cole said. "And my mother got a really good man to help her run the ranch," he added. After a moment, he shrugged. "I still help out once in a while, during branding season, if Will's shorthanded."

Ronnie tried to put a face with the first name. "Will?"

"Will Jeffers," he clarified. "The man my mother hired to help run the ranch after…" Cole's voice trailed off for a moment, his discomfort with the topic more than mildly evident.

Ronnie pressed her lips together. She hadn't meant to inadvertently dredge up a painful subject for him. Cole's father had died suddenly last year, coming down with and succumbing so quickly to ALS no one even knew what was happening until it was almost all over. Her father had told her about that last night, after she'd put Christopher to bed.

"I was sorry to hear about your dad," Ronnie said haltingly.

She had to stifle the urge to put her hand on his shoulder, to communicate with Cole the way she used to, with a simple look, a touch. They'd had their own unique way of "speaking" without words once. Back when the world was new and their paths hadn't diverged so very sharply and far apart.

"Yeah, well, these things happen," Cole replied, his voice distant as he made an attempt to shrug off her sympathy.

He didn't want sympathy from Ronnie. He didn't want anything at all from her.

And then he made the mistake of looking directly at her again.

Cole could almost *feel* her getting under his skin, shaking his world down to its foundations. Just the way she always used to. Searching for some way to distract himself, he asked, "When did you get in?"

What went unsaid was that he was surprised that he hadn't heard about her arrival. Redemption was a small town and most information became general knowledge within the space of a few hours. Usually less.

"Late last night. My father didn't even let me know about the accident until just two days ago." When she'd received the call from her father, she'd known, the moment she heard his voice, that something was terribly, terribly wrong. She vaguely remembered sinking onto the sofa, both hands wrapped around the receiver to keep it from dropping to the floor as she listened to her father tell her about the accident.

He told her about Wayne being in a coma. The moment she'd hung up, she'd galvanized into action. Calling the company where she worked, she cited a family emergency and put in for a leave of absence. Then, packing up everything she thought she would need, she'd strapped Christopher into his car seat and then drove straight from Seattle to Redemption, covering close to six hundred miles in just a little over nine hours.

She'd been too wired to be exhausted until after she'd put Christopher to bed and talked at length to her father who was surprised that she'd driven all the way to Montana to see them.

Ronnie shook her head as remnants of disbelief still clung to her. "A whole two weeks and he didn't think to call me." She and her father were closer than this. Or at least she'd thought they were. Now it felt as if she didn't know anything.

"You know your dad," Cole told her. "He's a stubborn son of a gun. Doesn't want help from anyone." He looked at her pointedly. "Not even you."

For a split second, some of the hurt, the anger and especially the fear she'd been harboring since she'd received the phone call—harboring and trying to deal with—surfaced and flashed in her eyes.

"I'm not *anyone*," Ronnie retorted. "I'm his daughter," she emphasized, then struggled to get her temper, her feelings under control. "I'm his family," she said in a softer, but no less emphatic voice. "He's supposed to call me when something like this happens. I'm not supposed to learn that he and Wayne were nearly killed because I just happened to call to ask him what he wanted for his birthday."

He could see why she was upset, but he was having trouble dealing with his own issues, his own hurt feelings, so it was difficult for him to be sympathetic about what she'd gone through.

"Yeah, well, maybe Amos lost that page in the father's handbook for a while." And then he told her something he wasn't sure she was aware of. "Your father's been busy beating himself up because he was the one behind the wheel, driving the truck, and he feels responsible for what happened to Wayne."

Cole saw her clench her hand into a fist at her side. He could all but see the tension dancing through her. "Wayne's going to be all right," she declared stubbornly. "I called Wayne's attending surgeon as soon as I got off the phone with my father. Dr. Nichols said all my brother's reflexes seem to be in working order and that sometimes a coma is just the body's way of trying to focus on doing nothing but healing itself."

Cole saw no reason to contradict her or point out that a lot of people never woke up from a coma. She was dealing with enough as it was. Besides, what she thought or felt was no longer any concern of his outside the realm of her being a citizen of Redemption—or a former citizen of Redemption, he amended.

"Have you been to see your brother yet?" he asked as they walked past his truck.

"No. Not yet. But I'm going this afternoon," she added quickly. She'd wanted to go the second she'd arrived in Montana, but there was more than just herself to take into account. She had Christopher to take care of. No one had ever told her, all those years ago when she had so desperately longed to become an adult, that being a mother required so much patience. "I wanted to get a couple of things squared away for my dad first," she added.

Ronnie took a deep breath, debating whether or not to continue. The easy thing would be to terminate the conversation here. But in all good conscience she couldn't ignore the particulars that had been involved in the aftermath of the accident.

She approached the topic cautiously. "Dad said that you were the first one on the scene after the accident."

His expression gave nothing away, neither telling her to drop the subject nor to pursue it. "I was," he acknowledged.

He said it without any fanfare. How very typical of Cole just to leave the statement there, she couldn't help thinking. Another man would have thumped his chest. At the very least, he would have basked in the heroism of what he'd done, risking his very life in order to save someone else.

But this was Cole. Cole, who stoically did what he did and then just went on as if nothing out of the ordinary had taken place. Cole, who wanted no thanks, no elaborate show of gratitude, no real attention brought to him.

But she couldn't let it go. She had to thank him, to give him credit where credit was so richly deserved.

If not for Cole, the only family she'd have at this very moment would be a five-year-old.

"He also said that if it wasn't for you practically lifting the cab of the truck single-handedly and dragging Wayne out of the mangled vehicle, my brother—" her throat went dry as she pushed on "—would have been burned to death when that old truck of Dad's suddenly caught fire."

Again, Cole shrugged. And this time, he looked away. He found it easier to talk if he wasn't looking at her face. Wasn't fighting off feelings that were supposed to be dead by now.

"I didn't do anything that anyone else wouldn't do," he told her.

"Maybe so," Ronnie allowed, even though she sincerely doubted that many men would have rushed in to do what he'd done when faced with the definite possibility of their own death. Good people though they were in Redemption, not everyone was that brave or that selfless. "But I still want to thank you for saving my brother's life. And saving my dad."

Cole shoved his hands into his back pockets and stared at leaves chasing one another in a circle along the street.

"Just part of the job," he told her.

They'd stopped walking and were standing before what, in his estimation, was undoubtedly a very expensive and utterly impractical vehicle. It was a late-model black sedan, a Mercedes, far more suited to a metropolitan area than a town that still shared its streets with horses from the surrounding ranches on occasion.

She had changed, he thought. The old Ronnie would have been the first to point out how impractical and out of place a car like that was. Was she trying to impress him and show him how very successful she'd become in her new life?

He didn't measure success the same way she did. Something else they didn't have in common anymore, he thought.

"You renting that?" he asked her, curious. If so, she had to have gotten it somewhere other than in Redemption. The town's one rental agency was run by the town car mechanic and he sincerely doubted that Hank Wilson had a car like that in his possession.

"No, it's mine," she told him. She suddenly felt self-conscious about owning the car and told herself she was being needlessly uncomfortable. The car was reliable and she liked it. That it was also out of place here wasn't her concern. She wasn't about to feel guilty because she'd made something of herself. "I had a few things to bring with me," she went on to explain, "so I drove here."

She saw his mouth curve ever so slightly. There was a hint of a smile on his lips that she couldn't begin to fathom.

It was official, Ronnie decided. She was on the outside, looking in. And it was by her own design.

So why did it feel so lousy?

Chapter Three

"You drove here," Cole said, repeating what she had just stated.

"Yes."

Ronnie said she'd just learned about the accident two days ago. That meant she had to have left almost immediately after that. No matter what else she was, the woman still had the ability to amaze him.

"All, what? Six, seven hundred miles from Seattle to here?" he asked.

"Five hundred and ninety three," Ronnie corrected tersely.

"Oh, five hundred and ninety three," he echoed, as if enlightened. "Big difference. And I suppose that you drove straight through."

The tone of his voice hadn't changed, but she could swear he was mocking her. Ronnie raised her chin, brac-

ing herself. Waiting for a challenge or a careless statement tossed her way, which would, to her, amount to
fighting words. "Yes, I did."

Cole's eyes held hers, as if he was looking directly
into her head. "No breaks?"

Of course there had been breaks. She wasn't a robot.
Besides, she hadn't taken the trip alone. But then, he
didn't know that, she reminded herself.

"Well, I had to stop to eat a couple of times," she
told him, then decided she wanted to know what he
was up to. "Why?"

"No reason," he said a tad too innocently. "Just guess
some things never change." Ronnie had been stubborn
as a kid and she was still just as stubborn now. Maybe
even more so.

Don't go all nostalgic on her now, Cole warned himself. *So she drove like a maniac to get to her father. This
doesn't change the fact that she didn't even try to get in
contact with you to say she was sorry. Hell, she's not
even saying it now. Time to give up on this and move
on with your life.*

As if he could.

There was something about Cole's mouth when it
quirked that way…

Belatedly, Ronnie realized that her breath had backed
up in her throat. Clearing it, she began to move away.
"Um, I'd better be getting back. My dad's going to be
wondering what happened to me."

Aiming her keychain at her car, she pressed the
button. The vehicle emitted a high-pitched noise and
winked its lights flirtatiously as all four of its locks
stood up at attention.

Cole glanced at the dark car, unimpressed. "He'd

probably think that fancy car of yours broke down somewhere."

Ronnie narrowed her eyes. Well, he wasn't going to make her feel guilty because she'd bought a car that she had secretly fantasized about ever since she'd hit her early teens.

With a toss of her head, she informed him, "It's a very reliable car."

His mouth quirked again, this time a half smile gracing his lips. It was obvious he didn't believe her. "If you say so."

"I say so," she retorted as she slid in behind the car's steering wheel. Yanking the door to her, she shut it. Hard.

She knew she had to go before she found herself suddenly caught up in an argument with Cole. It was all too easy to do, and the last time that had happened, Christopher came along nine months later.

Christopher. The little boy was the absolute light of her life.

After pulling away from the curb, she glanced in the rearview mirror. Cole was still standing there, in the street, arms crossed before him, and watching her drive away.

God, the man was just too handsome for her own good.

And when he finds out you never told him about Christopher, he's going to be one hell of an angry man.

No way around that, Ronnie told herself, sighing as she drove back to her father's ranch.

Think about it later, she ordered herself. Right now, she needed to touch base with both her father and her son before she drove down to Helena to see Wayne in the hospital. She had too much to do to let herself get bogged down in her thoughts of what could have been and what, in actuality, really was.

One final glance in her rearview mirror, one last glimpse of Cole, and then she focused her eyes and her attention on the road before her.

But her mind insisted on remaining stuck in first gear. With Cole. And their son.

There were a lot of reasons why, six years ago, she hadn't told Cole she was pregnant with his baby. Right now, she was damn sure that he wouldn't accept any of them, but that didn't change anything. Certainly didn't change the fact that she knew she was right in doing what she had.

She knew Cole, knew how honorable he was, and how very, very stubborn he could be. If she'd told him about the baby, he would have insisted on marrying her and at the time, marriage hadn't been in her plans.

Neither was having a baby, but there was nothing, given her convictions, that she could do about that— other than what she'd done. She adjusted and found a way to deal with it, the same way she did with everything else. Consequently, she had her baby and also went on to get her education. All she had to do in order to accomplish that was give up sleeping. Permanently.

Cole, if he'd known, would have insisted that she stay in Redemption instead of going off to college. Would have pointed out how much better it was for the boy to grow up in a place like this town rather than in a large city.

She could see the scenario unfolding before her as if it was a movie. She would have given in and stayed in Redemption. And every day she would have felt a little more trapped than the day before. And a little more resentful that she'd been made to stay.

Leaving Redemption hadn't been an easy decision for her, even before she'd known she was pregnant. Part of her would have wanted to take the easy way out, would have wanted to stay here because, after all, this was where her family was.

And this was where the only man she'd ever loved or would love was.

But a part of her craved to explore the unknown, desperately wanted to spread her wings and fly, to see how far she could go if she pushed herself. She didn't want to live and die in a tiny corner of Montana because she had no choice in the matter. If she decided to live in Redemption, she wanted it to be by choice, after having experienced an entire spectrum of other things— or at least *something* else. She didn't want to become one of those people who died with a box full of regrets.

Didn't she have them anyway? Not having Cole in her life had made for a very large, very painful regret. But then, nobody had ever said that life was perfect and any choices she made of necessity came with consequences.

Besides, she was happy.

Or had thought she was, Ronnie amended. Until she saw Cole again.

"You still did the right thing," Ronnie said out loud to herself, her voice echoing about the inside of the sedan.

If she'd told Cole that she was pregnant, there was no question that he would have married her. The question that *would* have come up, however, and would continue to come up for the rest of her life was would he be marrying her because he loved her—really loved her—or because it was the right thing to do? The right thing to give his name to his child and make an honest woman out of her so that there would never be any gossip about her making the rounds in Redemption?

Ronnie knew she wouldn't have been able to live with that kind of a question weighing her down.

What she'd done was better.

Not that Cole would ever see it that way.

But that was his problem, not hers, she thought, pushing down on the accelerator.

Cole watched her car become smaller and smaller until it disappeared entirely, then he went back to his office on the next street.

He'd barely sat down at his desk after muttering a few words to Tim—the overly eager deputy he'd hired last year after Al St. John retired—before the door opened again and his mother walked in.

Midge James was a lively woman, short in stature but large of heart. Over the years she'd gone from being exceedingly thin to somewhat on the heavyset side. But each time she tried to make a go of a diet, her husband Pete, Cole's father, would tell her that she was perfect just the way she was and that he really appreciated having "a little something to hang on to."

Eventually she stopped trying to get down to the size where she could fit back into her wedding dress. She figured if she was lucky enough to have a man who loved her no matter what her size, she should just enjoy it. And him. So she did.

As she walked in now, Cole saw that his mother was carrying a basket before her. A very aromatic basket that announced it was filled with baked goods—muffins most likely—before she even set the basket down and drew back the cloth she'd placed over the top.

"Something wrong, Ma?" Cole asked as he started to rise to his feet.

"Sit, sit, sit," Midge instructed, waving her hand at her son in case he hadn't picked up on her words. "Nothing's wrong," she assured him. "Why?" she asked. "Can't a mother visit her favorite son without there being something wrong?"

Cole's lips curved in a tolerant smile. "I'm your only son, Ma."

"Makes the choice easier, I admit," Midge responded, punctuating her statement with her trademark cherubic smile. Crossing to his desk, she placed the basket smack in the middle. "Just thought you might like a snack." She pulled the cloth all the way back. Beneath it were at least two dozen miniature muffins. "They're tiny. Makes it kind of seem like you're eating less," she explained, one of the many diet-cheating tricks she'd picked up along the way.

Glancing at the deputy who was eyeing the basket contents longingly from where he sat, she assured him, "There's enough for you, too, Tim."

She didn't need to say any more. Tim was on his feet, his lanky legs bringing him to Cole's desk in less than four steps. And less than another second later, he was peeling paper away from his first of several muffins. His eyes glowed as he bit into his prize.

"Good," he managed to mumble, his mouth filled with rich cake and raisins.

Midge beamed. "Glad you approve, Tim." She pushed the basket closer to her son. "Have one, Cole," she coaxed him.

Cole eyed the contents and then selected a golden muffin. There were also chocolate ones and he suspected several butterscotch muffins in the batch, as well. His mother never did do things in half measures.

"Not that I don't appreciate you trying to fatten me up, Ma," he said, "but why are you really here?"

The expression on his mother's face was the last word in innocence as she lifted her small shoulders and let them fall again. "I just felt like baking today, and then, well, you know what happens if I leave this much food around. I get tempted and I absolutely refuse to go up another dress size."

He eyed the basket. "You could have given them to Will," he pointed out, mentioning the ranch foreman.

Midge dismissed his suggestion. *Been there, already done that.* "Don't worry, Will and the other hands already got their share."

Cole regarded the muffin in his hand for a long moment.

"It tastes better if you eat it without the paper around it," Midge prompted in a pseudo stage whisper.

For a moment, he wrestled with his thoughts. And then Cole raised his eyes to his mother's kindly, understanding face.

"You know, don't you?" he asked.

For a brief moment, Midge contemplated continuing to play innocent. But Cole was too smart to be fooled for long—she doubted if she'd succeeded in fooling him even now. With a shrug, she decided to let the pretense drop. After all, she'd come here to offer him a little comfort if comfort turned out to be necessary. And if Cole let her.

God knew Cole was as self-contained as his father

had been. Her son certainly didn't get his stoicism from her. She had always been more than willing to talk about what was bothering her.

"Yes," she admitted quietly.

"How long have you known?" he asked. Just because she lived on a ranch didn't mean that his mother was out of the loop. Hell, she *was* the loop.

"Not long. I stopped by Amos's place late yesterday afternoon to see how he was getting along." Amos had been there for her to offer his support when her husband had passed away; it was only right that she return the favor. "I saw her car pulling up as I was leaving."

Cole nodded slowly as he took her words in. His expression gave none of his thoughts away. "Did you talk to her?" he finally asked.

She'd debated stopping to exchange a few words, then quickly decided against it. Midge shook her head in response now.

"No, I thought it'd be better if she just saw her father first. After all, Ronnie had just come much too close to losing both him *and* her brother. She *would* have," Midge emphasized, "if it hadn't been for you."

Taking credit, even when he deserved it, wasn't what he was about. "Maybe," Cole allowed vaguely.

"No maybe about it," Tim piped up jovially from his corner of the office. He looked at the man he considered to be his role model. "Folks are saying you're a regular hero, Sheriff."

Cole had never cared for labels, and praise had always made him uncomfortable. Now was no different.

"And what's an irregular hero, Tim?" he asked.

Caught off guard, Tim opened his mouth to answer

and couldn't even begin to form one. He blinked, summarily confused. "What?"

"Don't mind him, Tim," Midge told the younger man. "He's just being surly." Looking at her son, the woman shook her head. "Don't know what that girl ever saw in you, Cole." Her exasperation with her son could only last a few moments, if that much. He was as close to perfect as a man could be. Just like his father before him, she thought with a pang. "Must have been your charm and your silver tongue."

"Must've been," Cole deadpanned, finally taking a bite out of the muffin he'd selected. As always, the muffin all but melted on his tongue. His mother had a knack for making baked goods that turned out to be practically lighter than air. But Cole wasn't given to gushing effusively. Instead, he gave her an approving nod. "Not bad."

"You always did lay on the flattery," Midge told him with a laugh. "I swear, Cole, you're getting to be more and more like your father every day."

And that only reminded her how much she still missed her late husband.

Squaring her small shoulders, Midge left the basket where she'd placed it and took a couple of steps toward the front door.

"Leaving?" Cole asked, finishing the muffin. Rolling the paper that was left between his thumb and the first two fingers of his hand, he tossed the small ball into the wastebasket.

"Well, if you don't feel like talking, I figured I'd better be getting back to the ranch." And then a thought occurred to her. "Come over for dinner tonight," she told her son. "I'll make your favorite," Midge added to seal the deal.

Cole sighed. He knew what she was up to. She was trying to draw him out of what she referred to as his "shell." She'd all but undertaken a crusade to accomplish that the summer Ronnie took off.

"I'm okay, Ma," he insisted.

The very innocent look was back. "Didn't say you weren't," Midge replied.

She looked at the deputy as she walked past his desk. Tim McGuire hardly looked old enough to shave despite the fact that he was edging his way toward his twenty-second birthday.

"Tell your mother and father I said hello," she told him.

"Sure will," the deputy cheerfully assured her. As he spoke, a golden crumb broke away from the muffin he was in the midst of consuming and fell onto his shirt. Looking down sheepishly, Tim laughed and brushed the crumb—and several others—off. "You sure do bake the best things, Mrs. James. I wish you'd teach my mother how you make these."

Unlike her son, Midge absorbed praise, fully enjoying each compliment.

"I'm sure she does fine without my input, Tim." Her bright blue eyes danced as she paused at the door, one hand on the doorknob. "But I can teach *you* anytime you'd like."

"Me?" the deputy asked incredulously.

He glanced up at the sheriff's mother, stunned. Tim was the stereotypical male who had yet to master the art of boiling water—not that he felt he had to. He still lived at home and thought that was what mothers were for—among other things.

"Nothing wrong with a man knowing his way around a stove, Tim," Midge told him.

Cole rolled his eyes. "That's all I need," he grumbled. "A deputy in an apron, his face smeared with blueberries as he's burning the muffins he's trying to make." With a shake of his head, Cole slanted a sidelong glance toward his mother. And then he raised another muffin as if to toast her with it. "Thanks for bringing these."

"Don't mention it. And don't forget about dinner tonight," she pressed, opening the door. "Six-thirty. Don't be late."

"Or what, you'll start without me?" Cole teased.

"Don't get fresh," his mother warned. But she was smiling at him as she said it. "Goodbye, Tim," she called out.

"Goodbye, Mrs. James," Tim responded with enthusiasm.

"Your mom really is a nice lady," the deputy said with feeling, his eyes on his task. He was preparing to eliminate his third muffin.

Cole marveled at the way Tim could put food away and still look like a walking stick. Had to be all that enthusiasm he kept displaying, Cole thought.

"Yeah, I know," he replied.

He took a bite out of his muffin, thinking. It occurred to him that this wasn't the first time his mother had mentioned stopping by Amos McCloud's place. Seemed to him that she was doing that quite a lot.

He made a mental note to ask her about that the next time he got a chance. He didn't recall his mother and Amos being all that close before.

But then, loss had a way of bringing people together, and his mother wasn't the type who liked being alone. He could recall her taking part in whatever needed doing around the ranch, never worrying about getting her hands dirty or complaining about having to work too hard.

In that respect she was a lot like Ronnie, he mused, breaking off another piece of the muffin.

Except that, growing up, Ronnie had been even more so. Part of the reason, he knew, was because she'd grown up without a mother. Margaret McCloud had died shortly after giving birth to Ronnie. Never a strong woman, according to his mother, one morning Margaret just didn't get out of bed. When Amos came in to see why she wasn't up yet, or at least tending to the baby, who was screaming her lungs out—Ronnie was loud even then—Amos found that his wife was dead.

The doctor who had to be called in from the neighboring town said she'd suffered from a ruptured aneurysm. Just like that, she was gone.

Life could change in an instant.

Cole got up. "I'll be back in a while," he told Tim as he walked out.

"What's 'a while'?" Tim called out after him.

"Longer than a minute," Cole called back. And then he was gone.

Chapter Four

Ordinarily, patrolling Redemption and the area just outside its perimeter helped Cole clear his mind whenever he found it too cluttered.

Ordinarily.

But not this time.

This time the tension he felt from the moment he merely *thought* he saw Ronnie had increased and refused to dissipate. This would take a lot of patience. He would just have to wait it out, work through it and give himself some time.

What bothered him the most was that he couldn't simply shake the effects of seeing Ronnie off or block them out. The feeling hung in there, wrapping its tendrils around him like a vine determined to grow a hundred times its size.

Ronnie had always been his Achilles' heel.

Everybody had a cross to bear and this was his.

As he drove slowly up one street and down another, patrolling the town, everything seemed to be in order—rather an interesting aspect seeing as how his whole world had been turned upside down. But nothing was going on in Redemption today that required his attention. No visible disputes to mediate the way there sometimes were when tempers flared up between friends and neighbors. Not even Mrs. Miller's damn cat to coax out of a tree.

As he passed the woman's Prized Antique Furniture Shop, Cole could see Lucien, Mrs. Miller's smoke-gray Persian cat, curled up on a rocking chair just to the left of the large bay window. Lucien was sound asleep.

He'd lost count how many times that cat had to be rescued out of a tree. And the one time he needed the feline to act accordingly, it was sleeping.

Figured.

Cole sighed impatiently. There was nothing to divert his mind from—

The string of muttered curses scissored through his thoughts. Had he not had his windows down, Cole was pretty sure he wouldn't have been able to hear them. But he definitely would have noticed the distressed looking store owner outside of the Livestock Feed Emporium, kicking one of the tires of the truck that had the store's logo painted on the side.

Cole stopped his vehicle in front of the all-too-recent scene of the assault on his soul.

It was obvious that Ed was at odds with the store's truck.

Cole stuck his head out of the driver's-side window.

"Something wrong, Mr. Haney?" he asked the man mildly.

Ed's head jerked up. For a second, he appeared surprised that he'd been overheard. And then he scowled. Deeply.

"Two somethings," he corrected, annoyed. "First the truck won't start, and then Billy calls in. He only works part-time for me," Ed explained. "Says he's got a cold and he's taking a sick day. You ask me, he just wants to spend time with that girl of his, Judith Something-or-other—"

"Julie," Cole corrected. "Julie Gannon."

It still astonished him, though he gave no indication, how much his memory seemed to have sharpened ever since he'd become sheriff. It was almost as if the responsibility had caused him to suddenly pay attention to the comings and goings of all the locals—something he'd never had time for or interest in before.

As for names, up until four years ago, they usually eluded him. They were incidental, beside the point. Only faces had left an impression. Now every face had a name and a history.

"Yeah, her," Ed agreed, waving his hand vaguely. "Point is that I've got this here order for Ronnie's dad and nobody to take it out to the ranch." He raised his eyes to Cole's at the end of the statement, as if he was waiting for something. When Cole maintained his silence, Ed prodded a little. "You wouldn't be going out that way anytime today now, would you, Sheriff?"

Cole had wondered how long it would take for the store owner to get around to this. "Wasn't planning on it," he replied.

"Oh."

Had he not heard it himself, Cole wouldn't have thought it was possible to pack that much emotion and distress into a single two-letter word.

With a sigh, he decided to put the man out of his misery.

"Guess I could look in on Amos," Cole allowed. "Seeing as how there doesn't seem to be anything going on in Redemption that needs my immediate attention."

Ed instantly brightened. "You'd be doing me a huge, huge favor, Sheriff." He beamed at the younger man. "I *told* everybody that you were the right man for the job."

Now the man was going a little overboard. "Being sheriff doesn't include making deliveries for the local stores," Cole pointed out.

"No," Ed readily agreed. "But looking out for the town citizens and going that extra mile—or ten—for them kinda does." He moved in closer, dropping his voice as if he was sharing a timeless secret with him. "People remember a man who looks out for them. You never know when that might come in handy."

Cole laughed shortly. "First snow hasn't come down yet and you're already busy shuffling, Mr. Haney," he marveled. "Okay, you want me to send Hank on over to take a look at your truck, see what's wrong?" Approaching the back of the defunct vehicle, Cole began transferring the load that was intended for Ronnie's ranch from Ed's truck to his.

Ed joined in, eager to get the job done before Cole had a chance to change his mind. "No, no, I'll give him a call myself. You're already doing way more than I've got a right to expect."

Humor quirked the corners of his mouth. "You remember that, Mr. Haney," Cole told him.

And that was how, fifteen minutes later, Cole found himself on the road to the McCloud ranch despite the fact that after this morning's run-in with Ronnie, he'd had absolutely no intention of going anywhere *near* the sprawling horse ranch.

Damn, who the hell was he kidding? Nobody *ever* made him do anything he didn't want to do at least somewhere deep down in his soul. Being a pushover was for men without spines or convictions, and he had always possessed both—in spades. If he had wanted to avoid seeing Ronnie again, he wouldn't have agreed to take Haney's order over to the ranch.

Truth was that he was in the market for an excuse so he could put himself in her path again. To give her yet another opportunity to explain *why* she'd taken off that way six years ago. Because up until that devastating day, he'd thought she loved him. Been *convinced* she loved him. He damn well *knew* that he loved her.

But she'd taken off without saying a word. Love meant talking things out, at least once in a while, didn't it?

Apparently not for Ronnie.

Glancing down at the speedometer, Cole saw he was pushing his truck hard without realizing it. The intensity of his thoughts telegraphed themselves through his body, making him press down on the accelerator. He was going ninety-one miles an hour. Cole eased back on the pedal.

There was nothing else out on the open road—mostly a given in these parts—but still, if someone did suddenly come around and clock him, how would it look to see the sheriff going more than twenty-five miles over what was posted as the speed limit?

Cole frowned and kept one eye on the speedometer. Being the sheriff of the town could be really confining.

Ronnie was definitely not looking forward to the long drive to Helena, not coming so soon on the heels of her marathon drive over from Seattle. She really wanted to curl up somewhere and take a very long nap. After seeing Cole, she felt drained.

But then, she also felt incredibly wired. Cole had always managed to do that to her, to get everything inside of her moving at top speed with just a look or a touch.

Especially a touch, she remembered, her mind drifting.

She wasn't here for a reunion, Ronnie reminded herself sternly. She was here to help her father run the ranch while he—and Wayne—recovered. And she was here for Wayne.

To see her older brother before—

No, there was not going to be a "before," she upbraided herself. Wayne would be fine. Just fine.

Positive thoughts, she would only have positive thoughts, Ronnie silently ordered herself. She wasn't one of those people who believed in transmitting energy or "vibes" or any of that kind of far-out nonsense, but on the other hand, keeping a good thought couldn't exactly hurt, right?

At this point, she wasn't about to rule out trying *anything* short of waving a chicken over Wayne's head and chanting some kind of strange, unfathomable incantation.

Wayne was going to be fine, he was going to be fine, she silently insisted again. No reason to think otherwise.

Glancing over her shoulder, Ronnie looked in the direction of the house. She'd left Christopher to entertain her father—the boy had actually succeeded in making her father smile a couple of times since they got there.

She'd also left Juanita, the housekeeper who had been with the family for as long as she could remember, watching over her father *and* her son. That freed her up to go see her brother.

She had to brace herself, she thought, for what she might see. She'd never known a day when Wayne, six foot four, tanned with wide shoulders, a small waist and powerful arms, wasn't the absolute picture of robust health and strength. Seeing him any other way would be a shock to her system.

But she couldn't let on that it was because, despite the fact that he was still in a coma, she felt that on some level, he would be able to see her reaction. She didn't want anything daunting his spirits and keep them from rallying.

Ronnie opened the door to her sedan and then stopped dead.

Cole's truck came up the road toward her. Trucks were as plentiful in and around Redemption as storm clouds in January, but she would have known that beaten up grill anywhere, even at this distance. She'd been with him when it had gotten that dent. Jared Calloway's prize bull had gotten loose and the animal had rammed them before Calloway and her father had manage to divert the bull and finally get him penned up.

What was Cole doing, coming here?

Ronnie felt her heart start accelerating.

This was absurd. She wasn't a teenager. She was a grown woman. A woman with a business degree and a career, not to mention a child.

His child.

That meant maturity, didn't it? And mature women didn't react like dewy-eyed adolescent girls eyeing their first major crush.

With supreme effort, she got herself to move. Closing her door again, Ronnie walked a few steps away from her vehicle to meet him.

As he pulled up closer, she called out, "Something wrong, Cole?"

You mean other than you being here, messing with my mind? He left his first response unsaid.

"Ed's truck broke down and his driver called in sick. He was worried that you needed the order you placed this morning right away."

"So you volunteered to bring it?" she asked incredulously.

Once upon a time, he would have volunteered without hesitation. But "once upon a time" had faded away a long time ago. And after their conversation this morning, she would have bet money that Cole would have gone out of his way to keep from having their paths cross again.

"More like Ed volunteered me," he told her honestly, getting out of the truck's cab. "Said it was part of why I got elected. Because everybody in town felt I always came through for them, 'going that extra mile.' After that, it was kind of hard saying no to the man. So I didn't."

She thought of several incidents out of their shared past. "Does he still have that hangdog expression when he's playing on your sympathy?"

Cole laughed shortly, nodding. "Hell, it's even worse."

Amused, Ronnie laughed. "That man would have gone far if he had ever decided to go into politics." The laughter faded and she realized that she was standing much too close to Cole. She took a couple steps back. "I'll get Rowdy to unload your truck," she said, referring to her father's foreman. "Just back the truck up to the barn," she requested.

Cole gave her a slight two fingered salute. "Yes, ma'am."

She flushed. She knew she could get overbearing without being aware of it. Either way, Cole didn't deserve to be ordered around. He was doing her a favor. And he was the last man she'd ever thought would actually be willing to do her one.

"Sorry," she apologized. "Did that sound as if I was ordering you around?"

"Little bit, yeah," he allowed.

He wasn't scowling or smiling. That left her with no clue how he actually felt. "Didn't mean to," she told him.

Leaving the sedan where it was, Ronnie hurried off toward the corral, where she knew that Rowdy was working with some of the newest crop of quarter horses.

Standing beside his truck, Cole watched her go, appreciating the rhythmic sway of her hips as she quickly made her way over to the corral.

There was no use denying it, he thought, resigned. Ronnie still had an effect on him. And most likely always would.

"You just caught me in time," Ronnie told him as Rowdy and another hand unloaded the bags of feed she'd purchased this morning from the back of Cole's truck. "I was just about to leave for the hospital."

He recalled she'd said something about not having been to see her brother yet. "First time?" he asked just to be sure.

"To see Wayne? Yes." She thought she'd already told him that earlier, but to be honest, that entire encounter was blurry to her. She'd been acutely aware of her racing pulse and her desire to be anywhere else.

He nodded. Another moment passed before he asked, "Anybody going with you?"

Given that he knew how independent she was, had often commented on it when they were growing up, sometimes in a flattering sense, sometimes with exasperated adjectives surrounding the word, it struck her as a rather odd question for him to ask.

"Dad's kind of tired. I want him to rest and get his strength back. Why do you want to know?" she asked him.

"Just thought you might need some emotional support, that's all, what with seeing Wayne for the first time and all."

Ronnie deliberately ignored the implication behind his statement. He was telling her that Wayne was so bad that it would be a complete shock to her system to see him that way. Instead, she focused on something else. On the way he'd just phrased his answer. "I guess you have changed a little after all."

"What makes you say that?"

She laughed softly. "The Cole James I knew didn't even know there was such a thing as emotional support, much less was concerned about it being given."

"I knew," he protested. "Just didn't think it was necessary to slap a label on everything back then, that's all."

"We're done, Miss Ronnie," Rowdy announced, his voice rising from the rear of the truck. Cole turned in their direction as the foreman added, "You can have your truck back now, Sheriff."

Out of the corner of his eye, Cole saw Ronnie covering her mouth as if to stifle a laugh. He didn't see anything particularly funny about what Rowdy had just said.

"What?" he asked her.

"Nothing." She dropped her hands, but there was a trace of amusement still in her eyes. "It's just hard getting used to everyone calling you 'Sheriff,' that's all." The title belonged to someone in authority—or to a little kid pretending to be all grown up. "Reminds me of the game we used to play as kids."

He nodded. "Cowboys and Indians. And you were always the Indian."

The proud toss of her head was automatic. Cole watched the sun filter through her hair, highlighting the golden strands. "That's because I was always better at riding bareback than you were."

"Matter of opinion." Besides, as he recalled, that wasn't the reason for the division of roles. "Way I remember it, I always liked the order behind pretending to be a sheriff and you were always wild."

The next words came out of his mouth before he had a chance to talk himself out of them. He seemed to forget that more time with Ronnie was a very bad idea.

"I can go with you to the hospital if you want. To see Wayne," he added needlessly when Ronnie made no response.

She made no response because she was dumb-founded. But when that passed and she regained the use of her mind and her vocal chords, she was about to tell him "Thank you but no thank you"—until she saw the back door to the main house opening.

Christopher was coming out with her father.

Mercifully, Cole's back was to the house and he didn't see her father *or* Christopher. But he would. Any second now, she knew her exuberant son would call out to her and Cole would turn around to receive what could amount to the shock of his life if he put two and two together.

She definitely wasn't up to dealing with that situation, with introductions and partial explanations even if for some reason she lucked out and Cole didn't make the connection. It was all she could do to pull herself together in order to see Wayne for the first time, see how badly her beloved brother had been hurt.

It was an act of sheer self-preservation that caused her to grab Cole's hand and pull him over toward his truck, making sure that his back remained toward the house.

"Well, what are you waiting for?" Ronnie asked.

Taking a calculated risk, she released his hand and hurried around the hood of the truck rather than the back of it so that Cole would remain facing the way he was. She lucked out and he did.

Yanking the passenger-side door open, she deposited herself in the front passenger seat. He was still stand-ing where she'd left him, staring at her.

"Let's go," she urged impatiently.

He hid his surprise well, appearing to take her sud-den change in stride.

That hadn't changed any, either, Cole thought. Ronnie still acted impulsively, blowing hot and, just when he'd gotten used to it, cold. Back then, it had kept him on his toes, second-guessing her—and getting it right only half the time.

"Sure thing," he murmured. And with that, he got into the truck's cab.

Putting his key into the ignition, Cole started up his truck. It rumbled to life.

Over the last ten years, the vehicle had acquired its own set of sounds and noises, loud enough to mask any outside sounds that were not at a louder pitch.

Which was why he pulled away from the barn without hearing the little boy call out to them. And he missed seeing that same little boy break into a run, heading toward the barn.

But, glancing into the rearview mirror, Ronnie did and felt a pang.

Sorry, baby. Mama'll make it up to you. But right now, I can't let you meet your dad. I'm not ready for that and neither are you.

And probably, she added silently, neither was Cole.

Chapter Five

Despite the various noises of the truck, the silence seemed to grow larger, more pronounced and uncomfortable with every mile. Cole thought of simply turning on the radio. They used to like the same kind of music, although that had probably changed, too.

But he hadn't offered to come with her to the hospital in Helena so that the two of them could ride there in prickly, awkward silence like this. Granted, no one had ever accused him of being gregarious, but one of the best things he recalled about their relationship was that they could always talk to each other. About anything. She'd been his best friend and he hers.

He missed that. There had been no one to fill the void these last six years. Not for either position she'd left vacant.

Cole drew in a subtle deep breath and then plunged

in. "So, what have you been doing with yourself these last six years?"

The question—and his voice slicing into the silence—really caught her off guard. It took Ronnie a second to gather her wits about her. Where did she start? What was there to say? "I went to college, got my MBA and went to work for Peerless Advertising in Seattle."

He'd never heard of the company. Probably some company that advertised things people could do without.

"And that's it?" he asked. He'd been expecting something more than just a single sentence in response from her. At least a short paragraph. After all, it *had* been six years.

Oh, yes, and I had your son. What do you say to that, Cole James? "That's it," Ronnie replied out loud with a forced smile gracing her lips as she glanced toward him.

"Doesn't seem like enough to fill up six years," he commented. Was there someone in her life? Was she serious about him? Engaged? Married? But her hand was bare, he reminded himself. So she wasn't committed to someone, but that didn't mean she hadn't been, or didn't intend to be, maybe even any day now.

The thought chewed a hole in his insides.

"You'd be surprised," she commented. And it was true. Every moment of her day was spoken for in one way or another. And she felt as if she never managed to get everything done. "I barely have enough time to sleep." Afraid of where his question might lead, Ronnie deliberately shifted the conversation away from herself. "What about you? What have you been doing?"

He shrugged. He never liked talking about his life, never cared for diverting attention to himself. "Worked on my folks' ranch and then got voted in sheriff when the old sheriff had to leave."

And I missed you like crazy every day the first couple of years or so.

Cole kept his eyes on the road, afraid that they might give him away if she looked at them. "Guess we're all caught up, then."

"Guess so." Silence rose up and began to penetrate the cab of the truck again, nudging them each into their respective corners.

This is ridiculous, Ronnie thought. This was still Cole, the guy who had been her best friend since they were toddlers together. She should be able to talk to him without having to chew every word twelve times before spitting it out.

And now that she thought about it, there *was* something he could tell her.

"Tell me everything," she said, suddenly turning toward him. There was an urgency in her voice that hadn't been there a moment ago.

Well, this had certainly come out of the blue, he thought. "How's that again?"

"Tell me everything," Ronnie repeated. "About the accident," she added when he looked at her again, puzzled. "You were the one who got there first, so tell me. Tell me everything that happened. I don't want you to leave anything out."

He'd seen what her brother looked like when he pulled Wayne out of the wreckage. She suspected that her brother's condition was a great deal worse than she was allowing herself to believe. Positive thoughts notwithstanding, she needed to know what to expect when she walked into the hospital's intensive care unit.

"You didn't ask your dad?" Cole asked, surprised. To him that would seem to be the most logical way to start.

She had, but the answer she'd received from Amos McCloud was more disheartening than informative. "My dad can't seem to remember anything from the time the truck collided with the cross-country van until he woke up lying in the hospital emergency room."

Cole could see that her father's temporary amnesia just added to Ronnie's worries. "That's not uncommon from what I hear. Mind can just shut down when it doesn't want to process something."

Unfortunately, her father had processed just enough to blame himself. But the older man had no reason to be so hard on himself, Cole thought.

"He might've been the one behind the wheel, but it wasn't his fault from the information I've put together. That trucker was operating on four hours' sleep three days running. He fell asleep behind the wheel without even realizing it. It was just your dad's bad luck to be out there when it happened. Any other time, the only one that trucker would have wound up hurting— maybe—was himself."

Which brought her to another point. According to her father's reluctant admission, the ranch—whose main focus was to raise and train quarter horses—was already having financial difficulties. If for some reason the trucker took it into his head to sue her father, that was a whole shelf-load of problems she just wasn't up to sorting through right now.

But she might as well know the worst of it, she decided stoically. "How badly was the trucker hurt?"

"Not as bad as your dad," Cole could readily attest. "Some cuts and scratches on his arms and face, and he bumped his head against the dashboard. He was okay, but the truck was a loss. As was your dad's," he said in case she hadn't realized that yet.

"And Dad and Wayne were both pinned inside the truck?" She already knew the answer to that, but it seemed incredible to her that they had been and were still alive now, considering what happened next.

As if reciting a story to a child for the umpteenth time because hearing it repeated gave them comfort, Cole nodded and said, "Your dad's truck rolled two, three times and landed upside down on the road. Both your dad and Wayne were strapped in." He'd just been coming down the ridge when he saw the whole thing from his vantage point. He drove down as fast as he could. "I had to cut their seat belts to get them free because the locks wouldn't work. I got your father out first—he was easier to get loose even though he fought me."

Her eyes widened. That didn't make any sense. "He fought you?"

To him it made perfect sense. A parent's desire to save their child at all costs took precedence over everything else, even their own safety. That didn't change just because the "child" was six foot four. "He wanted me to get Wayne out first, but Wayne was really pinned down. The door on his side had caved completely in, pressing his torso up against the dashboard." Cole shook his head, reliving the incident. "To tell the truth, I really don't know how I got him out. But I did and a lucky thing, too, because the whole damn truck blew up not thirty seconds after I got Wayne clear of it."

She was hanging on Cole's every word. "Was he conscious?"

"No. And his pulse kept cutting in and out, but the emergency medevac attendant I called in managed to stabilize it and took him to the trauma center at the hospital in Helena. The chopper took your dad there, too, just to check him out to make sure there wasn't any internal bleeding even though he kept protesting that he was okay."

That sounded just like her father. Ronnie's mouth curved in a fond smile. "He's a stubborn old man."

He spared her a glance. "Runs in the family." His meaning was clear.

She had that coming, Ronnie thought, so she didn't contest his comment. Instead, she expressed her gratitude. "Thanks for saving them."

Cole heard the emotion brimming in her voice like unshed tears and it stirred up old memories, memories he'd forced himself to lock away. Memories that he'd hoped would eventually fade away, given enough time.

He should have known better.

Deflecting her thanks with a careless shrug of his shoulders, he said, "I didn't do anything someone else wouldn't have done in my place."

Not everyone, she'd come to learn, could rise to an occasion. The men she'd encountered these last few years weren't good enough to walk in Cole's shadow. But that was something she had to learn on her own.

Education had its price. She had paid for hers by losing Cole. Because even if he forgave her for leaving like that, he'd never forgive her for shutting him out of his son's life. Even though she still believed that all the reasons she'd had for *not* telling him were right, it didn't really help the situation.

"I don't know about that," she replied honestly. She

gave credit where it was due. "There was always something heroic about you."

Damn it, he wasn't supposed to want to pull over to the side of the road so that he could take her in his arms and kiss her. He was supposed to be angry at her, so angry that he was immune to her. Immune to the sound of her, the scent of her. He was supposed to want to wash his hands of her, not take those hands and hold them.

What the hell was wrong with him? Where was his pride?

Cole shrugged in response to her comment and muttered, "If you say so." The next moment, he reached over and turned on the radio.

He decided it was better that way.

Ronnie had thought herself fully prepared. Hadn't she just spent the last fifty miles bracing herself? The last two days, actually. Ever since her father had called, she'd been preparing herself for what she'd see when she walked into Wayne's intensive care cubicle.

The moment she saw Wayne, her heart constricted in her chest.

She wasn't ready at all.

Tears were in her eyes before she had taken more than two steps into the tiny space that was crammed with machines and monitors buffering both sides of Wayne's bed.

Ronnie could feel her throat tightening even as it, too, filled with tears.

She wasn't even aware that Cole came into the cubicle behind her, or that he remained standing there. She wasn't aware of anything except for the man in the hospital bed, the man whose face was battered and swollen almost beyond recognition. The man with a highway of IVs crisscrossing along both arms.

Her breath hitched in her throat. She couldn't even hug Wayne because she was afraid she'd dislodge something important. Something that was undoubtedly keeping him alive.

Ronnie tried to push down the lump in her throat.

Her mind was having trouble accepting that this was Wayne. Wayne, who'd always been a huge tower of strength in her life. Wayne, who had seemed so invincible to her when she'd been growing up. Oh, they fought a lot and she accused him of being overbearing and dictatorial, but in her heart she always knew that if she needed him, he'd be there, watching over her because he was her big brother.

For a second, she thought her knees would crumble. But even as she thought that, she couldn't let it happen, couldn't allow herself to break down. Wayne needed her to be the strong one this time. He needed her to be his strength until he could access his own.

So, summoning all the fortitude she had within her, Ronnie moved slowly toward her brother's bed. Taking one of his hands in hers, she wrapped her fingers around it. His hand felt cold.

It chilled her heart.

Digging deep for some inner strength, she managed to keep her voice sounding incredibly chipper.

"Boy, you don't do things in half measures, do you, Wayne?" she asked. But even as she spoke, she found she needed to lower her voice because she was afraid that it would crack on her. "When you get into an accident, you *really* get into an accident. Well, okay, I get it. Fun's over. You've had your fun. But I'm here now and I'm going to see to it that you stop this little charade and get back on your feet. Dad can't run the ranch alone, you know. Rowdy's a good guy and all, but we both know that he's got the IQ of a boot—and not a very smart boot at that."

She paused a second, afraid that she would lose it. But she didn't and in another moment, she was able to continue.

"So you've got to get back on your feet and that's all there is to it. I can stick around for a little while, and I'll do a better job than you can, but I've got a job in Seattle I've got to get back to so I can't stay here indefinitely."

She was babbling now and she knew it, but she couldn't stop. She kept hoping that her brother would say something to her, tell her to "stop all that racket" the way he always used to when he insisted that she was talking too much.

"I'm putting you on notice, Wayne. You've got two weeks. Three tops. And then you've got to stop fooling around like this and get back to work. You hear me? Squeeze my hand to let me know you're listening. C'mon, Wayne, squeeze my hand."

His fingers remained still. She pressed her lips together to keep from crying.

"Okay," she allowed, her voice quivering. "You don't want to squeeze my hand now. Squeeze it later," she said. "But you *are* going to squeeze it. And you *are* going to get up and walk out of here, you understand me?" she demanded, her voice finally cracking.

Ever so slowly, Ronnie became aware of someone standing beside her, offering her something. Forcing herself to turn her head, she saw Cole holding out a handkerchief.

"I don't need that," she told him, waving it away.

Instead of arguing with her, Cole gently took her chin in one hand and slowly wiped away the wet tracks that ran down both her cheeks with the other. Only then did he say, "I think you do." Pocketing the handkerchief when he was finished, he asked, "Want me to take you home now?"

Ronnie didn't want to go home, she wanted to stay. To stay here and somehow *will* her brother to come out of his coma and open his eyes.

But she knew there was no way she could do that. Getting her brother to come around was way beyond her sphere of control, no matter how stubborn she was. So she nodded and whispered, "Yes, please."

Cole's heart twisted to see her like this. To witness her pain and know that he could do nothing to make it better for her. That was entirely out of his hands. He could pull bodies out of a wreckage, but he couldn't heal them. That kind of thing belonged to another realm entirely.

As he slipped his arm around her shoulders ever so lightly, Cole doubted Ronnie was even aware of it. She seemed to be lost inside of her own world. Maybe it was better that way. She was insulating herself. God knew that he knew a few things about that.

As gently as possible, Cole guided her out of the intensive care unit and into the antiseptic-smelling hallway. What renovations had been undertaken at the hospital over the years had involved their equipment, attempting to keep them up-to-date if not innovative. Since there was only so much money to be had, aesthetics were overlooked. Hence, the institution, while exceedingly reputable, had the look and smell of an old-fashioned hospital circa 1970.

Ronnie hardly remembered walking back to the parking lot or getting into Cole's truck. In essence, she had slipped into her own coma-like state, afraid to think, afraid to feel. And Cole, whether out of respect, intuition or because he hadn't known what to say, hadn't attempted to try to talk to her, or make her come around.

When she finally pulled herself together and looked around, Ronnie realized that they were almost back at her father's ranch.

"He's going to be all right," she said suddenly and fiercely. Whether to convince herself or make a believer out of Cole even she didn't know. All she knew was that she needed to hear the words. Needed him to hear them, too.

"No reason not to believe that," he replied as if this was part of an ongoing conversation between them, rather than a statement she'd made after forty-seven miles of silence.

His response surprised her. That was definitely not something she had expected to hear coming out of Cole's mouth.

"That's one of the most positive things I've ever heard you say," she marveled.

But even so, Ronnie knew better than to press her luck and ask Cole if he really believed what he'd just said, or whether he just saying it for her benefit. Instead, she clung to his words as if they were a guarantee, or better yet, a magic talisman. Because the strength of those words was going to have to see her through. She knew that there was no way she could look to her father for strength and support. This time around, he was the one who needed her to be strong for him.

"Thanks for going with me to the hospital," she said to Cole. "I know you've got better things to do than to play nursemaid."

"Not at the moment," he told her, a sliver of humor quirking his mouth. "And you're welcome," he added.

His voice gave no indication that he ached for her. Or that he foresaw more pain for her in the near future. From what the doctor had told him, Wayne's chances were definitely not the best. The man would need a small miracle to pull through and be his old self—or close to it.

"You can stop here," Ronnie told him abruptly.

Cole looked at her quizzically. They had a bit of a way to go in his opinion. "You don't want me to drop you off at the door?"

"No, this is fine. You've already gone more than out of your way," she told him.

Doing as she instructed, Cole cut the engine and then looked at her for a long moment. Was she trying to keep him from coming in with her? Or was he reading too much into this? Was it just a matter of what she'd said, that she felt she'd taken up too much of his time already? He wanted her to know that he was available to her if she needed him.

Ronnie got out of the truck. "Well, bye. Thanks," she threw in again.

This felt suspiciously like he was being bum-rushed. Rather than start up the truck again, Cole got out of the cab.

"What are you doing?" she asked uneasily.

Since it was pretty clear what he was doing, he didn't

bother answering her question. Instead, he crossed to her. "Look, Ronnie, if you need someone to talk to, I just want you to know that I'm around."

"I know that, Cole." Damn it, he was being so nice, it made her feel even worse. "And I appreciate it. But right now, I just want to go inside and lie down."

This had all been too much for her. He could appreciate that. "Sure, I understand. Offer still stands, though."

Just as he turned to go, the front door to the ranch opened. Instead of her father or the housekeeper walking out, Cole saw a towheaded little boy come flying down the porch steps.

Before he could even wonder out loud who the boy belonged to, he heard the child all but sing out, "Mama, Mama!" uttering the mantra almost at the top of his lungs—which demonstrated considerable strength, given his young age.

Breaking into a run, the little boy made the distance between himself and his target disappear in a blink of an eye.

As Cole looked on, stunned, the boy flung himself at Ronnie, who had knelt down, her arms opened to receive the little blond missile.

Chapter Six

Even as she embraced Christopher, returning the little boy's fierce, enthusiastic hug—something she never took for granted—Ronnie prepared herself for what was to come.

The seconds ticked by and her feeling of foreboding grew. It was like waiting for a bomb to go off.

Cole wasn't saying *anything*.

For a long moment—most likely because he was completely stunned—there was nothing but silence from the man standing next to her.

And then she heard Cole's low, rumbling voice. He said rather than asked, "You have a son."

Releasing Christopher, Ronnie slowly rose to her feet and drew in a long breath as subtly as she could manage. *Steady as she goes, Ronnie,* she coached herself.

Making an effort to avoid looking at Cole, she affirmed, "I have a son."

Cole frowned, glancing toward the house. Bracing himself even as he asked, "Where's his father?"

Okay, here's the big question. You can get through this. Just don't blow it.

Ronnie turned toward him almost in slow motion, praying she wasn't revealing anything in her eyes or that he couldn't see through the practiced, patient expression on her face.

"His father and I aren't together anymore," she told him stoically.

Taking the snippet of information in, Cole nodded as if he'd expected nothing less. "Ran out on another one, did you?"

She had to keep from exploding. "What's that supposed to mean?" she demanded angrily.

He'd already turned away from her and started walking back toward his truck. "Way I remember it, you were always really smart, Ronnie. I think you can figure that one out on your own."

Yes, she could, and even thinking about it ripped open old wounds that hadn't healed so much as had been shoved away and ignored.

"I didn't run out on you," she cried, summoning indignation even though she knew she had done *exactly* that.

Cole stopped walking and glanced at her over his shoulder. "No? Then what would you have called it? Walking really fast?" he suggested sarcastically.

Putting her hands on Christopher's shoulders protectively, she told Cole, "Making the right decision for me."

Cole took a breath, trying very hard not to let his imagination go. Trying not to think of her in someone else's arms. Making love with someone else.

Jealousy threatened to consume him.

He looked at her for a long moment, then his eyes skimmed over the boy's bright, wide-open face. The kid, he thought, had an infectious smile. He looked happy. And well.

"I guess maybe you did," Cole finally said. He opened the truck door on his side. "Tell your dad I said hey."

Breaking loose, Christopher ran up to him just as he was about to get into his truck. The boy tugged urgently on his sleeve.

Nothing shy about this one, Cole thought, then couldn't help adding, *just like his mother.*

When he paused to look down quizzically at the small face, the little boy asked, "Are you a sheriff?"

"Yes, I'm a sheriff." Out of the corner of his eye, he saw Ronnie shift nervously. Did she think he was going to interrogate the kid?

The little boy's brilliant green eyes—Ronnie's eyes, Cole thought—grew until they were almost the size of huge emerald-green saucers.

"For real?" he asked the question breathlessly.

Despite himself, despite the fact that this was a child that Ronnie had had with someone else—something that ripped the hell out of his soul—Cole found he had to struggle not to laugh at the boy's earnest wonder.

"For real," he assured the little boy as solemnly as he could.

The questioning session wasn't over. Somehow, he hadn't thought he'd get away so easily, Cole mused. "Like on TV?" Ronnie's son asked.

Cole leaned down and pretended to whisper in his ear, "Better."

The shining green eyes were now dancing. "Wow," he cried, clearly impressed. Turning on his heel, Ronnie's son looked at his mother. "I'm gonna be a sheriff, too, when I grow up," he announced, making up his mind then and there.

Tension telegraphed itself throughout Ronnie's body. Watching Cole interact with Christopher this way was causing all sorts of bittersweet feelings.

Her eyes were all but riveted to his face. To her relief, there was no discernable spark of enlightenment.

He doesn't realize he's talking to his son, she thought, willing herself to relax.

"You've still got a couple of days left before you grow up," Ronnie told her son so solemnly for a second Cole thought she was serious. "We'll talk about it then, Christopher."

"'Kay." Christopher nodded solemnly. He still wasn't at the stage where he contested everything his mother told him. Ronnie counted herself lucky.

"That his name?" Cole asked. "Christopher?"

She nodded. "Yes."

"Christopher what?" he wanted to know.

"McCloud," the boy piped up, then declared proudly, "My name's Christopher McCloud."

McCloud. That was Ronnie's last name. Did that mean she'd never married the boy's father? Or was that just her perverse independent streak coming to the surface? For now, he kept the question to himself.

"Nice to meet you, Christopher McCloud," he said, shaking the boy's hand.

The moment he released her son's hand, she took it in hers, as if reestablishing her claim to the boy. And then she looked over her son's head at Cole. "Thanks for the ride and the company."

"Don't mention it," he murmured.

For the moment, it was a toss-up whether he was more stunned or angry that the woman he'd been pining for all these years had hooked up with someone almost the moment she'd been out of his line of vision. Right now, the thought left him numb.

"Let's go inside and see your grandpa," Ronnie coaxed her son. Turning, she started walking toward the house—and shelter.

Rather than follow along, Christopher glanced over his shoulder at the tall man he had just met. "Wanna come to dinner, Sheriff?" he called out hopefully. "Juanita's got chops."

Amused, Cole crossed back to the boy and dropped down to his level. Christopher couldn't be talking about the woman's courage. He doubted if someone as young as the kid looked knew what that expression meant—even if he did sound a little precocious.

"Excuse me?"

"Grandpa's house helper said she was making chops," Christopher explained agreeably, then confided, "She let me help get them ready."

Cole looked up at Ronnie for an explanation. "He must mean pork chops," she said. "I saw Juanita defrosting them this morning."

On the one hand, she felt on edge having Cole here for two reasons—because she was afraid he might guess he was Christopher's father and because just being around him made her mind wander to places it had no business revisiting. On the other hand, though, he *had* been helpful taking her to the hospital to see Wayne and if she encouraged him to leave, he might get suspicious about her reasons.

Stuck, she decided that maybe it was safer to invite him to stay—and to hope that he would turn her down. That way, her conscience was clear and she was still safe in the bargain.

"You're welcome to stay if you'd like," she told him pleasantly.

Cole looked at his watch. It was a little after six. If he hadn't heard from his deputy by now, that meant there was nothing going on in Redemption that required his attention. In other words, it was business as usual at the police station. Most likely, Tim had already left for the day.

They both had cell phones whose numbers were a matter of public record. And whoever was the last to leave the office programmed the official police landline to forward any calls to their cells so that if one of the town's citizens felt that they had an emergency on their hands, he or she could immediately get a hold of at least one of them.

Cole turned Ronnie's invitation over in his head and then nodded. He knew the invitation was forced, but he found himself wanting to stick around a little longer. He refrained from enumerating the reasons why. He made a mental note to call his mother, let her know that something had come up and that he was taking a rain check on that dinner.

"Well, I haven't had pork chops in a while." He looked down at Christopher. The kid really did have just about the sunniest smile he'd ever seen, Cole thought. Before he knew it, he had ruffled the boy's hair. "Okay, you talked me into it."

"Yay!" Christopher cried, happy and excited at the same time. Breaking away from his mother, he ran into the house. "Grandpa, Grandpa," he called out, all but bursting in through the door, "we're gonna have a real live sheriff eatin' chops with us!"

Cole looked from the house to Ronnie. "He always get that excited?" he asked.

"He's a happy kid. Takes almost nothing to get him going," she said, affection weaving through every word. Aware that it was just the two of them again, she roused herself. "I'd better go in and tell Juanita to put another plate on the table."

Maybe this wasn't such a good idea, he thought, hearing a note of hesitation in her voice. "You don't mind, do you?"

Was it his imagination, or did she just square her shoulders as if she was about to go into some kind of a battle?

"If I minded, I wouldn't have invited you." She paused uncertainly. "Why? Are you having second thoughts about staying?"

Cole looked at her for a long moment. The trouble with life was that people overanalyzed everything, insisting on holding each speck up to the light and trying to examine it from all sides. Hell, he was guilty of that himself, but only when he thought about Ronnie and what had gone so damn wrong with something that had seemed so very right at the outset.

"Nope," he answered. "Not me."

Which was a lie. Having dinner with her and the boy—and most likely Amos—would just drive home what he didn't have. What he could have had if she'd stayed in Redemption with him instead of running off to that college. And then staying away after she'd graduated. If she'd stayed here, they would have been married by now.

And maybe even had a son like the one she had.

The thought twisted in his gut like a double-edged serrated knife.

Ronnie realized that her lips were almost stuck together, they were that dry.

This was absurd. She had to get a grip on herself. She'd known if she came back, there was a very good chance that she'd be running into Cole. And once she had, she also knew that she had to act relatively friendly—not spooked, not nervous, but friendly. Otherwise, he'd see right through her in a minute and come to the one conclusion she wanted to avoid.

"All right then, you're having dinner here." She started walking toward the house again. He trailed after her. "Unless Juanita doesn't have enough pork chops to go around," she quipped, mentally crossing her fingers, hoping against hope.

Juanita had enough. When the question was put to her regarding the number of pork chops available for dinner, the housekeeper appeared affronted for a moment, then regarded Amos McCloud's daughter as if she'd lost her mind.

"Of course I have enough pork chops. I have enough to feed everybody. Why would I not? Mr. Amos and Mr. Wayne, they have always had good appetites." For a moment, sadness streaked across her face as she referred to the person who was not there with them. And then the short, powerful-looking housekeeper rallied. She beamed at Cole. "Good to have you here, Mr. Cole."

Christopher, who had come running in announcing the dinner guest to anyone with ears, looked a little confused. "Is that your name?" he asked, then repeated, "Cole?"

Ronnie could see where this was headed. "You have to call him Sheriff or Mr. James," she instructed. She definitely didn't want her son calling Cole by his first name. Other than the fact that she had taught Christopher to address people respectfully by their surname, calling Cole by his first name was just all wrong on several levels.

Christopher's head bobbed up and down, his flaxen-colored hair swaying. He was eager to do whatever it took to get the sheriff to like him. Just meeting a real live sheriff had sparked his very fertile imagination.

Amos McCloud, his gait temporarily impeded as a result of the accident, came slowly shuffling into the living room, leaning heavily on the cane Midge had brought over for him. It had belonged to her late husband, Cole's father.

It was obvious that moving at this snail's pace annoyed Amos despite the fact that his daughter had pointed out to him that it could have been a great deal worse. The accident could have landed him in a wheelchair. Permanently.

He didn't want to hear about how lucky he was. Not until his son woke up from his coma. Until then, life had been put on hold. For his grandson's sake, though, he tried to put on a happier face than the grieving one that had become second nature to him.

Amos looked at the man who had saved his life— and his son's life, as well. He forced a smile to his thin lips. Life these days consisted of various related events, all of which encompassed some form of forced action. He struggled to hold bitterness and guilt at bay. So far, he was winning, but he had no idea how much longer he would be able to succeed.

"Hello, Cole, glad you could join us," he said, nodding at the sheriff. "Looks like it took Ronnie to succeed where an old man couldn't." He glanced toward his daughter and explained, "Been trying to get him to come over for one of Juanita's dinners so I could say thanks for saving my boy."

"And you," Ronnie tactfully reminded her father. She knew exactly what was going on in his head. At the same time, she hoped to God he didn't know what was going on in hers.

Amos snorted at her addition. "Lot of good I am to anyone like this."

"Not true," Ronnie contradicted. Very gently, she slipped her arm through one of his. She gave him a light squeeze. "Who else could spin those bedtime stories?" she asked.

Despite the fact that his visits to Seattle were few and always far too short, there was a strong bond between her father and her son.

For a while, in the beginning, she'd been afraid that her father would turn his back on her. A man of simple, old-fashioned values, Amos had been surprised by her pregnancy. And even more so when she'd told him that the father was someone she'd met in passing. Someone who was now absent from her life and would remain that way. She was determined not to let him—or anyone else—know that the baby was Cole's.

Her father had been annoyed that she hadn't even given him a name to help with identifying the boy's father, but by the time Christopher was born, all had been forgiven. Her father had shocked her by coming up to the hospital in Seattle to see her the day after she delivered. A call from her best friend in college had alerted him that Ronnie had gone into labor. Wild horses couldn't have kept him away, he'd told her.

He'd asked after his grandson's father only once, then let the matter drop. What mattered most, he'd said, was that she and the baby were all right. He didn't want to risk losing her. Her mother's loss had been bad enough, he'd added sadly, recalling the woman who had died so long ago. He concluded that pushing away a daughter was not on his agenda.

"Is that all I'm good for?" Amos asked now, feigning indignation as he looked from his grandson to her. "Bedtime stories?"

Rising on tiptoe, Ronnie kissed the sunken cheek with its grizzled white stubble.

"You're good for so much more and you know it, old man," she teased. "Now stop fishing for compliments. You know how special you are to me." And then Ronnie turned her attention to the housekeeper. "Dinner almost ready?" she asked.

"Just waiting on you," Juanita replied with a toss of her head. Hair that was still incredibly blue-black and encased in a thick, long single braid, sailed over her shoulder. "Wash, sit, I bring the food," she announced, shooing them all out of the kitchen she considered her personal domain.

Doing her best to appear completely at ease, Ronnie turned toward Cole. "You heard the lady. Juanita's word is law around here."

"And don't you forget this," the feisty housekeeper

underscored with feeling, still waving them all out of the room.

Cole heard himself laugh. The sound surprised him as much as it apparently did Ronnie.

Time seemed to freeze as he looked at her.

For one long, shimmering split second, it was almost as if no time at all had actually passed. Almost as if they were back in the years where he and she were constantly over at each other's houses for meals, studying or just hanging out.

Coming to, Cole inclined his head and said to the older woman, "Yes, ma'am."

"Please." The woman pointed to something definitely offstage. "You know where the bathroom is, Mr. Cole. Go wash your hands," she instructed for a second time.

"I'll show him where the bathroom is!" Christopher volunteered eagerly.

But Cole had no intentions of setting the boy straight. Instead, as Ronnie looked on, utterly stunned, he allowed himself to be navigated.

Grabbing his newfound idol's hand, Christopher began to pull Cole toward the bathroom.

Amos looked on, amused. "I'd say your boy's in awe of the town sheriff," her father speculated.

She nodded. "It certainly looks that way," Ronnie agreed.

The problem was, she added silently, she didn't know, in the bigger scheme of things, if her son's awe was a good thing or a bad thing. She definitely didn't want Cole finding out that the boy was his son. Not after so much time had gone by. She was more than mildly convinced that the man would never forgive her if he knew. And she felt isolated enough without adding Cole to the tally.

Rousing herself, she looked at the housekeeper. "Anything I can do to help, Juanita?"

"You can wash your hands and sit down at the table," the woman informed her in that deep, no-nonsense voice of hers that said she would not brook rebellion, or even, at the very least, independent action.

Amos and his family members could behave as independently as they wanted to, as long as, in the end, they all obeyed her. Juanita demanded and accepted nothing less.

Ronnie smiled to herself. In an ever-changing world, at least she could rely on the family housekeeper remaining a constant in her life. That was a very big "something" as far as she was concerned. Bless the woman.

Smiling at her father, Ronnie said, "You heard Juanita. Let's go wash our hands." And with that, she threaded her arm through his and very tactfully guided her father toward the downstairs bathroom.

Chapter Seven

If she had any concerns about uncomfortable silences over dinner, Ronnie needn't have worried.

Given the slightest opening, Christopher filled the air with chatter. The boy seemed to have an endless supply of topics available to him and he conducted narratives like someone at least twice his age, if not more.

To begin with, Christopher recited the events of his day, citing them chronologically from start to finish. He then proceeded to bombard Cole with question after question, demonstrating his unending curiosity about what it was like being a "real live sheriff."

Cole, who had never been all that talkative as far as Ronnie could remember—and when it came to Cole, she remembered *everything*—patiently answered each and every one of the boy's seemingly endless font of questions. It got to the point where Ronnie felt she had to come to Cole's rescue.

Reaching over to place her hand on top of Christopher's to snag her son's attention, she admonished, "Christopher, the sheriff didn't come here to be interrogated."

Along with an ever growing rhetoric, Christopher had an unending thirst for knowledge and was ready and willing to absorb whatever came his way. "What's in-terror-gated?" he asked to know.

"It means having to answer lots and lots of questions," she answered.

"Oh." Christopher slanted a thoughtful look at his newly appointed hero. His expression became contrite. "Sorry."

"Nothing to be sorry about," Cole responded amiably. "Asking questions is how you learn things. And for the record, I don't mind answering," he added for Ronnie's benefit.

The answer made Christopher brighten immediately and he launched into a second, even more extensive volley of words.

This time, all Ronnie could do was grin at Cole. She didn't bother attempting to hide her amusement. "You asked for it," she murmured to him under her breath as Christopher's questions continued to pour out and multiply.

Her grin caught him right where he lived. He'd forgotten just how much he liked her smile. Liked watching that pretty mouth curve over something they were sharing. Some inside joke, or—

Damn but he wished…

He wished…

What was it his father used to say? Something about if wishes were horses, beggars would be kings. In any event, wishing wouldn't change anything. The situation—as well as his life—was what it was and there was no point in letting his imagination drift, bogged down with "what ifs" that would only result in further frustration.

Juanita bustled in from the kitchen, carrying a sponge cake adorned with strawberries embedded in cream. After setting it down with a touch of pride, she stole a look in Cole's direction.

"This was your favorite, yes?"

"Yes," Cole answered, surprised not only that she remembered but that the venerable housekeeper just happened to have that for tonight's meal.

"Everything was excellent," Ronnie told the woman. Reaching over, she picked up the plates around her and stacked them to her left.

"Thank you," the housekeeper replied, beaming. She said nothing about being well aware of her abilities in the kitchen, which she usually did when given a compliment. Ronnie knew the woman was behaving modestly only because she was playing a role, possibly because there was a guest at the table. Juanita did not lack any self-esteem or pride. She always knew *exactly* how good she was.

"I will miss doing this for you," the older woman added.

The quietly voiced declaration took Ronnie utterly by surprise. "You mean when I go back to Seattle?" That was, she decided, the logical assumption. What else could the woman mean? She couldn't be saying that she was leaving. Juanita had been with her father for as long as she could remember.

"No, now," the housekeeper corrected, looking none too happy about the situation.

"I don't understand," Ronnie confessed, lost. Had she missed something? "You're not going to cook anymore?"

"Juanita's going to Texas for a while," Amos told his daughter. It was obvious that while he was resigned to the fact, Ronnie's father wasn't happy about the state of affairs.

Before Ronnie had a chance to ask for someone to fill in the blanks, the housekeeper provided the missing information. "My youngest sister has to have an operation. I will be taking care of her four children until she gets better."

Oh God, when it rains, it really pours, doesn't it? Ronnie couldn't help thinking. Until a few minutes ago, she'd been trying to figure out how she would manage all the things that were necessary on the ranch. Replacing Wayne, even temporarily, was no easy feat. He ran the ranch, took care of the books and worked alongside the men when it came to caring for and training the horses. In addition to that, she would also be taking care of her father and looking in on her brother whenever she could find a few free hours to make the trip down to Helena.

Now she had to add household chores to that. She knew that her father was vaguely acquainted with cooking, but not to the point that anyone—including him—would want to eat what he produced. No, cooking would be up to her.

She suppressed a desperate sigh. She was just going to have to take it in stride, she told herself. She had no other choice.

"How long will you be gone?" she asked the woman.

"Not long," Juanita assured her. The next words brought a crushing depression in their wake. "Two months or so."

"Oh."

Right now, from where she was standing, two months looked to be just a little bit shorter than eternity. *You can do this,* she told herself. If she could raise a son single-handedly and still attend classes to get her degree, she could do this, she silently insisted.

"Well, we'll miss you," Ronnie finally said, doing her best not to allow her desperation to show on her face or in her voice.

She caught Cole looking at her. Was that amusement in his eyes or just a trick played by the lighting? He was probably enjoying this. Watching her struggling as she tried to pick up the reins of the life she'd abandoned.

Juanita smiled in response to Ronnie's comment. "I do not feel so bad about leaving," she told her. "Now that you are here."

"Ronnie to the rescue, that's me," Ronnie murmured, forcing a smile to her lips.

Cole's amusement increased, filtering down to his face. "Never knew anything you weren't equal to," he commented.

She knew a challenge when she heard one. Ronnie raised her chin. "And you won't," she informed him. She would do this if it killed her.

The healthy slice of cake on his plate had occupied his attention. But it was gone now and, his mouth empty—he knew he wasn't allowed to speak with it full—Christopher launched into yet another volley of questions in Cole's direction.

With Cole's attention diverted, it freed Ronnie to try to figure out what in God's name she was going to do with this extra set of bouncing balls she'd just been given to juggle.

Cole found himself staying a lot later at the McCloud ranch than he'd intended.

Hell, he hadn't intended on staying at all, Cole thought hours later as he took his leave of Amos. The latter remained sitting in the worn armchair that had seen him through the first years of his marriage and all the years that followed. Cole was fairly certain that Christopher would have accompanied him to his truck if the small boy hadn't—finally—run out of steam. Ronnie's son was presently curled up, sleeping on the sofa.

"I can carry him up to his room if you like," Cole heard someone with his voice volunteering. Since when did he do things like that? he silently demanded, stunned.

"That's okay," Ronnie said. "He might wake up if you do and then you'll be subjected to another round of eager questions." It amazed her the number of questions Christopher could come up with. His mind never rested for a second. "I think you should make your retreat while you can," she advised.

Cole nodded, then picked up his hat where he'd dropped it on the coffee table. Practice had him confidently putting it on without benefit of a mirror. "You know best."

He was mocking her, Ronnie thought, even though nothing in his expression indicated this. But she knew how his mind worked. And, most likely, he hadn't forgiven her for the way she'd ducked out on him six years ago.

I did it for your own good, Cole. For both *our own good. I wouldn't have been happy here back then. And I would have taken it out on you eventually—and you would have hated me for the way I behaved.*

"Some of the time," she allowed, responding to his offhand comment.

His eyes washed over her, as if he was doing a re-assessment. And, in a manner of speaking, maybe he was. "You've gotten more humble." With that, he started walking toward the door.

She didn't like the word *humble* or what it implied. The only time she'd actually felt humble was holding her newborn son in her arms and that was because, in her opinion, she was in the presence of a living, breathing miracle.

"I see things a little differently now," she informed him.

Cole reached the front door, opened it and crossed the threshold.

For just a moment, she debated saying goodbye and closing the door after him, terminating the exchange before it went any further. But, for the most part, the evening had gone a lot better than she had thought it would. She wasn't entirely ready to see it end just yet.

So she followed him out and then eased the door shut behind her.

Just before she did, she glanced one last time toward the living room. By now, not only was her son asleep, but her father appeared to be dozing, as well. She noticed that her father was given to dropping off when she least expected it. She fervently hoped it was just because he was recovering from the accident and not because he was wearing out.

Her father had always been a strong, vital man. He'd been her very first hero. She didn't want to think of him any other way. Heroes didn't wear out, they suffered temporary setbacks after being injured, she thought fiercely.

"Thank you for being so patient with Christopher," she said as she joined Cole on the porch. "I know he can get to be a bit much."

"Nothing to thank me for," Cole told her honestly. "Kid's a regular live wire." He watched her and wondered how even *she* was going to handle this latest development. "I've got a feeling he's going to be tough to keep up with in a few years."

"A few years?" she echoed with a laugh, forgetting, for a moment, to feel tense. "Try now. Christopher is pure energy from morning until night. I was really surprised he conked out just now. And really, I mean it. Thanks for answering all his questions like that."

Another adult would have lost patience and told the boy to go away and play. Christopher would have gone, but she knew it would have really hurt his feelings. He'd taken to Cole faster than she'd ever seen him take to anyone.

There's a reason for that.

She shut out the voice, refusing to let it get to her.

"I know he took it to heart," she told Cole. "I think it's safe to say that you've just become his new hero."

"He doesn't interact much with his dad?" Cole asked.

Not until today.

The thought flashed through her mind. Ronnie did

what she could to seal herself off, to lock away any stray, telltale emotion that could unwittingly betray her.

With a stoic voice, she said, "No."

"Shame." Cole shook his head. There were situations beyond his understanding. "His dad doesn't know what he's missing."

"No," she agreed. "He doesn't." She needed to change the subject before her guilty conscience got the better of her and had her confessing everything. And ruining everything. "This was nice. Tonight," she explained when he looked at her quizzically—at the same time causing her stomach to knot itself up. "Thanks."

The slight noise that escaped his lips sounded like an abbreviated laugh. "You keep thanking me for things you shouldn't be thanking me for," he told her. And then he paused to weigh his words, debating whether or not he wanted to commit to them. He decided to forge ahead. It wasn't as if he had anything to lose. "It's not like I exactly suffered through this tonight."

Her eyes on his, she asked, "You didn't?"

Was that her playing these games? Being coy? What had come over her? She'd always been blunt, honest, meeting every challenge head-on. What you saw was what you got, that was her. This was suddenly a different side—and she didn't think she liked it. And yet, here she was, playing it.

"No," he replied quietly, meeting her gaze with his own, "I didn't."

Damn it, she still had that power over him, he recognized to his dismay. The power to make him want to forsake everything else in his life just for the chance to spend time with her.

Not true, a voice in his head countered. *If it was, you would have gone with her when she left town.*

The thing of it was, in the end, he would have. But she had never given him that last chance. Never asked him one last time to come with her. After they'd made love, she'd just left, without a note, an explanation, nothing. Left and cut out his heart with a jagged seashell.

More than his heart had been wounded that day. His pride had been shredded. The latter he'd pieced together, vowing never to allow such vulnerability again. But here he was, thinking things he shouldn't be, wanting what would only wind up being bad for him in the end.

He noticed that the moon was out, surrounded by a blanket of stars. So many that if he'd wanted to, he would have been hard-pressed to count the number. It was the kind of night that people fancied that they needed to have when they discovered love.

Not that it existed.

He felt fairly certain love was a myth. A myth just like unicorns and flying horses were myths. Just when you thought you had this "love" thing nailed down, it disappeared on you as if it hadn't existed to begin with—mainly because it hadn't.

But if he *did* believe in it, and it actually *did* exist, he knew he would have been moved to kiss Ronnie just now, even after everything that had gone down between them before.

The moonlight was kind to her, bathing her in soft, compelling light, stirring up his insides again. It was beginning to feel as if they were permanently set on spin cycle.

For a moment, he stood there, looking into her eyes, struggling to win a fight he didn't want to win. A fight, nonetheless, he *knew* he had to win. Because he'd been down this road before and it had led him nowhere, except to frustration.

And a great deal of pain.

He didn't want to revisit that. Once was more than enough.

Ronnie held her breath, feeling her heart hammering against her rib cage. Just *feeling.* And knowing she shouldn't be letting herself feel anything.

My God, six years away and the second she was back, the second she saw him, she was his all over again. Crazy about him all over again. How insane was that?

The years were supposed to bring wisdom, but all they seemed to bring, at least in her case, was age. Nothing more.

Still she stood there, willing him to take that last step. To take hold of her shoulders or lean over her and just do it.

Just kiss her.

Please, she silently begged.

The moment stretched out between them, until it threatened to snap.

Chapter Eight

What the hell was he thinking? Was he really that much of a glutton for punishment?

Kissing Ronnie would just take him down that same old road again—even more than he'd already gone. But even taking all that into consideration, that she was scrambling up his insides again, at least he had a fighting chance of getting over her once more if he didn't give in to temptation.

If he kissed her, he'd be a goner. Any immunity that he might have hoped to build up would instantly vanish. Taking a deliberate step away from Ronnie, he touched his fingers to his hat, politely tipping it as if she were any other one of Redemption's citizens and not the woman who had permanently vivisected his heart.

How could one woman manage to turn everything in his life on its ear this way? he couldn't help wondering for what seemed to him to be the umpteenth time.

Cole had no more of an answer this time around than he'd had the first time he'd wondered about this— the first time he realized that he was in love with her. Even back then his very strong self-preservation streak warned him not to. Not to love Ronnie. Because loving someone made you vulnerable. It gave them a power over you that no mortal should have. A power they could so easily abuse. Just the way Ronnie had, however unwittingly.

It wasn't fair, Cole thought. But then, he already knew that.

"I'll see you around, Ronnie," he told her. "Call if you need anything." And with that, he got into his truck and drove away.

Call if you need anything. His voice echoed the parting sentence in her brain. *Yes, I need something,* she thought, as exasperated as she was frustrated. *I needed you to make the first move. I needed you to do it so I could pretend it was all out of my hands.*

Disappointment seeped into her bones as she stood there, watching Cole's truck disappear into the all-consuming darkness.

Damn it, what was she asking for? To be sucked back into that wild roller-coaster ride? Didn't she have enough to deal with? Just exactly how much did she think she was up to handling? Running the ranch, looking after her father and Christopher, checking in on Wayne and now taking Juanita's place. Even a superheroine had her limits, right?

Adding to her already spirit-breaking load by renewing her affair with Cole would be nothing short of disastrous because it wouldn't be romantic and wonderful; it would be like trying to cross a tightrope on one foot. She'd be holding her breath the entire time, waiting for him to stumble across the truth—and then when he finally did, he would wind up hating her for the rest of both of their lives.

She knew she would in his place, if he'd kept something this huge from her.

Chilled, Ronnie ran her hands along her arms, trying to chase the feeling away. It wasn't the kind of chill to respond to friction.

Ronnie reminded herself that she had to get up early tomorrow to get started on what seemed like an endless mountain of tasks. There was no time to linger, being lovesick and shadowboxing with regrets for things passed. That stagecoach had left town a long time ago.

Drawing in a very shaky breath, Ronnie turned on her heel and walked back into the house.

Standing calf-deep in fresh straw, Ronnie paused to wipe away yet another wave of sweat from her brow. She couldn't seem to stop perspiring.

Like yesterday and the day before, she'd been up since before dawn, working first in the stalls, then out in the corral, eventually working her way back into the house and the books that needed updating and balancing.

But right now, she was entrenched in mucking out the stalls.

She'd forgotten, happily, what that was like. Forgotten what it felt like—and especially what it *smelled* like—to clean out the hay and everything it contained within each horse's stall before putting down fresh straw for them.

She'd also forgotten what it was like to get up an

hour before even God woke up in order to get a jump start on the day. But she had to get up at four if she had a prayer of getting to the long list of chores that were waiting to be done.

To her way of thinking, she was attempting to replace not just her brother but her father, as well. Amos McCloud might be up and about, but she wanted him to do nothing except concentrate on getting well. She couldn't afford him suffering a relapse and winding up in the hospital. Though she wasn't about to tell him to his face, the man wasn't as strong as he used to be.

Damn, but her hands were aching from holding on to the pitchfork so tightly. Ronnie looked down at her palm. No wonder her hands hurt, she thought ruefully. She was forming calluses.

She looked at her other palm. If anything, it was even worse.

"Great, just what I wanted. Hands like a weather-beaten ranch hand," she muttered in disgust and with maybe just a smattering of self-pity.

"That's why the good Lord invented gloves. To keep a woman's hands softer."

The female voice made her jump. Swinging around, Ronnie found herself looking into the round, almost angelic face of Midge James.

Cole's mother. What was she doing here?

Ronnie swept back her hair from her face. There was absolutely nothing she could tuck, smooth or dust away in order to make herself presentable, she thought self-consciously.

"Mrs. James, I'm sorry," she apologized. "I didn't hear you coming in."

"Small wonder," the woman observed, amused.

"You're moving so fast, that pitchfork you were holding was almost humming like a tuning fork. And please," the older woman requested, coming closer, "at this point you can call me Midge. Hearing 'Mrs. James' always has me looking over my shoulder, expecting to see my late husband's mother standing behind me, scowling and passing judgment. I wasn't her favorite person," she confided.

Resting the pitchfork against the side of the stall, Ronnie moved forward through the fresh mounds of straw she'd just set down. She took a deep breath and smiled at the woman, still wondering what she was doing here. "Is there anything I can do for you?"

"Lord, no." Midge laughed, waving away the mere suggestion of putting the younger woman out. "The way I hear it, you've got more than enough to do right now. But there is something that I can do for you," the woman added cheerfully.

Ronnie had no idea where this was going, or what Cole's mother was talking about, but she was more than a little grateful for the excuse to grab a momentary respite from what she was doing.

"And that is?" she coaxed, recalling that Cole's mother had always had a tendency to go the long way around when telling a story.

This time, apparently, would be no different. "Cole told me that your housekeeper, Juanita, had a family emergency to tend to."

Ronnie nodded, hoping to egg the woman along. "Juanita's sister needed an operation, so Juanita went to help out with the kids."

Was Cole's mother here to suggest the name of another housekeeper? If she was, the woman could have saved herself a trip. Her father was not about to allow a stranger to come live in his house. The story went that it had taken him a full year to get used to Juanita living with them and she knew how his mind worked. Her father would feel he was being extremely disloyal to Juanita if he allowed someone to come in to take her place, even temporarily.

Just as he'd felt he was being disloyal to his wife for bringing Juanita into the house all those years ago. Only his late sister-in-law Katie's badgering had managed to convince him that this was the only way he could continue working his ranch and still be fair to his two motherless children.

"If you've got someone in mind to help out at the house," Ronnie told Cole's mother, anticipating her answer, "I'm afraid you've come all this way for nothing. My father's a wonderful man but he's not exactly the picture of hospitality when it comes to letting someone come live in his house."

"Oh, I think he'd be amenable to this," Midge replied, and then her eyes—they looked so much like Cole's, Ronnie couldn't help thinking—seemed to all but laugh on their own. "I've already been to the house. I went ahead and made a few meals for the three of you and took the liberty of putting them into the refrigerator for you." As if anticipating Ronnie's reaction, the woman quickly added, "I've got a few spare hours so I thought I'd help you out."

"Thank you," she said with genuine feeling. "But I really can't impose on you like that." She didn't want anyone thinking she couldn't take care of her own. Or that the McClouds needed help.

"You're not imposing. I'm volunteering. There's a big

difference," the woman pointed out with confidence. "Besides, I've already gotten started. I just wanted to come out and let you know I was here."

This just didn't seem right to her. This wasn't the woman's problem, it was hers to handle. "Mrs. James—"

"Midge," the older woman corrected patiently, then added, "Please."

"Midge," Ronnie repeated, doing her best to be agreeable and to not let Cole's mother see how awkward she felt about calling her by her first name. "I can't let you do this."

Gathering herself together, Midge made her pitch. "Veronica, I have much too much time on my hands. I really need to feel useful. Cole's so self-sufficient it's painful. Besides, his place is as big as a matchbox. Cleaning it takes half an hour—moving slowly. My own place is so clean you could eat off the floors if you had a mind to," she allowed with a touch of pride that shone through. "I've got a very good man—Will Jeffers—running the ranch and there's just not that much for me to do. If a body's not being useful, they start to dry up. I don't want to dry up, Veronica."

Ronnie sighed. She had no choice but to give in. "I wouldn't want to be responsible for you drying up," she said as solemnly as she could manage.

Midge laughed. "Good girl. I've got lunch waiting for you whenever you feel like taking a little break," she told Ronnie, retreating from the stall. And then she paused, as if suddenly remembering something. "Oh, by the way, that boy of yours—"

The very breath in Ronnie's lungs turned solid. Did Cole's mother suspect? Did she see something in Christopher's face that made her think of Cole when he was that age? For the most part, Ronnie felt that the boy looked like her, but every so often, she saw traces of his dad in him. Did Cole's mother see it?

She already had an excuse ready for that, that all little boys tended to look alike at his age. But she knew that it was a flimsy excuse at best.

"Yes?" Ronnie asked, bracing herself for the worst to happen.

"He's just about the cutest little guy I've ever seen," Midge told her. "And so polite," she marveled. Smiling at Ronnie she added, "He's a great credit to his mom."

Relief was all but overwhelming as it washed over her. Ronnie was barely aware of nodding.

"Christopher's a great little guy," she agreed. "And smart as anything." She took great pride in that. Picking up the pitchfork again, she said, "I'll be there in a little while."

Midge nodded. "I'll come after you if you're not," the older woman promised. "You're not going to do anyone any good if you wind up working yourself half to death and fainting from hunger, you know."

Cole hadn't inherited any of his mother's penchant for exaggerating, she thought.

"Yes, ma'am," Ronnie replied. The other woman began to walk away, back to the house. "And Mrs.— Midge," she corrected herself at the last minute, calling after Cole's mother.

Stopping, Midge turned around again and looked at her, waiting. "Yes?"

Ronnie smiled at her, her gratitude coming into her eyes. "Thank you."

Again, Midge laughed dismissively. "Nothing to

thank me for, Veronica. It's what good neighbors do," she told her, then punctuated her statement with a wink.

What did that wink mean? Ronnie wondered as she got back to work. Was that just a conspiratorial wink or was there more behind it? And if so, what?

Did the woman suspect that she and Cole had produced more than laughter, and then hard feelings, between them? And if she had them, would his mother mention her suspicions to Cole?

Okay, she was officially being too paranoid. Mrs. James was being exactly what she said she was being. A good neighbor. That wasn't exactly unheard of in Redemption. People did look out for one another here. She'd been away so long, she'd forgotten about that. Forgotten a lot of things about life in this small, scenic little town, she thought, unaware that a thread of fondness had woven through her.

"I really don't know how to thank you," Ronnie told the woman standing to her left as she pushed her empty plate away on the table. She couldn't remember the last time she'd felt so full. Certainly not on the meals she made. She could cook well enough to keep herself and Christopher—and now her father—alive. But what she couldn't do, she would be the first to admit, was cook with flair.

The way Cole's mother obviously could.

"You already have." Midge chuckled. "By cleaning your plate," the woman explained when Ronnie looked at her quizzically. "Nothing makes me feel better than to see someone enjoying a meal I've made." She sighed happily, looking at the other two occupants at the table. "With Cole out of the house and my Pete gone, there's nobody to cook for, nobody to appreciate my efforts. Letting me help out here, you're doing me a bigger favor than I'm doing you," she assured the younger woman.

Midge's line of vision shifted to Amos, who not only had eaten the serving that had been placed before him, but had gone on to do justice to a second helping, as well. Midge beamed at the man, satisfaction all but radiating from her every pore.

The woman looked softer somehow, Ronnie caught herself thinking. Younger even. And her father, well, he had brightened considerably in the older woman's presence. Oh, he couldn't have exactly been accused of being morose and he was interacting with Christopher, but it wasn't on the same level. Ronnie could see that something had been missing.

And now it wasn't.

It hit her like a ton of bricks.

Cole's mother and her father were sweet on each other. Who would have ever thought it?

She stole another look at her father. Did Amos even realize that he was sweet on Midge James? She was fairly certain that Cole's mother was aware of how she obviously felt about her father. But as for her dad reciprocating, well, men could be so obtuse.

Rising, she announced, "Christopher and I are going to do the dishes."

Instantly, Midge blocked her way into the kitchen. "No, you're not. Amos and I will take care of the dishes, won't we, Amos?" She eyed Amos pointedly, but her smile was wide, coaxing.

Amos never stood a chance. Before Ronnie's disbelieving eyes, he easily agreed to do what she had once heard him refer to as "woman's work."

"Sure thing, Midge."

This didn't seem fair to her. "But you cooked," Ronnie protested.

Midge was not about to budge on this. For such a small, amiable woman she was quite a force to reckon with. "And you, from what I hear, did everything else. You're not a superwoman, Veronica, no matter what you think. You can't do everything and you'll wear out much too fast if you try."

Ronnie slanted a covert look at her father. He had definitely perked up today ever since Cole's mother had arrived.

Okay, Ronnie decided, maybe she should just back off and retreat. Standing in the way of this just didn't seem right.

"All right, then I'm going to go and look in on Wayne if it's okay with you," she said to her father.

It was obvious that he wanted to stay here with Cole's mother, but his sense of obligation compelled him to go see his son.

"Maybe I should go with you," Amos told his daughter.

He was acutely aware that he hadn't been to see Wayne since he'd first conferred with the doctors at the hospital about his son's injuries and the unnerving coma that had Wayne in its grip.

"No, what you should do is stay here with Midge and Christopher," Ronnie told him calmly. "I called the hospital this morning."

The way she did every morning and every night since she'd gotten the news about the accident. She knew someone would notify her the moment her brother came out of his coma, but she still called, just in case it *had* happened and they hadn't gotten a chance to give her a call about this newest development.

"Wayne still hasn't woken up," she continued. "There's no point in you going."

She knew how hard all this was on her father, seeing Wayne unconscious and unresponsive. Her father was still very much a prisoner of the guilt he'd assigned to himself because of the accident. Despite any arguments, he still felt that he was the one who had put Wayne in that hospital bed.

Even though it was the other driver who had run into them.

She paused beside her seated father to kiss the top of his head affectionately. "I'll tell Wayne you send your love," she promised.

"Can I send my love, too?" Christopher asked, jumping up out of his chair, ready to stay or go, whatever his mother decreed.

Laughing, Ronnie knelt down beside her son and hugged him. "Absolutely. I'll tell Uncle Wayne you send your love." *I only hope that somehow, he can hear me.* Rising again, she looked over toward the other woman. "Thank you."

"Nothing to thank me for," Midge scoffed, waving away the words.

But she was beaming, pleased, as she said it.

Chapter Nine

It felt as if no time had passed at all even though it had been more than a week.

Ronnie was standing in approximately the same place, in the very same small cubicle she had stood in the last few times she had been here at the hospital to see her brother.

Nothing had changed.

Wayne was still wired to the same machines and monitors, still lying immobile with his eyes closed while all around him the subdued humming, buzzing and vibrating sounds wove one into the other to produce a disturbing dissonance. All involved in sustaining her brother, tethering him to the life he had almost left behind more than three weeks ago, functioning for him until he was able to function for himself.

If he was ever able to function for himself.

The sight ripped at her heart, but she refused to give in to pity, either for Wayne or for herself. He wasn't going to get better if she tiptoed around him softly, talking in hushed, quiet tones. She knew her brother. Wayne was only going to get better if he became determined to do so; if he became angry that his body was confining him like this.

Ronnie felt desperate.

There had to be *some* way to get through to him, to make him rally.

"Doctors told me that everything seems to be healing well. They also said that they can't find a reason why you're still in a coma."

C'mon, Wayne, get up. Open your eyes and get up. Please, she silently begged. Taking a breath, she went on talking to the inert body in the hospital bed. To the brother whose facial bruises were healing but whom she didn't recognize.

"But they don't know you like I do. They don't know that you were always the one who wanted those five extra minutes in bed when you were a kid. Or that you slept in every chance you could. They don't understand that you're just being lazy, but I do," she told him, her voice hitching just a little. "I do," she repeated more firmly. "And I want you to stop it. Do you hear me? Just stop it." She could feel her insides trembling as she added, "That's an order, damn it!"

When there wasn't even the slightest sign that her words had penetrated the haze surrounding Wayne, she pressed her lips together—willing herself to remain together, as well.

"I know I always said I was twice the man that you were when we were growing up, but I never thought you'd call me on it." She drew a little closer, leaving no space at all between her and the side of his bed. "I can't keep this up indefinitely. I need you back to take over, to do what you've always done." She paused, slowly releasing a shaky breath, desperately trying not to break down or start sobbing.

"I'll stick around for a little bit longer, to help, but the running of the ranch, that's your job, you know that. By the way, your handwriting stinks. I wouldn't have to spend as much time on the books if I could read that chicken scratch you call writing. Don't you know it's the computer age? Why didn't you use the laptop I sent you?"

As she talked, Ronnie watched her brother's face for even the tiniest glimmer of movement.

But there was nothing. The desperation inside her grew.

"You've got to start coming around, Wayne. I really don't know how much longer I can keep this up." She stopped for a moment, banking down the sob she felt rising in her throat. "And every day that you're here like this, Dad sinks a little deeper into that hole he's digging for himself. He's not going to start getting better until *you* start getting better. Do you hear me?"

She took Wayne's hand in both of hers and squeezed it, *willing* him to hear her. Terrified that he didn't. And that he never would.

"Do you hear me?" she demanded, repeating the question. "Damn it, Wayne, I *know* you can hear me. I'm not going to let you fade away like this. Do you understand? I'm *not*. You're going to open your eyes and wake up. Your life's waiting for you. *I'm* waiting for you and so's Dad and Christopher. Stop being so selfish and open your eyes, Wayne," she ordered angrily. "Open them *now!*"

"That sounds scary enough to get the dead to open their eyes and sit up."

Stifling a yelp, Ronnie swung around, her heart temporarily launching into double time. She was so wrapped up in what she was saying, in trying to get her brother to wake up she hadn't heard anyone entering the area.

Her eyes grew wide when she saw Cole standing behind her, looking laid-back and casual. As if he didn't belong anywhere else but exactly where he was.

How had he even known she was here?

"Cole, what are you doing here?" Ronnie cried.

"Looking in on Wayne," Cole answered her matter-of-factly.

And on you, he added silently. His mother had called to tell him where Ronnie was going and that she thought perhaps the younger woman might need a "strong shoulder to lean on."

Cole had patiently told his mother that he was busy, but somehow, thanks to the fact that it was yet another peaceful day in Redemption, he'd found himself driving toward Helena and the hospital anyway.

Self-conscious, Ronnie quickly swiped the back of her hand against her cheeks, wiping away the tears she only now realized had slid down her face. She'd been too involved trying to bully her brother into waking up to notice that she was crying.

"I thought maybe if I yelled at him, he'd hear me and wake up just so he could yell back," she explained wearily. Still holding tightly onto her brother's hand, she exhaled slowly, doing her best to center herself. "I guess maybe I didn't yell loud enough."

"I don't know about that," Cole contradicted in his even, emotionless voice. "My guess is that there were people out in the parking lot who heard you and snapped to attention." Sympathy for Ronnie had him asking, "Did the doctors say anything positive?"

That was just it, they had. It was just Wayne who was behaving so negatively. "They said he's healing—and that according to everything they know, Wayne should be out of his coma by now." The despair she was experiencing seemed bottomless. She was doing her best to keep from slipping into that abyss. "I guess they don't know all that much," she murmured, looking at her brother.

Raising her chin to keep a fresh crop of tears from falling, Ronnie stared out the window. She wasn't standing close enough to see anything but a blue expanse of sky.

"I don't know what to do," she said in a small voice, then repeated the words, her voice growing stronger in her frustration. "I don't know what to do."

"Stop."

Hearing the very hoarse entreaty, she looked at Cole, puzzled. "What did you just say?"

But Cole shook his head. "I didn't say anything. I thought you did. Why'd you suddenly say stop?"

"I didn't."

In unison, they both turned their attention toward the man in the bed. Wayne's eyes were still closed, just like they had been this entire time.

They couldn't have *both* imagined hearing the word,

Ronnie thought. She was almost afraid to hope—and more afraid not to.

"Wayne?" Ronnie said hesitantly. "Wayne, did you just say something?" As she asked, she leaned over her brother, her ear near his lips—just in case.

And then she heard that same raspy voice.

"Man…can't…rest…with…all…this…racket." The words were almost inaudible. Almost.

"He talked!" Ronnie cried. Thrilled, shocked, excited, she found herself verging on being utterly hysterical with relief. Immediately, she looked up for confirmation. "Cole, he talked. You heard him talk, right?"

Rather than stand there, answering her question, Cole had already crossed toward the outer room and was striding toward the nurses' station located at the outer edge of the ICU. He was intent on corralling the first doctor or nurse and bringing him or her back with him.

Returning to Wayne's bedside inside of three minutes, Cole brought with him a tall, efficient-looking woman with pinched features and a no-nonsense attitude. She immediately proceeded to move Ronnie out of the way in order to do a very basic exam of the heretofore immobile patient.

"Mr. McCloud, can you hear me?" the woman—a nurse it turned out—asked as she shone the pencil-thin light in her hands first into one of Wayne's eyes and then the other.

"Sleep." The single rumbling word emerged with a maximum of struggle.

"Yes, you're right. Sleep's the best thing for you right now," the nurse agreed.

Looking at the monitor that was continuously screening his blood pressure, heart rate and body temperature, the nurse nodded as if conducting a conversation on some higher plane that only she was privy to.

Only then, when she was finished making her assessment, did the nurse turn toward Ronnie. "He's out of his coma," she said guardedly. "At least for now."

"Does that mean he could have a relapse?" she asked the nurse. When the woman didn't answer her immediately, Ronnie pushed herself to ask the rest of it. She might as well know the worst now. "Could he sink back into another coma?"

"Yes," the nurse replied, pulling no punches.

"What are the odds on that?" Cole asked.

He shifted so that he was standing next to Ronnie in order to physically give her the support she needed. Under the circumstances, he thought that she was bearing up rather well, but even she wasn't superhuman. Everyone had their breaking point. Family apparently was hers.

"Remote," the nurse was forced to admit. "More likely, this is the beginning of his recovery."

Suddenly feeling weak all over, Ronnie went on automatic pilot. Struggling against dissolving in a puddle of tears, and because she and Cole had been friends for so long before, she buried her head in his chest. With a huge effort, she dammed up the tears that threatened to flow.

She felt his arms close around her, felt Cole holding her to him, not tightly but with just enough pressure to allow her to take comfort from knowing that she wasn't alone. That he was there for her whenever she needed him. And always would be.

Stroking Ronnie's hair so lightly, he had a feeling

she wasn't even aware of it, Cole looked over toward the nurse.

"Thank you," he told her quietly.

The woman nodded. "Just doing my job. I'll call Dr. Nichols in, alert him to the change." What most likely passed as a smile for the woman graced her lips. "Nice to have something positive to tell him."

Ronnie fought hard to keep her composure, to keep the tears from falling. It took a great deal of effort and self-discipline. She had a feeling that if she gave in, if she started to cry, there would be nothing left of her by the time she stopped.

Taking a long, shaky breath, she separated herself from Cole.

The air hit her cheeks and she could have sworn they felt damp. Annoyed at the lack of discipline, she scrubbed her palm over both cheeks, getting rid of any telltale signs of dampness. She was stronger than this. She wasn't going to fall apart now, not when the news was basically good.

What was wrong with her, anyway?

Pulling herself together, Ronnie looked back at her brother. His eyes were still closed, but that was all right. She'd heard him try to talk, heard that drawn-out, labored sentence. He was coming around. She could wait as long as she knew that was going to be the end result.

"Knew you were faking it," she sniffed, so relieved she couldn't even begin to take measure of the feeling. It filled every single tiny space within her.

Wayne's attending physician walked into the cubicle at that moment. "I hear your brother finally decided to join us," he said kindly to Ronnie.

Cole only managed to partially suppress a grin. "He told her to stop talking."

The doctor nodded understandingly. "I have a sister like that. Never lets me get in a word edgewise. Ronda promised to bring me back from the dead if I ever needed her to do it. Turned out I did. It was a skiing accident," he tacked on vaguely and then Dr. Nichols smiled at Ronnie. "He's lucky to have you."

She sniffed, trying to regain control over herself. "He probably doesn't see it that way," she said. She felt so drained, it was as if someone had opened her up and let everything just flow out. She felt beyond exhausted.

"Then he's wrong," the doctor told her. "It's the ones who drive us crazy that keep us going," he assured Ronnie.

Another, different nurse stuck her head in. "I'm afraid time's up," she told the two visitors at the bedside politely. Hospital procedures allowed only a maximum of two visitors per bedside, and in the ICU area, those visitors were only allowed to stay for ten minutes every hour.

Ronnie nodded. "I'm not greedy. I've had my miracle for today," she told the nurse. "So I'll be going home now."

She felt like embracing both the doctor and the nurse, but she refrained. She didn't want them thinking her brother was related to a crazy woman.

Oblivious to the fact that Cole seemed to be leaving the ICU with her, she paused at the very last possible moment beside Wayne. His eyes were still closed. That no longer worried her.

Ronnie bent over and whispered in his ear. "I knew you were in there somewhere," she told him triumphantly. With that, she straightened, flashed a smile at the doctor and said, "Please call me if there's any other change. Anything at all," she underscored, silently praying that there was only good news from now on.

Dr. Nichols patiently nodded, acting as if this was a new instruction rather than something that was already a standing order.

"You okay to drive home?" Cole asked the moment they stepped into the hallway.

Ronnie slanted a look at his face. She'd felt stronger in her time but she wasn't about to admit that just yet. "Why?"

"You look a little flushed, that's all," he answered. And with what had just happened, who could blame her for being a little off her game?

She *was* feeling rather wobbly and unsteady, Ronnie thought. But precision driving wasn't required for making the trip back to Redemption. She'd seen maybe three other vehicles before she'd entered Helena proper. Driving here was a completely different experience from driving in Seattle. Between traffic and practically daily encounters with at least sporadic rain, driving in Seattle was challenging at best.

"I'm okay," she said after a beat, then added with a smile, "Better than okay."

Even though he could have stood there, easily getting lost in her smile, Cole still had his doubts about her fitness to drive.

"Tell you what, why don't we stop for coffee first?" he suggested.

"Coffee?" she repeated.

What had made him suggest something like that? And wasn't he supposed to be on duty? That meant he was supposed to be back in Redemption, not here. The last time he'd technically been a guide for one of the ex-citizens of Redemption, so he'd had an excuse to be away from the small town.

But he didn't have that excuse anymore.

Did he?

As if reading her mind, Cole said, "Doesn't have to be coffee. It can be a bite to eat. Or just sitting, not saying anything. Just being immobile long enough to get our bearings," he told her.

He was saying "our" but he meant hers, Ronnie thought. She knew what she had to look like to him. Just on this side of deranged.

There was a time when she would have found his concern, his being practically in touching range every time she turned around, downright confining and insulting. It showed what he thought of her ability to take care of herself.

But after being on her own for so long, forced to make all the decisions for herself and Christopher and having really no one around to lean on, Ronnie found it comforting that he worried about her.

Even if he was probably only going through the motions.

She had no doubt that in no time at all, he would transform back into the town sheriff and would be making noises like the town sheriff.

Still, she saw the merit of his suggestion. "I guess sitting down and having a cup of coffee while I pull myself together isn't all that bad an idea," Ronnie allowed slowly.

He had to admit he wasn't expecting her to give in

so easily, not without a fight. That meant that he'd been right in guessing at her present state.

But then, Cole thought, he'd lived in isolation a long while now. He was well aware that good news could grab a chunk out of a person just as easily as bad news could. It was no secret that emotions could provide the bearer a wild roller-coaster ride, filled with ups and downs, even at the best of times.

He ought to know.

Cole felt as if he'd been perpetually attending a damn amusement park every single day since Ronnie had come back to Redemption.

"Good," he pronounced in his low-key voice, showing no feeling one way or another about her acceptance. "I saw a little coffee shop on the next block. We could stop there."

He was leaving it up to her, Ronnie realized. But it wasn't as if she was all that familiar with this area anymore. A lot more buildings had gone up here since she'd left the state.

Almost as many as there had in Redemption. The little town seemed to have doubled in size as far as the stores went. That still didn't make it on its way to becoming a city. At least, not yet.

"Lead the way," she told him.

He tried not to look surprised that she would relinquish the lead so very easily.

The woman was full of surprises, but then that really shouldn't come as such a surprise to him. Like a gaily wrapped, mysterious Christmas present, Ronnie had always been full of surprises.

Right from the very first moment he'd laid eyes on her.

Chapter Ten

Though he wasn't holding her hand, Cole became aware that Ronnie's hand was shaking before they'd gone very far down the block.

A closer scrutiny of the woman made him realize that she was about to come apart. Given that she had just been on the receiving end of some very good news, he was concerned about the frailty of her mental state.

"Ronnie?"

"What?"

Incredibly anxious and shaky, Ronnie tried very hard to concentrate on—literally—just putting one foot in front of the other on the sidewalk. Right now, it felt as if her entire body had turned on her and she had no idea why.

"You're shaking," Cole said.

"No, I'm not," she denied as vehemently as she could.

What was the matter with her? The worst was over. Everything from here on in would be all right, maybe not as fast as she'd like, but eventually. Right?

Coming to a dead stop, Cole tugged on her hand to get her to stop walking, as well.

"Yes," he said firmly, "you are." She really was shaking, and it wasn't restricted to just her hand now, but all of her.

His eyes searched her face for a clue as to what she was feeling. He was vaguely aware that emotions could be very complex and tricky. While he didn't have a handle on what Ronnie might be going through right now, he was pretty sure he could make an intelligent guess.

"When I was a kid, I'd sometimes find my mother crying. The first time I did, I asked her what I could do to help and she said, 'Nothing.' Sometimes she just needed to have a good cry and said that she always felt better afterward." He drew his own conclusions from that. "Maybe you just need to work whatever's going on with you out of your system with a good cry."

"Right," Ronnie said sarcastically. But then she looked into his eyes. "You're actually serious," she realized.

He'd figured out that she had to be under an enormous amount of tension. Ronnie was working on overload and even though the last piece of information she'd been given had been positive, she wasn't emotionally equipped to handle it. Crying was the only thing he could think of to help her.

"Yes."

Ronnie pressed her lips together, afraid she would do exactly that. But there was no way she would break down like that in public. She gestured around. The streets were filled with people. "Even if I wanted to, I can't just stand here crying in the middle of the city like some pathetic idiot."

Cole looked around for a second, not at the people, but searching for an opportunity. Spotting it, he took her hand and pulled her into the recessed doorway of an abandoned store that, from the fly-specked signs in the bay window, appeared to have once been a bakery.

He had her back up against the door. "What are you doing?" she demanded.

Cole placed himself between the rest of the world and her. "Now you're not standing in the middle of the city," he answered quietly.

Maybe it was his tone that got to her, or maybe it was the fact that he was going out of his way for her, being so kind.

Being protective.

Or maybe the weight of everything she'd been trying to deal with had finally gotten to her. Or maybe it was that the immense relief that Wayne's coma had receded had overwhelmed her.

Most likely, it was a combination of all of the above, with a dose of an anxiety attack thrown in on top of it. Whatever the reason behind it, as if on cue, Ronnie suddenly couldn't maintain another pseudobrave moment. She broke down and cried.

Silent sobs wracked her body, causing her to shake even more. And during the entire episode, Cole just held her. Held her close to him, wordlessly letting her know with his presence that he was there for her if she should find that she needed him.

Rather than talk, he let her cry everything out of her system. The fear, the weariness, the relief. Everything.

The only thing he did say was to assure her that, "It's okay. It's all going to be okay."

The rest of the time, he was busy struggling to keep his own feelings at bay and under control. He was trying to keep a tight rein on his own reaction to having her this close to him, to having her body turn into his, reminding him—as if he needed reminding—how much he still wanted her.

But this wasn't about him. This was about letting her know that she wasn't alone in this. That he was here for her and would continue to be for as long as she needed him. And a little bit longer than that.

She cried for what seemed a very long time, becoming progressively exhausted, progressively drained. And through it all, she was aware of the man holding her, giving her shelter, shielding her from prying eyes and the aroused curiosity of passing strangers.

More than that, she was acutely aware of Cole. Of everything about him. His scent, the gentleness of his hands, the texture of his shirt. Aware of the warmth of his body that radiated through his clothing and hers until it seemed to touch her very skin.

Aware of him.

As the last sob faded away, Ronnie slowly raised her head and looked up at Cole. Her body was no longer shaking because of an impending breakdown. But it *was* vibrating ever so slightly from an inner need that had materialized in the wake of her purging herself of all the rest of it, rising out of the ashes of anxiety like a resurrected phoenix, spreading its wings and taking to the sky.

Before she knew what was happening, Ronnie had raised her lips up to Cole's. Whether or not she was responsible for initiating that first kiss, she honestly couldn't remember. All she knew was that she had wanted it. Had tasted it before it became a reality.

Rather than keep her arms pinned down to her sides, she picked them up and threaded them around Cole's neck, still kissing him.

Damn it, this wasn't supposed to be happening, Cole thought. He hadn't pulled her aside to kiss her. He'd done it so that she could have a private moment, away from possible prying eyes, and either cry out all the emotions weighing her down, or just pull herself together.

There was no denying that she'd been through a hell of a lot this last week and a half. There was only so much a body should have to take. At a loss how to help, he'd fallen back on something incredibly elementary and simple and hoped he was right.

But there was nothing simple about this.

Nothing simple about the extent of the desire hammering through him, nothing simple about the things that this kiss was generating.

Damn, but he had missed her, Cole thought, gathering her even closer to him. If he could, he would have absorbed her, taken her very essence into his, mingling their spirits and whatever else he could manage so that she would be a part of him even more than she already was.

She would think he'd taken her aside for this, he warned himself. She might think he'd had an ulterior motive and he didn't want her thinking that way, didn't want her believing that because it wasn't true.

So why are you still kissing her? Why aren't you trying to put a stop to this and put some space between you? an annoying voice in his head demanded.

The annoying voice was right.

He had to stop kissing her. It was the right thing to do, just not the easy thing to do.

Reluctantly, Cole removed her arms from around his neck and drew back his head. A sense of almost bereavement came over him when his mouth left hers.

There was a dazed, quizzical look in Ronnie's eyes, as if she didn't understand why he'd stopped.

Cole fought with the very real, very strong urge to lose this battle he waged with himself and kiss her all over again. But Ronnie might think that he was just preying on her vulnerable state.

"Ronnie, I didn't..."

How the hell did he begin to phrase this? How did he begin to tell her that he didn't mean for this to happen, even though it made him happier than he'd been in six long years?

As it turned out, he didn't have to phrase it at all.

The dazed expression in Ronnie's eyes faded, to be replaced by one of understanding.

She nodded her head. "I know." There were unspoken volumes behind the two words.

She got it, Cole thought, surprised. Ronnie somehow understood how much he wanted her, but that he was trying his best to hold himself back. For her sake. God knew it wasn't for his own.

"You'd better be getting back," he told her quietly, stepping out of the doorway.

Ronnie raised her head and her eyes met his. A beat later, a sliver of amusement entered those same crystal green eyes.

"Are you trying to welsh out of that cup of coffee you said you were buying me?" she asked him.

"What?" For a second, Cole had forgotten all about the coffee, and everything else for that matter. The universe—his universe—began and ended in Ronnie's green eyes. "No," he answered with feeling as the suggestion he'd made in the hospital came back to him. "The coffee shop's right down there." He nodded to the left in the shop's general direction.

She moved out of the shelter of the temporary haven he'd formed for her, her step just a little surer now than it had been a few minutes earlier. She was ready to reclaim her position in the world.

"Well then, let's go."

He grinned. Okay, the old Ronnie was back. And all was well with the universe.

Inclining his head, he said, "Yes, ma'am."

Ronnie didn't remember much of the drive back to the ranch. Only that Cole remained right behind her the entire trip to make sure she didn't suddenly veer off into a ditch—or worse.

Her guardian angel, she thought, amused. But then, that was what he'd always been, right? Hadn't he always watched out for her, been there to deflect any possible blows, verbal or otherwise, aimed at her? She'd acted as if that annoyed her, independent tomboy that she tried to be, but secretly, it had pleased her.

The coffee shop had been fairly empty when they arrived and they had sat outside with their containers, talking for a little bit. The conversation had centered around Wayne, the ranch and his mother. No mention was made—by silent agreement—of the explosion that had rocked both ends of their worlds in that bakery doorway.

After they left the coffee shop, she'd wanted to go back to the hospital to see Wayne one last time before heading home. So they stopped by his cubicle and found Wayne sleeping.

For a moment, her heart sank and she was afraid that Wayne had slipped back into that awful coma. Cole went searching for the doctor, who came back and assured her that wasn't the case. Wayne was no longer comatose. Instead, he was simply sleeping again, resting his exhausted system. The good news was that while she and Cole had been having coffee, Wayne had completely woken up. The coma had gone just as mysteriously as it had descended on him.

Part of her wished that she had remained on the hospital premises the entire time so that she could have seen this for herself rather than hear about it secondhand.

But she was forced to admit, albeit silently, that another part of her was glad that she hadn't been here. More specifically, she was glad that she had been exactly where she had been. In the doorway, in Cole's arms. Lost in his kiss.

And just where is that supposed to lead you? her conscience demanded.

She didn't want to explore that avenue. Didn't even want to think about it. Because thinking about it would most likely only ruin the joy she was feeling right at this moment.

Wayne was conscious, that was the important thing and all that mattered right now. Ronnie focused on that.

By the time she reached the ranch, pulled up the handbrake and jumped out of her car, Ronnie had to restrain herself to keep from bursting through the front door. She deliberately hadn't called home from the hospital because she wanted to deliver the news in person. Wanted to be there to see her father's face when she told him that Wayne was awake.

The minute she was inside the house, Ronnie called out for her father. There was no one in the foyer.

"Dad? Dad, are you around?" She raised her voice and called again. "Dad? I'm back and I have news!"

Her father, moving far more stiffly than he was obviously happy about, shuffled into the room as quickly as he could, leaning on his cane. His face was the picture of dread.

"I'm right here," he grumbled. "Stop bellowing." And then he came to a stop in the middle of the room, as if he couldn't listen and walk at the same time. Steeling himself for the worst, Amos McCloud asked his daughter, "What's the matter?" Before she could answer him, he swallowed and nervously added, "Is Wayne—?"

He couldn't bring himself to ask the question. As a young man, Amos had been a soldier sent overseas. He'd faced death for his country. As a struggling rancher and family man, he'd been forced to face the death of his wife and deal with that. It had been painful going and he'd all but lost himself to the bottle for a couple of years back then. Eventually, he'd come out the other end and triumphed.

But facing the death of a child was something he wasn't sure that he would ever be prepared to face.

"Out of the coma, yes," Ronnie cried, ending the sentence for him with far different words than Amos had anticipated.

Cole had come in directly behind her and now Cole's mother and Christopher had come into the room, as well. But it was to Cole that Amos looked for confirmation of his daughter's words.

"Is this true, boy?"

Cole nodded. He didn't bother correcting the older man on any count, neither pointing out that it had been years since he'd been a boy and that he was, after all, the sheriff of the town and as such deserved to be addressed by his title. At the very least, he shouldn't have to respond to being referred to as a "boy."

"Wayne complained about your daughter's talking too much," he told the older man.

The relief that came over Amos's gaunt face was nothing short of astounding. Right before Ronnie's eyes, the old man seemed to shed two decades.

"I always thought she would talk someone to death." Amos chuckled, glancing toward his daughter. "Not the other way around."

Because she knew it pleased her father to kid around this way, Ronnie played along.

"Very funny, Dad," she sniffed. "But all that really matters is that he's finally, *finally* awake." And then she filled her father in on the details. At the end, she said, "The doctor wants to watch Wayne for a few more days, so for now Wayne's going to have to stay at the hospital but he'll be coming home before you know it," she promised her father.

"And then Uncle Wayne'll give me horseback rides?" Christopher asked eagerly.

She laughed and ruffled her son's silken hair. "Not right away, but yes, in a while, I'm sure he will. You just have to let him get better first."

Cole didn't think the boy meant the term the way

he was familiar with it. "Horseback rides?" he asked Ronnie quizzically.

"They're actually piggyback rides," she explained, lowering her voice in deference to her son's feelings, "but Christopher really has this aversion to pigs, so he calls them horseback rides."

Nodding, Cole looked down at the boy. "Would you like a horseback ride right now?" he asked.

The blond head bobbed up and down enthusiastically, stray strands of his flaxen-colored hair moving independently.

"You can do that?" he asked, barely able to contain his abundant energy.

Cole got down on one knee, his back toward the boy. He held his hands up shoulder-level, ready to receive the much smaller ones in them.

"Well, why don't we see?" he suggested. "You get on my back and give me your hands," he instructed.

"My mom always helps," Christopher told him.

"That's nice that you let her," Cole commented, guessing that was where this was going. "Moms like to feel helpful."

"Yes, we do," Ronnie agreed, amused, as she helped get her son properly seated on Cole's back. Stepping to the side, she said to Cole, "Okay, Trigger, you're good to go." She punctuated her assessment with a swat to his butt to launch him on his way.

As Cole gave her son—their son, she amended in her mind—a ride, Ronnie watched. And the lump in her throat that had materialized earlier in the day grew in direct correlation to the smile on her lips.

Chapter Eleven

Dr. Nichols, Wayne's attending physician, called Ronnie a couple of days later. Her heart all but stopped when she heard the man's gravelly voice on the other end of the line. Up until this point, Wayne had been due to be released tomorrow. Her gut told her this couldn't be good.

"Is something wrong, Dr. Nichols?"

"No," the man on the other end of the line was quick to reassure her, "but I just wanted to let you know that I've decided to keep your brother here a little longer than we first discussed."

What wasn't he telling her?

"Why?" she asked, the single word rising out of a suddenly parched throat. Had the last CAT scan shown something the doctor had missed seeing earlier? All sorts of possibilities appeared, her mind hopping from one thing to another.

"Because like all the men working on ranches around here, the second I release him to go home, he's going to start trying to catch up. I'm well acquainted with his type. They all think they're invincible. I just want to give Wayne a little more time for his body to make that a reality."

Wayne wasn't going to be happy about this. "What are you going to tell him?" she asked.

"That I want to run a few more tests to make sure that there's no further internal damage that we might have overlooked."

She supposed that sounded plausible enough. Especially since he'd mentioned the other day that he was thinking of ordering more tests for Wayne—just to be certain all was well.

Ronnie thanked the doctor for calling and then replaced the receiver in its cradle.

A sigh escaped her lips. She would have to call the administrative assistant at her firm and request an extension for her leave of absence. Though she really didn't want to be away from work for such a long period of time, there was no way around it. Besides, the doctor was right. Wayne would have to remain where he was for a few more days. If he was released too early, the chances were fairly good that he'd wind up having to go back to the hospital because he'd pushed himself and done too much too fast—before he was ready.

They were cut from the same cloth, her brother and she, and Ronnie knew exactly what drove him, what Wayne was capable of. In order to make sure he didn't overdo anything, he had to be kept in the hospital, waiting for the doctor's release.

And she had to keep to this overwhelming schedule just a little longer.

That included somehow finding the time to go look in on her brother at the hospital. She was well aware that part of healing was having a feeling of well-being. You couldn't exactly have that when no one visited and you felt as if you were being abandoned.

She knew that she wouldn't be able to stay as long as she would have liked, but something was better than nothing.

Besides, Wayne would understand. The trick would be to keep him from feeling guilty about it. They were officially two men down and there was no extra money to hire anyone until Wayne was ready to take over again. Money was better spent getting feed for the horses and paying off a startlingly large vet bill.

Not that the vet was really a problem. Dr. Starling was a very patient man, but a sense of pride was involved here and she wanted to make sure that her father owed no one. Things would get better once the twelve quarter horses her father had arranged to be sold to Bart Walker, a cattle rancher located a hundred miles to the south of Redemption, were delivered. That was in approximately three weeks. The payment coming from that sale would be readily applied to the mortgage on the ranch. Her father had been forced to refinance four years ago after a bout of cholera had taken out half his herd and set him back worse than he could have ever predicted.

Glancing at her watch, Ronnie decided she could squeeze in a quick visit to her brother if she left right now. She went to find Midge to let her know she was leaving. Cole's mother had become part of the family these days, a development that had contributed a great deal to her father's infinitely improved spirits.

Ronnie heard laughter coming out of her brother's room a second before she opened the door. Wayne had been transferred—finally—from the demoralizing ICU cubicle with its grating metallic sounds and placed in a semiprivate room yesterday. The other bed had been empty, but she assumed from the laughter that someone was now occupying it.

When she walked in, she saw that the other bed, located closer to the door, was still empty. The laughter she'd heard was coming from the four people gathered around Wayne's bed. Female people. Wayne, apparently, was holding court. Ronnie recognized all four women. They were all from Redemption.

For a moment, no one realized that she was even in the room. And then Wayne saw her. He gave her a wide, toothy grin. "Hi, Ronnie."

"Hi yourself." Relieved, Ronnie smiled. There were still a few bruises, but they were fading and Wayne was looking more like his former robust self. She shook her head. "And here I was afraid that you were lying here, lonely, pining away for some company. I guess I've been gone from Redemption too long," she commented. "I forgot that you never lacked for female companionship when we were in school." She nodded her head at each one of Wayne's visitors. "Cheryl, Dorothy, Lori, Annie." She acknowledged each woman in turn warmly. "Nice to see you ladies all here."

This was the best thing in the world for Wayne, Ronnie thought. Attention from the fairer sex was bound to lift his spirits. He was a far cry from the patient she saw lying downstairs in the ICU almost two weeks ago.

Ronnie stayed for a very brief visit, part of which was spent talking to Dr. Nichols for a more complete update. Satisfied that her presence wasn't needed, Ronnie gently made her way to the head of her brother's bed and told him, "I'm going to be heading back."

"But you just got here," Cheryl protested. She exchanged looks with the other women, all of whom looked a tad guilty.

"Our being here isn't chasing you away, is it?" Annie asked.

Ronnie laughed. "Just the opposite," she assured them. "Your being here is a godsend. It means I won't have to worry about Wayne wasting away here. Trust me, seeing you ladies is the best medicine my big brother could have." She paused to kiss her brother's cheek. "Boy, the lengths you'll go to just to get a little attention. It really boggles the mind," she teased.

For a moment, Wayne looked serious. "You know you don't have to go."

She knew he meant it, but she really did have reason to get back to the ranch. "Yes, I do. I've got twelve quarter horses to get ready for delivery, whole sections of fence that still need mending and right now, I'm still two men short."

Wayne grinned weakly. It was obvious to her that her brother still had a ways to go before he was completely back to normal. "Not with you on the job."

She nodded her approval. "Good answer. See you, big brother." Surrendering her space, Ronnie looked at the other women around her brother's bed. "Take good care of him."

And with that, she hurried out of Wayne's room as quickly as she had hurried into it less than twenty minutes ago.

The trip back to the ranch was monotonous, but quick. With terrain so flat that it enabled her to see an approaching vehicle from miles away, she was relieved of the added pressure of watching for any law enforcement officer with too much time on his hands and a virgin ticket book on the seat next to him.

She made it back to the outskirts of Redemption in record time. Since she'd gotten everything she needed to get right to work after her visit and had put it in the back of the Jeep, there was no need for her to stop off at the house. Instead, she drove up toward where she'd seen the decaying section of fence the other day.

In its present state, that section was a problem waiting to happen. Horses had an uncanny knack of being able to find the one section that would offer them the least amount of resistance and then break out. After all the trouble that had gone into raising, feeding and training these horses, she was not about to take a chance on losing any of them because no one had gotten around to fixing several yards of rotting boards.

It looked like she'd been concerned for nothing, Ronnie thought as she drove closer. From a distance she spotted a lone figure doing exactly what she'd intended on doing. One of the ranch hands had obviously taken it upon himself to fix the fence. Whoever it was had stripped down to the waist and his shirt was hanging down from about the waistband of his jeans. No wonder. The day had turned out to be unseasonably warm and, worse, humid.

She could see sweat glistening along the ranch hand's muscular back as she drove closer. She couldn't recall any of the men who were left on the ranch being built that well—

Because they weren't, she realized as the man, obviously hearing the car approach, turned around from the fence.

Cole returned her stare with a lazy smile curving his mouth. Good though his back view was, the view from the front was astonishingly superior to it. A layer of perspiration glistened along his bare chest. His abdominal muscles appeared to have been chiseled out of rock.

He'd always been handsome, but for the life of her, she didn't remember his chest looking so damn good, Ronnie thought.

The inside of her mouth had turned to cotton, making it exceedingly difficult to form any audible words. She took a second to pull herself together. A second during which Cole seemed to be enjoying himself.

It was as if he could read her every thought. She did her best to look disinterested. It was damn near impossible.

"You're back early," he commented when she drew close enough to hear him.

Ronnie pulled up almost next to him and got out. "Early?" she echoed. "In comparison to what?"

How did he know when she was supposed to get back? How did he even know she'd been gone? Wasn't the man supposed to be in town, sheriffing?

"Your dad told me you were going to visit Wayne in the hospital." Stripping off his gloves, Cole reached for the bottle of water he had on the ground beside the fence and then paused as he took a very long gulp of water.

Ronnie could feel her throat tightening just watching him drink.

"Can I have some of that?" she asked, hating that she had to. Knowing if she didn't, she'd wind up croaking out her words like some octogenarian on her last legs.

"Sure." He held out the bottle to her as he wiped his forehead with the back of his other hand.

Ronnie found that she not only had to remind herself to breathe, she also had to struggle to draw her eyes away from his incredibly appealing upper torso. The latter was far from easy.

Addressing the air just past Cole's left ear, she murmured, "Thank you." Taking the water bottle from him, she quickly started drinking.

"Hey, careful," he cautioned her. "I don't want you drowning on me." Cole said it with such a straight face that for a moment she thought he was serious. Until she saw the grin. "I know you've been away in the big city all these years and forgot a lot of stuff about living out here, but you really shouldn't be driving around without bringing along some water," he told her. "You break down here, it's gonna be a while before someone comes along to help you out. On a hot day like today, that could really be murder. I really wouldn't want to come across you all shriveled up inside your car."

The need to argue was all but acute. Still, she forced the urge back. Cole was right in what he was saying. She just didn't like being reminded of that, or treated like some damn brainless tourist who didn't have sense enough to come in out of the rain. Or the unexpected hot sun.

"Guess I just got out of the survival mode habit,"

she said with a careless shrug meant to terminate the conversation.

It didn't.

"Out here that could be dangerous," Cole told her seriously. This time there was no smile at the end of the sentence.

She really *hated* being lectured. "You made your point," she bit off, then reined herself in for a second time. "What are you doing out here, anyway?" she asked. "I mean, besides sweating."

And looking good enough to eat, she couldn't help adding silently. Was he always going to have this effect on her? Was her stomach always going to tighten like a drying piece of leather? Didn't people eventually get over feeling like that about someone? So then why wasn't she?

"I decided to take today off," he told her. He went back to working a rotting board loose so he could replace it. "I left Tim in charge and I'm around if something happens he can't handle. But I needed some time off and Tim needed to find out that he can take care of things on his own." He paused, spreading his hands wide. "See, a win-win situation."

Not from where she stood. From that position, she was swiftly losing ground—and control over her thoughts.

"Very altruistic of you," she commented with more than a touch of sarcasm. "That still doesn't explain what you're doing out here—" she gestured at a length of fence "—working. Most people don't opt to engage in this kind of tedious physical labor on their day off. They do fun things."

"What makes you think I'm not having fun?" he

asked, amused. For a moment, his mouth quirked, and then he became serious again. "I figured you were at least one man down, what with Wayne being in the hospital and your dad still just getting the full use of his legs back. So I thought I'd give you a hand." A hammer in his right hand, he pried the board loose and then looked at her significantly. "In case you've forgotten, that's what friends are for."

Needing something to do with her hands, Ronnie had started unloading the lengths of wood she'd brought out of the back of her father's Jeep.

Before she realized his intentions, Ronnie found Cole beside her. Elbowing her out of the way, he took out the rest of the boards. She pulled on her gloves and picked up a hammer and a box of nails.

"I haven't forgotten," she answered. She looked up at him. "And don't get me wrong, I'm grateful for everything you've done. Most of all, I'm grateful that you were the one who was first on the scene because you saved them."

"Anyone would have done the same thing," he reminded her.

Ronnie shook her head. "I'm not that sure. Stop being so damn modest," she ordered. "But the bottom line is that I'm here now and I can take over. You can go home and use the rest of your day off to do something that *you* want to do."

He made absolutely no move to either get into his truck or even stop what he was set to do. Applying the back of the hammer just so, he pried off another rotting board, then stepped back to keep it from falling on his foot.

"I am," he answered as he picked up another length of board.

Ronnie laughed shortly, shaking her head. Arguing with Cole was like trying to argue with a rock and win it over to her side. It just couldn't be done. "Nothing's changed," she told him. "You are as damn stubborn as ever."

Taking the brim of his hat, he pulled it a bit lower in order to keep the sun out of his eyes as he paused to study her. Stetson not withstanding, she could see humor in his eyes.

"Isn't that a little like the pot calling the kettle black?" he asked her.

"I wouldn't know," she replied coolly. "I haven't got any talking cookware."

Cole turned back to his work. "You know," Cole said as mildly as if he was just commenting on the weather, "nothing and no one ever made me as crazy as you could—and still do."

"If I make you so crazy," she challenged, "what are you doing here on my ranch, working on my fence?"

He spared her a glance over his shoulder, then went on working. "You know, I keep asking myself that same question."

"And what is it you answer yourself?" she asked.

Stopping, he turned around and looked at her for a very long moment. She could swear she could literally *feel* him looking. The entire area suddenly felt a little hotter to her.

"That I'd rather be here, being driven crazy by you, than anywhere else, without the added aggravation." He leaned a length of board against the fence as he began to pry away another broken section. "I guess that means I've got a problem."

If you do, I've got the same damn problem. But her expression didn't give her thoughts away. "I guess people would say that you do."

"I don't really care what other people say. Never have." He wasn't saying anything she didn't already know. And then his next question blindsided her. She never saw it coming and was definitely *not* prepared with an answer. "What do you say?" he asked.

There went her mouth again, Ronnie thought, annoyed with herself. Going drier than dust. She had a feeling that no amount of water would help.

She took a breath, as if to fortify herself. If she had a prayer of functioning, she needed to have him get dressed.

"I say that you'd better put your shirt on before the sun winds up blistering your delicate skin and it starts coming off in sections, like this rotting fence."

"You always did have a silver tongue," he commented wryly. The moment seemed to freeze and linger. Just when she was afraid that it would go on forever, Cole laughed. "There you go, always thinking of me," he said so drily that, once again, she wasn't sure if he was teasing or being serious.

Pulling his shirt out of his waistband, he shook the shirt out. But instead of putting it on right away the way Ronnie had requested—mandated, really—he bunched it up and began to wipe the sweat off his chest.

It was one hell of a hypnotic sight. "What are you doing?" she finally managed to ask.

The answer was a simple one. "I'm so wet there's no way this shirt is going on unless I dry off." He held the shirt out to her. "Here, mind doing my back for me? I can't reach it."

She took the shirt from him and steeled herself. He was doing this on purpose, she thought. Well, if he thought that this was going to have her crumbling to her knees in anticipation, he had another damn think coming. "Sure," she told him. "I can do that."

But not without feeling hotter all over myself.

Drying off his sculpted back was as close to an out-of-body experience as she'd had in a very long time. Almost never, really. The very last time she'd felt even close to this was that last night she'd spent in Redemption. With Cole.

The night Christopher had been conceived.

She rubbed the length of his back hard. "Here," she said, thrusting the shirt back at him. "I'm done."

Cole's eyes held hers. His mouth curved slowly at her last words. She could almost *feel* his smile unfurling. And as it did, the pit of her stomach contracted. "Whatever you say, Ronnie."

Her pulse raced. They weren't talking about something as minor as drying his back anymore.

Chapter Twelve

"Feel free to pitch in," Cole told her offhandedly, as if he was the one in charge and not the other way around. "Most likely, the work'll go faster if two of us are going at it. Unless, of course," he theorized, glancing in her direction, "it's getting too hot for you out here."

He thought he could scare her off, she realized. Well, he was in for a surprise. She wasn't that innocent, smart-mouthed kid she'd once been.

Ronnie drew herself up to her full five-foot-four height. "I can put up with the heat if you can."

Her own words echoed back to her. She could almost *feel* the chip on her shoulder. Except that she knew he really could outlast her. Cole had worked on a ranch long before he'd taken on this new mantle of town sheriff. She had worked on a ranch, too, before she'd left to start another life in Seattle. The difference between them was that she'd never felt dedicated about the work. To her it had always been just a way to help her father out, a chore to get over with as fast as possible so that she could move on.

For Cole it *was* something else. More like a statement, an almost loving assertion that this was the life he would have chosen for himself without any hesitation if it had remained exclusively up to him. He wasn't without ambition. His was just a different type from hers.

His ambitions revolved around being the best at what he did. Quietly, without fanfare, for his own satisfaction, not for any kind of outside reinforcement or accolades. He didn't live and die by other people's assessment of him. That wasn't the kind of man that Cole was.

There weren't many men around like Cole. He was in a class all his own.

It only stood to reason that by now some enterprising young woman living in Redemption would have snapped him up. But no one had. If so, her father or his mother would have mentioned it by now if for no other reason than to make small talk.

"Why aren't you married?" Ronnie suddenly asked him as she threw down another length of wood she'd gotten from the back of her Jeep.

His eyes swept over her before he went on with what he was doing. "I had someone in mind once, but she took off on me."

Ronnie blew out an impatient breath. "Besides that," she pressed pointedly. "Wasn't there ever anyone else?" He was far too good-looking for there not to have been.

The jealousy at the very thought of that, of Cole with someone else, making love with someone else, came bolting out of the shadows, sharp and prickly, all but taking her breath away. She wasn't accustomed to that feeling and she didn't like it.

Jealousy spiked higher as she listened to his very next words.

"I got engaged to Cyndy Foster a while back," Cole told her, displaying no more emotion than he would have if he had recited all the things he'd had to eat in the last month.

Ronnie almost dropped the hammer in her hand. "Cyndy Foster?" she echoed, struggling not to appear stunned.

They'd all gone to school together. Cyndy had been in their small graduating class. She vividly remembered Cyndy, who had been one of the school's cheerleaders. Back then, Cyndy's hair had been too blond and, in her estimation, her clothes had been a size too tight. Half the guys in high school would have given their right arm just to go out with her.

Cole stopped working to look at her. He was mildly amused by the way Ronnie had said the other woman's name. "Yes. What?" he questioned. "She doesn't meet with your approval?"

Ronnie shrugged carelessly. "Not my business to approve or disapprove." She paused, knowing she wasn't going to be able to work if he didn't tell her why he wasn't still engaged—or married. Knowing, too, that he wouldn't tell her unless she asked him. She held out all of ten seconds before the question finally burst out of her.

"So, what happened?" she asked. "You didn't marry her, did you?"

Oh, God, did that sound as hopeful to him as it did to her own ears? She didn't mean it to, even though a cloud of disappointment waited to descend—depending on what his answer was.

Had he married Cyndy and then divorced her?

"No," Cole answered after a beat, "I didn't marry her. We were engaged for a year and a half, but it didn't seem right, marrying someone when part of me was somewhere else," he said matter-of-factly. "Cyndy deserved better than that." He laughed softly to himself. "When I told her that, she broke it off."

Cole shrugged. It was all in the past now and he wanted to leave it that way. He should have never gotten engaged to the other woman in the first place. It had happened because he'd thought that would be a way to finally get over Ronnie. He realized now that he never would be over her. Not entirely. He'd resigned himself to that.

"She's better off that way," he added after a beat.

She knew him, instinctively knew that Cole had orchestrated it so that Cyndy would be the one to break off the engagement, enabling the other woman to save face and get the opportunity to tell her friends that she'd been the one to end the relationship.

But for now, Ronnie kept her theory to herself. Obviously Cole didn't want to be prodded. "Sorry to hear that."

He raised his eyes to hers and paused, his hammer suspended in midair. "Are you?"

Why was it he could always see right through her? "Okay, I'm not sorry to hear that," she admitted, giving up the pretense. After another few seconds had gone by, she told him with certainty, "But Cyndy wouldn't have made you happy."

Ronnie was probably right, he thought. Still, he

pointed out one glaring difference between her and the former cheerleader. "Maybe not, but at least she wanted to try."

Okay, she needed to have this out with him, Ronnie thought. He deserved it after everything that had happened. "Cole, I'm sorry about the way things ended. I'm sorry I just ran out that way. But I knew that if I'd said anything to you about it, if I told you that I *had* to do this, you would have talked me into staying."

"And would that have been so bad?" he asked her quietly.

She could feel helpless, angry tears sting her eyes. Damn it, she wasn't going to cry about this. He wasn't going to make her cry. She'd done the right thing—for both of them. *And* for Christopher, too, once she'd realized that she was pregnant.

"For me, yes," she retorted firmly. "At the time, I couldn't stay. I would have felt horribly trapped and resentful."

"At the time," he repeated. Did that mean she'd changed her mind? Had the lure of the city worn off for her? "And now?"

That was an unfortunate choice of phrasing, Ronnie thought. She wasn't in the mood to get sucked into an argument.

"And now I have to get this fence finished. There's a whole list of things waiting for me to get to. Wayne's doctor is keeping him at the hospital a little longer because he's worried Wayne will start to push himself too hard once he's home. On top of that, if I have a prayer of getting that payment from Bart Walker, I've got to have the quarter horses checked out one last time before we get them ready to be sold."

She was throwing up a smoke screen. It wasn't the first time. "Still trying to lose me in the shuffle?" Cole asked.

Ronnie tossed her head, dismissing his question. She avoided looking at him. "I don't know what you're talking about."

The hell she didn't.

Dropping the hammer he'd been holding, Cole crossed to her so quickly, she didn't even realize what was happening until he was right there, his hands on her arms.

His hold was gentle, but firm, meant to keep her in place as he talked.

"Tell me you don't feel anything for me, Ronnie," he challenged. "Look me in the eye and tell me you don't feel anything for me."

She couldn't do it and they both knew it. "Whether I feel anything or not isn't the issue."

"Then what is?" he demanded. "What the hell *is* the issue?"

They couldn't start walking down a road that still wouldn't lead them to the same destination. Especially after all this time. He had to see that. "We have different lives now, Cole. You're the sheriff here and I've got a career waiting for me in Seattle."

"And a man?"

She stared at him. "Excuse me?"

How much clearer could he make it? "Do you have someone in Seattle?" he asked, enunciating each word carefully.

It was an excuse. A way to end this. She knew that all she had to do was say yes and he would back off. He was too honorable not to. But that would mean lying to him.

Skirting around the truth was one thing, but outright lying didn't sit well with her. She couldn't bring herself to do it, even if it did ultimately save her some grief.

She chose an evasive reply. "Not anyone right now," she told him.

"Right. Christopher's father," he naturally assumed. The way she had worded it had him drawing his own conclusion. "He's still in the picture."

Oh, God, Cole, there's no right way to tell you the truth. She looked away. "No, not really."

"Fakely?" he asked sarcastically.

He was still holding on to her. Angry, upset, Ronnie tried to yank away and found she couldn't. His hold was too strong. But then, she already knew that.

Frustrated, she cloaked herself in her anger. "Look, if you want to help, help. If you don't, then go. But either way, damn it, let go of me!" she demanded.

"You don't think I would if I could?" he fired back, his emotions breaking through. They were running just as high as hers were.

Cole had no idea how he went from point A to point B. It was almost as if those emotions that he had kept under control had just staged their own jailbreak and then took over the very prison that had incarcerated them for so long. One second he and Ronnie were shouting into each other's faces, the very next second, he was kissing that same face. Kissing her for all he was worth.

And she was kissing him back with enough fervor to set an iceberg on fire.

Oh, God, she had missed this, Ronnie thought, sinking into the sensation his lips created for her. Missed this, craved this.

Wanted this.

That taste she'd had the other afternoon, in the doorway of the boarded-up bakery, only served to remind her how celibate and deprived she'd been these past six years.

Because her knees had gone weak and threatened to buckle beneath her, rather than pushing him away, Ronnie threaded her arms around Cole's neck to keep from crumbling as well as to strengthen the connection.

Leaning her body into his as the kiss flowered and consumed her seemed to be merely a natural progression. Everything within her sang. It was as if she'd finally come home. Cole had been her first love and her first lover.

He was also her only lover because there had been no one since she'd given birth to Christopher. All her emotions were focused on the son that she'd had and adored.

Over the past six years she had managed to talk herself into accepting a life without romance, without intimate male-female interaction of any sort. To talk herself into believing that she didn't need that part of life to be happy. But all it had taken was just the smallest of connection with Cole to show her just how wrong she could be. And to show her how very incomplete she'd been until this very moment.

Even as the power behind his kiss fed her, Ronnie could *feel* the fire within her very core consuming her, begging for more. Desire seized her in its grip, ripping away her common sense and leaving behind a trail of ragged, raw and throbbing emotions. She ached for him.

As if reading her mind, Cole ran his hands along her body. They felt wonderful as strong fingers caressed every curve, every dip. She raked her own hands over his body, as if to assure herself that he was really here with her now and not just another one of her dreams. The initial years without him had been hard on her. She'd dream of him incessantly, filling her dormant nights with him even as she wasn't able to fill her days.

But this was no dream.

Cole was real. His body was hard beneath her touch. Hard and demanding. She felt the pull as her body longed to be possessed by his.

With the crystal blue sky above and a carpet of grass beneath her, she ripped away the cloth barriers that kept him from her. All the while, her mouth went questing over him, over his face, his neck, his upper torso, singeing him with the contact, needing more.

Cole groaned as desire filled him. The control that had kept him functioning, had kept him sane all these years, had cracked badly under this last assault. His resolve was no match for the desire that had remained trapped within him for so long. That now soared out of his every pore.

Once released, he could only follow its lead, availing himself of the opportunity that had suddenly opened up before him and presented itself at his feet. The taste of her skin as he pulled the layers of clothing away from her was tantalizingly tempting and sweet.

He wanted to be everywhere at once, touch everything at once, kiss everything at once.

The excitement that throbbed through him was at a level that he'd never experienced before, not even that first time with Ronnie. It was as if he felt that if he ceased going at this breakneck speed, he wouldn't be allowed to go at all. Something would happen to derail this. But as much as his body begged him not to stop, to take what was before him, he couldn't continue without knowing that she wanted this as much as he did.

Struggling harder than he had ever struggled before, Cole pulled himself back and searched her face. Looking for an answer he didn't quite see in her eyes.

Bereft, afraid, confused, Ronnie looked at him questioningly. "What's wrong?"

Nothing was wrong yet—and he wanted to keep it that way. For her if not for himself. "Ronnie, are you sure?" he asked.

He was being considerate. If she hadn't lost her heart to him already, this would have done it. "Oh, God, Cole, this is no time for a debate," she cried impatiently. Sealing her mouth to his, she sealed both their fates then and there.

Cole made love to her with a zeal that took him by surprise.

It didn't surprise her. Nothing about this man could surprise her. It could only thrill her.

They sank down onto the velvety green grass carpet, aware only of the heat that radiated from both their bodies, a heat that threatened to burn them to cinders unless they joined together and became one.

Pulse throbbing throughout him in double time, his lips taking hers over and over again, Cole threaded his fingers through hers. Holding her eyes captive with his own, he drove himself into her very core.

The heat and tempo increased, being driven up to a height that neither of them had expected or ever experienced before.

The rhythm in his head drove him, as did her response. In a world all their own, they went faster and faster until the summit had been captured.

Embracing her and holding her to him for all he was worth, Cole absorbed every sensation that thundered through his veins. Absorbed it and shared it with Ronnie, because, even though he couldn't express it, she was all things to him.

And always would be.

Cole continued to hold her even as the crescendo their lovemaking had created died away and faded into the shadows.

The urgency slowly left him. The desire did not.

Cole knew that no matter what happened after this, no matter where life might take each of them, the desire for Ronnie would always be there, always be a part of him. He knew he needed to make his peace with that. In time, he would.

He exhaled slowly, as if to empty himself of the force that had driven him. He might as well have made a wish to grow wings and fly. It wasn't about to happen. Not in this lifetime.

"I've missed you, Ronnie," he whispered against her temple, curtailing the very strong desire to stroke her hair.

He felt Ronnie smile as she turned into him. "I noticed."

He tucked her in against him just a wee bit closer. They would have to get dressed, but that could wait for a while. He just wanted to enjoy the sensation of having her here next to him like this. Naked and his. "Glad that I didn't bore you."

She laughed softly to herself at the improbable notion. "You, Cole, could never bore me. Even if all you did was sit by the window, reading the newspaper."

It was an odd scene to conjure up. To his best recollection, he'd never sat by a window, reading a newspaper. "Nice to know your expectations aren't high."

Ronnie raised herself up on her elbow, looking down into his face, her naked body brushing unselfconsciously against his. She ran the tip of her forefinger along his lips.

"On the contrary," she told him. "My expectations are very high. And I might as well admit to myself that only you can live up to them."

When had longing turned to love? he wondered. Or had he always loved her like this? He couldn't remember the exact moment, or even the day that it had happened. Only that it seemed always to be a part of his life.

"Careful what you say in the heat of the moment," he warned her, running the back of his hand along her cheek. Exciting himself with the thoughts that filled his head. "I've got an excellent memory."

She laughed again, even more softly this time than before. "You're right. No more talking," she declared with finality.

And before Cole had a chance to ask her if that meant she wanted to get back to repairing the fence that was only halfway done at this point, Ronnie answered his unspoken question by sealing his mouth with her own.

He drew his head back for a moment and grinned at her, his eyes sliding appreciatively over the dip of her waist.

"Who am I to argue?" And with that, he kissed her back—and lost himself in her all over again.

It was a long while before they had a chance—or the strength—to get back to working on the fence.

Chapter Thirteen

This wasn't supposed to have happened.

The sentence throbbed in Ronnie's brain as she upbraided herself. She'd been doing that, telling herself that she was making a grave mistake, at least once a day—if not more—ever since that idyllic interlude in the field by the fence with Cole the week before.

Because, she knew, the moment it *had* happened, she had opened up a floodgate of emotions. It was like having a suitcase that had been packed to capacity and then jammed shut. When she'd inadvertently opened it, there'd been an explosion that had sent the suitcase's contents flying out all over the place. To even contemplate returning the items into the suitcase again was hopeless. It just couldn't be done.

One taste of heaven made her loath to walk away

and once more settle for what had been, until that delicious moment, her life.

Making love with Cole just made her want to do it all over again.

And again and again.

She had become completely insatiable. The very nature of that required, at the very least, a readjustment of her own self-image. She hadn't realized, until it was there, staring her right in the face, that there was this other side of her—this woman who, the more she got, the more she craved.

Who knew?

With the enthusiasm of the teenagers they had once been, she and Cole found creative, inspired ways to be together.

Stealing moments.

Stealing interludes.

And always, always, she found herself wanting more. Looking forward to the next encounter, the next excuse to be with Cole.

To make love with Cole.

What in God's name would she do when she had to return to Seattle? Eventually, the horses would be turned over to their new owner, her brother, who was coming home Friday, would be back on his feet, ready to get back to work again, and she would be free to go back home.

Home.

The word echoed in her brain. *Was* that home to her? That high-rise apartment that she and Christopher lived in, in the shadow of the Space Needle, the one that she had been so excited about when she found it and moved in without a stick of furniture to put into it. Was that really home to her now?

Or was this home again? The ranch, Redemption. Cole.

Ronnie leaned against the kitchen sink, shaking her head as she realized that she'd been standing there, staring at the water flowing from the faucet, the glass she'd come to fill still empty in her hand. What was going on with her? Wasn't she supposed to have all the answers by now, not just all the questions?

Oh, God, she'd never felt so confused before.

"You look as if you've got the weight of the world on your shoulders, honey. Something the matter?"

The quietly voiced inquiry came from Midge James. The older woman had walked into the kitchen, no doubt looking for her.

"No," Ronnie answered a little too quickly as she snapped to attention.

Get a grip on yourself, Ronnie, she silently ordered, annoyed that she'd let her guard down like this. She'd been doing that a lot lately, letting her guard down and thinking on two levels. Arguing with herself—and getting nowhere.

"It's not about any bad news about Wayne, is it?" Midge gently prodded.

"No," Ronnie repeated, this time with feeling. "It's nothing, really."

Rather than accept her answer, Midge remained standing in front of her, thoughtfully regarding her expression for what felt like an extra long moment. And then, in purely motherly fashion, Cole's mother cupped her cheek and said, "You know, sometimes it helps to talk things out. Maybe I can even help," she offered. "Telling me certainly wouldn't hurt."

Want to bet?

Ronnie forced a smile to her lips. It fluttered weakly before dying. There was no use in pretending that everything was fine. Cole's mother seemed to see right through her.

"Nobody can help, Midge," Ronnie replied. "This is something I have to deal with on my own. But thanks for the offer."

Midge stepped back, nodding before gently asking Ronnie, "Are you trying to figure out a way to tell Cole?"

Though she gave no outward indication, Ronnie could feel herself freezing inside. Just what *did* his mother know? She would have staked her life that Cole hadn't said anything to anyone about their being intimate with one another again.

Ronnie pressed her lips together, looking for a way out. "Tell Cole what?" she asked innocently.

Midge watched her for a long moment, as if debating whether or not she should say anything further, and, if so, how much she should say. Where was the line between interested party and meddlesome mother?

The wide shoulders squared just a tad before she plunged in. "That Christopher is his."

And just like that, Ronnie felt her orderly world being blown to smithereens.

"What?" Ronnie cried, surprised she didn't croak out the word.

Midge leveled a penetrating look at her. "Do you really want me repeating that?" Cole's mother asked her quietly.

"No! Of course not!" The response had been automatic. It wasn't what someone with a clear conscience would have said. She cleared her throat, as if that could somehow explain away her rudeness. "I mean…you're wrong. About Christopher," she added with feeling, then released a long breath before asking, "But just out of curiosity, what makes you say that?"

The expression on Midge's wide, amiable face was patient, sympathetic. And maybe just a little amused at the deception.

"I have eyes, honey. And, don't forget, Cole was my little boy just as Christopher is yours. Your son's the spitting image of Cole at that age. Just looking at that little boy running around the ranch brought back so many fond memories of when Cole had been a little boy, into absolutely everything. He had to be all but tied down for bed each night."

"Lots of kids look alike at that age," Ronnie pointed out evasively.

"Very true," Midge agreed, inclining her head. She gave no sign that she intended to continue to argue the point. Instead, she offered Ronnie a warm smile. "Like I said, if you need to talk, I'm around."

And with that, armed with the cup of tea she had come for, Midge began to walk back toward the family room.

"He'd never forgive me," Ronnie said suddenly to her back. Midge turned around slowly, her body language indicating that she was listening and deliberately keeping her silence unless asked to speak. Ronnie appreciated that. "If I said anything to him about Christopher now, after all this time had gone by—after not letting him know right away—I know Cole would never bring himself to forgive me."

Midge's tone indicated otherwise. "A woman has her reasons for doing what she does."

Ronnie stared at her, her eyes wide. She had to concentrate not to let her jaw drop. "My God, you're being awfully understanding about all this."

Midge dismissed the compliment. "Wouldn't do me any good to rant and rave now, would it? Most likely, if I did that, it would drive you away and I surely wouldn't want to have that happen." She smiled warmly at Ronnie from across the room. "I've always liked you, Veronica." She crossed back into the kitchen and next to Ronnie. "Now you've given me one more reason to like you."

Ronnie was leery of what was coming next. "And that is?"

"You've given me a grandson," she said simply. "And I think you've underestimated Cole. Oh, he'll be madder than a wet hen for a while, but eventually, he'll come around. In case it escaped your notice, my son loves you, Veronica."

She didn't believe it for a minute. "Did you know that he was engaged to Cyndy Foster?" she asked, as if that countered anything that Midge could tell her or bring up.

Midge laughed shortly. "The whole town knew. Cyndy saw to that. The important thing for you to take away from that is that when it came right down to it, Cole couldn't go through with it. Couldn't marry one woman when his heart clearly belonged to another."

"He told you that?" she asked as her pulses began doing their own little dance.

"Didn't have to. It was right there in his eyes. Still is."

The woman didn't look as if she was drifting on her own cloud. But Ronnie still couldn't get herself to believe what Midge was telling her. "I don't see it," Ronnie protested.

"Then look closer," the older woman advised. "Look, why don't you stop being the brave little soldier and just tell Cole how you feel about him? You might try leading with that before you say anything to him about Christopher."

Ronnie desperately tried to maintain her facade. "No offense, but what makes you say that I feel anything for him?"

Her smile was tolerant, her manner indicating that there was no lying to her. "Like I said, I have eyes, Veronica. And I've seen the way you look at Cole when you think that no one's paying attention. Don't look so worried," she added quickly. "I'm not going to say anything to Cole. Sons hate having their mothers butting into their lives. You'll learn that soon enough," she predicted with a bittersweet smile. "Somewhere around when Christopher turns twelve. Thirteen if you're particularly lucky. At thirteen all boys claim to have arrived on this earth through spontaneous generation—mothers were definitely not involved in the process. They continue to maintain that for years on end. It's a rare son who gives up that myth by the time he hits twenty."

The liquid-blue eyes suddenly looked over Ronnie's head. A wide smile moved over her thin lips.

"Ah, speak of the devil," Midge declared warmly. "We were just talking about you, Cole," she said to her son as he came in from outside and joined them. "Jed Winchell still vowing to be sober?" she asked, referring to the man who Cole periodically brought into the jail so that Winchell could sleep off a bender before going home to his less than understanding wife.

"Been close to a month now," Cole said with a nod. He looked from his mother to Ronnie. "Why am I the devil?" he asked.

"You're not, darling," Midge said cheerfully, patting his cheek to assure him that he was no such thing. "I didn't raise you that way. I was just telling Veronica how you always come through for everyone and how proud I am of you."

He knew there had to be more. His mother sounded way too innocent just now. What was she up to? And had she dragged Ronnie into it? She was the most level-headed of mothers, but right now, she was making him suspicious. "And that's why I'm the devil?"

"It's just an expression, dear." She turned to face him completely. "Just an expression." Midge shook her head as she regarded her only child. "You really do need to loosen up a little, Cole. Otherwise you're going to wear yourself out right before my eyes. Can't have that, you know."

He grinned at that, sending a significant look toward Ronnie. If he wore out, his loosening up wouldn't reverse the process.

Ever since they had rediscovered one another last week, they had been making love at least once, if not twice—or more—a day. It was what he focused on these days, as well as looked forward to. He got to the point where he needed contact with her the same way he needed air. To sustain himself. He felt he would just expire if he did without it.

The fact that he was dependent on Ronnie for anything bothered him to no end. He didn't like that he was so tangled up inside because of her. It also bothered him that he couldn't just take it or leave it when it came to Ronnie, to making love with her. Whether he liked it or not, he couldn't do without her.

The more they did make love, the more he wanted to. It made thinking ahead by more than a day particularly difficult. He knew better than to put himself on the line and ask her to stay.

He'd gone that route before and it had all but ripped him apart when he found her gone.

He wanted her to stay—there was no point in pretending that he didn't—but the decision had to be hers to make, not his to request. Only two things he knew for sure. That he was not about to apply any sort of pressure on Ronnie. And that this waiting for her, wondering what she was going to do, was killing him slowly by inches.

"I'm not wearing out, Ma. I'm fine," he told her. "I just stopped by to ask Ronnie if she wanted to go to Bill Haines's barn raising this Saturday." His eyes shifted to Ronnie. "That's the day after tomorrow in case you've lost track," he added.

"I haven't lost track," Ronnie assured him. Especially not since she was bringing Wayne home tomorrow. "Barn raising?" she echoed, suddenly realizing what he was saying. "They still do that out here?" she marveled. It felt like something from another era, although she could remember there being more than one instance where all the neighbors got together to help out and build a barn—or stable—for one of their own. That all seemed like a whole other lifetime ago.

"Times being what they are, can't think of a better way to save a little money and have a party to boot than holding a good old-fashioned barn raising," he answered her. "I figure we could all go," he continued, looking at his mother before turning his attention back to Ronnie. "Might be a good thing for your dad, too," he pointed out. "Amos's been cooped up here for a while now. Do him good to see a few friendly faces. Other than your own, of course," he clarified, glancing at his mother pointedly.

It wasn't lost on him that his mother seemed to light up a little more each time she was in the same room as Ronnie's father. Amos McCloud was an honorable, hardworking, decent man and he had no problem with his mother finding a little happiness with him.

Everyone deserved to find happiness, he thought, looking now at Ronnie. Including him.

Ronnie laughed, surrendering. There was no point in objecting. She didn't mind the thought of visiting wholesale with some of the people she'd grown up with. Besides, if they were out among their neighbors, she wouldn't be able to give in to the urges that seemed to be with her now, night and day.

"You always did have a silver tongue," she recalled, grinning at Cole. "Maybe you should have made a run for state senator instead of just the sheriff."

"Being 'just the sheriff' is as far as I want to go up the public servant ladder," Cole told her, echoing the phrase she'd uttered so carelessly. He was teasing her because he had taken no offense, knowing she had intended none. He watched her now, obviously waiting for an answer. "So is that yes? You'll come to the barn raising?"

"That's yes." And then she laughed. "As if you had any doubts."

Maybe not exactly doubts, but he had never counted chickens until well after all the eggs had hatched. "With you, Ronnie, I take nothing for granted."

Hearing that should have gone a long way to reassure her that she was still free to return to Seattle. That he wouldn't try to keep her here because he knew she was her own person. But the bottom line was that it *didn't* reassure her. She couldn't begin to explain why, even to herself. So she focused on something she didn't need to explain or explore. The invitation. "It really is going to be a barn raising?" she asked.

"Barn raising, dance, barbecue, you name it, it's going to be taking place at Bill's ranch this Saturday," he told her. "All day. Bill plans to put everyone to work, then reward them."

"Reward?" she echoed. Had neighbors started paying one another for services rendered since she'd left?

He nodded. "Man makes a mean barbecue chicken. Makes you feel like you've died and gone to heaven, just eating at his table."

Ronnie nodded. The memories all came back to her. "I remember."

"Nice to know," he said. "I can stop by at eight on Saturday, take you, your dad and Christopher to Bill's place, get you started working early."

"I'm going to work?" the high-pitched voice asked, confused, as Christopher bounced into the kitchen at the tail end of what Cole was saying.

"You, too, little man," Cole told the boy, stooping down to his level. He restrained himself from ruffling the boy's hair although the urge to do so was almost always present. The boy had taken a shine to him. And it was mutual, Cole thought fondly. "It's going to be a barn raising."

Wheat-colored eyebrows scrunched together over Christopher's close-to-perfect little nose. "I'm going to be helping pick up a barn?" he asked, giving it careful consideration. And then his face brightened, his eyebrows parted company and, unfurrowing his brow, he grinned. "Cool."

Laughing, Cole couldn't resist scooping the boy up into his arms. As he rose up, he tucked Christopher against his hip the way he'd seen mothers do with their younger children. The boy was small for his age, Cole had already noted more than once, but that was of no consequence. Christopher would fill out.

Just like he had.

He could remember despairing at the boy's age, worried that he would remain peanut-sized, a nickname his father had pinned to him without realizing how demoralizing it was. To his overwhelming relief, he'd shot up over six inches the summer between his sophomore and junior year. His father was forced to stop calling him "Peanut."

"Yeah, 'cool,'" Cole agreed.

Because he was looking at the boy in his arms, Cole missed the look his mother exchanged with Ronnie as both women took in the scene of man and boy and pressed it to their hearts.

For different reasons.

Chapter Fourteen

As she got ready to go pick up her brother from the hospital, Ronnie debated asking Rowdy to come with her. She decided against it despite the fact that she might need a hand with getting Wayne into the truck. He claimed to be fine, but she knew he was still weak. She didn't want him exerting himself needlessly because he was thickheaded and macho.

But she instinctively knew that Wayne would be less than thrilled if she brought the ranch foreman along with her to help out. A visit from any of the men who now, or at any point in the past, worked on the ranch, was one thing, but having to possibly lean on a man who was, after all, the hired help for physical support was another matter entirely.

She didn't need to be told that the possibility of such a scenario offended her brother's sensibilities and troubled his sense of the natural order of things. Hired hands were never put into the position of strength if that position directly affected their boss and cut into the whole power hierarchy thing that men seemed to have going for them, Ronnie thought, shaking her head. Even being justifiably weak because of surgery and prolonged bed rest was not enough of an excuse to have Rowdy propping him up. It all had to do with ego and pride.

And they said women were complicated.

As she stopped in the kitchen to get a drink before she left, Ronnie saw Midge. The other woman was in the middle of baking up a storm. Her father had a weakness for her cinnamon apple pie, especially with its hint of Amaretto.

After satisfying her thirst, Ronnie turned to the other woman and said, "I'm going to Helena to pick up Wayne from the hospital. I've got a feeling I might need a hand getting him squared away in the truck. Got any suggestions?"

Midge paused, her friendly face cheerfully dotted with a smidge of flour. "You mean like who to take with you to help if you need it?"

"Yes," Ronnie answered.

The other woman eyed her as if the answer was self-evident. "Why don't you ask Cole to come with you? I'm sure he'd be glad to lend a hand."

Would Cole see it that way? Or would he view it as an imposition on his time? Granted they had become intimate, but she had no idea what the ground rules were between them. No promises had been made, no requests, either. Six years ago, he'd told her he wanted her to stay, that he wanted to build a life together. Now, while he made her blood sing in her veins, he never made any reference to their future together, or even *if* he thought they *had* a future together. For all she knew, he'd taken it for granted that she was going back to Seattle once Wayne was home and back on his feet.

Why shouldn't he? You said as much, remember? she upbraided herself.

That didn't change the fact that she still had no idea how to read Cole. Her mind insisted that nothing had changed since the last time she'd been in Redemption. Her gut told her otherwise.

How could it not have changed? They were both six years older, both had gone separate ways to forge a life for themselves and there was a child now, a product of the first night they had spent together.

Yeah, a child he knows nothing about. At least, not in the way that it counts. Nice going, Ronnie, she silently mocked herself. *This is a disaster waiting to happen. A disaster of your own making.*

"Any particular reason you're not asking Cole?" Midge finally asked when she made no response to the initial suggestion.

Ronnie shrugged evasively. "He's the sheriff. I don't want to bother him. He's probably busy."

"Any reason that actually makes sense?" Midge specified. She raised her eyes to Ronnie's face, pinning her in place as she waited for an answer.

Ronnie sighed. Cole's mother was right. Wayne and Cole were friends. Wayne felt comfortable around him. That made Cole the likely choice.

Besides, no matter what did happen, it would all be over soon. The horses were being shipped out on Monday. Everything would be neatly tied up and paid off by the end of next week. There would be no real reason for her to stick around. She'd be free to go back to Seattle.

And away from Cole.

She bit her lower lip, trying to ignore the wave of loneliness that thought generated. She might as well avail herself of Cole's company as much as she could now. She had a lifetime of being without Cole looming ahead of her.

"I guess not," Ronnie finally admitted, answering Midge's innocent inquiry.

Finished making the pie crust and mixing together the filling, Midge turned her attention to the cookie dough she'd prepared earlier. Pinching off a piece, she rolled it between her fingers, then placed it on a cookie tray, smoothing out the uneven sphere until it was capable of rolling around on the table if she gave it a push. Especially after she gave it, and each cookie that followed, a dusting of powdered sugar.

"Good," she pronounced. "Glad you agree. Now give my son a call." It was almost a direct order. "I can give you his cell phone number if you don't already have it," Midge volunteered.

"No, I have it, thanks," Ronnie murmured, taking out her own phone.

Seeking a little privacy away from Midge, who actually gave no indication that she wanted to listen in on the exchange, Ronnie quickly pressed the numbers on the keypad.

Within less than a minute, she heard the phone on the other end being picked up. Her pulse instantly accelerated and she cursed herself for her adolescent reaction.

"Cole? Cole, this is Ronnie," she began, aware that she was talking a little too fast.

"No need to tell me," she heard him say. "I could always recognize your voice. What's up?" he asked amiably.

For a second, she went utterly blank. Why did the mere sound of his voice scramble her brain like this? What was the matter with her? She was a grown woman with a child to support and raise, not some air-headed teenager, daydreaming about the hunk in math class.

Taking a breath, she did her best to sound nonchalant—feeling anything but. "Are you busy?"

"Depends," he drawled into the phone.

This was a bad idea. She never liked putting herself on the line, asking for favors and leaving herself vulnerable. But she'd started this, which meant she was stuck now. She might as well see this through.

"On what?" she heard herself asking.

"On whether you consider talking to you as qualifying me to be busy." She heard him chuckle. The deep, rumbly sound undulated through her entire system. She was absolutely hopeless, Ronnie thought in disgust. "What do you need?" he asked her.

I need to start behaving like an adult. "I thought that if you weren't busy, you might come with me to pick Wayne up from the hospital. Doctor said he could come home today and he's chomping at the bit." Wayne had already called her twice, reminding her of his release and asking her to come as soon as possible.

"Oh, that's right, he's being released today, isn't he?"

Was it her imagination, or did that sound a trifle *too* innocent? She knew Cole—he hadn't forgotten. Cole *never* forgot anything. He had an amazing head for facts, figures and dates. If Cole didn't remember something, it wasn't worth remembering.

"Yes," she answered impatiently. "Look, if you have something else to do, that's okay. I can manage this by myself."

"Never doubted that you couldn't," he told her.

Now what was that supposed to mean? she wondered, feeling her temper flare. Reining it in, she was about to ask him what he meant by his comment, but before she could put that into words, she heard someone knocking.

"Hold on," she said into the wireless receiver. "There's someone at the door."

"Better open it, then," he agreed.

Now he was giving her permission to answer her own door? Just who the hell did he think he was?

The love of your life, an annoying little voice whispered in her head.

Already at the door, Ronnie yanked it open a little too fast.

And found herself looking up into Cole's face.

"You could have told me that you were standing on my doorstep," she said accusingly.

Cole walked in, grinning. "And miss the expression on your face just now? No way," he told her, more than a little amused.

Behind her, from within the house, she could hear a set of size three boots flying down the stairs and then hitting the wooden floor as Christopher came bounding over, drawn by the sound of Cole's voice.

"Hi, Sheriff!" the little boy all but crowed happily.

"Hi yourself, short stuff." Cole returned the boy's greeting, as well as the grin on Christopher's face.

"You gonna go to get Uncle Wayne, too?" the boy asked him.

Ronnie looked down at her son. "What do you mean,

'too'?" she repeated. She'd brought Christopher with her a couple of times when she'd gone to visit Wayne, as well as bringing her father. She thought it important that Wayne have contact with his family and that both her father and her son got to see Wayne. But this was different. She wanted to be in and out as quickly as possible. Having an entourage along would only get in the way. "You're staying here with Grandpa," she informed her son.

Christopher looked crestfallen. "Aw, Mom. I wanna go help Uncle Wayne walk."

She stared at the boy. Where had he picked that up from? It was obvious that she would have to be more careful what she said and where she said it. Christopher had apparently developed superhearing since they'd come to Redemption.

But before she could tell her son that she really needed him to remain here with his grandfather, Midge came to her rescue.

"Hey, Christopher, I'm going to need a cookie taster for the next batch of cookies I'm making. Know where I could find one?"

The boy's eyes instantly lit up. "Me," he declared, puffing up his very small chest. "I can help you. And Grandpa, too," he added brightly. "He'll taste cookies for you."

Midge struggled to suppress her grin. "But I thought you were going to the hospital with your mom," Midge said with the most serious face she could manage under the circumstances.

For a moment, Christopher appeared torn between the two choices. His expression was solemn as he looked from his mother to the offer he really didn't want to turn down.

Then he pronounced, "It's okay, she's got the sheriff with her. He can help. He's real strong. I saw his muscles," he confided, then lowered his voice as he added, "He let me touch them."

Midge glanced from Ronnie to her son and smiled. "Yes," she agreed easily, "your mom certainly does have the sheriff."

His eyes darted toward his mother, a warning look in them. Sometimes, his mother just went too far. But then, he supposed he couldn't fault her. She just wanted what most mothers wanted: to see their son or daughter married and surrounded with kids of their own.

Cole looked down at the animated boy in front of him. He'd never been that partial to children, but he had to admit that he'd taken to Ronnie's son. The boy was a regular crackerjack. And he'd be lying if he said that he didn't get a kick out of interacting with Christopher.

"Be sure to save me a few, kid," he instructed Christopher.

Delighted to be given the go-ahead by his hero, Christopher almost crowed, "You bet! A whole bunch," he promised with enthusiasm.

"Tell Uncle Wayne I'll play with him when he gets home!" Christopher piped up as his mother started to walk out of the kitchen.

"I'm sure that'll make him very happy," Ronnie told her son. She paused for a second to kiss Christopher goodbye. With an eye toward his hero, Christopher squirmed a little bit. Her little boy was growing up, she thought sadly. It really did happen much too fast. "Be good," she instructed.

"Take care of your grandpa and my mom while we're gone," Cole said to the boy.

Christopher beamed, then struggled to look serious and worthy of the responsibility he'd been awarded.

"I will, Sheriff," he promised solemnly.

"Good man," Cole told the little boy just before he followed Ronnie out of the kitchen and then out through the front door.

Once outside, Ronnie paused.

"Forget something?" Cole asked her.

These days, it felt as if she was constantly second-guessing herself. She really didn't care for the feeling. "I'm just wondering if I should bring my dad along."

"Why?" he asked. "Isn't that why I'm coming with you? Just how big do you think Wayne's gotten?"

She waved away his words. "That's not it. I just don't want my father to feel like I'm trying to exclude him."

Cole laughed quietly and shook his head. His truck was parked right out front and he approached it now, making the assumption that he was the one driving. Which was fine with him. On the way back, he figured that Ronnie would want to remain in the back of the extended cab with Wayne.

Cole laughed. "I think your dad would rather hang around my mother, supervising the baked goods coming out of the oven."

"Really." It wasn't a question but rather more of an expression of surprise. She didn't think that Cole was even aware of what had been going on.

"What? You didn't think I noticed?" Cole asked, amused. He would have to be blind to have missed the sparks between Amos and his mother. "My mother's sweet on your father, and from what I can see, he seems to be sweet on her."

Ushering Ronnie gently over toward the passenger side of his truck, he then rounded the front and got in behind the wheel. He waited for her to buckle up before turning his key in the ignition.

"The way I see it," he continued matter-of-factly, "it's just a matter of time before we become brother and sister."

"*Step*brother and *step*sister," Ronnie corrected, inserting the key prefix that he'd so cavalierly left out. "Otherwise it becomes something that would have pestilence and wrath being rained down on our heads—not to mention that we'd both probably wind up being turned into pillars of salt." That said, she stopped teasing. "You really think that your mother and my father would…?"

Her voice trailed off as she tried to find the right words. It was hard thinking of her father as having the same kind of feelings that haunted her.

"Do what we did out in the field? And in the barn and in the back of my truck, not to mention in—?"

She raised her hand to stop him. "Point made," she declared loudly. "And I was about to say, 'Get married,'" she informed him. "I really wasn't going for that kind of a visual."

Amused, Cole made his apologies. "Sorry. But yeah, to answer your question, I do. I think that they might get married. They're both intelligent people with a bit of life tucked under their belts. At their age they realize that everybody's got a limited amount of time assigned to them on this earth and if they're lucky enough to find someone they care about, someone who cares back, well then, why not grab that bit of happiness while they still can?" Cole glanced at her. "You have any objections to that?"

"To what? My father marrying your mother?" she asked to make sure they were talking about the same thing. Try as she might not to, she couldn't help drawing a parallel between their parents and them. She just hoped he wasn't doing the same thing. "No, no objections. I think it's great," she said honestly. "Your mom only lost your dad eighteen months ago. My mother's been gone for the last twenty-five years. That's a really long time for someone to be alone."

"He wasn't exactly alone," Cole pointed out. "He had you and Wayne for most of that time and he had— has," he corrected himself, "the ranch to run. The accident put him out of commission for a while, but he'll be back in the field again before long. Your dad's a rancher. Ranchers don't retire. They keep on working. It's in their blood."

She knew what he was trying to say, but he was wrong. "It's not the same thing," she pointed out. "Work keeps you busy, but it doesn't take the place of loving someone or being loved by them."

There was silence for a long moment. Cole turned his attention away from the long, desolate road that seemed to spread out to infinity before him. Instead, he looked at her.

"No," he agreed quietly, "it's definitely not the same thing. Not even close."

The tone of his voice made her a little uneasy, warning her that she might not like where this could go if she wasn't careful. Because if he asked her what she was afraid of, she wasn't sure what her answer would be. Confused, she wasn't sure what the right answer was in this case.

Was she supposed to follow her heart, or her brain?

When in doubt, Ronnie decided, change the subject. And she did.

Quickly.

They talked about Wayne and tomorrow's barn raising and everything else she could think of to put between them and the one topic she didn't feel up to discussing.

At least not yet.

And perhaps not at all. Because, more than anything, she admitted to herself, she was afraid that what he would say was *not* what she, in her heart of hearts, really wanted to hear.

It was better never to know than to know when it was the wrong answer.

Chapter Fifteen

Ronnie decided that going to the barn raising at the Haineses' ranch and seeing all his neighbors would do Wayne more good than harm. But first she made absolutely sure that she extracted a promise from her brother that he was would remain seated on the sidelines for the entire time they were there. Under no circumstances was he to join in the work.

To help out, Gene Haines said he and his oldest son, Rick, would bring an old armchair out of the house and have it waiting for Wayne on the back porch. That way he'd have a clear view of the event.

Still somewhat worried about how stubborn her brother could be, Ronnie also made Wayne promise to let her know the moment he started to feel tired. She was determined that he wasn't going to push himself too much. They would go home the second she saw him beginning to fade.

This was an entirely new experience for Wayne. He wasn't accustomed to being dictated to. He was always the one who made the rules. Grumbling, telling Ronnie that she was behaving like some power-crazed dictator, Wayne finally surrendered and gave her his word when, looking to Cole for backup, he found himself turned down and standing alone against his younger sister.

"Traitor," Wayne accused his friend, only half-kidding.

Like everything else, Cole took it in stride. "Hey, don't look at me. Ronnie'll have my head if I take your side. And right now, I'm betting she's a lot stronger than you are."

"She's also making more sense," Ronnie interjected, referring to herself in the third person, something that didn't go unnoticed by Wayne.

"See? What did I tell you? She's turned into a dictator. She even talks like one," Wayne pointed out as he eased himself into the front passenger seat of his truck. "Boy, give someone a little power—"

"Complain all you want, it doesn't change anything. Face it, boy, you're outnumbered," Amos told his son as he climbed into the truck behind him. Christopher was already in his seat, strapped in and impatient to get going.

Ronnie smiled to herself as she drove to the Haineses' ranch. For the first time since she'd arrived in Redemption, her father sounded like his old self. Things, she thought, were going to be all right. At least for them, she added as her thoughts shifted to Cole.

As far as her own life went, well, that continued to

be a very messy situation. But just for today, she was going to pretend that all was well there, too. Worrying about it wasn't going to change a thing. It would just make her waste what precious time she had left.

When they arrived at the ranch, Ronnie lost no time in getting her brother situated. The armchair was just where Mr. Haines had said it would be.

"Consider it your new throne," she teased.

"Don't feel right about not helping out," Wayne complained.

She kissed his cheek. "You can supervise," she told him. "God knows you were always good at that."

Cole and his mother had both already arrived. On the lookout for Ronnie and her family, the two made their way over a few minutes after the foursome had arrived. Christopher was the first to spot them and excitedly made the announcement to his mother—just before he ran up to Cole and launched himself into his hero's arms.

Cole carried Christopher as he crossed over to the rest of the McClouds. Ronnie couldn't help seeing how happy her son looked in his father's arms. How natural.

"I believe this is yours." Cole grinned at Ronnie as he put the boy down on the ground again. He nodded at Wayne and Amos. "Nice to see you all could make it."

"I'm not talking to you," Wayne said, pretending to still be annoyed.

Cole nodded. "I can live with that." Glancing toward Ronnie, he leaned over and whispered into her ear, "You realize that you look like the cat that swallowed the canary."

She was willing to bet any amount of money that Cole had no clue as to why she felt so happy. Most likely he thought it was because her family was attending this social function all together. That might have contributed to part of it, but watching Cole with their son was what brought a glow to her heart.

"Haven't the slightest idea what you're talking about," she said, playing along.

"Yeah, right."

She could feel his breath along her neck and did her best not to react—or at least not allow him to see her reaction. Although, after the last couple of weeks, she had a pretty damn good feeling that he knew he sent shivers up and down her spine.

"Shh," she shushed him. "Mr. Haines is about to speak."

Suppressing a grin, Cole kept his peace. Gene Haines, all four of his sons standing behind him, held up his hand to still the buzz coming from the various conversations that were going on. When the noise level had died down sufficiently, Haines told his friends and neighbors just how lucky and proud he was to have such good people around him he could rely on.

He went on to say several other things, as well, but Cole really wasn't paying attention. Standing beside Ronnie, her very essence filling his senses, he couldn't help thinking how lonely it would be once Ronnie and her son left. Not for the first time he wondered what he could legitimately do to keep Ronnie in Redemption a little while longer. Battles were won one inch at a time.

Finished with his halting speech, embarrassed that he had gotten so emotional, Gene Haines clapped his massive hands together and loudly declared, "All right, let's get to it!"

As everyone who'd come to help moved, almost en masse, toward where the new barn would be erected, Ronnie realized that Cole was still standing where he'd been when the rancher had started talking.

"Planning to take root?" she asked Cole, mildly amused.

Coming to, Cole realized she was talking to him. "What?"

Ronnie nodded toward his boots. "Your feet, they're not moving. Are you planning to take root?" she asked.

Cole frowned. "Very funny."

Confused, Christopher got in between his mother and his hero. He looked from one to the other. "No, it wasn't," he protested, confused.

"You're right," Cole agreed, slipping a protective hand on the boy's shoulder. "It's not. C'mon," he urged the boy. "Let's go build us a barn, Christopher."

Christopher lit up like the proverbial firecracker on the Fourth of July. "You bet!" he declared with enthusiasm.

Walking behind them, watching Christopher and Cole together, Ronnie felt her heart warming again. At the same time, she wished with every fiber of her being that she could somehow go back five years, back to the day that her son had been born. She would have sent Cole a note, telling him that he had a son and that she wanted nothing from him, she just wanted him to know about the boy.

If she could only have done that, then she'd be able to enjoy scenarios like this without enduring the guilt, the pain that was an ever-present part of every waking moment.

This isn't the time to get maudlin, she told herself. She was here to work, not to lament things that couldn't be changed.

Everyone who could wield a hammer did. Those who couldn't, such as Christopher and Cole's mother, served as backup. They saw to it that the wood being used was easily accessible and that there was always plenty of water and lemonade to drink as well as food to eat for those who needed to take a break.

Much to his frustration, on the advice of the doctor in Helena, Gene Haines was forced to remain on the sidelines. Along with Wayne and Amos, he supervised the work. The rancher provided the blueprints for the barn and Amos coordinated the different groups of men and women working on the structure, insuring that no one got in any one else's way.

Consequently, building progressed like a lyrical poem and at a pace that Ronnie wouldn't have thought possible if she hadn't been there herself to see it.

By the time they ran out of daylight, they had also run out of building materials—which was fine since Haines, with tears gathering in his eyes, drove in the symbolic last nail.

The new barn was finished.

"I don't know what to say," the rancher told his neighbors honestly, emotion filling his throat, choking off words.

"How about 'drinks on me'?" someone called out. Laughter greeted the suggestion. All around them, lanterns that had been hung up by Haines's wife, Katie, went on, illuminating the area.

Shaking off the emotional moment, Haines responded, "Absolutely!" Beckoning to his sons, they came forward, bringing out ice chests filled with ice and bottles of beer.

The barbecue began in earnest as laughter and music filled the air, the latter courtesy of several of Redemption's citizens who took out the instruments they'd thought to bring with them.

Delighted, excited, Christopher talked up a storm, taking it all in and giving absolutely no indication that he was about to wind down anytime in the near future despite the fact that he had put in a long day.

On his second helping of spareribs, Cole marveled at the boy's boundless energy. "Doesn't he ever come up for air?"

"Not very often," Ronnie answered. One helping of spareribs was enough for her. She cleaned off her fingers with the napkin Midge had handed her. "I've gotten used to it," she confessed, "although I have to admit that being on the ranch seems to have increased his energy levels."

He watched the boy talking to a couple of other boys close to Christopher's own age. He wished he could tap into some of that energy, he mused. "If I hadn't seen him fall asleep that one time, I would swear that boy runs on batteries."

"He's pure energy, all right," she said fondly.

"Gets that from you, I take it," Cole observed.

"I guess maybe he does," she agreed. She was completely unprepared for what Cole said next. Or rather, what he asked next.

"What does he get from his father?"

For a split second, her mind went blank. Did he suspect? No, the look on Cole's face was guileless. Ronnie thought for a minute, trying to be both truthful and vague at the same time. "His intelligence," she finally said. "He got his intelligence from his father."

The look on Cole's face turned slightly skeptical. "You're not exactly dumb, Ronnie."

"I know." She took the comment for the assessment that it was. "It's a different kind of intelligence," she explained. "Christopher has an innate savviness, a unique way of looking at things that I don't have."

"And he got that from his father?" Cole asked.

She had the impression that Cole was trying to fit the pieces of a puzzle together.

Change the subject, change the subject, she silently pleaded. She didn't want Cole stumbling across the truth, not tonight. Not here. This wasn't the setting she wanted when she finally told Cole the truth.

"Dance with me?" she asked.

Well, that had come out of the blue, Cole thought. Wiping his hands carefully, he dropped the napkin onto his paper plate. "Yes, ma'am," he responded "obediently."

With that, he led her to the area where all the other dancing couples had gathered.

Taking her into his arms, Cole began to dance.

"You still look like the cat that swallowed the canary."

"Just enjoying the day—and the company," she replied.

He said nothing, not wanting to mar the moment. This was the way it was supposed to have been, he couldn't help thinking. This was the life he'd wanted her to share with him. Maybe—

Someone bumped into them. Stumbled into them,

really, he realized as he looked at the party who was responsible. It wasn't another couple, it was Cyndy. An inebriated Cyndy from the less than faint smell of alcohol about her.

Rather than apologize, Cyndy took an unsteady step back. Her eyes swept over Ronnie. "I heard you were back." When she said it, it sounded more like an accusation than anything else.

Jealousy and a feeling of foreboding shot through Ronnie at the same time. This was the woman Cole had been engaged to. The one he had planned to marry.

But he didn't, did he? she reminded herself. There was no reason to be jealous. At least, not on her part, she thought.

"Hello, Cyndy." Ronnie did her best to sound friendly, even though she felt anything but. The truth was, she had never really liked the other woman, even when they had gone to school together. They were complete opposites. "How have you been?"

"Frustrated," Cyndy retorted. "I thought for sure that once you ran out on Cole, I'd have a clear shot at him." She shook her head, then stopped because it seemed to make her dizzy. "But I guess your hooks just went too deep."

Cole took hold of Cyndy's arm and firmly moved her over to the side, away from the makeshift dance floor. "Cyndy, I think maybe you should try switching to lemonade for a while."

She drew herself up indignantly. "I will when I want to." She glared at Ronnie. "Did you know we were engaged?" she asked Ronnie, raising her voice. "But he dumped me." Anger and disgust echoed in each word she uttered. "Because he just couldn't get over you."

She tossed her head. "There's nothing so great about you," the woman observed. Turning toward Cole, she underscored her point. "There isn't."

Aware that there was a scene in the making, Midge hurried over to the trio. With a forced smile on her lips, she told her son's former fiancée, "I think you've said enough, dear."

The expression on Cyndy's face was pure belligerence. She stood her ground, albeit unsteadily. "Doesn't matter what I say—or don't say. Doesn't change anything."

Cole lowered his voice. "Cyndy, you're making a spectacle of yourself."

"*I'm* making a spectacle?" Cyndy scoffed indignantly. "What about little miss fancy-pants here?" She jerked a thumb at Ronnie. "She comes waltzing back after six years, leading the man I love around by the nose. I'd call that a spectacle." She turned toward Midge. "How about you?" she asked.

Exhibiting a great deal of patience, Midge tried to take hold of Cyndy's arm to lead her off before they began to attract too much attention.

With an angry cry, Cyndy attempted to yank her arm back.

Just then, Christopher came barreling over to them, his eyes seeing only his hero. "Can you get me a soda pop, Sheriff?" he asked. "I'm really thirsty!" He looked up at Cole hopefully.

Cyndy blinked, trying to focus. She stared at the boy. "He yours?" she asked, turning toward Ronnie.

Ronnie could feel the muscles in her stomach tightening. She had a really bad feeling about this. "Yes."

Her hand on Christopher's shoulder—more to hold

herself steady than to keep him in place—Cyndy looked directly into his small face. Then she looked at Cole, and finally, at the woman she blamed for her broken engagement. It was apparent that she was trying to think and having less than an easy time of it.

"How old is the kid?" she asked.

Never having had a shy moment in his life, Christopher answered the question for his mother. "I'm five."

"Five," Cyndy repeated as if digesting the single word carefully. And then she looked at Ronnie, a smirk on her lips. "He doesn't look all that much like Cole, does he?"

Alarmed, afraid of what else the other woman would blurt out, Midge took hold of Cyndy's arm and forcibly moved her away from the others. "You're making a fool of yourself, Cyndy," she warned.

Cyndy tossed her head, then turned a light shade of green as a wave of nausea found her. "I'm not the fool in the group," she declared. Pulling free of Midge, Cyndy took an unsteady step back. She raised her hands, as if to indicate that she could leave on her own power and didn't need anyone to usher her away.

Then, weaving, she retreated.

Despite the fact that the noise around them continued as loudly as before, a silence descended on Ronnie, Cole and his mother.

Midge recovered first. "Can I get anyone anything to drink?" she asked brightly.

Ronnie hadn't realized that her father, seeing Cyndy gesturing and looking angry, had made his way over to lend his support.

"I'd like some iced tea if you don't mind, Midge," he requested. And then he thought better of it. "I didn't mean to act like I expect you to wait on me. I can still get around," he told the older woman. "Just point me in the right direction."

Midge looked uncertainly at her son, as if she was hesitant to leave him alone with Ronnie after what had just happened without the benefit of her support.

"It's okay, Ma," Cole said. "Why don't you take Christopher with you and go show Amos where the iced tea is." Without waiting for her to answer him, he turned toward Ronnie. "Can I see you for a second?"

There was absolutely no emotion in his voice and his expression was stony. Ronnie's hands went cold.

Rather than answer, Ronnie glanced toward where her brother was sitting. She wasn't about to leave him if she couldn't be sure that he wouldn't exert himself.

But her brother appeared well taken care of. Several of the women who had visited him in the hospital were keeping him company.

You're out of excuses, Ronnie. It was bound to happen someday.

It was time to finally face the music. Ronnie braced herself, hoping it wouldn't be as bad as she anticipated.

Without another word to Ronnie, Cole walked away from the gathering and the focal point of the celebration, the newly erected barn. He kept on walking until he had gone around the front of the house to where all the various vehicles had been parked. He was hoping that the walk would help him get the anger, the growing fury he was feeling, under control.

It didn't.

The only thing he could hope for was that Cyndy had just been trying to create trouble and that her assumption wasn't true.

He knew he was grasping at paper straws.

When he finally reached his own vehicle and turned around, the wary expression in Ronnie's eyes destroyed the last shred of any hope he had. For a moment, he went numb.

"It's true, isn't it?" he asked her. "What Cyndy was implying, it's true. Christopher's mine."

Ronnie remained silent for a long, agonizing moment. If she lied to him, if she said no, that Christopher wasn't his, he'd believe her, she knew that, sensed that. She instinctively *knew* that, although the words remained unspoken, a part of Cole was actually asking her to lie to him.

But she couldn't.

She could be evasive, she could be silent and thus lie to him by omission. But when confronted with the question, Ronnie just couldn't bring herself to lie to Cole.

"Yes," she whispered.

"Who else knows?" he demanded. "Your father?"

She shook her head. "He suspects, but no, I never said anything and he never came right out and asked."

"Then no one knows?" He saw the wary look in her eyes and had his answer. Partially. "Who?"

"Your mother."

"My mother? You told her?" he demanded, his temper cracking his voice.

"No, but she guessed," Ronnie told him. Regret warred with anger for being put on the spot like this. She hated it. "I couldn't lie when she asked me pointblank. Just like I couldn't lie to you just now."

A rage the likes of which he had never felt before—not even when he discovered her gone that awful morning—completely filled him, threatening to overflow with a force he knew he wouldn't be able to control.

Struggling now to somehow contain all the churning emotions, he ground out, "Is there any reason—any reason in the world—why you could tell my mother but you couldn't—wouldn't—tell me that I had a son? Any conceivable reason why you would let so much time go by keeping this from me?" Cole demanded, his voice rising with each word.

When she didn't answer, Cole took hold of her arms, fighting hard to restrain himself, to keep from letting loose the fury that had suddenly mushroomed inside of him and just shake her.

He clamped down his jaw hard to keep the harsh words at bay. "Well, is there?" he shouted.

"Cole, please, keep your voice down. People will hear you," she implored.

"I don't give a damn. *Is* there a reason, or did you just not care at all?"

"I cared," she insisted. How could he think she didn't? "And yes, there was a reason," she whispered again.

Cole stared at her, fury in his eyes. "What was it?"

Chapter Sixteen

"Well?" Cole demanded when several seconds had passed and Ronnie still hadn't said anything.

It was obvious that he was prepared to wait her out until she *did* say something. So, taking a breath to steady herself, Ronnie gave him the reason behind her actions—or lack of actions.

"I didn't tell you because I didn't want to spend the rest of my life wondering if you married me because you loved me or because you felt you had to give the baby a name."

"And you didn't think it was possible that it could be both?" he wanted to know. "That I could want to give the baby—*my* baby," he emphasized, "a name and love you at the same time?"

It was easy enough for him to toss that all-important word around as if it was nothing—but he'd never uttered it in earnest when it mattered. He'd never actually told her that he loved her.

Why should she believe him now?

Ronnie raised her head up proudly. "You never told me you loved me."

He'd taken it for granted that she knew. Why would he have hung around her so much if he hadn't loved her? If she hadn't meant the world to him?

"I thought that was understood," he growled out.

There were truths a woman might intuit, but there were others that she had to be told. *Needed* to be told.

"Well, it wasn't," she shot back.

She was trying to make him feel guilty, Cole thought. Well, that wasn't a one-way street. It ran both ways as far as he was concerned. "You never told me, either," he reminded her.

There was a reason for that, too. One he could have easily guessed if he'd been the slightest bit into her the way he was now claiming.

Her chin was out pugnaciously and her eyes were blazing. Damn, but he wanted to make her forget about this squabble—and everything else, as well. Everything in his entire being wanted her. He reminded himself that he was more than just a mass of desires and physical urges.

"Because I didn't want you parroting it back after I said it to you—or worse, not saying it at all." She pressed her lips together as a sob came out of nowhere and threatened to undo her. Very carefully, she took in a breath and then blew it out again. "And besides, I didn't want to stay here, and if you knew I was pregnant, you would have married me and made me stay here."

There it was again, that wall he kept crashing into. The one she'd placed between them.

"That's it really, isn't it?" he challenged. "You wouldn't let anything get in your way, wouldn't let anything keep you here a second longer than was absolutely necessary."

There was no point in denying it. She'd felt like that. Like she was fleeing for her life, for her peace of mind. Fleeing a stifling way of life. Funny how things changed. She no longer felt trapped being here. This was where her roots were, where her heart was.

"No, not then."

Enraged though he was, Cole caught the minute inflection in her voice. "And now?" he asked.

And now I realize that this isn't a trap, it's a haven. But it's too late for that.

She shrugged her shoulders and looked away. "Doesn't matter."

Cole stared at her profile for a long moment, unable to come to grips with everything going on inside of him. But like it or not, he would have to.

"No, I guess you're right," he told Ronnie stonily, his expression never changing. "It doesn't. It doesn't matter that you lied to me, that you kept my son—*my* son— away from me, that you stole that time away from me, time I can't get back. Time with him, time with you. None of that matters."

"Cole, I'm sorry," Ronnie began.

He continued as if she hadn't said anything. "Give my mother a ride home," he requested. And with that, he started to get into the cab of his truck.

"Why?" she asked. "Where're you going?" A cold chill ran up and down the length of her spine. Suddenly afraid, she tried to grab his arm, but he pulled it away from her so hard, she wound up stumbling backward. She caught herself at the last moment, avoiding falling down in front of him. "Cole, please, don't do anything stupid," she entreated.

His eyes all but burned holes into her. He'd gone way past the point where a mere warning would do him some good, he thought darkly.

"Too late," he told her, his voice giving absolutely nothing away.

And with that, he started up his vehicle and drove away as if it was all one fluid movement, leaving Ronnie to try to figure out exactly what he meant by his glib comment.

All she managed to do was go around in circles in her head.

Ronnie drew in a ragged breath and turned on her heel, intent on going into the house and getting something for her very parched throat. Instead, she caught herself stifling a shriek when she all but walked into her brother.

Wayne shook his head, as if reassessing what was before him. "And here I always thought you were the smart one."

This was no time to argue about intelligence and the difference between their IQs and brain power. Her heart pounded wildly in her chest and had yet to settle down.

"How long have you been standing there?" she asked.

"Long enough," was Wayne's vague response as he continued studying his sister. "You know, Cole's right. You should have told him about Christopher."

This would wind up spreading like wildfire during a drought. Maybe it was a good thing that they were leaving. She didn't want Christopher finding out about his father from anyone but her.

"Water under the bridge," she informed her brother crisply.

"Ronnie," he began.

"I don't want to discuss it, Wayne," she retorted firmly, doing her best not to snap out the words because as far as she was concerned, Wayne's recovery was still in the fragile stages. "And you're not supposed to be wandering around, remember? You promised to take it easy if we agreed to let you come along," she reminded him.

"I guess you're not the only McCloud who stretched the truth."

She'd had just about enough. Christopher was her son and this had been *her* choice to make, not anyone else's. "I didn't stretch the truth," she informed her brother coldly as she began to lead the way back. "I never said anything at all."

"Sins of omission are still sins," Wayne told her as he followed her to the back of the house where everyone was still gathered, enjoying what had turned into a barbecue.

"Very profound," she dismissed. "Maybe I'll get that embroidered on a pillow for you," she added crisply. There was a finality to her tone.

Obviously, Wayne knew better than to push the subject.

"Do we hafta leave, Mom?" Christopher asked, clearly unhappy about their leaving the ranch for the more confined life in Seattle. There were no horses to ride there and he was just another kid in his class. "I like it here."

Ronnie and Christopher were sitting on the back porch for what she assumed was the last time before they got into her car and drove back.

There was nothing to keep them here any longer.

Mr. Walker had come up to pay for his horses and arrange for their transport down to his ranch himself. With the agreed upon fee safely banked, her father's outstanding accounts could now be paid off and the ranch would be back in good standing again. Wayne was getting stronger every day and had been chomping at the bit to get back to work. All the reasons that had forced her to take a leave of absence and come out here to Redemption were now gone.

She and Christopher had a life to get back to. Such as it was, she thought without a flicker of joy.

"I know you do, sweetie. But we'll come back and visit, I promise," she told him, hugging her son to her. "Christmas isn't all that far away."

"We don't hafta come back for a visit if we stay," the boy pointed out. "We can stay here and take care of Grandpa."

"I think Mrs. James has her eye on that job," she told her son with a fond smile. Things had heated up rather quickly in the last few days since the barn raising. She'd even caught the two of them embracing. At least someone was happy, she thought. "Who knows? She might even be your new grandma," Ronnie told him. *Actually,* she thought to herself, *as your dad's mother, she already is your grandma.*

"Then we gotta stay here," Christopher insisted with

new conviction. "I don't have a grandpa and a grandma in Seattle."

"I know, honey." She fully empathized with her son. "But I have a job there and we need to eat."

"You can find a job here," the boy pleaded. And then he hit her with a question she hadn't anticipated. "If we go, who's going to take care of the sheriff?"

The question had come out of the blue. They hadn't even mentioned Cole for the last couple of days. It was as if her son sensed that talking about the man would upset her. But now, apparently, the rules seemed to have changed.

"He doesn't need anyone taking care of him," Ronnie told her son. Cole hadn't been by since the barn raising and his distance had said it all. He'd made his decision. He wanted nothing to do with her. With them.

"Yes, he does," Christopher insisted, jumping off the two-seated swing and suddenly becoming a pint-sized advocate for the absent sheriff. "He's all alone. You always said that everybody should have somebody taking care of them."

This was one time she didn't appreciate her son's rather remarkable ability to remember things. "The sheriff's the exception."

Christopher scrunched up his face as he tried to puzzle out what his mother had just said to him. "Why?"

"It's complicated."

"Is it because he's my dad?"

Ronnie's world came to a skidding halt. He knew. Oh, God, Christopher knew. She searched his face, looking for some telltale sign that the news upset him. She saw nothing apart from his reluctance to leave.

"Who told you that?" she asked, keeping her voice as level as she could.

"Nobody," Christopher answered solemnly. "I heard Mrs. James talking to Grandpa about it. It's okay, Mom," he said quickly, as if he could somehow sense his mother's uneasy feelings. "I like the sheriff. I like that he's my dad." He smiled brightly at her, mercifully devoid of a single devious bone in his body. "He's fun and nice. I never had a dad before. Can't we stay?" Christopher pleaded, then played his ace card, hoping to tip the scale in his favor. "I'll eat broccoli if we stay. Every day. Honest." To seal the bargain, the boy crossed his heart. Twice.

Ronnie didn't know whether to laugh or cry. The one thing that she knew was that she was out from beneath the burden of that very large, weighty secret. And her son had taken it in stride like a trooper.

"Boy, that is a really big sacrifice for you," she acknowledged, doing her best to keep a straight face. "You hate broccoli."

The small head bobbed up and down with enthusiasm. "But I'll eat it," he promised again. "Just please, can't we stay? Please, please, please, Mom? I'll go to work, too, to help out."

Ronnie closed her eyes and sighed. She hadn't thought it would be this hard. But it didn't change anything. They still had to leave. "You're not making this any easier on me."

Christopher was almost jumping up and down with joy. How could she have ever guessed he could grow so attached so very quickly?

But he was still very much her son, which meant he could be enthusiastic, but he was still cautious and that meant taking nothing for granted and assuming nothing. "Then we can stay?"

Saying no outright to that face was not an option. She chickened out. "Let me think about it."

"Okay. You think about it," Christopher echoed cheerfully. "Real hard," he added as if that was the answer to winning her over to his side.

With that, he ran off to share this hopeful possibility with his beloved grandfather—and anyone else he encountered.

Ronnie continued sitting where she'd been, on the two-seated swing she'd spent so many summer evenings on, dreaming of her life away from Redemption. But right now she wasn't dreaming. She was feeling hopeless and rather lost.

With a pronounced sigh, she shut her eyes, as if that could somehow help her see things more clearly.

But it didn't.

Her head told her to move on, her heart wanted to please her son. The result was that the sum total of her felt so terribly confused that it was almost more than she could stand.

If only there was some way, some magical way, that—

"I've loved you ever since I was born, did you know that?"

Her eyes flew open, positive that she had somehow conjured up the deep voice with its solemn declaration. Positive that she would be looking at no one, only the same scenery that had been there when she'd shut her eyes a few moments ago.

For a moment, she was right. All she saw was the same scenery.

And then Cole shifted, coming into her line of vision.

Her heart stopped, holding its breath. Or maybe that was her.

"Maybe even longer than that," Cole speculated. "I guess I never said it before because I didn't want to be standing here like this, looking at you looking at me and not speaking. Making me feel like some village idiot." He took a breath, pushing on. "I'm not saying this to keep you here. I know you want to go back to Seattle and your life and I understand that, I really do. I'm just hoping that somewhere in that life, you can find a place for me because I haven't stopped loving you, not for one day, not for one hour. I wanted to. Damn, but I wanted to," he confessed with feeling. "Even tried to talk myself into loving someone else, but I knew I was lying."

He shrugged, resigned. There was no escaping what was. The truth always had a way of finding you. He knew that now.

"Some people get to move on—like my mother and your dad—which is good," he added quickly, wanting to make it clear that he was glad for them. "Some people can't. I guess I'm one of those."

Out of things to say and having resigned himself to the fact that he might not have moved on with his life but she had, Cole murmured, "I just wanted you to know that before you left."

And with that, he turned on his heel and began to walk away.

He had almost gotten to the point where he had to disappear around the side of the house when he heard Ronnie sharply ask, "And that's it?"

Turning around, Cole looked at her, unable to make sense of her question. "Excuse me?"

She was on her feet, walking toward him in deliberate, measured steps. "And that's it?" she repeated. "You're retreating? Just like that?"

He'd just spilled his guts to her without a single comment on her part. What did she expect him to do? Cheer? "I'm the sheriff. I'm not allowed to grab you and drag you behind the barn."

"How about into your arms?" she asked, her face a sheer portrait of innocence. "Can you do that?"

His face broke into a wreath of smiles. "I can do that."

There were still a couple of feet between them. Ronnie stopped walking and looked at him expectantly. "Well?"

The next moment, Cole was doing exactly that, dragging her into his arms and kissing her, kissing Ronnie to make up for all the moments of agony he'd suffered since he'd driven away from her the evening of the barn raising.

"So what does this mean, Ronnie?" he asked her when he finally came up for air. There was a rushing sound in his ears, but he could still hear her answer—provided there was one. "Where do I stand?"

Ever cautious even in euphoria, she asked, "Where do you want to stand?"

This time there was no hesitation. "Next to you," he breathed, pausing to press a kiss to each one of her eyelids. "For the rest of my life."

She could feel a warmth spreading through her. A comfortable warmth along with the passion that was sizzling through her veins. "That could be arranged."

He ran the tip of his forefinger along the perfect

ridge of her nose. "Think there's a place in Seattle for an ex-sheriff?"

"I'm sure the police department would love to have someone of your dedicated caliber," she assured Cole, "But I was thinking more along the lines of my staying here."

She saw the surprise in his eyes. Along with a flicker of relief. She couldn't blame him. He'd known what he had wanted all along. It had taken her a lot longer to come to her conclusion. There'd been wings to try first. But she was done with that stage now. Done with it and ready to settle down where she belonged.

"My dad's getting on a bit and Wayne can't run this place on his own, not with the plans I have for it." Plans until this moment she had decided were best to leave unsaid. But now everything was different. "I can get some significant capital from these investors I know and the ranch can really get on the map as a place where ranchers can find not just good quarter horses but the *best* quarter horses."

Cole laughed softly, shaking his head. "You really do think big."

"I thought so, too," she agreed, "but somehow, I managed to miss the biggest thing of all." The look in her eyes left no room for doubt about her meaning. "I love you, too, you know," she said, threading her arms around his neck. "And that 'since birth thing,' I guess that about sums it up neatly," she confessed. "I've been waiting for you to tell me you loved me forever and I just about gave up hope. But—"

He tightened his arms around her, holding her to him and reveling in the heat that generated within him. She was staying. The three-word sentence kept replaying itself in his head like a wonderful refrain.

She was staying.

"I'll love you forever," he said. It was exactly what she'd been waiting to hear.

And then he kissed her with all the feeling of a man who intended to do just that, to love her forever.

He paused only for a moment to add, "How do you feel about making an honest man out of me?"

"You mean marriage?" she asked breathlessly, afraid to hope that she hadn't ruined things after all.

"I mean marriage," Cole answered with a smile. "I think Christopher would like that. How about you?" he prodded.

As if he didn't already know the answer to that. "I'd like that very much."

Cole grinned that grin that he reserved for when he was really, really happy. The one she loved so much, and said, "Me, too."

It was all either one of them said for a long time.

* * * * *

SPECIAL EXCERPT FROM

HARLEQUIN®

American Romance®

Can't get enough of the **TEXAS RODEO BARONS**
miniseries? Read on for an excerpt from

THE TEXAN'S SURPRISE SON
by Cathy McDavid…

"Excuse me, Jacob Baron?"

Jacob turned. The woman looked vaguely familiar, though he couldn't recall where he'd seen her before.

"Yes."

She started toward him, managing to cover the uneven ground gracefully despite her absurdly high heels that had no business being at a rodeo. "May I speak to you a moment?" Her glance darted briefly to his brothers. "Privately."

"We were just heading home," he said.

"This is important."

After a moment's hesitation he said, "Go on, I'll catch up with you."

"No rush, bro," Jet said, a glimmer in his eyes.

"It seems you know my name." He gave her a careful smile once they were alone. "Mind telling me yours?"

"Mariana Snow."

Jacob felt as if he'd taken a blow from behind. "I'm sorry about your sister. I heard what happened."

Leah Snow. That explained why he'd found this woman familiar. Three years ago he'd dated her sister, though describing their one long weekend together as dating was a stretch. He hadn't seen her since.

Still, the rodeo world was a small one, and he'd learned of Leah's unexpected passing after a short and intense battle with breast cancer.

"Thank you for your condolences," Mariana said tightly. "It's been a difficult three months."

"I didn't know Leah had a sister. She never mentioned you."

"I'm not surprised." Mariana reached into her purse. "Leah didn't tell you a lot of things." She extracted a snapshot and handed it to Jacob.

He took the photo, his gaze drawn to the laughing face of a young boy. "I don't understand. Who is this?" He started to return the photo.

Mariana held up her hand. "Keep it."

"Why?"

"That's Cody Snow. Your son."

For a moment, Jacob sat immobile, his mind rebelling. He hadn't been careless. He'd asked, and Leah had sworn she was on birth control pills.

"You're mistaken. I don't have a son."

"Yes, you do. And with my sister gone, you're his one remaining parent."

The photo slipped from Jacob's fingers and landed on the table, the boy's laughing face staring up at him.

Look for
THE TEXAN'S SURPRISE SON
by Cathy McDavid,
*part of the **TEXAS RODEO BARONS** miniseries, in October 2014 wherever books and ebooks are sold!*

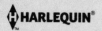

First love, last chance?

Coming home to the south Florida ranch that's been in his family for generations holds bittersweet memories for Hank Judd. Time and distance haven't dimmed his feelings for Kelly Tompkins, who broke his heart when she walked away from their future. But now he needs her.

Twelve years ago, Kelly fell in love with a Judd—her grandfather's sworn enemy. Now she needs Hank's real estate expertise to sell her family ranch before she hightails it back to Texas. In exchange, she'll help the interim ranch manager reconnect with his daughter. But Hank is rekindling desire Kelly can't resist. Has her cowboy really changed? And how can they try for a second chance when neither of them plans to stick around?

Look for

HIS FAVORITE COWGIRL
by LEIGH DUNCAN

From the *Glades County Cowboys* miniseries from Harlequin® American Romance.

Available October 2014
wherever books and ebooks are sold.

Mr. Right-There-All-Along

Since she was a kid, there's been one guy that restaurateur
Dani Pettit can always count on—her best friend,
Nick. Their relationship is purely platonic, until a single
kiss changes everything. Now Dani is falling hard
for the one man she shouldn't—the one who can
truly break her heart.

Although rancher Nick Kelly knows he's to blame for his
string of failed relationships, Dani is the only woman he's
ever trusted. Nick doesn't want to be just another guy who
lets her down, but his new feelings for Dani are too strong
to resist. Do they dare risk their lifelong friendship for a
once-in-a-lifetime love?

Look for

A RANCHER'S REDEMPTION

by ANN ROTH

From the *Prosperity, Montana* miniseries from
Harlequin® American Romance.

Available October 2014
wherever books and ebooks are sold.